THE LAST OF THE TORLOCS

Irissa the Torloc stopped, watching as stone melted from under stone of her ancient home, while the crumbling towers shrank into each other and vanished. Finorian the Eldress sat on the broken battlements of one partly dissolved tower.

"I cannot hold the gate much longer, Irissa," she said. "All the rest are gone. You, too, would have passed with us—but it is too late now. I go to a green world, child, and I leave you in this one, already growing rusty. Your courses are set and you must run them as I must follow mine. Farewell. Do not forget that you are the last Torloc . . ."

Air spoke to them, only air, where Finorian had been.

"Gone," Kendric marveled. "You are alone, as am I. We Six of Swords are fallen —upon each other, fallen upon fear . . ."

Six of Swords

Carole Nelson Douglas

A Del Rey Book

BALLANTINE BOOKS • NEW YORK

For Sam,
who is my
husband, best friend,
sounding board, wailing wall,
computer co-pilot, occasional typist,
perpetual advisor and unsung co-conspirator,
unfailing partner and fellow creator,
ever-ready shield and sword,
And my home.

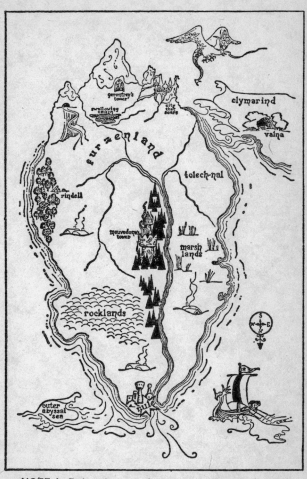

NOTE: *In Rule, when one faces south, the sun rises to the right and sets to the left.*

Chapter One

◆◆◆

Irissa of the Green Veil bent to the forest pool. The greens hung heavily over the still water, casting such shade that she could not see her own reflection. That was well; to see oneself in any mirror was a weakening of power. It had been so since the days of the Torlocs of Edanvant, and so it was with the Torlocs of Rindell, though these were lesser days and, perforce, the Torlocs were less than they had been.

But Finorian the Eldress, it was said, had not so much as looked at the moon, lest its lighted surface reflect the slightest sliver of herself. Finorian was a moon-sliver of a woman in her own right, straight and narrow as a snow-season ice-dagger, with silver eyes in a pale face. It was said that Torloc women's eyes grew more discernibly amber with each glance at self in polished brass or motion-silvered water—or at even the eye of another, although that took deep looking.

Nevertheless, the women of Rindell who would practice the power that remained became adept at looking to only the edge of eyes, a habit that did not encourage commerce with mankind, those direct beings who dwelt beyond Rindell. Mankind could always look one directly in the eyes and still lie. There was another kind of power inherent in such an attribute, and Irissa bit her lip as she considered it. For Rindell was on the wane. Those such as Finorian were merely remnants. But the power must be hoarded in the few vessels that remained to the Torlocs, and Irissa was such a one.

From Irissa's birth it had been plain. Even her mother's irredeemably amber eye had seen the purity of her new

1

daughter's vision. She had risen herself from the birthing
bed to empty the basins of reflecting water, strip the
servants of their decorative metals, and order the trophy
shields in the great hall veiled. No glimmer had intruded
into Irissa's unwinding life.

Every forest pool was thick-grown with shade, an obsidian surface whose reflections were absorbed into some
sable recess beyond sight. Now Irissa's fingers dappled the
dark water. Silver ripples undulated outward. She thrust one
hand wrist-deep in the element; the dim reflection braceleted her—or manacled her.

Irissa shook her hand free, scattering her liquid bangle
into drops that sparkled like the coldstone mined deep in
the Torloc rins. The rins also yielded Iridesium, the metal
which mailed Torloc men and made them resistant to
swordstroke or the piercing of arrows, a phosphorescent
metal that sprang back like grass from most blows aimed
upon it.

There were few to wear the Iridesium now, though the
other Realms cherished it and had once imported it like
water diverted from an upland farmer's pasture. Now the
rins were abandoned and the Iridesium almost gone, as were
Torloc men. Most Torloc men were old—or simply gone,
none knew quite why. Irissa had been kept apart for the
protection of the sight, so she had seen few males of her
race even when a child; armored men were walking mirrors, likely to draw the untrained child's fascinated glance
and thus wreck the work of years. Her own father had long
since vanished into the mystery of male missions from
which such emissaries seldom returned. It was the women
who clung to the overgrown castles, who made Rindell
of the Shrinking Forest a vague reality even as the other
five Realms encroached upon it . . .

Irissa stood, wiping her damp hand on the green veil
that floated from her narrow headdress like the cloudy
flaw that moved within Finorian's great emerald touchstone. The old woman would expect her soon, as would her
mother. Not that the time to take the rite of Far Focus
had come—no, that was still a turn of the moon's head
away. But Thrangar was to come. Irissa had never seen
a Wrathman of the Far Keep before.

She dusted her palms on her veil again, tossing it behind
her shoulders as if the alien cloth held the long familiarity

of her own hair, as it did. Except for two narrow, dark braids looped around her ears, her hair was caught tight under the Iridesium circlet that bound the veil to her temples. She paused again, studying the quiet clearing where even the moonweasels dared not come. She was slight but tall. It was the Torloc race's stature that the people of the other Realms held against them. They said the Torlocs were apart, from another land, time, or even reality. It made easy their encroachment on the Torlocs' deep glades and mines. They made more of the Torlocs and thus less of them. And then they swallowed them whole.

Yet a Torloc was always first among the Wrathmen, and it had always been so. Irissa did not have to pass through the Far Focus to see that. Thrangar, who had borne the great five-foot-long sword in the service of the Circle of Rule, was coming soon. Thrangar was the last of the Torloc leaders, when that race was no longer even represented within the Circle itself; his arrows were feathered with peacock colors and could insinuate themselves into any chink. Always the Torloc, among the Six Wrathmen who guarded the Circle of Rule, was armed with the bow and arrows. His bow was bent from seven feet of yew wood, and only Thrangar could direct its arrows true and far—and deadly.

It must be an unusual quest that brought one of the Wrathmen away from the City at the point where all Six Realms met—weighty business, beyond the work of mail and men. It would be work for Finorian.

Irissa rustled through the forest. The young shoots bowed away from her passage as if windblown. Her veil wafted behind her. She walked more quickly, aware of a certain urgency tracking her like a pursuer. She broke into another clearing centered on a similar pool, but this glade was open to the daylight that shone from the sapphire sky above. A sudden glitter below, on the pool's verge, caught her attention—a rich vein of glitter, black, midnight green, vermilion, violet, and black again, so deep it swallowed sight.

Irissa arched her veil over her face. There was little Finorian and her amber-eyed mother had let her see from birth. Nothing within that limited spectrum had prepared her for this. With the veil a filter before the rare silver eyes that made her race feared in other Realms, Irissa advanced on the pulsating shimmer that danced like a cluster of fireflies ahead. Before she came to it, she had to bow to some overdraping foliage. The glitter softened, and she and it were in the sylvan semidarkness surrounding the pool. The gleam damped like a snuffed candle. She advanced on something dark, awkward, and long, very long, like one of the sleeping-water-beasts that circled the nomad island of Clymarind. Bulky and lethargic, it was perhaps something dead—a stray bearing-beast from the Rocklands, seeking pool water and finding death . . .

It was not a beast, but a man. Irissa knelt by the now strangely colorless form and reached out a finger to the substance which had dazzled her from across the pool. It was metal, linked into mail. It rusted there, turned mocking red-brown. The quiescent colors still trembled in it, but out of direct light it was tamed. Iridesium, such as the Wrathmen wore! Thrangar!

A new meteor of glitter struck her eyes. The black metal helmet had swiveled toward her. For the first time, Irissa found herself staring, unprotected, into the living eyes of a fellow creature.

"My sword."

Thrangar? The man's words could have been assertion or threat or question. Irissa did not answer and kept her eyes fixed at his helm's edge, as she had been trained.

"Sword!" His voice rasped like rough metal.

She glanced down again to the puzzling rust spot on his mailed shirt of Iridesium. Blood, mortal blood, flowed as red as hers or that of any Torloc. But he was not Thrangar. Nor, did she think, was he Torloc.

Chapter Two

◆ ◆ ◆

"Sword!" he cried again.

Irissa scanned the ground. Against the gnarled trunk of a weepwater tree, his shield lay askew, slashed diagonally with bronze that glimmered even in the uncertain light. Instinctively, Irissa averted her glance from its pseudomirrored surface. Her eyes came back to the rim of the black metal helmet that edged the fallen knight's face. Despite her indirect glance, she felt his gaze pool on her like liquid suspicion.

"Torloc," he said. "You are Torloc. I must be near Rindell."

"Near Rindell, yes, what remains of it. From which of the Realms do you come?" She felt rather than saw his smile form.

"From all and none of them. Torloc lady, can you not see that? My sword!" His voice had become demanding again, urgent and impolite. "I see it there, near that twisted weepwater root. I thought for an instant that the tree had spawned serpents and wrested it from me—but I had taken Fiforn's lance blow by then and may have dreamed it . . . Fetch it to me."

Irissa skittered over to the venerable tree's foot to search among its massive roots, feeling oddly like a dimwit ordered to be of some use. But the sword's haft thrust into her hand on her first probe; its blade was half-invisible, impaled in the marshy water that was as brown as blood. "I have it!"

"Commendable." The voice was stronger, growing impatient again. "Then bring it to me."

Irissa clasped both fists around the crossbar and tugged

5

upward. It was as if she sought to raise a ship's heavy anchor. "I cannot move it," she told him over her shoulder, giving a useless last pull.

The knight behind her was silent for a while. "Then look upon it, Torloc."

"I cannot!" Another would have whirled to face him so that the incredulity of tone would strike home. Irissa was used to addressing the edges of things, even with her emotions. She kept her veiled eyes carefully on the mossy weepwater trunk that loomed over her like a wall. "I have not undergone Far Focus. I must not look—"

"What do I care for your Torloc rituals? Was it not some trick of Thrangar's that brought us to this pass—to Fiforn's hacking at me as if I were his favorite rack of lamb? Has Thrangar come? Is that why you delay me?" He must have read Irissa's blankness in her back, for his words were milder when they came again. "I need it for a cane, not a weapon, lady. It is not mortal metal. Look upon it; the forge that fired it was pure."

Irissa heard weariness enough in his voice, weariness strung on an endless cord of despair. She had never discerned that emotion before; it demanded an extraordinary answer. She cast back her veil and dropped her glance slowly to the blade of bright metal bridging its own longer reflection in the murky water. A brilliant clarity struck her eyes, a clarity as rainbowed with color as the black Iridesium of the knight's mail had been previously. She saw something spinning and glittering at the center of that brightness, something dangling like a star—herself, but a shifting self, twisting beyond reach. The light lengthened and attenuated until it was as high as she and as narrow as a moonweasel. It was a ladder. It was a bar.

Irissa was standing by the woodland pool, a great silver sword in her hand. She held it as lightly as a wand and returned to the recumbent knight, laying it at his side. The moment her glance left it, the metal faded to pewter, rough along the edges where it had dulled its fang on armor. The knight clasped a mailed hand around the haft, then slowly levered himself up until the sword bit into the earth and stood vertical at its full five-foot length. Irissa's eyes rested on its dully worked, almost plain hilt. It was a noncommittal point of view. The knight's Iridesium-gauntleted fingers laced themselves over the hilt, and she felt him draw up, propping himself on his sword, until he loomed over her as surely as had the weepwater tree.

"You are a Wrathman," she said, not troubling to look up even to the edge of his helm, now towering nearly seven feet from the ground. "But you are not Thrangar."

"No. I am a mere mortal from the marshes, one whose youthful tendency to knock his head on lintels saw me into the Circle's service. I am not Thrangar, I thank Rule, though you may not. There is another Torloc service you could do me."

Her glance dropped instinctively to the rusty seepage at his side. "No," she said, still wondering that she had lifted the heavy sword. "Finorian will aid you—if she sees fit."

"Ah. A Torloc who can see, instead of slinking around the center of things. But you have aided me; if you stumble not overmuch on the way, take me to your Finorian."

For answer, Irissa whirled and strode swiftly through the underbrush, hearing with some satisfaction the Wrathman lumbering hard behind her in his armor. Satisfaction was another original emotion for her to meditate upon between this day and that of her initiation into the use of her inborn gifts. She could recognize the feeling only because she knew its obverse all too well. The rite of Far Focus would make her wise, she had been told. Perhaps it came too late. But these were the poolside questions with which she teased her shuttered mind; there was more to think on behind her than within.

For the first day in her life, Irissa felt she was living within an event, not a dream. The sword had arched into her hand like the back of a favorite pet when one stroked it, because she had done what she was never to do—look upon a thing freely and fully . . .

Irissa stopped, reined by a phantom inner twitch she had never felt before. The questioning of her place in life had brought unease; this was what one got for shaking one's head at the bridle of Finorian.

The Wrathman towered to a halt behind her, catching a pair of ragged breaths before he spoke. "What is it?"

Irissa resumed walking, but more slowly. "Nothing. And everything. I thought I saw something—a bridge of ether or some eldritch vapor. Since I looked upon your sword, I am aware of— Nothing, it is nothing. We will go to Finorian."

She moved more quickly, leaving the Wrathman to blunder on behind, using his massive blade for a walking stick. She stopped again, with a soft cry that brought the Wrathman's sword up to duel the air or whatever had made his guide draw back.

"What?" he demanded, a bit impatiently.

Irissa clasped her side, where the twist of pain had passed. It must have been merely a walking cramp. But she was not susceptible to such troubles.

Irissa clasped her side and ran past strands of underbrush to the clearing she knew so well, which broke suddenly on level ground to reveal the ancient Torloc stronghold rising up like rock, with sprays of ivy on its crumbling sides. There Finorian the Eldress waited with her answers . . .

She saw the familiar lines of stone, the high, arched windows, as secret as hooded eyes—solid, safe, with nothing dangerously reflective about it. Irissa saw her home and stopped, watching as stone melted from under stone and the crumbling towers diminished and shrank into one another like fog.

Finorian sat, her white hair bare to the light, her deep-set eyes serenely lidded, on the broken battlements of one dissolved tower. Her forefingers each touched the massive emerald cabochon upon her breast. It cast a glow that pulsed around the Eldress' figure in a kind of phosphorescent breath.

The Wrathman rattled behind Irissa like death, but she was immune to mortal metal. Something new was being forged here, something . . .

"I cannot hold the gate much longer. It has closed beyond your passing, Irissa. It takes all my powers—and yonder Wrathman could tell you something of those—to keep my image in your eyes." Finorian's voice was creaking, mechanical; it emanated from her body as if from a stone. Irissa put her hands to her ears at the foreignness of it.

Finorian laughed shortly. "Ah, it will be a time for you now, child, to live within the Five Realms. Yes, the Six are broken. Thrangar was called out of time, and the rest of us Torlocs must follow."

"My mother—?"

"Gone over, child, as the others before her. You, too, would have passed from the Realms with us, if only—

But it is too late, Irissa; there is little I can do for you.
You are awash on the ground that is breaking, the bridge
that is falling . . . The time of the Six Realms is over, and
the Five shall turn upon one another like a pack of moonweasels when the prey is scanty. It was meant to be. We
Torlocs have been fading into a more beneficent world for
generations. Thrangar alone held this last Torloc remnant
to this world. Now Thrangar—"

"Thrangar is a traitor!"

Irissa whirled to see the outlines of the Wrathman behind her.

"Ah, you know so much, Kendric of the Marshes," the
old woman replied without lifting her eyelids or her voice.
"Tell me, then, O Discerner of Traitors, how came you
here? Do you know?"

"Yes. Thrangar was gone, vanished. For the first time in
memory, the Six Wrathmen were five. We fanned out
across the Realms, seeking Thrangar, seeking an answer,
seeking—"

"Each other, Wrathman. That is what you sought. And
whence came the rust that reddens your mail? It ran from
the blade of another Wrathman, Fiforn of the City That
Soars, he whom you called bondbrother. Do you still
swear you know so much of traitors? Or Torlocs?"

"No!" But the Wrathman was not answering Finorian; his
cry was confused, as certain a form of denial as the turning away of his eyes. Irissa wished for a paradoxical moment that she dared read his face.

"The Six are now five," Finorian declared. "It is not a
harmonious number. Irissa." The Eldress lifted a long,
admonitory finger from the emerald. It dotted the air with
a brief pulse of green. "I have not long. I can give you
one moment of the Far Sight. Come, look at me."

Twenty years of constant training held Irissa's eyes
oblique to the old woman's.

"Come! You will have to walk upon the shifting air of
this world. I must show you. Look."

Irissa brought her eyes to the Eldress' face. The pale
lashes screening Finorian's eyes rolled upward. Irissa dived
into an endless silver sea, as blank and bright as death.
"Nothing, I see nothing," she protested.

"That is the beginning of vision," Finorian said, wavering

in Irissa's unshielded gaze like moonlight. Her finger flexed
to touch the emerald. "I go to a green, green place. Another time, place, and people. A green world, child, and
I leave you in one growing as rusty as your Wrathman's
mail—"

"He is not my Wrathman; it is not my world—" Irissa
objected, while the pale slivers of smoke shifted in her
vision.

"No?" The word seemed to emanate from the hot, green
heart of the emerald. "Your courses are set. You must
run them as I must follow mine. Farewell. Fare well. Do
not forget that you are Torloc . . ."

Air spoke to them, only air, a vaguely green exhalation
that rose dustily from the last of the tumbled stones that
had been Irissa's fortress home. She stood still a long moment. Then the mail behind her shifted. It sounded like
hail. The Wrathman clattered around her to study the
leveled clearing.

"Gone," he marveled. "As Thrangar is gone. She said
he was called. And she is right; I do not recall much of my
meeting with Fiforn, only the bite of his famous flying
lance—and I ran, ran from Fiforn as if I feared him,
feared something other than he even more. Truly we Six
are fallen—fallen upon one another, fallen upon fear . . ."

Irissa heard the Wrathman's words, but they were merely
bitter counterpoint to her internal keening. Gone, all gone,
truly gone! And what reason had she to stand above vanished stones and long for home fires and for even the rite
of Far Focus? She had seen nothing when given the gift
of Finorian's silver gaze; there had been nothing to see.
Something else which Irissa had never seen before flashed
in her eyes and ran moonweasel-swift down her cheeks.

The Wrathman glimpsed the furtive silver and cupped
his hands beneath her chin. Something clinked into his
mailed fingers. "Torloc tears," he said, his voice softening.
"It is true." He held up a palmful of glittering coldstones,
like the ones found in the rins when they were mined.
Irissa averted her eyes from the flashing white gems.

The Wrathman tossed them once in his hand and closed
his fingers upon them. They rattled within his palm like
coins. "I'm not afraid to look upon them, lady. Among the
men of the marshes, they call such stones wealth; many

labor a lifetime to earn as much as one small coldstone. They will buy you a mount, at least. It appears your talents, while bizarre, are not useless." The coldstone tears slid into the deep recesses of the boarskin purse at his belt while Irissa stared stonily ahead.

"I need no mount, nor guardian of my talents, Wrathman. Keep them as recompense for your inconvenience; I would not profit by my own mourning, though it appears mankind is not loath to leech on another's sorrow."

"Have you never wept before?" he asked curiously.

"No."

"And I have never bled before." His hand touched the severed mail at his side. "A woman who has never wept and a warrior who has never bled. It strikes me the elusive Finorian was righter than we knew; we had best make our way together for a while until some harmony is restored."

Irissa shrugged and turned away.

"Wait." The Wrathman's hand upon her arm was insistent. "Your tears are done, but I still bleed." His mailed palm opened like a bright red blossom.

"I may weep again," Irissa pointed out.

"And I may bleed again. My blood has no value in its wasting. I assure you no rubies form. You have the means—"

"I don't know what you mean."

"You Torlocs can heal with a glance. You can do that for me."

"No! I have not taken training in such things. Perhaps my glance may draw the blood from you in a sunset river. It's best you heal of yourself."

"I cannot. Fiforn's lance eats deep. I do not know how I came away from that encounter, or crawled to yonder pool. And I have walked far since. I will risk your looking awry; I have no other choice."

Irissa's glance fell to the mailed hand clutching her forearm, then to the open palm washed in streaks of red. Her eyes slid reluctantly to the Wrathman's side, where the broken Iridesium glittered dully in the waning daylight. She focused on the rust-rimmed break in the mail, looking hard, until it hurt her eyes; then she looked beyond that hurt to the hurt within, mining the essence of the Iridesium from within the metal's shifting colors, burning through into riven flesh below, seeing bone bridging to bone, blood flowing into blood, flesh knitting into flesh . . . Before her eyes, the crushed links of Iridesium writhed and reached for one another, joining, linking, and forging themselves together. She saw only a rainbow of ridged black metal and a rising blackness as the ground leaped up at her.

Chapter Three

A feeling of constriction dragged Irissa back to consciousness. Her wrists were bound. She tugged on the binding and felt her head snap back. She was sitting, and her conveyance rocked her. She focused forward, saw that her wrists were tied to a chased metal ridge of some kind, and looked beyond to a furred throw. She glanced left and then quickly away from a smoothly rounded expanse of Iridesium.

She was on the back of a bearing-beast, tied to its elaborately worked saddle as firmly as that contrivance was buckled around the sleek creature's belly.

"Awake?" The Wrathman swiveled his helmeted head, which was level with her own, though she rode and he walked alongside. But she felt another tug on her wrists, and the rope slid away. "Hang on with your own power, then, if you have any left. I did not know you would be so taxed."

"You are well?"

"Better than even before I met Fiforn's lance—or your eyes." He gestured expansively, his mail sending off a shower of iridescence. "Veil yourself; we are in full daylight now. They do not call it the Shrinking Forest for naught. We are but a few minutes from your home clearing, and already the hamlets of ordinary folk cluster around us."

Irissa followed his pointing arm to wisps of smoke curling over the nearby hills. "You found your bearing-beast," she noted, studying the distance to the ground. She had never been aboard such a mount before.

"No. Willowisp found me, as any worthy mount must." Kendric gave a friendly tug to the silken red mane. The creature turned its massive head and rolled a faceted brown eye at Irissa.

"It does not like me."

The Wrathman's hand slipped down the creature's well-muscled neck and gave it a slap. Willowisp shook his head until the crimson mane twisted around the short ivory horns atop it. "I do not doubt that," said the Wrathman. "You Torlocs are light for a war mount to bear; I think he senses you may be a heavier burden than is apparent."

"Then ride him yourself; I would rather walk."

"Soon enough, we shall both have mounts. I see a village smoking over the next rise. Stay back by the road." He tied Willowisp to a slender larch stripling, started away, and then returned, binding Irissa to the silver-shelled saddle before she could pull her clasping hands away.

"You do not like my race," she said, keeping both her glance and her head down.

"No. Why should you not turn to vapor as easily as that old seeress among her shifting stones? If you are indeed the last of your kind left in the Six Realms—"

"Five."

"Say you. I am not certain that is true."

"Finorian said it, and she cannot lie."

"Nor, it seems, can she remain to see her sayings tested. You may prove as elusive. Stay a while, Torloc." His mailed hand rested once firmly on hers, and then he was striding away to the grinding accompaniment of his armor.

Irissa stirred on the brocaded saddle cover. Willowisp moved his massive hooves in a short dance that indicated he was as restive with the arrangement as she was. He was a fine, high beast of polished red-gold hair smoothed to bronze along its muscular body. Willowisp seemed to read her grudging assessment, for the long neck arched and he shook his flame-colored mane until sparks seemed to fly.

"Hush," Irissa said, stroking her hand along the whipping

strands. The beast quieted instantly. But she was seething, as if ignited by some ember caught from her fiery mount. She pulled again on the thick rope that bound her, then hissed in disgust. The Wrathman's disappearing form still bobbed blackly over the green hill brow. Mortal thanks, that was what one got for aiding a mortal man. Irissa studied the rope strands. If metal could weld together under her glance, perhaps rope could part. She stared at her bonds, concentrating until all she saw was the rough hempen strand, and then that was merely an impression dissolving . . .

Only mist manacled her now. She slid off the high saddle and jolted to the ground. The Wrathman and his hamlet were beyond the bearing-beast's polished bulk. She turned, heading for the underbrush and the not-too-distant green outcropping of forest behind it. A sheet of burnished hair rose like a hedge before her. She ducked around it— and found herself caught in the reflection of a glittering brown eye and whirled again. A rope of crimson tail hair circled her wrists and held her fast. Irissa looked to the edge of the bearing-beast's eye, which was elegantly fringed with bright gold bristles.

"No wonder you found your master," she remarked softly, but in surrender. "You are wiser than he. And as untrusting."

For answer, the creature dipped his head to the sweet long grasses and munched a casual bouquet. He swung his tail once, pulling her around to face the unseen village. Soon after, the helm of Kendric of the Marshes rose over the hill brow.

"Beast," Irissa snarled over her shoulder. The mount whistled then, a high, soft sound that echoed over the hill. Another bearing-beast swayed into view behind the Wrathman, a fog-gray creature with ebony horns and sharp hooves to match.

The Wrathman came up without comment and patted his mount's tall flank. The imprisoning tail strands melted away in a crimson flicker. Kendric laced his mailed fingers together and stood by the new mount. Irissa didn't bother resisting; she put her foot into his hands and felt herself sprung into the black leather saddle. She brushed a vagrant strand of smoky mane off the high pommel.

"I should have bought you boots as well," the Wrathman noted.

Puzzled, Irissa glanced down at her tattered hemline. She always walked the forest bare of foot—now she had left it shoeless. She shrugged and gathered up the bell-strung reins. "I am glad you spared yourself further efforts in my behalf. This is an oddly knitted beast. I hope he did not cost you dear."

"No, only a tear or two, and those borrowed. He is yours, lady. Name him well, for he will serve you as he is named. And as for his configuration—well, I would hardly ride him into battle. But he has an elusiveness I thought would appeal to you. I think he hails from Clymarind, or some forebear did."

"Impossible. There are no four-footed beasts in Clymarind."

"Nor Torlocs in the Six Realms, if one would believe what some say." The Wrathman mounted and urged his beast forward. The creature flashed like fire and sped down the road. Irissa waited, then shook the belled bridle once. "Very well, nameless one, follow." The tall gray bearing-beast obeyed, floating smokily behind its fiery leader.

Flames danced through the soft, green gauze veiling Irissa's face. Across from her, the fiery tongues' reflection licked the Wrathman's helmet. As if feeling that heat, he suddenly stripped the helmet off, revealing a head hooded in Iridesium like some samite snake. Irissa dropped her glance to the fire. Behind her, the tethered bearing-beasts whistled softly to each other and occasionally stamped powerful hooves as punctuation to a colloquy in which no human could partake.

She pulled her unshod feet under her coarse linen hem, wishing for the moonweasel fur with which the lordlings lined their robes, and clasped her hands around her knees. "Am I the last Torloc?" she asked the thoughtful Wrathman.

He stared for a while at the ardent flames he had coaxed from gathered hazelwood. It burned sweet and warm and would keep any moonweasels off until dawn. But perhaps moonweasels were extinct, like Torlocs. Perhaps they had never really existed, save to frighten the young, the old, and the feeble into keeping to the home hearth. Perhaps.

The Wrathman pulled his sword closer to his side. He glanced across to his fireside partner as if anticipating a questioning look. There was only the tightly clasped hands, the slightly bowed and veiled head. "Moonweasels," he explained tersely.

"Have you ever seen one?"

"No." Again she heard a smile in his voice. "But then I had seen only one Torloc until now."

"Thrangar. Is he dead?"

The Wrathman pulled off his head mail; Irissa was startled to see dark hair spring from the retreating mesh like a woodland creature from a trap. He suddenly looked more human. "Is Finorian dead?" the Wrathman inquired in turn.

Irissa folded her arms deeper in her wide sleeves—another choice spot for moonweasel pelt; perhaps they would come, and the Wrathman could halve one or two and procure her some fur. "Where do you go?"

"We go to the City where the Circle of Rule meets."

"We? What does a mighty and muddy mortal from the marshes need with a Torloc?"

"Not conversation, I vow. Talking to you is like addressing a log. It's uncanny how great a thing a mere glance is when it is absent. I will sit at any angle to you so that you may look ahead and not see me." She heard him settle near her side. "Have you a name?"

"Irissa."

"And have you named your mount?"

She thought for a moment. "We Torlocs had no need to harness beasts to our purposes. I know not what to call him; he is like meadowmist, like rock, like smokeshadow . . ." A whistle vibrated from behind them.

"You have named him. It is good not to be too ponderous in these things; the wrong name can weight a beast's hooves."

"Yet you would misname your fellow beings."

"Torlocs? In the marshes we grew up and grew old fearing what we heard of Torlocs. When I came to serve the Circle, I found less fear of your kind, but no love for them either. And, of course, there was Thrangar. He was ever one of our company, yet isolated from it. When he—vanished, do you say?—when Thrangar was gone, it seemed we suddenly remembered a thousand suspicions."

"How did you come to be a Wrathman? Was it something passed down in your family line?"

The Wrathman laughed until his armor echoed the ring of it. "Passed *up* in my family, Torloc lady. I rose to my exalted position quite literally. Merely by being Halvag the smith's son and growing higher than his humble portal. There is but one primary consideration to becoming a Wrathman of the Far Keep among the marshmen." He slapped the sheathed sword that lay beside him. "The height to carry one of the Six Swords forged generations ago for the first Wrathmen. Among the people of Tolech-Nal on the world's rim, or the men of the City That Soars, or even the sturdy Rocklanders, family lines to rear Wrathmen have been established for centuries. We men of the marshes are too rough yet for such niceties; we rely on what has served men better than design—accident of birth. I am a Wrathman only because I am too tall to be anything other."

"You make light of your position. To be a Wrathman is an honor."

"Is it? So they have told me since I was fourteen years old and sent to the City of the Circle to study the arts of war. But of the Six, who alone has never carried an ancestral weapon? Thrangar had his bow and arrows; Fiforn has his singing lance, as I can well attest; Glent of the Stones, his granite-tipped axe; melodious Valodec of elusive Clymarind, his snakeskin gauntlet that never fails him; and Prince Ruven-Qal from Tolech-Nal has his burning crimson powder. For Wrathmen from the marshes, there is only the sword they take on with their oath and what little wit is left to them in such a company. You claim you have not undergone the Torloc ritual of power; perhaps you are fortunate."

"But I find I can do—things I had never thought to do . . ."

"Mere conjurer's tricks, rudimentary for a Torloc. One could find twelve wizard's apprentices in the City of Rule who could do as much for the eager market crowds and the few pence cast to them."

"The City of Rule sounds like a place that does not content you. Why go there?"

"It is the center of the Realms, Lady Irissa, perhaps center of our current riddle. I had been sent to Rindell to find and bring back Thrangar. Perhaps another Torloc will serve."

"I am prisoner of Rule, then?"

"No more so than I."

"It appears you are fond of riddles; no doubt the City of Rule suits you."

"No more so than you."

"Be careful, Kendric of the Marshes, or I shall look at you." She turned her head slightly and the veil fluttered around her face, like the green mist that had swallowed Finorian.

The Wrathman stirred, so that his mail protested. "Without having undergone Far Focus, lady, that would be more peril to you than to me, I think."

"Perhaps you overestimate my fear of peril."

The Wrathman stood, a metal mountain looming over her. "Enough word sharpening. We ride early."

Kendric returned from a check of the mounts with a great circle of cloak he fanned over Irissa. She caught it around her without demur and tucked it close under her chin. Moonweasel fur tickled her. Perhaps the City of Rule would not be so dreadful. Before the Wrathman's last rattles had died away, she was asleep, a Torloc trait she had never appreciated until now.

Another Torloc trait, that fine-tuning of hearing granted to those who did not rely on their eyes, woke her. The fire was snapping rhythmically, though its color had ebbed to a blood-dark glow. There was silence in the meadow. Even the bearing-beasts slept, their horn-crowned heads drooping. A slither sounded behind them. They did not stir. Again came a dry rustle, as of a leaf kissing the ground and then swept away, followed by silence and the crackle of fire. Then there was sound and motion behind her.

The night was waning, but not the moonweasels. It was said they were longer than the tallest man and crawled upon their bellies like a snake. Their amber fur was as soft as their numerous fangs were hard. And they had human faces, pale faces like the moon. Some said they had small, clever little arms and legs with which they could undo latches and wriggle over windowsills. They came in packs and preferred their victims sleeping; once their attack succeeded, they would hang on with their relentless teeth until human blood dyed their pelts crimson. After-

ward, they could be seen sitting in a moonlit circle, licking
one another's coats . . .

Irissa stirred, the wave of moonweasel fur against her
throat suddenly sinister. The heavy cloak rustled, but no
motion came from the sleeping Wrathman. She strained to
search out his figure in the dark and saw a crimson glimmer beyond him where the tall grasses whispered together
—two crimson glimmers, matched and symmetrically balanced . . ."Wrathman!" Her voice was as dry as the graze
of claws across grass. "Wrathman!"

He rattled to life, and the crimson gleams blinked out.
She heard the spine-chilling rasp of the great sword drawn
from its sheath. Its blade caught the moonlight as he swung
it almost contemptuously.

"Moonweasels, I think." Irissa pointed behind him and
he whirled, the mail and metal clanking around his figure,
jingling into silence as nothing more presented itself.

A fugitive wisp of fur wound around Irissa's throat. She
reached for the cloak and found it had ebbed to her ankles.
The fur at her neck pulsed, twined—was warm. She
screamed. Then the Wrathman's blade hung over her.

"Wait!" Irissa cried, daring to face the furred thing that
coiled around her. "Wait. It's only Finorian's cat Felabba."

The sword sighed through the air and touched earth. The
Wrathman knelt by her, his eyes upon the small creature
balanced on Irissa's shoulder. "Another Torloc?" he inquired in no good humor.

"Merely Finorian's old cat. It has no Torloc powers,
simply a nose for the table when fresh meat is upon it and
a liking for licking its whiskers in an opportune spot of
sunlight. It must have followed us."

"Half a day's ride? Are you certain it is not a dog? No
powers, you say? Well, it has a gift for disturbing a man's
sleep, as do you. I suggest you accommodate your familiar
and settle into rest so that, if any moonweasels do arrive,
I shall not be too tired to deal with them."

"It's merely a cat," Irissa complained as the Wrathman's
armor grumbled to silence again. She pulled the creature
off her neck and tucked it within the folds of her cloak.
Poor scrawny thing, poor Felabba, forgotten again. It was
a most unprepossessing creature, but having something
familiar about one was nice . . .

"Rude, that one," a voice purred near her ear. "And

you're learning it from him. No good will come of your
taking up with that mortal, you mark me. And move, you
great oaf of a Torloc; you're on my tail. We should have
stayed by the castle, both of us. You watch, Finorian can't
help you now."

Irissa looked fixedly at the creature that curled into her
cloak and shut its baleful eyes in sequence. Talked—it had
talked! Or it thought, and she had heard it. No powers? By
Thrangar, this was astounding. She opened her mouth to
hail the Wrathman's shadowed back, then shut it. He had
obviously not heard Felabba's comments on his manner,
and he just as obviously would not appreciate them, even
if they had been complimentary.

Irissa closed her eyes but did not sleep.

Chapter Four

Morning revealed that at least Felabba's outward appearance had undergone no startling transformation. The
cat was as lean and sharp-boned as ever, its white fur
somehow ruffled-looking. The only remarkable thing about
it was a pair of limpid eyes that reflected a spectrum of
green as various as the colors of the Shrinking Forest.
Irissa did not gaze long into the creature's eyes, only
enough to distill a certain smug twinkle.

Felabba leaped to the broad leather saddle a moment
after Irissa had mounted. The Wrathman cocked a dubious eyebrow, then shrugged and pulled on his helmet. As
he mounted his own beast, Smokeshadow danced lightly
on the grass, testing its ability to dislodge the new pas-
senger. Felabba balanced easily and twitched her unim-
pressive tail. The procession resumed, the Wrathman in
the lead with his great sword slung diagonally across his

back like a bow, Irissa behind on Smokeshadow, who shook the dew off his ebony hooves so smartly that not a bell on his bridle rang.

Felabba leaped to Irissa's shoulder and curled her tail around Irissa's mouth to smother any startled exclamation. "These men from the marshes are most lacking in chivalry. He made no offer to assist *me* into the saddle, as he did you. And at my years, it's quite a bound from the ground to the top of a bearing-beast's withers. You weren't entirely helpful either, my girl. It *would* be my misfortune to be stranded with the last Torloc in the Six Realms, and she is a silly fool who goes traipsing meekly along on a most uncomfortable—and fruitless—journey to the City of Rule. City of rue, my girl, that's what you'll find. Now don't bother arguing; I'm going to nap now, for I certainly didn't sleep all night with you about to roll me into oblivion . . ."

They rode all day, Felabba artfully curled into the high curve of Irissa's saddle, sleeping and silent as promised. The landscape was changing, gentle hills turning broken as they thrust up through the earth. Soon rocky prominences blocked the roadside view. The sapphire sky took on a grayer hue, and finally great, fast-moving masses of smoky clouds roiled across it. The heavens seemed suddenly lower, as if they were scowling down on the rough countryside. Once a small rock slide danced across the road, and Willowisp jigged to avoid it, his ivory hooves striking sparks from the ricocheting rocks. That small shower of light was somehow comforting.

Kendric finally reined in Willowisp. He lifted a hand to signal Irissa to stop. At that moment a flash of violet lightning wracked the clouds from left to right; they rolled back to unveil a blacker layer.

"A dry-storm is coming," the Wrathman said, nudging his mount up a roadside gully. "We'd best shelter here." He dismounted near an overhang of rock. "Small chance of fresh food in these Rocklands—and if we found it, I doubt it would be edible fare—unless Torloc tastes run to the reptilian."

Irissa shuddered and slid off Smokeshadow. Her feet hit bruising stones and she hopped about, each jump landing her on something sharper.

The Wrathman frowned. "It's boots for you once we

reach the City. Torlocs must truly hail from an elder world if they care not for such conveniences as shod feet. Sit down and I'll fetch you supper. Felabba can fetch for herself."

The cat growled faintly and leaped lightly to the rocks above Smokeshadow's back, padding silently out of sight.

"Now you've injured her feelings," Irissa objected.

"Nonsense! The creature's just following its natural bent. Are you saying the thing can understand me?"

"Not words, perhaps, but tone. You forget, we Torlocs have sharp ears for unsaid things."

"Do you?" The Wrathman looked at her oddly. For a moment Irissa was glad her powers required avoiding direct glances; but she could read tension in the way the skin tautened over his cheekbones.

"How long is it to the City of Rule?" she asked.

"Longer than you would like," he answered, tossing her the cloak from the back of his saddle. Irissa caught the garment without donning it.

"Why do we go there? What will you do there? If Thrangar and the rest of my people are truly called into another world, what use is it to worry? I might as well live on in my clearing, forgotten . . ."

"The Realm Lords and the Circle of Rule forget nothing. The last Torloc would be a prize or a pawn over which they'd fight until you or they broke. You have powers. What does it matter if they are dormant? They are still dangerous."

"And I ride to the City of Rule with you because, for the first time, the men of the marshes and their Wrathman have a weapon beyond the sword to match the other Wrathmen, the other races."

"Yes." Kendric handed her a packet of dried meat and cheese.

Irissa let it lie in his hand. "What makes you think you can use my powers when I cannot?" He withdrew the food without answering, and Irissa realized she had asked the wrong question. "What makes you think you can use *me?*"

"Someday you will look at me, Torloc lady, and know the answer."

Irissa shrugged herself into the cloak. A wind gust blew her veil back, but she shut her eyes to the dust it carried.

Another gust lifted the heavy cloak folds and riffled moon-weasel fur across her cheeks.

"No fire," the Wrathman said. "A dry-storm can be as dampening to wood as a wet one."

She heard him rustle about, unsaddling their mounts, then settle under the rocky lip to chew methodically on the food she had rejected. A low growl of hunger came from her stomach, but Irissa ignored it and shrank further into the cloak on a hard chair of rock at her back. The wind whistled shrilly, piping through the rocks with an almost intended melody. She opened her eyes briefly to find the horizon glowing sulfur violet. It was eerie; there were no trees to break the wind and turn it back against the overhang, only the Rocklands, yet wind struck her, a fierce wind that glued her to the stony shelter. The Wrathman's head was flat against the rock behind him, his eyes shut to the infinitesimal pieces of sand that massaged their faces with a dry tattoo of sensation. Another branched lightning struck, phosphorescent pink. Irissa squeezed her irritated eyes shut and thought of Felabba. When she opened them, the cat stood there, a rock-gray lizard with six legs dangling limply between her neatly pointed teeth.

"Ahhhh!" Irissa edged harder into the rock. "Take that thing away!"

Felabba dropped the lifeless prey and blinked her emerald eyes. Her back was to the wind and the dust was ruffling her coat, turning it an evil ocher shade.

"Away!" Irissa begged.

A thick point of steel flashed over the lizard and flicked it suddenly an arching distance away. "Torloc tastes," Kendric commented, pulling back his blade and shutting his eyes again. Felabba gave him one poisonous glance, then glided after her scaled dinner.

A clatter like hail pelted around them—not ice crystals but rock crystals; it seemed to be raining faceted pellets of amber and violet.

"Glent of the Stones was homesick for these dry-storms when he served in the City," Kendric said sardonically. "I suppose you yearn for your forests. It occurs to me there are worse things than springing from marshes one will never mourn . . ." A vagrant violet crystal fell upon the tip of his sword where it protruded from the overhang. The crystal shattered in a fan of color.

"It's unnatural," Irissa said, shutting her eyes against it. The Wrathman's silence was her only answer. She decided to forget about the Wrathman, the dry-storm, and even the obstinate Felabba, who was now quite probably becoming minced cat out on some exposed rock. The thunder cleared its throat and burst forth in a rumble, followed by the crack of more lightning. A violet branch burned itself through her closed eyelids and the dark behind them. Another clatter of thunder followed.

"Shield-shakers, Glent called them—the thunder-gods," the Wrathman said, speaking as much to remind her that they were, after all, merely mortals caught out in a mortal storm as to make conversation.

"Perhaps they know you bear a sword and would do battle," Irissa responded dreamily. "Go shake your sword at them, Wrathman, and remind them how mighty mortals are. But do not disturb me with your battle rumbles. I did not sleep well with Felabba anchored around me . . ."

She was gone, suddenly, into that blank, memoryless land the dreaming mind painted under all the pictures it etched on the surface. She did not dream, or remember dreaming, until she saw the Shield-shakers advancing from the dark-clouded sky, their boots making the rock towers around them shudder, their shields striking together like cymbals. Tall—they were taller than a Wrathman, three Wrathmen tall, their blue-black beards and long, wild hair streaming around their shining armor . . . It was too shining. She must not look upon it, though her eyes were drawn to the gleaming surface, so like an obsidian pool, with a dream desperation she never would have tolerated awake.

Look, some inner voice urged. *Look, Torloc!* The Shield-shakers drew near, forked lightning flaring from their sword tips as they swung the great blades around their helmeted heads. There were three—no, four—of them, each the mirror image of the others, and they engaged a shadow, a flat, black shadow that absorbed their blows and ebbed backward.

Look, look, the inner voice urged. A flash of violet lightning struck toward her, branching and stretching to touch her. A sizzle of pain streaked along her neck. *Look!* Irissa looked, her lashes sweeping upward like a curtain on a scene. It was dark; and still the dry-storm howled around

them and the Shield-shakers dueled in front of her eyes . . .
Something burned along her neck. She touched it and
found blood on her fingers.

A pair of implacable green eyes glared over her shoulder.
"Sleeping?" the cat asked. "Just like a dull-wit. Look, look
at what transpires before you. Your knight is sore-pressed,
lady; he fights himself and another and three shadows.
Look."

Irissa glanced to the place where the Wrathman had
settled for the night; it was vacant. And figures were bat-
tling in the open space beyond. She discerned now the
glitter of Iridesium lit by frequent flashes of the unnaturally colored lightning and saw another figure contending
with Kendric. A twin, identically armed, was swinging a
great broadsword two-handedly. It rose and fell on the
bronze slash of Kendric's shield. The other Wrathman had
forsaken his own shield and came cleaving toward Kendric
with swordstroke after swordstroke crashing down thunderously. Kendric parried with his shield and backstepped,
bringing up his own sword and thrusting fiercely. The
blow caught the strange Wrathman under his upraised
arms. He staggered backward, then rallied and hacked
forward, his lethal sword falling again and again on Kendric's ringing shield.

"Stop!" Irissa commanded, before she even knew she
had spoken.

The other Wrathman only swung his sword sideways,
aiming a blow that could cleave a man in half. Kendric
genuflected to the onslaught, then scrambled away, his
sword carving an arc that hit the ebbing Wrathman in the
backs of the legs. The Iridesium-clad figure staggered and
sank to the ground.

Irissa unclasped her tautened fists. It was done. Kendric
towered over his fellow warrior, his sword and shield
dragging on the battle-beaten ground. The only sounds were
the rasp of both knights' breathing and a soft complaint
from Felabba, who sat on a small rock and cleaned her
tail of battle dust.

The fallen Wrathman rose without warning and had at
Kendric, his blade pointed straight ahead, lancelike. The
point caught Kendric's shield off-center and wrenched the
protective bronze away. Kendric swayed, his shield-bereft
arm still limp from the impact. He sidestepped in groggy

surprise as the other Wrathman charged again, this time
raising his sword for an axe blow.

"Wait! I implore you, stop!"

Neither man so much as paused to attend Irissa's plea.
Kendric clasped his sword with both fists and drove it at
his opponent in a lethal arc. It plowed the side of the
ebony helmet and drove a furrow in the metal.

"Stop!"

The alien Wrathman staggered to his knees. Surely this
time the battle was ended, over . . . He pulled up his sword
slowly and swung it feebly at Kendric. The blow was weak,
but it caught Kendric on the thigh. Kendric toppled, re-
gained his knees, and aimed another ribbon of steel at his
adversary.

Stop! This time the word echoed only in Irissa's mind.
They would clearly hack at each other until they were
animated by their limbs rather than by their brains, like
slain animals that twitched in a mockery of life. She felt
a great anger toward such a pointless contest. She had
looked on a Wrathman's sword once and had made it light.
If only she could wrest away their weapons, force the
combat to an end . . .

Irissa shut her lids, seeing as always the dark and the
formless shapes of light upon it. She sculpted the amorphous light into a line—the long, forged line of a sword—
and met it with another line until the images were etched
on the blacks of her eyes, as the lightning fork had been
earlier. She made the images burn bright in her mind and
then she thrust them back, deep away from her. She would
not accept them. She saw them dull and recede. A distant
clang of metal shook her from the task. She dared open her
eyes.

The two knights were still reeling from the fight, but the
other Wrathman had staggered to his feet again and was
laboriously drawing up his immense sword, readying it for
a slash at the still-kneeling Kendric, who was dragging his
sword around in a great, slow arc to counter the inevitable
thrust. The five-foot-long blades were grim, unshining, the
color of dull lead, or the color of the gray rocks around
them. More color seeped along the blades and ran into the
ground, leaving them drained. The standing Wrathman
pulled more intently on his hilt. His sword point seemed
buried in the hard ground; it would not lift. Kendric

strained to raise his own lowered blade. It lifted a moment and caught a bit of vagrant light. Then it clanged back to earth like metal embracing a magnet.

The Wrathman hovering above Kendric screamed in triumph and wrenched his earth-bound blade into the air, as if uprooting a tree. His scream died, and so did his gesture. The upraised sword toppled backward, taking him with it. The two exhausted knights stared at each other, their hands still cleaving to their useless swords, their eyes still engaged in combat.

Chapter Five

"Traitor," the intruder gasped finally. "This is some Torloc trickery. You were always wont to side with Thrangar. Where is he—hiding to come out and slay me?"

"Glent," Kendric said, taking in a great gulp of air. "Glent, you came upon me by surprise and attacked me. I am no traitor; I but followed my mission to seek Torloc strongholds and Thrangar. But they are gone, as he is gone. The Torlocs are vanished from the Six Realms. You must seek your traitors elsewhere."

"No, you! You would have slain me; I read the blood lust in your disloyal eyes. You have broken oath. We who remain true Wrathmen will slay you on sight, with no warning called for. Who need exercise honor against a creature of slime and mud from the marshes?"

Kendric stirred, pulling again on his dormant sword. He fell back, unsuccessful. The dusty face shrouded in Iridesium across from him grinned. At least the teeth flashed white in the face.

"So your sorceries have snared even you. Kill me if you will; I will die with the memory of you groveling on the ground, where a marshman belongs. The elders were mad to admit your kind to the Fellowship of the Far Keep."

"Glent of the Stones, it seems you have little regard for the people of either the forest or the fen." Irissa had risen and walked between the two men. "In this you outdo Kendric of the Marshes, who has contempt only for Torlocs. So two Realms out of six discontent you. It seems your Circle of Rule grows smaller."

Glent's mailed hand grasped convulsively on his sword pommel. Irissa shook her head. "Forget your sword, mighty Wrathman. I have looked upon it, and it now bears the weight of every life it took. You will not be able to lift it until you atone for that toll, or until I release your sword from the dark of my mind." Irissa sat upon a rock set back from the fallen knights and regarded the air between them. "Now, then, what has brought two Wrathmen of the Far Keep to each other's mailed throats? You speak of Kendric as a traitor, Glent. Is that why he fought with Fiforn?"

"Fiforn? Did you kill him, marshman? Is that why we have not heard from him and must wander alone until, one by one, we perish of your treacherous sword and Torloc magic?"

"I know not if I slew Fiforn, Glent," Kendric said wearily. "I know only that his singing lance played a less pleasant tune upon me than it is wont when I hear it arrayed with me in battle. We came upon each other in the Shrinking Forest and fought as madly as we two have here. I came away wounded, in body and in mind. There was a great darkness over me—over Fiforn, too, I think . . ."

"The darkness of the traitor," Glent snarled, his face pinched with pain and hatred.

"You seem to sing only one tune, Glent," Irissa noted calmly, "and that a sour one. Is this the Fellowship of the Far Keep, then? Is this how the bondriders of the Circle of Rule, who from legend immemorial have defended the Six Realms against enemies outer and inner, speak when they meet one another?"

Although she had addressed Glent of the Stones, it was Kendric who answered. "She is right, Glent. Despite our differences, the Wrathmen have always held firm. So it has been in elder times, and so it was with us Six, until—"

"Until Thrangar the Torloc vanished," Glent finished sourly. He stirred and struck the pommel of his leaden sword. "And he vanished by sorcery," he continued stubbornly. "For I felt a great pull, as if something inward had been wrenched away . . ."

"I, too," Kendric said. The two Wrathmen stared at each other across the ground that was ruffled by their recent battle; a fleeting sympathy for the other's loss was in that look.

"Perhaps Thrangar did not go willingly," Irissa speculated during the neutrality that prevailed betwen the temporarily immobilized warriors. "Thrangar would not break bond with his fellow Wrathmen. Nor would he fail to come to Rindell when he had so intended. And why did he seek Finorian? Perhaps he anticipated his—"

"Treachery," Glent interjected, with more stubbornness than feeling.

"—his disappearance. Or death. Have neither of you thought that Thrangar might be dead? That that is why the balance of your bond is turned against you? That someone other than Torloc may be your enemy? For if the Six Wrathmen are compassless and turn their great swords on one another, who is to say the Six Realms may not do the same?"

There was a pause while both men stared reflectively at their swords.

"Five," Kendric said, shifting to his knees and leaving his blade ground-bound. "Five Realms now," he repeated, standing and flexing his shield arm painfully. Glent stirred defensively, grasping again at the hilt of his useless sword. "Glent, I shall not attack you. We ride to the City of Rule to delve to the root of these matters. Ride with us."

"With a Torloc?" Glent growled. When Kendric moved to protest, Glent's dark brows loured, as thunderous as the dry-storm which had buffeted them earlier. "And with a man from the marshes, always a slippery breed? The marshlander was always the least among the Wrathmen; I will not follow one's behest now. Nor will I promise to spare you battle, should we cross paths again."

Kendric's hand squeezed once, as if clasping a sword of air or making a fist. "Neither Rocklander nor marshborn ride now, whether first or last. Our duel has weakened us both. We must join forces, not contend with them."

Kendric clasped his side, spent from speaking, and sat slowly on a nearby rock. Glent rustled and rattled, attempting to rise, then subsided.

"Perhaps when we mend, Glent will listen to reason," Kendric told Irissa. "We are not greatly hurt, thank Rule and not our intentions, but we cannot ride yet."

"Nor can we wait." Irissa stood and contemplated her steepled fingertips. "You say Glent will recover in a day or two . . ." Kendric nodded. "Then we leave him. If he wishes to pursue us, it will be a bitter ride."

"But I myself cannot ride for half a day, at the soonest."

"I will restore you."

"This is no simple axe slice, lady, for a facile knitting of flesh and mail," Kendric protested. "Glent and I battered at each other like Shield-shakers until our bones are bruised. You have not that kind of general power . . ."

"I think I do, but whether I can focus it properly—" Irissa knelt by the sitting Wrathman, aware of a shield of silent hostility at her back. "You have no tolerance for Torloc sorcery, Glent," she remarked without turning. "Be thankful I am not of a mind to aid *you*."

Irissa did what she guessed she must, for on this occasion the entire man required healing. She brought her eyes from the dusty, bronze-colored marsh emblem on his tunic to the ring of Iridesium circling Kendric's face. She knew the borders of that face, for she had looked that far, though never to its center. She brought her eyes slowly, tentatively, to his.

Kendric reared away slightly. He had seen the silver coinage of her Torloc eyes before, but always edgewise, spinning away from him in an elusive glitter. He had not looked fully at her, and by now he was as certain as she of the danger of such an enterprise. For power she had, though perhaps neither of them knew its limits; it was raw force, unshaped, untutored, capable of cutting many ways.

Irissa herself was startled by the amber warmth of Kendric's eyes, like those of her unempowered mother. She felt a shock of familiarity as she probed their brown-gold depths; he had been her sole companion for two days, and that bred a certain knowing beyond sight. The more deeply she looked, the closer she would be to self-reflection. She must skim the surface, a leaf on water, and if her look were true enough and Torloc enough, she would smooth where she had passed.

It seemed Irissa entered a vast and velvet world. She became as small as a dust mote and she glittered through the topaz air of that world, something vagrant blown through a carelessly unshuttered window. She found the soundless force of physical pain barking at her like voiceless but alerted watchdogs. And confusion sentried the room, an anxious sort of restlessness that gathered itself into a corner to try to net her floating self, but she glided away, ignoring it, and addressed the presence of pain. I know you, she told it, as does everything mortal. In knowing you, I name you. And I banish you. Take up your company of ache and bruise and throb and burn and decamp to someone other. You are not needed or wanted here.

She felt the place's aura grow faintly yellow, then gold. Only at the center of it, the dark confusion persisted, a yawning, mobile pit that sucked her forward like an indrawn breath. It was a pool now, black and forest-shaded. She fluttered away toward the pinprick point of exit, while the black, blank vortex behind sucked on her departing will, threatening to swallow it.

Then she was staring into the black of Kendric's pupils. She moved her focus farther back and saw his face. It was not an unpleasant one, and now he was smiling. She remembered the vortex in his eyes and drew her attention back, as a skirt might be swept clear of that which would besmirch it.

Kendric's smile held a bit of wonder. "I feel—refreshed, as if I had sojourned somewhere pleasant . . . Torloc talents—I'll never libel them again!" He rose supplely. His golden eyes fell on the dull length of his ensorcelled blade. "My sword!"

They were the same words he had first spoken to her, but he seemed not to remember that. "My sword." He spoke to her as if she were a page whose duty was to equip him. Kendric grinned. He had found a world in which travail and pain could be banished with a look. He had always believed that such things were possible of Torlocs; now he believed that they were possible for him. His confidence radiated as certainly as the Iridesium that mailed him; its glow obscured the hesitation that clung to the figure of the Torloc woman before him more insidiously than her veil.

Irissa dropped her eyes to the spell-mired weapon. Her lids lowered, then flashed open and she looked upon it until the metal glowed with a white, rising gleam. Glent muttered an invocation to his stony gods, then was silent. Kendric plucked up the shining sword and held it aloft.

"My life is as worthless now as these stones on which I lie, Torloc lady," Glent wailed in his helplessness. "You have unweaponed me and given me over to a mere marshman to be slain."

The taunt to his heritage hardened Kendric's face; a shadow smoked across it, and the gleaming blade dulled to mortal metal. His knuckles whitened around the hilt.

"Kendric." Irissa knew how to meet his eyes now without seeing past him to the part of herself that lurked within them. "You must help me mount." It was a request, reminder, and plea.

Kendric elevated the great sword, looming over Glent. Then he sheathed the blade and slung it over his back, striding without farewell to the mounts waiting dumbly by the rocky embrasure. His good humor had returned by the time he bent to lace his fingers and help Irissa spring into the high saddle.

"You had best tie me to the cantle," she said softly, her voice colorless.

"Tie you?" He looked up, startled, from the bridle.

"Hush. I do not wish Glent to know how my powers tax me . . ."

He looped her proffered wrists efficiently to the leather and quickly mounted Willowisp. A soft, white shadow leaped to the back of Irissa's saddle, and the party began wending its way through the rocks. Soon Glent was as gray and distant as the stones for which he was named.

"You are tired," Kendric said, dropping back to ride alongside Irissa.

"As tired as you were," she admitted, glancing swiftly at him from lowered lids. His newfound buoyancy absorbed and rejected her meaning. He grinned.

"By the Circle Lords, but you are a pretty companion, Torloc. What need have I of my fellow five—or four now, with Thrangar gone—when I've an instant restorative at my elbow? I would ride into the mouth of the Swallowing Cavern itself with a Torloc for companion . . ."

"Glent would not," Irissa said wearily. "He has little use for Torlocs."

"Glent!" Kendric scoffed. "These Rocklanders are stern and stupid folk. They have not the imagination to see possibilities, as do we."

"We? You forget, I am no ordinary Torloc. It was always held that I had access to the greatest powers of my kind—"

"And so you do." Kendric's mailed hand patted her white knuckles. "We'll go straight to the Circle of Rule and, between your witchery and my will, we'll delve to the bottom of this riddle." He spurred Willowisp into a burst of orange color and trotted ahead.

"And what of the riddle that has no bottom?" Irissa mused softly.

Smokeshadow followed the Wrathman dutifully all day, his sharp ebony hooves striking a rhythm that lulled Irissa into an exhausted stupor. It was a long ride, for Glent's attack had aroused them early, and there was little point in not continuing their journey as long as what passed for daylight lanced through the still-continuous cloud-cover. The Wrathman sang, his deep voice ringing off the stony outcroppings that marked their way. It was a lively ballad, full of valiant deeds, wondrous beasts, and ladies so lovely the very air curtsied to them as they passed.

Kendric finally dropped back to her side again, riding in silence for a while. She felt his eyes on her bowed head. "What troubles you?" he asked at length, a begrudging seriousness in his own voice.

Irissa sighed. Their mounts' trappings creaked rhythmically in the silence. "I was thinking on something Felabba said—"

"Felabba?" Distrust crept into his voice and established residence.

"Did I say that? I was thinking of Finorian," Irissa said, lifting her eyes to his. He appeared nonplused, as if the new directness of her gaze were a phenomenon more unreal than the previous unnatural constraint.

"And what did your Finorian say?"

"She spoke of a man, a warrior, in contention with an-

other. And with three shadows of that other. And himself.
I thought I detected a certain parallel."

Kendric was silent for a moment. "We must be nearing
the City of Rule; you are catching the disease of riddles-
manship, Lady Irissa of Rindell. Torlocs should see and
not be heard." He had spoken sharply, and the words
thudded between them like a lance fallen short. "You are
weary," Kendric said more lightly. "And bootless in a
world full of stones. We will soon near the villages; a
night on inn feathers will lighten your heavy looks. Believe
me." He lowered his helmet visor and looked ahead, spurring Willowisp, so that the tall red beast took the lead
again.

Something soft brushed Irissa's cheek. A white tail, albeit a scrawny one. Irissa lifted a hand from her saddle
rim to stroke Felabba. The old cat curled into her lap
and stretched its neck upward. A low purr rumbled beneath the fur. "You did well, my girl," the cat said tartly,
her praise as rough as her deep pink tongue. Felabba
licked a rose-padded foot. "Well enough. Almost worthy
of Finorian, this healing. It's not easy to reach into another's eyes and come back sane. A shame you had to
lavish such gifts on yon thick-skull. But one must practice on something, whatever is at hand. You think I relish
rock lizards? There's little meat despite all those legs, let
me tell you. This knight is of their ilk. Much to chew
upon and little gained. Do not frown your Torloc brow
over such tough and thankless meat."

"Oh, Felabba." Irissa smiled faintly. "There was as much
danger of the light going out in his mind from that seeing
as there was a threat to my sanity. Yes, I began to see the
ways of my powers, and mazes within those ways. Riddles?
Perhaps, but there is a touch of sorcery in the oaths of the
Wrathmen. He said himself that the sword he carries was
not mortal-forged, nor do I think it is mortal-sheathed.
He bears magic, though he knows it not. And I saw the
black veil of the magic rended in his mind. He is as spell-
bound as ever Fiforn or Glent, but he admits it not. He
is dangerous, Felabba, this marshman, more dangerous
than you might think . . ."

"Dangerous?" The cat spoke in a protesting squeak.
"You have not seen dangerous yet, my girl. Wait until the
City of Rule, and then don't come mewing to me that one

puny Wrathman is dangerous. Wait till you close with the Circle, Torloc. Then you will know why your race was called elsewhere."

"The Circle? But the Circle of Rule will help us!"

For answer, Felabba regarded Irissa from slanted green eyes, elevated her rear leg gracefully over her shoulder, and began licking the base of her dusty tail.

Chapter Six

Whatever magic Kendric carried did not extend to prophecy. There were no feather beds for them that night, but a cushion of hay that insinuated golden needles through fabric into flesh. Perhaps had the Wrathman arrived at the rude country inn alone, there would have been lodging, despite the way his helmeted head rang periodically on the smoke-eaten rafters. But Irissa stood mutely alongside him. She kept her burnished gaze down; even with her head bowed she towered over the plump, swarthy women of the countryside who waited on travelers. Irissa was marked as alien from the first.

In the end, Kendric delved into his purse for another coldstone, which was received as much with loathing as with avarice. It won them loft space above their mounts' munching heads.

"I'd as soon lie on the marsh monarch's brambles as on this pincushion," Kendric complained, tossing in his mail. Irissa lay silently on the spread cloak, aware of the small prickles of hay needling through it and of Felabba's kneading claw-work on her midriff.

"And must that creature be up here with us?" the Wrathman muttered. "Doubtless its disreputable appearance did much to discredit us at the inn. It's useless; better we had left it as rations for Glent . . ." Felabba bridled, but Irissa stroked the arching back until the cat's kneading rhythm resumed.

"You fear for him?" Irissa asked.

"For whom—Thrangar? You know what I think about—"

"No. Glent of the Stones. Your bondbrother we left weary behind us. You fear for him."

"No." His tone was defiant. "He has passed beyond whatever bond bound us. He would have killed me; he spoke with contempt of my kind, my people—"

"Of whom you are so respectful. Oh, Kendric of the Marshes, Discerner of Traitors, have you not seen the traitor in yourself?" she mocked gently, sounding like Finorian. He was silent, and only the old cat's feeble purr rumbled between them. Irissa sat up, dislodging Felabba. "There's moonlight streaming through the loft window. Oh, I wish I might look at it; I feel it is a peaceful thing, the moon. Finorian was wrong to fear it."

The Wrathman's hand restrained her wrist. "No. You must not risk your powers." His gauntlets were gone. A circle of warm flesh ringed hers. But his hand was large and strong; she did not resist its pressure.

"I have healed you, Wrathman. Would you deny me comfort?"

Kendric held her still, watching her sharply in the moonlight that flooded across her back. "Your hair is dark," he said abruptly. "It glitters like Iridesium in the moonlight." He looped a finger through the gleaming braid at the side of her face, watching the rainbow shift in its sheen. The straw crackled beneath them as he pulled her closer, by wrist, by hair. "There is one thing I have never known of Torlocs," he said contemplatively. "I do not know if they can mate outside their kind."

The warmth of his hand pulsed at her wrist. Or perhaps it was her own pulse she felt, throbbing with something— protest? Irissa sat very still as his finger set her braid brushing her cheek with a pendulum's regularity.

"None of us mate—or hate—outside our kind, whatever we may think," she said finally, turning her face toward him. "Do you know upon what you embark?"

By the time she faced him completely, there was only the recumbent shadowed figure of the Wrathman in the hay. Only that and a certain warning tingle at her wrist.

But she heard his breath, a trifle rapid, as that of something that lies in wait.

"I think that even Torlocs require sleep," he said at last. "I know that marshmen do."

Irissa lay back and turned her face upward into the low rafters, where nesting doves cooed a peasant's lullaby. The straw between her and the Wrathman crackled. She swiveled her head sideways to find the great length of his blade between them. As her glance paused upon it, the dull metal flared brighter, casting a wink of light that made her look upward again.

Felabba edged away and blinked upward also. "Mortal men," the old cat's thoughts whispered into Irissa's ear. "Trust neither them nor their swords." Feline eyes shone gemstone green in the dark and stared up again. "I go hunting," Felabba said. The narrow body sprang upward with ageless agility. There was a sudden fluttering among the doves. Irissa shut her eyes.

She must have slept, or something like that, for she was aware of moving footlessly from beyond some strange silver mist. She had dreamed of Thrangar in an ancient hall, his great broadsword rusting in its scabbard and a furtive ebony web veiling all his quenched Iridesium . . . She had seen Felabba there, stalking a skeletal bird that perched upon the hilt of Thrangar's sword; she had seen the flash of pale claws and the clattering arc of scattered silver bones . . .

Irissa glanced sideways to the sword of Kendric. It still lay between them, but its hilt—nearly a foot from its plain apex to where it crossed metal with the crossbar—caught an errant gleam of moonlight. It caught and amplified the gleam, until the pale glow grew and filled the hilt with lamplike light. The hilt grew rock-crystal clear, exuding moonlight with a white, nonlunar heat. The crude runic slashes that decorated it by ordinary light turned into a scowling, mythic face. Then even these fleeting features vanished, and the hilt seethed with bright white life that nestled into the surrounding hay and burnished the golden strands red. Smoke wafted upward and wreathed the empty rafters. A white, smoky form bounded down—the sated Felabba, her meager fur roughened until it fanned in a prickly ruff around her entire body.

"Wrathman! Your sword!"

Kendric roused instantly, his Iridesium mail dancing gaudily in the reflected brilliance of the sword hilt. The burning hay around the glowing haft crackled and spread red cheer on a broader swath. Kendric instinctively reached for the pulsing hilt, his hand retreating unwillingly from the heat.

"Torloc, what—?" he demanded urgently.

Irissa shook her unveiled face. "It is beyond any looks that I might give it. I have tried."

The illumined hilt lit Kendric's face from below, painting it heavy and sinister. But his mouth worked in perplexity even as the shrieking whistles of their mounts rose from below.

"They scent the smoke," Irissa said needlessly.

Kendric's fist formed and then dissipated. He spread his fingers and seemed to warm them above the lighted hilt and the pooling flames.

"No," Irissa warned. "Some spell is upon it. If my eyes cannot affect it, why should your hand not sear to ashes upon it?"

Kendric's eyes met hers so steadily that she glanced away, fearful of finding reflection there. His voice was as steady as his look, although it seemed to come over a vast wall of snapping crimson flame. "It is my sword. I swore Wrathman oath upon it and have borne it these ten years. If it wishes to take my hand, so be it."

She saw his splayed fingers hover above the throbbing hilt, then close upon it. The Wrathman gave a rending cry and rose to his full height in the flame-lit loft, as if drawn up by some mighty, invisible force. But his hand still grasped the sword hilt, though the rising flames showed his face in agony. Irissa rose also, drawn as unwillingly to her feet. She felt rather than saw Felabba twine around her legs and heard the sear of Kendric's flesh upon the pulsing hilt. He transferred the blade suddenly to his other hand and looked at the palm that had first grasped the pommel.

"It's . . . frozen," he said wonderingly. "Cold. But not hurt at all." Even now the smoldering straw was graying to ash, and a cold pall of moonlight lay across the loft.

"Some witchery?" Irissa asked. "In the sword?"

"Not in it," Kendric answered slowly, "but through it. Perhaps an enemy, some sorcerer, has sent a spell to destroy us."

"But who? And why? Did Thrangar's blade ever glow so? Or Glent's when he attacked you? It is your sword; you carry it as Wrathmen have done before you. I cannot believe some alien sorcery could turn it against you. If it is magicked, it is by you and you alone."

Kendric laid the sword's length gently upon the straw—not between them now, but on his other side. His brows met like enemy lances over the bridge of his nose. He settled down again wordlessly, deep in thought or some emotion.

"By myself!" he said finally when she had pulled the moonweasel fur to her chin and Felabba had resumed a post near her head. "Perhaps . . . But that is mad! It has never served as barometer to my thoughts before. Rest easy, Torloc woman, though I shall not put the sword between us again. It is too great for such a purpose—and too little."

A red sunrise painted false embers in the hay the next morning. Kendric and Irissa rose wearily, but Felabba stretched luxuriously and yawned until her dainty fangs showed to her throat. Kendric examined his hand—unhurt, his glance answered Irissa's darting look—and picked up the sword to sheathe it and sling it over his back in one long-practiced motion.

They broke fast upon the road with fresh inn-bought food and nudged their mounts toward the bold bronze sun that bobbed into sight above the towering hills like some teasing sort of good-luck charm.

Chapter Seven

The Circle of Rule was meeting in the high, domed chambers of the government house. The edifice was a marvel of concentric innovation, the work of the long-dead Torloc architect Griondel. But the heads of the gathering men never tilted up to regard the peacock gleam of Iridesium scales that feathered the dome's inner curves or to study the branching traceries of gilt wood carving that topped massive pillars made to mimic weepwater trees. Griondel was long dead, his name forgotten in the City of Rule, save by moss-bearded archivists in the municipal library.

But the Circle of Rule's thoughts were not bent on such decadencies as edificial genealogy. Members of the Circle of Rule spoke only in phrases, and those carefully nourished to buffer meaning with a thick padding of confusion.

Wooden trestle tables sprawled in clumsy yet meticulous order across the floors tiled in cobalt-blue porcelain, a color like the eye of the ocean on a cloudless day. The Circle of Rule sat on their moonweasel-skin stools and unrolled their somber parchments. They were now ten, though once they had been twelve—two men from each of the Six Realms, chosen, as the Six Wrathmen had been, to represent their people and the place from which each race sprang. But time had blurred the selection process as much as it had anesthetized residents of the City of Rule to any soaring Torloc architecture. The people of Rule did not look up.

"Here." Ronfrenc the executive implementor stabbed a pale finger into the parchment he unrolled across the rough table in one gesture. "There's still a nest of Torlocs here, I vow." Of a body, the nine other men crowded their

40

shorn heads into a circle and stared down at the faded paper.

The members of the Circle of Rule had become a breed unto themselves and reflected that exclusivity in their attire. Unassuming brown or gray was the color of their daily garb of plainly cut trousers and tunics that modestly belied the wearers' power. Occasionally, one of their number would affect some dashing touch of fashion—a saffron stripe in his tunic, perhaps, with matching yellow ribbons to lace his indoor boots. It became an inner-circle power game; if the innovation came from one who must be respected, Rulians could expect to see their leaders streaming yellow bands of color for a month or more as they darted about the City, taking sumptuous lunches at one another's ordered palaces or inspecting the latest fortifications or City sanitary projects, or simply went off to some deserved recreation in the form of folg, a game that involved pursuing a ball about the surface of highly polished marble while attempting to divert it from a series of traps below and a squad of trained ball-snatching falgons above. Then, one day, the golden banners would vanish and all would be normal—until a junior member would turn up at council on gilded platform boots and either remain solitary in his affectation or encourage a swarm of similarly shod imitators.

This day discretion had prevailed; after all, these were unfrivolous times. The Circle of Rule was sober-dressed, somber, and remarkably similar-looking—a conclave of dour faces, pale from too much sitting under airy roofs.

"Torlocs . . ." an elder meditated, pulling thoughtfully on the gray beard that blended into his equally gray tunic. "The Shrinking Forest is but a glade now, Ronfrenc. I know Rindell—an ivied keep for women near an empty Iridesium mine. What have we to fear from that?"

"We have much to fear from somewhere!" Young Tillack, who represented the men of the City That Soars, was speaking. But he had been reared at the feet of the Circle so long before they had finally clasped him to their appointed bosom that he secretly felt there was something vaguely ludicrous about his fabled mountaintop birthplace.

Eight disapproving pairs of eyes were raised to Tillack. Ronfrenc kept his firmly on the parchment, an ancient map that purported to tell the whereabouts of Torloc settlements when Torlocs had been one of the Six Realms in fact as well as in courtesy.

"Fear?" Ronfrenc asked finally without lifting his eyes from the map. "The Circle has naught to fear. Naught from a mangy remnant of sorcerer folk and naught from some mysterious wrongness the people prattle of."

Ronfrenc's breath stirred the parchment. Then he swept it away. "We are done with old fears, men of the Circle," he announced, meeting every eye with his own certain one. "If there's some witchery afoot, we'll stamp it out. We are not living in eldritch times. There's magic enough for us in our own heads to meet any sorcerous challenge from a pack of feeble smoke-manufacturers and shape-transformers—"

"Thrangar—" Tillack began tentatively. Once Tillack had seen the Wrathmen ride six abreast up the winding icy road to the City That Soars, and something about their Iridesium glitter still reflected off his mind.

"Thrangar!" Ronfrenc snorted. "Speak not to me of ponderous metaled stalks made heavy by their own outdated armor. Ours is an age of solons, young Tillack, though you are not wise enough to see it. We need no such anachronisms as ancient champions. The Wrathmen were ever soldiers of fortune, mere berserkers, held together by some flummery of oaths and bonds. That's a tale fit enough to warm a child's ears upon a cold night, but nothing for grown men to fasten upon. We have no need of Wrathmen, Tillack. Come, see the Work."

Ronfrenc's soft boots hushed across the marvelously tiled floor, a floor so deeply blue it looked as if he walked on water. He skated to the room's center under the overarching dome. Here some disruption had caused a great circle of tile to be canvas-swathed. The dulling dust of the caulkers still lay across the floor surrounding this dun-colored pool of fabric.

Ronfrenc raised his hand. A pair of anxious pages scurried from their posts near the foot of Griondel's pillars and swept the canvas back. It wafted away like a clumsy cobweb in their hands, laying bare a great circle of mosaic in violet, scarlet, bronze, cobalt, azure, and saffron.

Ronfrenc shuffled across the rainbow surface, pausing in its center like a great gray spider inspecting his dew-jeweled web. "This, Circle members," he began dryly, "is our City of Rule." He pointed to a symbolic six-pointed star at the map's edge. "Here are the borders of each of our Six Realms—the daub of green there is the Torloc lands you fear so, Tillack."

Ronfrenc began a slow round of the circle's limits, his soft-soled feet pausing to point out a landmark contemptuously now and again, much like a dancer's foot despising the ground. "Clymarind—that's this violet section here. Always hard to position precisely, Clymarind. We shall have to devise some method of anchoring this most unpredictable nomad island. For now, my technicians have made it movable." His foot sent a diamond-shaped formation of mountainous purple rolling like a child's toy. The mock island of Clymarind skated across the cerulean surface that represented the Abyssal Sea and crashed on the coastal topography that represented the City That Soars.

An indrawn breath shivered through the Circle members, and Ronfrenc lifted amused brown eyes. "My model is durable, gentlemen, more durable, perhaps, than these lands are in reality. And you fear Torlocs!"

Ronfrenc deliberately covered the small green spot at the Realms' remote outskirts with his engulfing gray boot. "Hear the results of my census and then say if you trust to Wrathmen and Torlocs," he boasted. "I have numbered our people by race, by degree, and by vocation. From the humblest reed-cutter growing bent-backed in the marshes to the haughtiest liege-master on elusive Clymarind. My— our—agents have ferreted out the last of the ditch wizards and sewer sorcerers from the City. Rule will be free of such nonsense, and then we can use what we have learned to build a single Realm of such power and admirable effectiveness—"

"But, Ronfrenc, we have from time unremembered been Six Realms. To propose only one means warfare at best. At worst—some kind of sacrilege. I recall old legends of how the races were split and the Wrathmen assembled to guard the difference . . ."

"You are old, Verthane. And I do not forget you came to the Circle as representative of proud Clymarind. Your service here has not erased that stiff-necked superiority in you. You are an eccentric, Verthane. My agents have seen the volumes you keep in your draperied votive room. You are old and remain in the Circle on sufferance, Verthane. Your opinion is not required."

Six of the Circle quailed at this uncustomary harshness toward its senior member, who still wore the floor-length robes of the Circle founders rather than the boots and trousers and tunics of its modern-day members.

Verthane tucked his palsied hands into his flowing sleeves, rather like an old cat gathering into himself before the fire. His gray eyes pricked Ronfrenc once and darted about the Circle with the agility of the mind behind it. Verthane marked embarrassment among the Circle members who knew him well and a certain hardened disrespect among those elected to the Circle more recently, those who seemed to share Ronfrenc's stamp.

"Clymarind shall not be as easy for you to pinion as you may think," Verthane answered formally. "Nor Torlocs as simple to stamp out as a piece of colored glass is to shadow with your executive foot, Ronfrenc."

"Perhaps not." Ronfrenc's innocently plump face hardened into a dangerous mask, like congealed fat upon a plate. "But one senile Circle member certainly is within my immediate power. I charge you with being sorcerous, Verthane. You have kept forbidden volumes in your palace. Your ways are old ways, and while we do not fear what mumble-jumble you might mutter over your moonweasel-fat candles, you are a detriment to morale. I hereby restrict you to your fusty palace and the company of your own mind, Verthane. Does the Circle uphold me?"

There was a mutter of protest mixed with approbation. Then the Circle closed ranks, and whatever objection there might have been to Ronfrenc's decision was drowned in the pooling looks of his lieutenants among the members. Verthane stood alone and abandoned in the center of his fellows.

"Take him to his house and see that he keeps there," Ronfrenc ordered.

Two men broke like shadows from the pillars' foot; in an instant they had engulfed Verthane's frail figure.

"I see you are well embarked on the road to tyranny, Ronfrenc," the old man said. "First you turn every citizen into a spy, then you turn every counselor into an enemy. The Oracle of Valna had a saying for this: 'Beware of that which sees without eyes. Most fear what you most despise . . .' "

"Riddles, old man? Aye, sorcerers ever boil over with cryptic nothings," Ronfrenc snorted, taking a quick round of his many-colored map. "Here. Every head is accounted for. I know who, what, why, and wherefore to every soul in the Six Realms. My figures, the energies of my census-takers, mean more than any ramblings from the Swallowing Cavern. Valna and its Oracle, indeed! Away with him! We have maps to study, and his interest is—magic!"

The Circle laughed uneasily as Verthane was dragged away, his feet trailing from under his old-fashioned robe. The Circle laughed more freely and leaned forward as Ronfrenc seized Verthane's cast-off staff and began to scribe a pattern on the Six Realms under his feet. "The Oracle of Valna, that has been silent these five centuries! And a remnant of Torlocs, as played out as their Iridesium mines! These are not matters for grown men to gnaw upon. What shall we do to depose imperious Madorian on Clymarind and to set marshmen against Rocklanders, so that we can install our own governorship, eh?"

The heads drew closer and lower, until it seemed the Circle of Rule drank deep of something at their feet, something pooled and poisonous on the floor—power, to slake their ambition.

Ronfrenc prodded gently at the miniature island of Clymarind with Verthane's abandoned staff. The violet-mountained landscape rocked across the cerulean surface, a ship in stormy seas.

"Clymarind next, I think," Ronfrenc said, "now that there are few Torlocs to play witchery war with us. Madorian *will* recognize our authority . . . Yes, Clymarind!"

Chapter Eight

❖❖❖

"What do you know of Clymarind?"

Irissa's question barbed through a silence that had webbed Kendric for most of the morning. He reined Willowisp and dropped back. "Clymarind? It's where the Wrathmen take sword-oath. Why ask of Clymarind?"

"Something made me think of it. Have you ever returned there?"

Kendric shook his head until the black helmet rainbowed in the sunlight. "Your vanished Finorian kept you truly in the dark, Lady Irissa; you are shockingly ignorant of such matters for a Torloc. One only comes to Clymarind once—once for oath-taking; if a Wrathman comes again, it breaks the bond."

"How do you know this?"

"It is—simply known."

"I may not know much, Kendric, but I know the sound of a piece of nonsense. Perhaps some people wish to keep the Wrathmen from Clymarind for a reason. You are marvelously trusting for a marshlander."

"Perhaps." Kendric ran his ungauntleted fingers contemplatively through Willowisp's fiery mane. "As I said before, I have not bled until of late. I suspect I shall have opportunity to do more of it. Look, there is Rule." His finger pointed through a break in the rocky landscape.

Irissa stood in her stirrups and looked over a valley that sprawled to a certain dark cluster near its center, a navel in a green whirlpool of countryside. The City's buildings appeared from this distance as unrefined as the hulking rocks still circling the riders, save that here or there some fanciful dome or spire thrust heavenward like a long, artistic finger. Even now these architectural digits caught the rays of a setting sun, so that their tips glowed garnet, as if blood-dipped.

"We'll stay the night here," Kendric said, dismounting with a series of creaks that set the weary Willowisp fidgeting.

"We can reach the City in but an hour or two more," Irissa objected.

"Rule is no place to enter past sunfall. The City keepers have a way of interrogating twilight strangers nowadays . . . I think your silver eyes would earn us too much suspicion."

Those eyes flashed at Kendric, but the Wrathman had turned and was attending to his mount. Irissa sighed and felt Felabba desert her saddle with a bound. The matter appeared to be a case of two against one.

"Dismount, then," Kendric urged. "Or can your Torloc eyes move the sun back to the apex of the sky?"

"No, I cannot do that. I doubt I could now move so much as a hair on Smokeshadow's mane," she admitted, suddenly aware that her insistence on reaching the City of Rule was more exhaustion than impatience.

Kendric materialized at Smokeshadow's side, remarkably quiet for a man in full armor, and lifted Irissa down. She was immediately aware of bare feet on rocks unwarmed by the sun and sank to a sitting position. Smokeshadow sidestepped wearily away.

"Aye," Kendric said, assessing the general fatigue. "We've traversed the spine of the Realms, for the City of Rule lies like yon setting sun, with the kingdoms radiating out from it and nothing beyond but the Abyssal Sea. So we rest and enter Rule under dayshine."

He pulled a piece of hardened cheese from his food pouch, broke off a moldy edge, then tossed it toward Felabba. The old white cat drew back from the morsel daintily, her baleful eyes measuring Kendric's faulty generosity.

Irissa laughed. "She won't eat cheese; that's for her prey to eat."

"She'll eat what there is, and so shall we," Kendric said gruffly. " 'Make Do' is the motto for Rulians nowadays, with the Circle taxing the citizenry for even the burlap in which they bear their tribute coins Cityward."

"Taxes? Torlocs never had to gather gold for such purposes."

"You had other things to give the Circle of Rule," Kendric said, falling heavily to the hard ground and dropping sword, helmet, and head mail beside him. "No fire this night; we're too close to the metropolitan patrols. The Circle has initiated all kinds of safety measures of late, though against what I cannot fathom." Kendric tore into his dry bread and cheese.

Irissa broke hers into many pieces so that whatever flavor remained would be detectable. Ah, for the life of the Rindell keep, with its fragrant herb salads and fresh roasted platters of white scalefish—blind creatures that dwelt in pools at the mine shaft bottoms and, some said, swam in from underground streams leading to the very Abyssal Sea itself; how tender and flaky their meat had been! And the honey-soaked puddings Dame Agneda would concoct in the warm bakery behind the salad garden! She remembered the great hall torches flaring, ever-lit by some trick of Finorian's, and her mother, tall and graceful at the great table, dark braids caressing her gentle face with each motion she made . . .

Something glittering fell on Irissa's repast. She plucked a coldstone off the bread and hid it in her palm from Kendric's glance. This man had a habit of turning grief to his advantage. If her tears were worth so much, it was her they would serve, not another.

She dropped the last bread crumbs for whatever Rocklands denizens might be about, then settled into her cloak —Kendric's cloak, actually; but his chivalry in forgoing ownership had somehow made it hers. Its blond moonweasel pelt would keep out the night's advancing icy fingers. The City and the Circle tomorrow, perhaps, would offer some answer for the last Torloc in the Six—no, Five— Realms. Perhaps there might be even some news to quiet Kendric. He was a troubled man, as Felabba had warned, and therefore troubling . . .

Dreams didn't come, or if they did, tiptoed on their way out past her dormant consciousness. Something teasing did come, though. A soft, tickling wind, circling around her forehead and throat. Warm and tight, comforting almost, a wave of dry pliability washed over her mouth, and an almost maternal circling pressure was on her body. A long-remembered voice hissed out of her undreamed dreams— attack!

Irissa's eyelids snapped open. She stared into a flat, pale face upon her chest, regarding her as unwinkingly as Felabba did when so ensconced. The eyes were amber and oval, lashless, rimmed in black. There was no nose, just slanted caverns in mid-face. And the mouth—no, maw— was slack, resting, but filled with black rows of savage teeth and a supple tongue of deep sylvan green which even now flicked in her direction, acknowledging her awareness.

The ringing warmth tightened; she was bound the length of her body by the creature's coils. The head slithered toward her face. She saw the tiny, black-nailed hands that fingered upward.

"You wear my kin." It was more purr than speech. The little hands were furless and wrinkled. They clutched the cloak folds and drew its entire body nearer still. The face hung flatly in her view. The voice was molten, its tones as insidiously swathing as its undulating body. There was something of Finorian in it, some elder wisdom.

The face bent abruptly to her throat, the teeth somehow glittering, though they were black and should reflect nothing. She would have screamed, but her voice was captive in her body, as she was held captive by the encircling presence. The creature rubbed its hairless face on the moonweasel fur around Irissa's throat, then drew back to regard her. Its maw opened leisurely in a yawn, and its thick, green tongue vibrated with a kind of high-pitched purr as it swooped toward her throat again, black teeth bared—

Bound, half-hypnotized, Irissa thought of looking fully at it with her inner sight, but knew the voracious evil behind the amber eye would devour her as surely as would the moonweasel's physical being. She looked instead to the bodyless fur still ringing her shoulders, an ironic hangman's rope of luxury. Every fiber in her body demanded that she watch the moonweasel head. Every Torloc instinct brought her eyes away from it to the long-slain moonweasel she wore.

And then the lifeless fur stirred, raised, and presented a mirroring form to the oncoming attacker. The expression of surprise in a moonweasel's face was merely a ripple across the pale flesh. Irissa's reanimated moonweasel moved from perfect duplication of its fellow to something darker from her Torloc mind, something larger, with scaled limbs marching down its ophidian sides, like those of the six-legged lizard Felabba had fetched once. A long, lethal snout formed, also like a lizard's, with strong white teeth that snapped together on chill night air and on warm moonweasel flesh. Then something warm soaked through the cloak and something heavy writhed away on the rocks . . .

Irissa screamed and threw off the blood-heavy cloak. She looked toward the sleeping Kendric and saw only a vibrating mound of pale, golden fur. She screamed again, stood, and saw a flash of white fur spring past her ankles. She saw it leap atop the throbbing golden mountain with a wrenching hiss of rage. The golden mountain bucked. Felabba—her back arched, tail bristled, and clawed feet splayed—was thrown off like a piece of volcanic flotsam. A moonweasel unwound itself from Kendric's motionless form and coiled into a thick basket of fur in the clearing's center. Its maw widened, and it circled its long body around the retreating cat, coiling tighter. The back behind the head was gemmed with ruby drops of blood in neat rows of four . . .

Felabba hissed and spat, turning in her narrowing isle of ground as the moonweasel slithered around her in ever-tighter loops of muscular, furred body. Kendric rattled slowly to his feet, seized his sword, and unsheathed it in slow motion. Bewildered, he moved toward Irissa.

"No!" she screamed. "Save Felabba. I am in no danger—" Something snaked around her ankles and tightened. She fell, facing once more into supple golden fur. The creature hissed and was answered from above by a slashing sword. A tiny, twitching hand grasped one of her braids. Then Kendric's spurred foot kicked something long and limp away.

"Felabba!" Irissa begged as soon as she could talk.

He finally turned back, but another moonweasel dropped down from the rocks above him and enmeshed his sword hilt in its toils. Kendric staggered, his face adrift behind a wave of pulsing fur. Irissa thought of the hilt the clever creature had immobilized, then remembered their innyard stopover and their bed upon the straw. A soft light flared somewhere in the rocky clearing and grew brighter, as if fighting smothering. There was a sudden stinging odor of burned fur in the air. A screech of agony sounded as the blazing hilt shone through the hand that held it until the fingers glowed red.

The moonweasel looped to the ground, and the sword followed it with a blow that cleft the body in half. A green tongue twitched in the glow from the sword hilt. Kendric changed hands upon his weapon and whirled to where the other moonweasel had Felabba's throat in its small, wringing claws and was drawing the cat's head toward its gaping maw. The slice of sword through pelt and muscle had an almost pleasant ring by now. Felabba fell and sidestepped the writhing body of her tormentor.

Kendric dropped his sword and looked toward Irissa. He glanced at the fading hilt. "Your work, I gather."

"Yes, but how—?"

"This time it gave heat as well as light," he grinned ruefully. "Thank your Torloc ancestors that there seem to be no more of this pack." His mailed foot prodded a limp body over. "I could not have held on much longer. Ach . . ." He blew on his blistered hands, while Felabba leaped up to a small rock and began preening her coat.

"Nerveless beast," Kendric complained. "If I hadn't bothered to preserve her scrawny hide, I'd not be nursing my own flesh now."

Irissa advanced apologetically, but he waved her back. "No, I'll heal myself, thank you. This time I'll pay the price of pain for a normal course of events. Enough witchery for me."

Irissa stopped. "She saved you, you know."

"Saved me? That ragged feline?"

"The moonweasel had you sleep-entoiled. Felabba distracted it with her claws so you could wake."

Kendric sighed and cast a dubious glance at the still-ruffled cat. "Well, kitty, it seems I misjudged you. You're a sorry sight and doubtless no more fond of me than I am of you. But you have your uses, as do all Torloc things. The next inn we reach, it's a fowl for your supper."

Felabba blinked and returned to her bathing.

Irissa concealed a smile and turned to the circle of motionless moonweasel forms. "So many—" she began.

"Many? They say moonweasels have run in more than fours before—but not so near the City of Rule. Of course, we had no fire to keep them away, but still . . ."

"Another sending?"

"Lady, you would have all the Six—very well, Five Realms peopled with sorcerers, dispatching sendings after us. No, it's some natural phenomenon—what the legends told of, perhaps a migration—" He began heaving the corpses out of their immediate vicinity.

"My cloak as well," Irissa advised, averting her face.

"*Your* cloak?"

"It's tainted with those creatures' blood. I'll not don it again."

Kendric lifted it, then regretfully hurled it away. "A cold night we'll have of it, then."

Irissa nodded, still standing dazedly in the clearing's center. Kendric sat against a rock wall, pulling her down beside him. "Sleep, then, if you can," he said. He leaned his head against the pillowing rock and shut his eyes.

Irissa kept hers open, even after the deep breathing beside her betokened a warrior's willingness to toss off past danger like a bad dream. Much later, Felabba jumped down beside her and curled into her lap, purring contentedly and, for once, absolutely without comment on the night's events.

Chapter Nine

◆·◆

They rode into Rule virtually unnoticed. Only the gate-keepers scowled silently at them, their hands tightening on their weapons as nervously as their lips tautened over their teeth. Few others were about. It was early morning, a time as rosy in its way as the previous day's sunfall. But the light was weak; it was unable to pierce the folds of Irissa's face veil, to burnish Willowisp's bronzed sides, or to catch more than a feeble reflection off Kendric's Iridesium mail.

Even the villages ringing the City had seemed damped and still when they had ridden past. True, they had risen early, a circle of moonweasel carcasses somehow no invitation to long slumber. But the City was strangely sluggish. No shutters swung open above the riders' heads. Not even a sudden shower of morning wash-water from above threatened to flood their progress. And the timbered doors of both shop and residence were closed. A nosegay of weeds was affixed above each of the latches or sprouted from doorside buckets. It was a dull growth of petrified green with no flower, only leaves. There was an odor of old fires about the weeds.

Kendric led them down Wormwinder Street, named as much perhaps for its circuitous length as for the weavers who dwelt along it. Irissa stared upward, surprised at the City's third-storey balconies and geometrically inventive windows shaped into triangles, circles, and stars. A row of yellow-feathered gutterhawks kept claw-footed company along some higher rooflines, chattering raucously.

"It's early," Kendric said to nobody in particular, scanning the streets that were deserted of even the solitary scavenging dog or cat.

Felabba's lean neck yearned upward, her eyes lusting for the washline of yellow feathers above. But the old cat kept her place behind Irissa, though she had eaten nothing since the Rocklands lizard. They stopped at the sign of a fanciful loom, and Kendric swung down into the street.

"If the shopkeepers are about, they'll outfit you here," he told Irissa. "You need shoes and a gown, perhaps, since we go to see the Circle." He dredged a fistful of coldstones from the mine of his purse.

"Now? They can attire me?" Irissa asked incredulously, unable to imagine any article of clothing that was not the time-consuming product of Dame Agneda's weaving.

"The ladies of Rule, when there was something to dress up about, used to favor the place," he answered impatiently. "It's all I know of it. And fashion in Rule comes in quantity. What is worn, all wear. So shops such as this cater to the mass desire of the moment. Choose what you will; it will be more correct than your archaic linens."

Irissa surrendered Smokeshadow's reins and brushed by a pot of the alien green weed and inside the sober shop door. Kendric paced to the street's end, peered down a cobblestoned byway, walked back, patted Willowisp's

horned forehead, stopped, looked at Felabba perched on
Irissa's saddle, shrugged, and paced again.

She came out sooner than he had expected. He heard her
newly shod step touch stone and turned, his jaw dropping
enough to be noticed by the edge of Irissa's vision. She had
chosen fine sillac-lined boots, embroidered over in diamond
patterns of Iridesium thread, trousers stuffed unceremoniously into the boot tops, and a knee-length tunic of matching worm-woven gray stuff, tied with a tasseled green silk
cord. She carried a black cloak that flaunted a lick of green
lining, almost like a moonweasel showing its tongue, and
another cloak of tanned orange sillac skin from the outer
Abyssal islands, collared in dark brown beaver fur.

"For you," she said, tossing the heavy fabric at him with
the satisfaction of paying debts fairly but unobsequiously.

Kendric caught it without comment and slung the cloak
over his shoulders. It came only to his knees but gave the
Wrathman a more civilian air as he doffed sword, helmet,
and head mail and attached them to Willowisp's saddle.

"Do you not fear for your weapon?" Irissa asked, springing into her saddle astride, the circle of her short skirt
lying across the bearing-beast's back like a ceremonial
drape.

Kendric laughed and mounted. "You've seen Willowisp's
talents before; he would not take kindly to any tampering
with his responsibilities."

"I hope you have no more stops planned," Irissa said.
"Your cloak cost the last of my tears. I trust you do not
lose it."

"Your generosity is as caustic as your glance," he shot
back. But he spurred Willowisp lightly, and the tall beast
trotted amiably up to the intersection. Irissa followed, trying vainly to keep Felabba from rubbing appreciatively
against the silkiness of her new garb.

"Oh, delightful," the old cat muttered between purrs. "I
shall not have to scratch my nose on those miserable linen
skirts of yours henceforward. Perhaps Rule will not be so
bad, after all." The green eyes flashed upward again and
lingered on a pair of yellow gutterhawk crests peering over
the gable edge.

Irissa wiggled her toes within the downy confines of her
new boots almost as contentedly as Felabba exercised her
whiskers at the bird-ripe rooftops. Both Kendric and Fino-

rian had been right, unlikely allies as they were. It was good to have shoes in a thorny-footed world. And her attire, albeit practical, made her feel competent to address the Circle of Rule and plead for some sort of intercession into the events that had banished her Torloc race like smoke. She was not a prisoner of some miserable lanky mortal with an imagination as short as he was long. She was her own mistress and about to demand accounting from a world which had proved unpredictable. She was about to do something for which her life in Rindell had not provided her, but she found she liked the challenge.

Kendric finally stopped at a long, low building ripe with the scent of hay and raw leather. An attendant scurried up. Willowisp and Smokeshadow bowed their horned heads and trod leisurely after her.

"We Wrathmen always leave our mounts here," Kendric explained, looking pointedly at Felabba. "Rule is not accustomed to seeing such strapping beasts on its streets."

"Felabba is not strapping," Irissa replied, picking up the cat. "And I'm sure the people of Rule are used to seeing a cat or two."

"Are you?" Kendric asked with a certain savoring as Felabba dug her claws into Irissa's stomach and springboarded off her keeper to the ground. "I've not seen a cat since we came to Rule. Nor anything that runs upon the cobblestones. All I've seen are these forsaken stalks of weed—" He brushed at a weed swatch hanging from the stable courtyard lintel and strode into the street.

Irissa had to trot to keep pace with him, her new boots beginning to pinch. An anxious backward glance showed Felabba stalking along behind, with frequent glances upward again. The streets were still oddly empty. When the party arrived at the great, star-shaped plaza before the governmental palace, a wave of yellow birds broke against the sky at Felabba's pounce among them, squawking protest.

"That's odd; it's as if they hadn't seen a cat," Kendric mused.

"No wonder Rule has no attraction for Torlocs," Irissa said. "Imagine a City that has no room for cats!"

A sprinkling of people crossed the space before them, and Kendric sensed a certain cold curiosity. "Come along."

He commandeered Irissa's arm and led her at a toe-stubbing pace across the ancient, uneven pavement.

"What a marvelous pattern," she noted in mid-passage, studying the glint of gilded mosaic as intently as Felabba had scanned the bird-filled skies. "There's a scene here in the center of the star—it looks the way Rindell must have been before the Shrinking Forest overgrew it."

"It's an old scene, lady, but probably as Torloc as you," Kendric said shortly. "A good part of the architecture in this section of the City was Torloc-made. Don't gawk like a country maid; you'll not impress the Circle with that." Kendric was slightly flushed as he paused by the great, arched double door that bore the inscription above: *Where Rule is, there is happiness.*

"Perhaps you'd prefer me to wait outside, like Felabba," Irissa suggested, allowing the slightest slice of angry silver to graze the Wrathman's eyes.

"And draw your veil. One look at your ill-starred eyes and the Circle will send you to a keep even deeper than your Torloc rins—and as empty."

Irissa pulled the screening veil over her face, noticing another harvest of dried weeds thrust into the huge Iridesium door handles. From behind her veil, she saw that the weeds shimmered with a phosphorescent glimmer, almost as if they were invisibly growing. She frowned, but Kendric irritably ushered her in when the twin doors swung away from them. This lintel, at least, was high enough for a Wrathman. They advanced down a vast and empty hall. Irissa was aware of a surrounding glitter above them from Iridesium-feathered domes. Everything seemed shiny—old but sleek.

She suddenly recalled her fear of reflection; this sort of glitter was exactly the thing from which Finorian had isolated her. At the edges of Irissa's eyes, a procession of shadows kept pace with her and the striding Wrathman. More Wrathmen moved in dim formation on either side, each escorting a Torloc lady. Mirrors! She had heard the word used only in hushed tones. She was foolishly drawn to take sidling glances at the parallel temptation that bracketed them. But seeing even enough to realize what they were was doubtless already dangerous. She gazed ahead, not looking, until she and Kendric came into the hexagonal center from which the building's wings pointed outward like lances.

"Your business?" a page demanded, impeding their progress. He was clad in black and had to tilt his neck to an awkward angle to face Kendric.

"I am the Wrathman from the marshes. I have come to report on my mission."

The page glided away on soft shoes. Irissa stood in the shadow thrown by Kendric and looked up at the distantly glimmering dome. Torloc architecture, he had said. And she had always believed that her forest fortress had been the natural expression of her people's artistic inclinations. She was aware of a far older, almost a more decadent, spirit animating the Iridesium-scaled curves above. Perhaps the Rindell keeps were not Torloc at all, but merely a refuge the vanquished Torlocs accepted as their own for a while before moving on to other, more alien places, such as that in which she had dreamed of Thrangar—vast and remote. Was that where Finorian had gone, where Irissa herself ought to have been transported? What was she doing here in the City of Rule and in the shadow of a Wrathman?

"The circle does not meet, Wrathman. Why have you presented yourself now? And without Thrangar?" Ronfrenc the executive implementor stood at the base of one sweeping gilded pillar, the shadow-garbed page trembling away in obeisance. Ronfrenc glided forward silently, until he stood in the slightly shifting light reflected from the central dome above him.

Kendric advanced in recognition of the executive implementor's presence, the Wrathman's every motion a protesting creak or click of mail, leather, or metal. He sounded like a great armored Rocklands lizard moving to meet a moonweasel.

"Thrangar is not to be found, Ronfrenc. That's why I returned. He was never seen in Rindell, and all the Torlocs have vanished as thoroughly as he. I saw one disappear with my own eyes—an old seeress, Finorian, who melted from the glade like the call of a wailwraith."

Ronfrenc snorted and came farther forward. "It's you who go blind in the world, then, Wrathman, not Torloc seeresses. Tell me they all died; tell me a raiding party from the Abyssal Sea brewed them into wind for its beaten

gold sails; tell me the moon drank them. But do not tell me
they vanished. No one vanishes from Rule these days, unless I order it. We are done with old sorceries. But if
Torlocs are gone, good. We have no need of them.

"Nor do we have need of your kind, Wrathman. This
quest was the last riding of the Six. Valodec lingers in a
Soarian abbey, ill of wounds contracted when he was set
upon by moonweasels—moonweasels, can you credit it?
What use are warriors who cannot stem a legend, a few
pests from the further forest? An army of moonweasels, indeed! And I have not heard from Glent of the Stones this
fortnight. Which, by the by, are you? Not Prince Ruven-
Qal, surely, else you would not want for oil to smother
your clatter. Ah, yes, you must be the unpruned marshlands
lad—I see you carry no weapon but that accursed sharp-
edged walking stick of a sword. I am collecting swords these
days, Wrathman. I have here Verthane's, taken when he was
found to be sorcery-tainted. Perhaps you would care to add
yours to the collection."

Ronfrenc reached out a small, pale palm with the contempt of a master demanding that some servant place a
token upon it. Kendric did not so much as creak for a moment, a very long moment. Then he abruptly unslung the
sheathed sword that crossed his back and laid it hilt-first
across Ronfrenc's hand. The weight bore the executive implementor to his knees on the intricately tiled floor, until his
pointed sleeves trailed in the blue that represented the Abyssal Sea. All eyes focused on the sword's point. It rested near
the amethyst mound of movable Clymarind.

"Enough," Ronfrenc ordered. "Take back your oversized toy. It is as outmoded as you."

As Kendric grimly reclaimed his blade, Ronfrenc gave
the representation of Clymarind a shove with his silk-clad
foot. The bit of wheeled topography skidded across the
tiles like a toy a child had tired of; it rolled destructively
toward the foot of the gilded weepwater pillar.

The star chamber was vast, the tiled floor variegated in
color. At the carved pillar's very root, it seemed a hedge of
Torloc green sprang up and deflected the spinning island
from its doomful course. The small construction spun away
into the room's center, where it wound to a stop. There was
no longer any hedge to be seen at the pillar's base. Ron-

frenc's eyes met Kendric's for the first time, and they were worried.

"What—?" he began, but Kendric shrugged carelessly.

Irissa stepped from his shadow into the light, and Kendric's shrug changed into a start of warning. Neither Ronfrenc nor Irissa noticed it, for they were staring at each other like long-lost enemies who had suddenly met.

"Torloc," Ronfrenc said, his voice as unguent as a moon-weasel's. "A Torloc with the seeress' silver eyes. I forgive you Thrangar, Wrathman."

"She is—untutored, Ronfrenc," Kendric said disparagingly. "Useless, really."

"All Torlocs are useless now, save for pestiness. But if she is indeed the last, as you say— I could keep her here to amuse my council. You could perform a few tricks with my Realm-map, as you did with floating Clymarind, eh, girl? It was you, wasn't it, who sent little Clymarind on a safer course just now? Such—entertainments—would do much to impress those who needed reminding of my purpose. And my power."

"I have not come here to propel toys across your pretty floor, sir," Irissa said. "There is dire danger to the Realms. As Kendric said, all the Torlocs have vanished. Some influence is abroad—I do not know if it is mortal, elemental, or alien, but some force tugs at our very survival—"

"So!" Ronfrenc interrupted. "Superstition! The basest metal in the mind's armament. I've banished you wonder-workers—you pretty, petty players with love potions and shape-slipping and small puffs of powder to dazzle weak eyes. Your kind has always lulled the population into pinning its hopes on wonder instead of work. I will have workers in Rule. I will have sensible, stouthearted armies with crossbows and firejectiles. I will have level streets in Rule, with intersections that meet at right angles. I will have buildings whose circling domes are mathematically mated. No diagonals for me, no ellipses. I will have none of these trickerish, Torlockian, sorcerous deviations from the right and the proper. It is time the Realms and their City answered to a consistent geometry. You are an improper fraction in my mathematics, Torloc. Either modify yourself and serve me—or leave me and be my enemy."

Ronfrenc's face had thickened with pallor; it was clear he spoke from the center of his convictions and power.

Irissa dared skim the surface of his implacable eyes. The light within them was the color of old blood, ancient blood spilled and never wiped away. Behind this curtain boiled a wall of flame, and beyond that lay ice, so clear and impervious that the blue within it froze even as the firelight danced upon it. She probed further, but beyond the wall of frozen hatred she could not penetrate. She looked through its clouded surface and saw a dozen leering, grinning faces trapped within, the small, human impulses of this man who led the Circle of Rule. And even these were malicious, spiteful creatures. She saw the familiars of a sorcerer who lacked inward power and thus wreaked misery outward. He was less even than a moonweasel, and therefore he was more dangerous, because he was a man.

"I will not serve you, Ronfrenc," she finally answered. "But neither shall I oppose you. I will return to the forest and live there with what spirit of my people remains. I will be the last Torloc in the Five Realms. And eventually, long after you precede me, I will die and your mathematics will at last come out even. I cannot help that I do not fit your calculations. It is my nature, and nature is the one thing in Rule you cannot change."

She turned and left, passing the hall of shadowed mirrors without giving them a thought.

Ronfrenc took a few steps after her, but they were silent ones. He paused beside Kendric, not bothering to look up at the towering Wrathman's face. "Kill her," he said. "Kill her and I will keep you, alone of the Wrathmen, in the Circle's service."

Kendric unslung his sword again and brought it whistling around his shoulder to the floor. He balanced it there, his hands folded over the hilt at his chest. They both glanced to see where the point had chanced to rest. It was on a vagrant spot of green that the mapmaker had meant to represent the shrinking Torloc lands.

"You have no need of Wrathmen," Kendric said stoically.

"In this instance, yes, I do. The ancient swords, the elder bond, may be sufficient to end her. I cannot be sure my merely mortal arrows would find her. She is dangerous."

"She has promised you no harm, no enmity, no interference."

"She is dangerous."

Kendric looked down at his sword point impaled on the

vibrant green before answering. "I come from the marshlands, Ronfrenc—a dreary place, whose inhabitants know
too well the world you sketch for the rest of the Realms.
I always thought I had no more than my height to recom-
mend me to the fellowship of the Six, but I was glad
enough to take oath and sword for my own—"

"I am not interested in your personal history, you overgrown varlet," Ronfrenc snarled, pacing impotently.

"I have served the Circle well in these years," Kendric
continued, unperturbed. "And though the bond that linked
the Six Wrathmen has grown weak in these days—else you
would never dream of loosing us from the Circle's service
like so many toothless moonweasels—though only a thread
binds us together, it is stronger still than the webs you
weave, Ronfrenc. She will not serve on your terms, and
neither will I."

On his last word, Kendric's fist struck his chest, and the
mailed fingers buried themselves in the bronze emblem
embroidered onto his tunic. He rent the decoration free
and threw it at Ronfrenc's feet. It landed on the blue that
represented the Abyssal Sea and reflected there like a
bronze sunset.

Kendric turned and strode away, the rattle of his with-
drawal echoing from all the overarching Iridesium and the
hard, tiled floor. It finally faded. Then all that could be
heard in the star chamber was the sound of rending cloth
as Ronfrenc retrieved the emblem and ripped it to pieces
until his pallid hands were abraded to red.

He scattered the shreds like a fistful of stars across the
Realm-map. When he had gone, the gilded threads winked
solemnly back at the Iridesium dome.

Chapter Ten

Irissa stood blinking outside the double doors that had shouldered shut on her like a householder dismissing a peddler. And what had she to peddle, beyond her silver eyes and a certain pride of self? Nothing, it seemed. She dropped her face veil and searched through its gauzy green hedge for Felabba, but the cat was gone. Somehow she had thought Felabba was one certainty left in this diminishing Realm-world. Irissa stepped further into the open plaza, feeling some unnameable lack—the creak of mail behind her, the presence of the Wrathman who had accompanied her these last several days. But he was in his City now, within his Circle; he had no need of her. And she, certainly, had no need of him.

She moved briskly across the plaza, peering down its capillary pathways. But they all ended in pointed little cul-de-sacs where townspeople gathered in hushed gossip and where hawkers paused to rest their burdens of weep-water-leaf baskets and the outspill of overland fruits and Abyssal Sea fishes that filled them. Fishes, ahhhhh! Even as Irissa fled a particularly pungent gathering, it occurred to her that here was where the lizard-surfeited Felabba might drift. But there was no sign of the cat. Was she truly on her own now, then? Irissa pulled the emerald silk tie at her waist tighter, merely to feel she was preparing for some outright action, and crossed the plaza again, this time never slowing to study the central mosaic. She reached the street through which they had entered the area and started down it. A soft growl, and something that made it darted into her path.

"Felabba! I thought I'd lost you."

The green eyes stared reproachfully up. "It takes more than a Torloc to lose a feline of my accomplishments," the cat said, sounding oddly muffled. "Well, take it, moon-weasel brain. I can't tell you what a strain it is not to puncture the creature. And quite plump it is, too."

Irissa cupped her hands under Felabba's mouth. Something soft and wriggling fell into them.

"A mouse! Felabba, you needn't share your prey with me. A mouse is not to my taste, I assure you. Or if you don't wish it, I'll let the little furry go—"

"No!" Felabba's response was more yowl than word. "I'd eat the vermin gladly, you great silly girl," the cat spat through her pointed white teeth. "It's no ordinary mouse, though you are being more than ordinarily stupid. Look at your mouse, Torloc."

Irissa unpetaled her palms and examined the tickling bit of fur that nibbled at her caging fingers. "It's a clever little thing, I'll grant you—and look, its tiny tail is scaled like a lizard's—but what's this? Braided hair . . . The creature wears a harness!"

"Yes, yes, yes," Felabba sighed, licking a paw and running it exasperatedly over one eye. It looked as if the cat were smoothing one superiorly arched eyebrow. "And we furred things, you know, don't wear jewelry—unless some human has inflicted it upon us. I suggest you unhand my catch and follow its tasty little golden tail. I will bring up our new pet's rear." Felabba licked her whiskers and trotted off alertly behind the creature.

Irissa debated, then followed her tailed guides along the deserted cobblestones.

The narrow byway had just swallowed the party when the great double doors split to emit Kendric of the Marshes. He stood for a moment blinking in the sunlight, then took off his helmet and head mail, like a man removing shackles. He started across the plaza, the sunlight winking from the metal he wore as if from a mirror. Pausing at the entrance to a narrow street, he turned and looked back to the government building with its spire and dome gleaming in the daylight radiance. He suddenly hurled his helmet at the distant double doors, like a small boy throwing stones at a mired carriage.

Both gesture and helmet fell short. The Iridesium helm

rolled down the shallow stairs leading from the great doors, ringing from step to step, like an out-of-tune bell. It stopped and lay rocking softly on its rounded side in the street. The people in the plaza all cast anxious looks at the abandoned helmet. Nobody picked it up until Kendric bent to recover it.

Light was dim along the narrow byway. Soon Irissa had only Felabba's twitching white tail to follow; she had lost all sight of the bit of golden fur that drew them on. Felabba paused abruptly. Irissa had all she could do to keep from kicking the old cat.

"Clumsy," Felabba sniffed. Irissa crouched to hear her better, staring into the wedge-shaped face. "Up we go, now," the cat said, looking intently at a mound of alley debris piled against a wall.

"There?" Irissa was dismayed.

"Aye, there." The cat prowled around the next corner and promptly returned. "There, all right. We have a welcoming committee with crossbows threaded on the other side. Up, Torloc, the scale-tail waits on the sill, and if I go first, I may consume our tender little guide."

Irissa scrambled up the pile of debris, not stopping to consider how she was to negotiate the small, dark, star-shaped window above. But once started, she wriggled through, her elbows just fitting into the star-arms and her boot heels catching stubbornly on its sharp angles; she tumbled inside, rather than entering in a dignified manner.

Felabba catapulted onto Irissa's prone stomach and rebounded off gracefully. "You've not squashed our guide, I hope," the cat commented sourly, casting green beams of greed around the dark space they occupied. "I deserve a snack after all this effort."

"Effort! It was I who served as springboard, you ungrateful feline. And now see where your advice has led me—to a prison hole blacker than a Wrathman's helm—"

"Hsssss," Felabba commanded. "Someone comes."

Indeed, a vertical line of light grew in front of them, rather like a door opening on a lighted space. But there was nothing behind the light, only something lean and dark within it that stretched and expanded. Then a narrow man stood in the room with them, his long robes dusting the unseen floor and a streaming golden beard lying across his chest like a chain of office. He extended a cupped hand and opened it. On it sat the mouse, its supple tail wound companionably around one of the man's attenuated fingers. Its harness gave off the gleam of braided gold in the unnatural light; Irissa saw it was woven of hair taken from the very beard before her.

"Away, my pet," the man ordered. The mouse gibbered faint protest, but the man's face crinkled into a smile, even as he shook his head. "Yes, that is a most noble and prescient creature, my little one, but it is feline as well, so be off." He bent down and the mouse leaped to the floor and scurried to the golden sliver of light behind its master, vanishing as if absorbed.

"I am Verthane," the sorcerer said, straightening. "I apologize for requiring your rear entry; my material doors are guarded by some of the grosser material products of Rule—namely, Ronfrenc's henchmen. Welcome, Torloc sorceress—and Torloc feline," he added, bowing solemnly to Felabba. "I trust your reverence will deign to consider some slight repast while I closet myself with your companion."

The bar of light broadened near its base to reveal an assembly of such feline delicacies as mouse-liver pâté and a fine plucked gutterhawk, garnished with catnip wreaths, all displayed on small silver trays.

Irissa found herself drawn through the needle of light by the sorcerer's hand, even as Felabba settled down to her meal. The light felt warm and rekindled a sense of security in her she had thought lost. She stood in a cluttered room ringed with deep purple draperies embroidered with gold thread in bizarre, geometrically alien designs. Flames of all colors burned in elaborately arranged spirit lamps on the chamber's many tables. The gray stone floor was swept pristinely clean. In its center, a pattern had been laid out in spider webs, dewed with drops of iridescent liquid.

"Forgive my untidiness. I am old; in the wane of life, one is wont to rebel against order. Some say I would rebel against Rule itself." Verthane looked sharply at Irissa from under thick white-gold brows as untidy as his chamber. "Methinks you would rebel as well."

"You are wrong. I will merely return to my forest and count the ripples in my shaded pools."

"And is that not rebellion?" Verthane smiled. He strolled

once through the room's center, his trailing robe somehow failing to dislodge a single strand on the pattern-webbed floor. "You are the last Torloc in the Five Realms," he said finally, "and I do not think there is retreat for you."

"You sound like Finorian, Verthane. Why did you draw me here? My powers are faint. I am alone in a world where what I have is held in little regard—or worse, in hatred. What use am I to Rule? What use am I to you?"

"To me? Naught. I do not use things; I only guide them to their natural conclusions. In some places, this facility is called science. Here in Rule, it is called sorcery." The old man plucked at his luxuriant beard; Irissa half-expected to hear a musical note struck by his strumming fingers.

"You wear a veil," Verthane noted abruptly. "Such is proper for a Torloc who has not passed through Far Focus. I suspect you have played with powers around the edge of that veil. Would you not wish to dispense with it utterly?"

"You can put me through Far Focus?" Irissa had thought her powers forever stunted by Finorian's departure. Departure? It was odd she had thought that word, as if the sudden leave-taking had been planned.

"I cannot, but you can initiate yourself under the proper circumstances, if you dare relinquish your veil and face what lives on the other side of mortal eyes—and what dies there. Sometimes it is souls, even Torloc souls."

"You challenge me, Verthane? Why should I bother? You think I have pride like Ronfrenc to chafe at the intimation that I am less than I could be? Power can be evil."

"And most often is. Nevertheless, it is power which will save the Five Realms, or those and that in them which deserve saving. It is power which will see you through the gate into the new Torloc world, where Finorian waits. And perhaps—Thrangar."

Irissa stepped close to the elderly mage, heedless of her boots' drag across his delicately arranged floor. "You mean that I can rejoin my kind?"

"If you are worthy," Verthane said, a twinkle in his gray eyes.

"Riddles," Irissa said, disappointed. "You may rebel against Rule, sorcerer, but you are of it." She turned her back on him—a mistake, for the wall facing her was lined with skulls of a very strange configuration.

"Ignore my hobby, Lady Irissa," Verthane coaxed as he saw her back stiffen. "But there is a gate, and more than one, for some of these smiling fellows were gathered outside them." He rested a palm on the bleached dome of a skull with three eye sockets. "But tell me, do you wish to become fully Torloc?"

"Yes . . . perhaps, but—"

Verthane chuckled softly and a bit sinisterly. "You should have avoided the affirmative if you wished to leave yourself qualifications. 'Yes' was the only word I required . . ."

He bowed away from her, and she glanced to the stones at her feet to see herself centered in the sorcerer's webbed configuration. She tried to lift an Iridesium-laced boot; her foot clung to the floor.

The chamber walls fell away as if knocked over by a mammoth breath. She saw them spiraling into the black distance, their angles distorting as they retreated. Verthane was gone—or was he the pale silver mist that hung at the edges of the web-strewn floor? She looked to the web and suddenly found it familiar. The design was similar to the mosaic that centered the great government house star that Kendric had hurried her past so ungraciously. If only she had studied it more, perhaps—

A violent wind sprang up from the dark reaches. It beat past her in folds of purple cloth, and she caught glimmers of alien constellations above and around her, golden things that glittered. The wind came stronger. She felt her veil flayed away as if it were skin, felt sudden, raw sensations that knifed at her sensibilities. She turned in the direction her veil must have drifted, but saw only the dark, and now dark, whipping strands—her own unloosened hair. She raised the backs of her hands to her eyes and swayed in the unreal wind.

"Look, Torloc, look." It could have been Felabba's voice. That was the only reason she dropped her hands and looked around again. No small white figure appeared in all that encircling darkness. And now she saw that what she had taken for stars were gleaming, predatory eyes, arranged in twos and fours—and threes and fives.

Something tugged upon her tunic hem. She glanced down. The web vined her boots and twined around her trousered knees. She cried out in denial and horror and made her hands into fists. The clinging webs caught her cloak hem and pulled her backward until her knees flexed and she feared she would fall into the web, become part of the web.

"Verthane . . . !"

Her call was an echo before it even completely escaped her lips. And now the supple twining was waist-high, seeking her throat with moonweasel single-mindedness. It was rubbery gray stuff that shone in the lightless light. The more she watched it, the more she realized its repellent texture and form—scaled, oozing, leprous . . . And to save herself, she must look into that, beyond it even, look until it fell back upon itself.

Look, yes. Verthane, yes. Her thought was almost physically sharp, a scalpel prodding her brain. She looked deep into the viscous stuff that netted her, stared into its most disgusting properties, and dived farther below the surface through muck, morass, and a vapid pink blood that animated it. She sucked it dry, absorbing all that ancient poison until she saw the encroaching strands shrink, wither, become brittle, and snap, to drop like desiccated moonweaselbane to the stones at her feet.

Irissa was amazed that she could absorb that much evil and still see. But the slit-pupiled eyes gathered around her yet—distant, loathsome, twinkling with some inner animation. A constellation of three loomed larger in the windy dark—eyes indeed, three eyes on a horned and plated head. The colors came and went behind those triple windows—all the colors of Iridesium, yet somehow tainted, the crimson become bloody, the green gangrenous, and the yellow clotted. Now the rest of the form loomed up. It was from beyond any gate of which Irissa could conceive. It was fanged and clawed and even, incongruously, armed. Its horny appendages clamped a sword and battle-axe, and an oddly designed helmet sat upon that most irregularly shaped head.

For once Irissa did not fear reflection in the creature's armor. Even that was better than regarding the thing outright. But the entity sought her recognition anyway, circling around to catch her evasive eye, lifting its clumsy sword and sweeping it past her ears until she was sick with the whine of it.

This she could not defeat by looking upon it. Its evil was a deeper drink than any bloated, climbing web. It was beyond her, as was the gate of escape into the new Torloc domain. It was a guardian, she sensed, one that Finorian might merely blink upon to banish, but not one that Irissa could vanquish even with her silver eyes. It seemed about to engulf her; an odor of fetid power wreathed her like a scarf. She raised her arms and thought to surrender. A voice came again, whining in the wind. "A Torloc can make as well as alter . . ."

She looked at her empty, clenched hand, filled it with a pommel of smooth Iridesium, lengthened it, and drained the sight of her eyes into a long silver stinger as light as a blade of grass and as strong as sunlight. She sliced it across the being that confronted her, hardly looking to follow the track of her slash. The apparition rent, a curtain slitting open, and then a noxious fume hissed around her sword blade. Irissa struck the wavering cloud, carving it into strands that webbed to the floor. It was gone, and Irissa looked at the weapon in her hand. She stared at the pommel until a great emerald cabochon grew there, a gemmed, gangrenous carbuncle.

The wind around her chuckled. "You Torlocs were always prone to embellishment," it noted.

The chamber walls reassembled rapidly. The stars of the limitless skies dimmed into rows of well-mannered skulls on display. The purple velvet curtain trembled back into place on the farther wall. At her feet, the web shone innocently, its star-shaped arms almost embracing. And Verthane stood outside the web, smiling.

"You have faced the pentagram within, the star without," he said, pointing to the design at her feet. "There is no less nor more any Torloc can do. You have made your own weapon and will never have to borrow from another. Now go, find your gate, and pass through it."

"Is that all? And what of the Realms you would have me save?"

"If you find your gate, the Realms will have been drawn through their own," Verthane promised. "Seek my scattered brethren for guidance, but do not believe everything you see. And you had better take your Wrathman with you—"

"He is *not* my Wrathman!" Irissa exclaimed, stamping a boot on Verthane's web. He laughed. As she turned to confront him, she saw only an ebbing crack of man-high light.

She was alone in a dim chamber with a star-shaped window high above. Her unbraided hair tumbled to her wrists, and a supple short sword with one great emerald eye drooped from her hand. She was alone with the cat Felabba, who even now glanced up from a pile of clean white bones and flicked a delicate tongue past her whiskers.

Chapter Eleven

Kendric the smith's son, formerly the Wrathman from the marshes and one of the Six of the Far Keep, lounged against an oaken settle in the Jade Bottle and contemplated the brown glass stem between his long fingers. The glass contained marshwine, a bitter, alelike brew, but it suited Kendric. His mailed shirt and Iridesium helm were gone, exchanged for a dark blue tunic belted in serviceable sillac hide. He wore high boots of dark brown leather, unspurred. A luxurious beaver-collared cloak of orange sillac pelt lay heaped beside him, and protruding from under its innocuous folds was the sheathed tip of a sword.

Kendric the smith's son considered alternatives. He could hie to Clymarind and offer his sword in service to Madorian there, though it was said that once a Wrathman had taken oath on that mysterious isle, he could not return, save to his death. But perhaps that only meant he would die if he left Clymarind a second time . . . Then again, perhaps the Torloc witch was right, and the entire place was mystery-shrouded simply to keep the curious away.

Kendric spun his glass and watched the murky liquid, dark as grasshopper bile, spill onto the tabletop. He glanced once from under lowered brows at the burly innkeeper. Just let the man complain about his client's quaffing habits; he would have Moonbane out of its sheath and give the fellow a volley across his backside with the flat of it. Strange, he had never named his sword when he carried it in Circle service. Now it seemed to require definition. And he was not wont to tease brawny innkeepers into directing an uncivil word at him, nor to linger in shuttered urban taverns. He would fetch Willowisp and ride out, then. He would go somewhere—but not back to the marshes; he was finally dry from the knees down, and the thought of sinking into the marsh, the image of Willowisp's dainty hocks immersed in mud . . . Kendric swallowed some of the bitter wine and ran a large hand through his wiry, dark hair.

He appeared more worried than dangerous to the innkeeper, who slipped Kendric sidling glances, despite the unusual size that sent his guest's legs sprawling far beyond the trestle table. The innkeeper surveyed the scanty crew of customers that littered the establishment. Only bravos and thieves came to drink after sunfall now, men with daggers in their boots and eyes whittled into looks as sharp. Those who were not afraid. These days that fellowship did not include the innkeeper, a man as sour as the wine he served and now a frightened man, who always drove the last customers out with him so that he did not have to walk the streets alone at midnight. The tavern door banged open, flat against the wall, and the small bouquet of dried weeds nailed to its face riffled a little in the incoming breeze. The innkeeper's attention forsook forever Kendric the smith's son. This was a far more interesting new client—a white cat.

The cat crossed the threshold daintily, as if sensing the mire-drenched boots that had trod that floor. Behind it came another figure. The innkeeper became aware of a tall, slight person with long, barbarian-black hair whipping around the head and the silver thorn of an unsheathed short sword. The fact that his new guest was a woman didn't impress itself upon the innkeeper until the figure had crossed half the room to pause and address the innkeeper's previous center of attention.

"You were willing once to ride out in search of Torlocs; will you do the same in search of gates?"

Kendric's eyes raised and his mouth dropped open

simultaneously. He uncoiled until his dark-thatched head loomed above the settle back like a sullen hillock.

"It's not my idea," Irissa said brusquely, striding nearer to Kendric's table. Her voice and eyes lowered. "A certain sorcerous Clymarindian has persuaded me that a demoted Wrathman is a necessary accouterment to a quest for a gate to another world."

"Why should I—?"

"To learn what breeds in Rule, besides fear. To see something of the world beyond the world. To keep me company."

Kendric frowned and met her silver eyes. Her glance was unwavering, as if she had learned to skirt reflection automatically now. Or had learned to meet and not see it? He was about to refuse when Felabba leaped upon the table. He looked at the cat, which dipped a fastidious paw into his goblet and licked a bit of marshwine off with a certain unfeline savoring. It waited, like its mistress, like a drinking companion making an offer across a taproom table.

Kendric stood, his hair brushing the cobwebbed rafters. "Innkeeper. A round of Clymarindian borgia for my companions."

"Perhaps Felabba would prefer a milk toddy," Irissa suggested, drawing up a stool and sitting at right angles to Kendric and the looming settle.

Kendric nodded once to the befuddled innkeeper and sat again, leaning his elbows on the wood. "You have acquired a fang since we last met."

"And you have not surrendered yours," Irissa said, nodding to the blunt point that almost nudged her knee.

"Ronfrenc was in the market for assassins," Kendric replied. "Not Wrathmen."

"He would have hirelings kill his enemies? Whom? Verthane?"

Kendric smiled and sipped from the new goblet the innkeeper had brought. "No. Torlocs."

"Torlocs? But—" Irissa smiled, too, and sipped her borgia. "There are no Torlocs left in the Six Realms," she finished demurely.

"Five," Kendric snapped. He lounged into the settle's shadows again. "There are only four Wrathmen left in the Realms also."

"Five," Irissa corrected sharply. "I do not count Thrangar lost yet."

"Then we understand each other," Kendric said.

"No. But perhaps it is not necessary."

Irissa drank slowly from her goblet, tilting back her head. Kendric watched the rhythmic swallows. Felabba brought her face up from her frothy libation. A milk mustache dotted her pink nose, looking comic. The cat's eyes were serious. Kendric avoided that disconcerting intensity and returned his attention to Irissa.

"Where do we ride?"

"Verthane suggested we seek the exiled sorcerers for clues to what rends the Realms apart. And he spoke of a gate. For me."

"As did Finorian. You'd forgotten that. She spoke of being unable to hold the gate for you."

"If we can find it and I can slip through to rejoin my kind—"

"I will remain behind and become a gatekeeper. A noble occupation, I think, for an unemployed warrior." Kendric slapped his palm upon the table, for once startling the composed Felabba.

"We'll ride, then, for I tire of Rule and I tire of bearing my sword in another's service. We will join forces, Torloc, but not fates. If your destiny threatens Realm survival, or my own, I will use Moonbane upon you as sharply as I would on any moonweasel."

"I hope it will not come to that," Irissa said, smiling. "I do not bite."

Chapter Twelve

Willowisp fairly danced down the road leading from Rule. His unarmored master accounted for half of the new spring in his ivory-hoofed steps. A long, hay-filled respite in the stables of Rule took credit for the other half.

Irissa, whose first chore on reclaiming Smokeshadow had been to strip the bells off his bridle, came abreast of Kendric without warning and caught the marshman looking doleful. "I thought you would be glad of leaving Rule," she chided. It was dusk, and they intended to ride all night to avoid Ronfrenc's agents.

Kendric nodded but still looked discontent. "One is glad of leaving an ill place only if certain of arriving in a better one. I do not know that your vague gate to an even vaguer other world holds much improvement over present places. Nor do I know where to find it."

"You are being as stolid as a Rocklander, Kendric," Irissa complained, tossing her flailing locks back over her shoulders. She had retained the Iridesium circlet, though its attached veil had disappeared in Verthane's purple wind. Her front locks had been braided for the sake of tidiness, but the evening wind ran its rippling fingers through and undid all her weaving.

Kendric considered his riding companion glumly. She was very different from the docile creature who had found him by the Shrinking Forest pool, and, in part, he must account for some of that. Different. He was different, too—not wounded now, but not well. Kendric plodded on, unresponding, and Irissa reined Smokeshadow to follow in Willowisp's rear.

"Ah, Felabba," she whispered to the oval of white fur

74

curled into her high saddle lip. "I hope Rule and the Circle have not wilted all the conversation out of you as well."

"It is a long ride we must make on account of you and your gate," the cat said, hardly bothering to unlid one reflective eye. "Such journeys knock my old bones about like a pair of Tolechian dice—ooooh! Finorian's lap was bony enough of a winter evening, but now I must be dragged from pillar to post on the back of a four-hoofed, dumb beast!"

"Sometimes, Felabba, I wish *you* were dumb."

"It was you who wanted chitchat," the cat sang back, sinking her triangular face onto her paws.

Irissa sighed again, prodded Smokeshadow gently, and trotted past Kendric. She rode on ahead most of the night, until she began to long for some horizon-high glow—the rising sun or something like it. She finally found one, nearer than the skyline and smaller than she had expected.

"A fire!"

Kendric goaded Willowisp toward the hot, round pit of light that lay on the dark landscape like a burning cherry. It turned out to be a blazing campfire, whose cheery glow illumined a disconsolate circle composed of a two-wheeled wagon, a one-horned, one-humped bearing-beast of gangly proportions, a scrawny wood owl charring on a spit, and a small disreputable rock sitting nearby—or a man of such equal proportions in height and width that he might very well have squared the circle in his person.

"Welcome, travelers," the mound of clothing greeted them, rising and revealing no more of itself than before. "If you hail not from yon scrofulous metropolis, nor from the accursed fens and Rocklands, nor from falsely fabled Clymarind, nor even from imperious Tolech-Nal on the selvage edge of the Abyssal Sea, ye are welcome. That is, if ye are not from the Five Realms, I will converse with ye. Otherwise, be on your way."

"Here, now," Kendric admonished, dismounting to loom over the ragged personage like a pine tree over a particularly unworthy mound of moss.

The creature's garments fluttered in umbrage. "Ho! Ye think because ye be long of limb ye can set Ludborg the Fanciful aquivering in his buskins. Ye be redundant, lad," he said, stretching to study all seven feet of Kendric. "I'd take ye for one of these festy Wrathmen, save ye do not lumber about in their great metal clothes. And I take your brain to be a flijibbon quicker." The creature's garments stopped quivering with his speech and settled closer to his rotund form.

"Will you share the warmth of your fire with us as well as that of your tongue?" Irissa dismounted and led Smokeshadow into the light.

The little round, dark heap shuffled over. "Ah. Another long straw of borgia to whet my curiosity. And so noble a beast she leads. Come here, Cato."

Smokeshadow ambled over and laid an obedient, fanged muzzle in the plump puddle of flesh that appeared at the end of a ragged and voluminous sleeve.

"The Ebony Eye of elder Clymarind . . . A fine beast, and one must know how to use it. Do you, Lady Longitude?" Irissa stood as unruffled as Smokeshadow while the stranger stretched up to peer into her features. "Ah, excellent." The rag mound giggled and skipped away in a wake of feathered clothing. It stopped on the fire's farther side, so that the flames etched a pale circle of something under a drooping hood and a fine, gleaming copper belt around the center of the globular figure.

"You are silver, bronze, and black, and these are the ancient heraldic colors of the moonwalkers—but there should be another, if my memory is as long as ye twain."

Felabba bounded off Smokeshadow's back and into the fan of bright light cast by Ludborg's flames. She rubbed ritually back and forth on the shapeless robes, roughly in the proximity of Ludborg's ankles—if, indeed, he had ankles. His draperies made such speculation relevant. Irissa and Kendric exchanged glances and inched nearer to the heat-giving flames.

"Yes, come closer, fair travelers, now that I see ye be not of the foul moonweasel-loving lot. Yes, my Queen of the Green," he added, folding into himself to run his sleeves over Felabba's head. "Old Ludborg the Fanciful knows ye. Let us have better light."

His sleeve arched away from his bulk, spraying something. The fire flared up and danced on the logs in a fountain of glancing colors. It lit up the landscape around them; it delineated little more of Ludborg's contours, save for the multicolored, tattered robe that garbed him from cranium to great toe, if he had either.

"Rest, friends." He indicated the bare ground. Kendric and Irissa settled upon it as if it had been a Clymarindian couch. Felabba sank onto her haunches and curled her tail as efficiently as possible around her paws. Ludborg danced among his guests and showered them with sprays of dust that made them cough.

"Moonweaselbane powder. I milled it myself. 'Tis far more effective than those dried-out tufts of weed the Rulians hide behind. The Hegira has bypassed us, travelers, but it never hurts to be overcautious in the Five Realms nowadays."

"There are Six Realms," Irissa interjected, testing him.

The hood swiveled abruptly to her. "Five. And you know that better than I, Torloc lady." The hood bowed profoundly.

"What is this Hegira?" Kendric sounded suspicious.

The hood shook dolefully from side to side. "The moonweasel pack, my friend. They course in a steady stream toward the City of Rule and the Abyssal Sea beyond. It is best not to fare far in these days."

"We have met moonweasels before." Kendric pulled the sword that lay beside him around into the firelight.

"Oh! Why did you not tell me you bore one of the Six? This alters everything, everything . . . I really oughtn't to delay a bit. Enjoy my fire, friends; I must be off. Octa, come."

The drooping bearing-beast revived like a flower in water and took up a position before the rickety wagon.

"Wait!" Irissa cried. "We are looking for—a gate. Can you . . . ?"

"A gate." The figure paused. "It was by a gate I was ushered out of the City of Rule not long since. Magician, they called me. Me! Scyvilla the Rengarthian—that is, of course, Ludborg the Fanciful. 'Tis my name. Ludborg. See it written on my humble vehicle."

They glanced toward the decrepit wagon and were astounded to see the letters writhing there like serpents in a kaleidoscope—multicolored, serifed letters that danced in the firelight as if alive. They had not been there before.

"You called yourself something other than Ludborg a moment ago," Kendric challenged.

"And did you not call yourself something other once, Wrathman?" The voice was sly, unguent, and ingratiating. "And this noble beast—" What appeared to be the white projection of a remarkably fluid finger peeked from under a ragged sleeve to indicate Felabba. "Ask this most sublime creature what her name was beyond the gate . . ."

"Ask a cat?" Kendric laughed. "You are devious, Ludborg, or whoever you are. But you will not convince me to seek answers from the mute."

"Then ask your Torloc traveling companion, Sir Wrathman Who Was. She is an excellent translator." Ludborg had scuttled to the bearing-beast and affixed a line that glimmered like Iridesium to its single horn.

"Clymarindian falgonskin! Valodec has that for gauntlets. Where do you come from?" Kendric stepped forward to delay the departing figure.

"From beyond the gate, of course. And soon Rule shall be beyond all gates. But I have matters to attend to." He mounted the narrow wagon seat.

"The gate! Is it my gate?" Irissa asked.

"No, no, no. If I could exit by any Torlockian gate, do ye suppose I would be dawdling about the Realms when there are wonders beyond words out there?" The hood raked a semicircle across the lightening sky. "Limpid, distant Rengarth the Lost?" Ludborg seemed to shrink.

"My gate—how shall I find it?"

"Oh, by Garnethian, you are festy. Single-minded and double-sighted, Torlocs. Always. And prone to embellishment, even in these latter days. Go to Mauvedona, silly silver-eyed one. Take your cat. And 'ware of moonweasels and mirrors—and Wrathmen!"

Ludborg's robes pinched shut on his iridescent rein and gave it a sinuous shake. The weary bearing-beast shuddered, staggered forward, unfolded great ribbed wings from either side of its hump, and was suddenly airborne, its lanky legs dragging the tops of the nearer pines. The odd vehicle shrank into the brightening horizon, until even the rubbery flap of wings had faded from hearing.

"Mad. He's mad," Irissa said in wonderment. "What he said meant nothing. Moonweasel Hegira and other gates and . . . move a, move a—a what?"

"—dona. Mauvedona. It's a name." Kendric's face was

even longer than her own, but an expression of amazement touched it, too.

"Mauve-dona? You know this Mauvedona?"

"Everyone in the City of Rule has heard of Mauvedona. She used to bring sleep to the wakeful and wonder to the dreamers. A minor-order sorceress only, but one with great delicacy of invention . . . If Ronfrenc has truly driven all practitioners of the fanciful arts from Rule, I don't know where we would find her, or that we care to. She is less even than this Ludborg, I would think. And he, or it, gave us no aid."

Irissa sank to her knees near the strangely shrinking fire. "He knew us. From my cat to your blade. Perhaps he knows where to direct us."

"Mauvedona can do nothing for either of us, believe me! If she could help us, do you not suppose I would have thought of her myself?"

"No," Irissa said, looking at him narrowly. "For some reason, I do not think you would have thought of her. Or if you had, you would have hoarded her in your own mind."

"You wanted company, Torloc," Kendric said evenly. "And I lent it to you. If you become as traitor-obsessed as Glent, I shall withdraw my bounty."

"Go, then. But tell me first where to find this Mauvedona."

"If I knew—" Kendric came forward and booted a loose stick into the flames, where it snapped to its destruction. The firelight painted his face as bronze as the emblem that had once decorated his chest and his shield. "Perhaps . . . She had a fascination for crimson castles and other sorcerous erections. She was Rocklands-born. If we bear south toward the rising sun . . . she would place her retreat within the easy angle of its rays."

"You will guide me, then?"

"I will go where I think. If you wish, you will follow." Kendric swung aboard Willowisp, who gleamed golden in the firelight. "But, like our airborne friend, I promise you no gate. Perhaps our quest is hinged on grief."

He reined his mount in a tight arc and galloped into the sunrise. Irissa scrambled atop Smokeshadow, barely waiting for Felabba to leap up beside her, and cantered after.

The fire of Ludborg the Fanciful flickered and went out.

Chapter Thirteen

With irony as the compass, the journey took a circular path. Kendric and Irissa were not quite aware of bending back on themselves like a tortoise-shell hairpin, but they rode from Rule on a route that paralleled their recent entry into that City of the Circle.

They rode for Feynwood, a bristling beard of fir and cedar that divided dry Rocklands from the watery wastes of Kendric's marshes. It was a place of which Rocklanders often macabrely jested, saying it was a place they "fain would" not go. Kendric went there, and Irissa followed.

The wood reared on the horizon, a sudden scowl of forestation, dark, ridged, and forbidding. On one side the low reedlands that had nourished Kendric fell away, and the broken rocky wastes that now nourished little more than new breeds of lizards and old varieties of contention rose on the other.

Kendric reined straight for the forest's narrow heart, directly into towering pines, poised like battle-ready lances against the murky skies.

"My forest was green," Irissa said, spurring to his side. "But it was a decent shade. This place speaks of the green that grows where the sun is ashamed to walk; it whispers of decay."

Feynwood widened and spread its pitchwood cloak around them as they moved implacably into it.

"You wished for Mauvedona's guidance," Kendric said a long time after Irissa had spoken, when they were already immersed in the wood's instant dusk. "Watch for a sunset tower, similar to the painted-fingernail turrets we saw in Rule. Only this one will wear a longer claw."

Daylight still lingered over the barren landscape beyond the wood. Within, the sun's light was a matter for speculation only.

"We must cleave to the heartwood," Kendric warned. "To our right lies bog that could suck us deeper than the Swallowing Cavern."

Irissa nodded, her Iridesium circlet sending off no glimmer in the tangible dark. Kendric deliberately searched out her eyes and found them dulled, a mirror upon which someone might have breathed and passed by, with the mist remaining. But they were sharper than he thought.

"There!" The tip of one long white finger arrowed toward a particularly tall pinetop, its needles burning scarlet in some sunset simmer. The glow resolved, and the pine tree was suddenly a narrow and soaring turret, delicately fenestrated with triangular, fanged notches.

"There," Kendric agreed grimly, drawing up Willowisp.

The bearing-beast whistled nervously and arched his supple neck as Kendric drew the reins even tauter, so that their pennants tangled in one another, a tousled, decorative mane. Smokeshadow shifted under Irissa's knees and blew out a sudden gust of air, almost a sigh. Felabba ran from a nest behind Irissa's hips to perch alertly on the pommel of the saddle.

"You are all impossible," Irissa said, nudging her mount toward the distant tower. She trotted through the elbowing pinewoods, her dark hair weaving through the air behind her like the product of some night-spinning loom. Felabba sprang to the rear of her saddle and stared back at Kendric. But the marshman was still for a long time before his boots finally brushed Willowisp's glossy sides and he brought up the party's rear.

They came upon the castle suddenly. One moment they were barred about by dark pine trunks, and the next all that loomed before them were pulsing scarlet walls, arrowing upward to a five-fingered hand of turrets stretching for the indifferently distant skies.

A fiery drawbridge lowered abruptly toward the mounted party, like a tongue lolling out of a voracious red mouth. The bearing-beasts pranced in unison, but Kendric prodded Willowisp. In an instant his pale hooves were flashing across the flaming bridge; Smokeshadow cantered after on his own, and Irissa felt a trellising sting as Felabba climbed, claw by claw, to her shoulder.

"Oh, my pride, my panache, my colors—my tail!" Something wafted in front of Irissa, something white and limber and slightly charred at the tip. "My ultimate pride—gone," the cat continued in a low, throaty moan. "An errant ember, and the growth of generations is so much ashes. Lift up your heels, my girl, or your boots will be but smoking memories. Curse Wrathmen who ride into walls of fire, curse Torlocs who follow, curse bearing-beasts who are so low to the ground they make matchwood of their riders."

Both mounts had slowed on the hard stone squares of a courtyard. Felabba sniffed and retreated to Smokeshadow's flanks, from where she morosely stared down at the ground while wrapping her injured extremity gingerly around her paws. Kendric dismounted and paced alertly through the empty courtyard, leading Willowisp by a very short rein.

Irissa looked around, puzzled. For inside, the construction was solid, golden, and somehow opaque. It was as if the castle had been built from blocks of topaz; it was infused with a hard yellow light that filtered the red, outer firelight as water would strain sunshine. And yet—something about the structure's inner reality disturbed Irissa more than its outer eccentricity of construction. It was an empty, vaulted sort of place, warmed by illusion, not by the heart of its inhabitant.

Willowisp shook his massive head free of Kendric's restraint and trotted across the court to a yawning, pyramidal portal. Smokeshadow followed; Irissa was unable to rein him up. Kendric ran over and pulled Irissa off her beast's back.

"No use to restrain him. He's been called." Kendric nodded brusquely toward the pointed door that had swallowed Willowisp already. "It's best only the bearing-beasts cross that threshold."

At that, Felabba deserted Smokeshadow's disappearing back and sprang down to the amber pavement, her steps a staccato clicking across the flagstones.

Kendric laughed. "Finorian's cat has no love for the

flames. It will be interesting to see what she makes of Mauvedona."

"You have seen her before, then?" Irissa followed him to another cavernous doorway, this one keyhole-shaped.

"I've seen her before, yes. Your arm, Lady Irissa. It is best to be formal when one calls upon Mauvedona. And I have not seen her in some time. I am not certain what we shall find."

They stepped through the black entryway almost in the precision of a dance, brown boot and gray boot striking the substance within together. Perhaps it was that which signaled a line of torches to life; flames sprang up, gelatinous, artificial spigots of reflective yellow flowing from stone serpents' mouths. The tongues of light flicked in and out of those basalt orifices, and the only sign that they were actual flames was that they had charred the ophidian fangs black.

Irissa's hand tightened on Kendric's arm, but he gave no sign of heeding her. Her right hand dropped to the short sword at her hip and she clasped the hilt, feeling the emerald warm in her palm. It was a more human kind of heat than that spitting from the rows of serpentine heads.

"I wonder some artisan did not execute these snakes in Iridesium," Irissa noted as they advanced down the hall. "It would be a natural substance for the subject matter."

"Mauvedona abhors Iridesium. It comes from Torloc rins, and the powers she practices are antithetical. You meet here a kind of shadow."

Irissa's hand tightened on her sword pommel; she had been taught not to trust in reflections. Behind her, the antithesis of a shadow, the white part of darkness, padded after her. Irissa heard the occasional scrape of claw on stone; and though she knew it meant even Felabba was nervous, it somehow softened her own uncertainty.

The parallel row of serpents opened out abruptly. Kendric and Irissa were in a wide, circular chamber centering on an oddly shaped table of polished weepwillow wood. Upon the gleaming, golden length lay a winking assortment of serving dishes richly ornamented with edibles. Dates were displayed on long silver salvers. Borgia, the brew that became as deadly as venom when improperly aged, glittered greenly from clear glass flacons shaped into dragonflies,

swans, falgons, and all sorts of airborne inventions, their
lacy, spun-glass wings folded into handles.

In the table's center rose a tower of shining candied
fruits—cherries, apricots, and sweet, scarlet pomms from
Tolech-Nal; lavender-veined pears from the Abyssal islands, obtained at great cost by the intrepid Clymarindian
merchant fleets; and heavy pendants of grapes, still frosty,
from the City That Soars. Berries as polished as coldstones
lay like great purple drops of blood on the confection's
summit.

They came close to the board and looked down upon
the outpouring of rich and elusive comestibles on it. Irissa
saw it was hexagonally shaped, and that among the familiar foods that bedecked it were rarities from each of the
Six Realms—or rather, the Five. Anything Torloc was
oddly missing. And if she looked at the tabletop quickly,
out of the corner of her eye, it was five-sided—a pentagon.

Two rows of servitors slid out from somewhere and split
to encompass the table. They were robed and hooded in
black velvet with trailing sleeves and trains that puddled
on the floor to form three tails behind each one.

"Borgia?" one asked, directing a green rivulet into a
carved garnet cup and extending it to Kendric. The green
seen through the red turned as brown as old blood. But
the pale arm extending from the enveloping velvet was as
smooth and cool as ivory, and the voice was as silken as
the best wares of Wormwinder Street. Kendric accepted
the goblet and held it against his chest; in the gold light
it sparkled more boldly than his bronze Wrathman's emblem once had.

"Our lady rejoices in your return," the servitor said
softly, bowing or perhaps just writhing a little and gliding
away.

"Borgia?" another servitor inquired in the same silken
tones to Irissa. This time the delicate, bare arm snaked
out from its velvet cave and seized upon an ebony glass
goblet. The green stream hissed into the shadowed bowl
and then was thrust at Irissa.

She took it, her palm still warm from the emerald of
her sword pommel. She peered into a deep pool of sable
green, as obsidian and shifting as a forest pond, within
the glass. She peered in and saw a woman's face floating
within it or upon it. A woman's face—her own, or not

her own? She must make sure, must name the reflection . . . Irissa's hand tightened on the cold glass stem; the pool above it rippled, shook the image, and broke into fragments—green splashing in a river down her gray tunic front, flying in fat globules to quiver on the polished weepwillow wood, to spray the golden flagstones and hiss there acidly.

"Clumsy!" came Felabba's voice, hissing into her ears. The old cat sidestepped a plummeting borgia droplet and shook her scrawny tail free of it. A shattered pile of black glass lay at Irissa's feet, and green borgia ran off her fingers like icy lava.

"Clumsy," a voice said from above, and this time others besides Irissa seemed to hear it. Man, woman, and cat turned their eyes up and saw someone poised there on a bare stair in the chamber's dark, upper regions. "Perhaps marshwine is more to your liking, Torloc, though it is a bitter brew, I hear, and inclined to muddle one's senses."

The head above nodded, and a shadowy servitor thrust a common pewter goblet into Irissa's still-curled hand. The acrid wine scent that had permeated the tavern in Rule poured from it. The servitor bowed away. Where the broken glass and a thick sea of borgia had been was only clean stone, swept so by a trailing sable broom.

The figure on the steps descended slowly into the hot amber light that suffused the lower chamber. Something in its progress proclaimed it female, though certainty was impossible from this distance, and its voice had been husky and elusive as to gender.

"And what will our hostess have?" Kendric asked, bowing and gesturing with his goblet, though he did not drink from it.

Mauvedona, who had obtained some small fame in the City of Rule in other days, advanced to her shining table and paused without answering. She was female indeed in the light of her serpent-tongued torches, though something sinewy underlay the suppleness of her body. She had a small, flat face, tawny like a sun-warmed apple, and dark-lashed almond eyes that tilted as subtly as her smile. Her hair was more golden than her skin and rippled to her shoulders, where it was caught into tufts wrapped in gold wire, so that she seemed to be surrounded by a pride of leonine tails.

"I am wont to have my will," Mauvedona finally replied gravely. "A heady concoction, so I will settle for some borgia, Wrathman."

A childlike arm proffering a topaz glass half-full of the vivid green liquor was before her. Mauvedona curled her short fingers around it, the rings upon them winking red, saffron, azure, and violet—but no green. There was no green in the room except for the bright, lethal emerald of the borgia turning brown in both Kendric's and Mauvedona's colored goblets.

Irissa sipped her marshwine, glad of its sour pucker on her tongue and its head-clearing aroma. Mauvedona popped a gleaming date into her mouth and followed it with a draught of borgia. Her eyes were on Kendric; he finally sipped from his semiprecious glass before speaking.

"I have come for aid, not entertainment, Lady Mauvedona," he said quietly. "We—I—was directed here by Ludborg the Fanci—"

"That senile, wandering curse?" Mauvedona popped another date into her mouth and munched implacably. "Truly, Kendric, in the old days you were unlikely to seek direction from any but your own inclinations."

"These are new days, Mauvedona, and we must seek direction and aid where we find them. I am no longer a Wrathman."

"I see." The slanted eyes slid obliquely to Irissa, who found herself fighting an instinct to return the insolent look, though her very bones rattled of danger at the idea. "Aid," Mauvedona said, juggling the word, datelike, between her teeth. "And I will lend my assistance—if I receive aid in return."

"Aid? What sort? I told you I am no longer a Wrathman. I can do your cause no good at Circle meetings."

"Your aid, no. If the Circle of Rule does not require you, neither do I. It is she, the aid you have brought me, I desire."

"I have brought you nothing . . ." Kendric began stiffly, his knuckles as white as baroque pearls on the garnet glass stem.

"Poor Kendric. It is your lot to serve others, even if you know it not. You are where I wished you, with whom

I wished you. The only thing I had not anticipated is that you would travel with a ragged feline for a familiar." Mauvedona's oblique gaze swept to Felabba on the floor, and the sage old cat flounced away with equal contempt. Kendric laughed shortly, as Mauvedona's tongue lashed lightly across her lips.

"Her!" She turned and thrust out an impolite, pointing arm. The nail on her stubby golden finger was long and buffed metal-bright. "Your skitterish eyes—I almost had them in the borgia pool, you know. You did not expect to meet me across the elements, and so I almost drank you in."

Mauvedona advanced upon Irissa, although she was perhaps several inches shorter, and certainly not armed with a sword. Irissa polished the emerald pommel with her hand; it warmed her like a fire. "If there is some service I may do you," she offered, "in return for your guidance in finding Thrangar and the center of the Realm troubles—"

"I do not need to search for others' troubles, Torloc. I am up to Kendric's eyebrows in my own." Mauvedona's expansive gesture found those eyebrows raised in polite disbelief.

The sorceress lashed her train behind her and began pacing the stone-floored chamber. Her hem was studded with six-pointed stars of some dark metal, and they chattered against the pavement as if accompanying her plaintive aria.

"Hounded out of Rule. And I had not even time to call up a shape-slipper to become an empress falgon and bear me away more conveniently. I must walk. Walk!" she spat, demonstrating this appalling necessity with a few more percussive sweeps of the room. "Such gray little men they sent, who would not look at me, like yon Torloc, though she at least has reason. Gray little creatures with sealed orders and minds as well glued. I had to abandon the accumulation of years—my best censers, my Clymarindian vials, my wonderful miniature unicorn in the bottle. They broke them all. All my spells melted and misted away. I had to begin from nothing here, like the greenest apprentice." Her arms waved outward to encompass the room. She paused to quaff a swallow of borgia.

"You have done nobly," Kendric consoled. "This palace quite outdoes your last."

"Yes, yes. I suppose we all must make the best of a bad thing. And I intend to make new beginnings better ones. But . . . Illusions are the cheapest of sorceries; so many exist already and only need a bit of amplifying. I must weave fresh magic and I have lost my loom. I must look to new methods." Mauvedona's blunt fingers toyed with the central amethyst ornamenting a broad belt around her hips, but her eyes fastened on Irissa.

"You said you wished me here," Irissa answered the woman's unspoken meaning. "Why?"

Mauvedona's yellow hands fanned like starfish on the table edge. She leaned intently across the wood toward Irissa, her eyes as passionately purple as mountain grapes. "Your eyes. That is all. It is so simple. They can be my tunnel through the mountain, they can take me faster than thought to the source of new power—or rather, the old power that was mine to draw from the well until my rope was cut. Please!" Mauvedona said, and her tongue vibrated on the "sssss" until the sound seemed an ophidian hiss and demanded an affirmative hiss in reply.

"No," Irissa said.

"No!" Mauvedona's blond brows met and shadowed her eyes for a moment. "But only a Torloc can provide me a gate to what I desire. And you—you are the only gate left in the Realms."

"A gate? But that is what *I* seek—my own gate out of the Realms. If you can help me find Thrangar, or some means to rejoin my vanished race, perhaps I can help you, but I am not to look deep at anyone, including myself."

"Am not to. Cannot. Must not . . ." Mauvedona mimicked. "These are Ronfrenckian words, Torloc. And Thrangar—do not speak to me of Thrangar. He refused me also and rode past without speaking or seeing, a great creaking, armored tree in his miserable overcolored metal—"

"Thrangar! You have seen him? When?"

Mauvedona's head tilted, so that her eyes took on an even more pronounced slant. "Re-cent-ly." Each syllable dropped separately.

"Mauvedona." Kendric stepped forward, and his boot sounded on stone with the old authority of a Wrathman. "It grows late for games. Tell us when."

Her angled eyes defied him momentarily. Then her head

straightened and she shrugged with a certain prowling grace. Nervous fingers polished the square-cut amethyst on her belt. Irissa and Kendric noticed jointly that her nails were dyed dark carmine.

"A moon ago," she said. "I saw that moon set upon his accursed Iridesium helm. I rejoice to see you wear not such metal now, Kendric."

Mauvedona came and stood so close within his shadow that Kendric's head had to bow to regard her. Irissa saw only a swath of studded metal train pooling on the floor and Kendric looking down upon a column of slim shadow.

"Sorceress!"

Mauvedona wheeled from Kendric at Irissa's word, her eyes and jewel winking in unison in a bit of flaring light. That was all that could be seen of her—the three glowing points of her body and the constellation scattered on her hem. Irissa stared at the brassy stars and faltered. They had five points now, not six. No, Six was gone. The Sixth and the Six. Five remained. And Mauvedona.

"Sorceress," Irissa repeated.

The woman finally stalked toward her, emerging from Kendric's shadow like a wailwraith unwillingly called from a weepwater root.

"Where did Thrangar go? If he rode through this wood, he was not bound for the Rocklands or the marshes. And certainly he sought not Rindell."

"Nor your Finorian," Mauvedona added with a feline satisfaction so tangible it could almost be seen upon her lips. "I know something of Finorian. My mother and she were . . . neighbors."

"Thrangar," Irissa persisted wearily, expecting no answer.

"To the dark towers of Geronfrey, which snap higher at heaven and root deeper in hell than even mine," Mauvedona replied. She fanned a hand against the air to illustrate some vague direction; for a moment, her vertical fingers resembled her own sunset-tipped spires. "Geronfrey," she mumbled, as if afraid, or ashamed of being afraid. Mauvedona brought her attention back to Irissa's face. "I have answered you. Now you must answer me with your eyes."

"I cannot. You must look elsewhere."

Mauvedona tilted her chin on the tip of one sharp nail

and studied Irissa while trailing slowly around the room and around Kendric. Her movements were random, perhaps even disjointed. Her train hissed across the pavement, occasionally rasping the metal on stone.

Kendric's face suddenly flared like one of the serpentine torches; he leaped at a certain patch of empty air while Irissa watched, puzzled. Mauvedona darted to anticipate Kendric's acrobatics, then pranced in a circle, her golden, clapping hands matching the shower of stars on her skirts.

"Done! Done, my great metal man, Wrathman Who Was. That is the trouble with you giants; you move a bit slowly for the wily of the earth. Now." Mauvedona swept her gown behind her and advanced on Irissa, her head lowered bullishly for her target. "Now, Torloc, you will deal with me."

Kendric heaved against air. And air rebuffed him, hurling him back as if he had been slapped. He stepped forward, lowered his head as stubbornly as Mauvedona, and pushed with his massive hands against air. Sweat blossomed on his face in crystal studs. And only air opposed him—only air.

"The pentagram," Mauvedona explained expansively. "You stand within my pentagram, and there you will stand until I free you with another sweep of my spelling skirt."

"I ought to have guessed ill times would have honed your temper, Mauvedona," Kendric said, baffled, furious, and centered in an invisible prison.

"Yes, you ought to have known a great deal, but you did not. Do not fret, I will free you. Or rather, *she* will, by complying with my desires."

Hand on sword, Irissa looked down at the advancing sorceress. The woman had no weapon of her own—or rather, no forged extension of her physical force. But power she had, and it was blacker than the robes of her evasive servitors. The great emerald flashed an arc as Irissa drew her sword and thrust warningly ahead. The blade engaged only air, only light—engaged them and drew back as if from a wall.

"You drank your pentagram, Torloc," Mauvedona said, laughing. "You feared my sweet green borgia and thus took the humble marshwine. But the marshes produce bitter fruits." She glanced at Kendric like a beast-master throwing a gibe to one of her leashed creatures. "And this tartness only masked a more dangerous nectar. You are contained."

Irissa looked at the dull pewter goblet still in her left hand and hurled it at Mauvedona. The cup rebounded from the air ahead of it and clanked to the stones, oozing marshwine like blood.

"You are contained, I say. And your sword is no stinger to me. So let me look at you and read what I must, what I wish, what I require."

Mauvedona neared, her small golden hands fanning on the air three paces ahead of Irissa as if touching a mirror that marked the distance between herself and some image equidistant in it. "Look."

"No, for your sake as well as mine."

Mauvedona laughed. "Favors? You would do me favors? Open your eyes to me."

Irissa glanced around wildly to Kendric. His face was whiter than his fisted knuckles still belaboring some barrier of air. He shook his head, silent, unwilling to advise when he was in no position to aid her. She found Felabba, crouched near the lavish table, the cat's brittle tourmaline eyes staring at her. If Felabba thought or said anything that could help Irissa, it could not penetrate Mauvedona's seemingly absent wall. Irissa's hands probed forward, seeking a limit. They found it—the icy, hard expanse of nothing that penned them both in. She would picture it melting, misting, but she could not see it. And not having seen it, she could not alter it.

"Look!" Mauvedona ordered, her voice thundering in confidence.

"No!"

Stars windmilled upward with a chain-swung rattle. Mauvedona stood four paces away, sweeping her trailing gown hem up and down until it clattered like hail on the floor. It crossed the invisible barrier in its jeweled arc, and so did the ornamental stars. They spun and grew larger than axe blades, their six wicked arms cartwheeling past Irissa.

"But—" Irissa's hands reached out, encountered the barrier, and withdrew.

"It is of my making," Mauvedona said. "My power can pass through it. Yours cannot." Mauvedona pointed at one of the spinning stars, and it paused in midair. She beckoned it lazily. It rested one sharp point on the golden pad of her outstretched forefinger. "Each of my—toys—obeys me implicitly," Mauvedona said, smiling. She looked quite beautiful standing there, calm in her power, with the large, glittering star balanced on her fingertip.

"But if I release my control only a bit—" Mauvedona's face winced and distracted Irissa's eyes to it. Irissa glanced instantly back at the star, afraid the magical weapon was now aimed at her. But it still balanced on Mauvedona's level fingertip, save that now its sharp point had sunk a bit into the flesh and something ruby pooled around it.

"Ahhhh," Mauvedona said, still wincing. The star elevated slightly, like something the sea bounces on its waves. It floated up into the air, then spun without warning and axed past Irissa's face so swiftly that her strands of dark hair stirred in its wake. One smoky wisp floated featherlike to the floor, where it lay curved atop the amber stone like a small, still snake.

Another lethal pinwheel of gold shot forward. Irissa lunged sideways and it hissed harmlessly past.

"I have many cards in my deck," Mauvedona said languidly, hurling another of the suspended stars haloing her toward Irissa. This one hovered in front of Irissa's pale Torloc face, its edge as fine as a sillac hair.

"Then slay me, and you break your last looking glass, Mauvedona. Slay me."

"No. I am neither that wicked nor that foolish. Killing is not the question. My pets only propose to caress you, to spin a slow pattern across your face. You are female, as am I, so I know your weaknesses as I know my own. I would send my blades slicing at you as randomly as a rainstorm—icy, scalding drops—here, there . . ."

Mauvedona's finger traced the air. The star in front of Irissa moved with her motion, puppetwise; it spun exquisitely and made a jagged pattern. Its passing cut a trail of reflected light into the air, like a scar.

"Now will you let me look?"

"No." Irissa felt calm and triumphant, though she dared not let Mauvedona read that in her expression. A few facial slices—was that the best Mauvedona could do? Irissa had the power to mend flesh and weave it whole again, as she had done once with Kendric, and could easily do for herself. Why did Mauvedona think her silly, star-shaped blades should be so menacing? Irissa glanced to the cat Felabba and saw the creature staring up at her and still mute. She found Kendric even paler, his fists pounding soundlessly on nothing.

"Mauvedona," he said, "you do not understand her. Your axes will elicit nothing but blood, believe me. You cannot mean—"

"I mean to attain my ends, to see what I must see in her eyes only. Refuse me, Torloc, and I shall scratch my mirror!"

The star blade floated on its side and edged nearer. Irissa stared at its spell-honed edges until it seemed her eyes should cross. She could not send it away, but she need not fear it if she did not fear pain. And pain was a very small thing to a Torloc.

"No," Kendric ordered from behind his spell-wall. "Mauvedona, Irissa, you're both mad. Both! By my sword, my oath, I swear you must not risk what either of you intends. No one will win if your wills lock. No one."

Irissa kept her eyes on the blade. Mauvedona also looked only at her suspended star. They were two planets struggling to draw the same moon into their orbit. The blade quivered, drew closer, and bit infinitesimally into Irissa's temple. The faintest vein of red appeared. Felabba twitched her tail across the topaz floor. Mauvedona swept back her skirt, and Kendric paced like a mountain cat in his tethered space.

"Irissa, accede to her! You have more seeing to share than anything Mauvedona can draw from you. You always said you could do more than you thought. Do it now, if you ever hope to see Thrangar again, or Torlocs, or if my aid is ever to be of value. This is a matter of petty pride. Don't you see that?" The irony of his phrase struck him then, and Kendric fell silent, watching her as mutely as Felabba.

Puzzled, Irissa unleashed her gaze and let it slip through the slits of Kendric's eyes. He jerked back from this unheralded invasion, then grew still as she dived through his mind as confidently as a wailwraith through underwater pastures.

There was the same amber haze she had encountered before. Only now that golden light betokened Mauvedona and her works, and thus seemed alien. Perhaps all non-

Torlockian eyes hid just such a smoky morass behind.
There was no pain to dog her this time, but she sensed a
tension as potent as a panther straining on its leash. And
still she perceived that foaming hazel uncertainty she had
noticed previously, that unanchored magic. Weren't they
all nomads of unanchored magic? Mauvedona, Kendric,
herself? She read all this and yet recognized the space's
central, abiding integrity. If Kendric advised her from
deception, it was not of his making.

Irissa retreated and glanced quickly around Mauvedona's chamber. Felabba was looking as simply feline as
she had seemed before joining the party riding from Rindell. She was an ordinary housecat hunched upon her hunt-
er's feet at the base of a victual-laden table, awaiting
bounty, not offering it.

Irissa sighed and glanced again to Kendric. His eyes were
like Mauvedona's dates, both soft brown and hard black,
entreaty encased in command. She sighed again and let
her glance fall to Mauvedona's feet—or hemline, rather.
It climbed the sculpted folds to the sorceress' embroidered
belt with its cyclopean amethyst, passed beyond, and
skimmed up the sinuous torso to the lean golden neck, small
chin, mouth, nose, and eyes.

As she met Mauvedona's eyes, Irissa gasped and felt
herself drawn through a space slenderer than a needle's
eye into a lavender mist. Heavy-lying violet seemed to
stretch from forever, with bolts of velvet overlaying a
rumpled landscape. A dark sky was above. This was an
alien land she wandered in. Twin moons glimmered in the
black heavens, and Irissa trod the rolling purple hills on
floating feet, looking slowly from left to right. She was
being drawn farther and farther into the dusky moors of
Mauvedona's mind. She felt the impulse reel her forward
like a fish on some silver line from a sunlit world above,
beyond, this place.

Someone walked toward her. A small figure rippled,
indiscernible save for a starry haze around it and two white
palms, each with five fingers, pale as the underbelly of some
subterranean thing, white with terminal decay. Irissa's
hands lifted and matched length with those straining toward hers. Their palm heels touched. Irissa felt a spongy
sinking; that was all. Her own fingers were longer than
those others, so long they seemed to grow and in growing

doubled back upon themselves. They curved like a stream of milk from a pitcher, poured down upon themselves, and flowed to meet the shorter fingertips beneath them.

This unhealthy self-extension horrified Irissa. She tried to withdraw but found herself unmoving, simply pooling on the tips of the entity's fingers like some melting ice-dagger, draining, dripping, and diminishing. The landscape around her darkened, then glowed with a heavy golden haze. A pair of amethyst daggers aimed toward her eyes and plunged. The dwindling pool that was Irissa was cool and still. The twin daggers with rubies on their hafts drove deep into the icy water. The water sizzled at their passing, boiled, and rose up in a wrathful cloud of steam. The daggers buried themselves deep with a rising whine. A scream corkscrewed upward and became an embodied entity. It widened, broadened, spread over the hills, and soaked into the black and voiceless sky. It was all a scream, all sound, no sight at all. Irissa put her hands to her ears, astonished that the gesture had reality, that she had hands and ears. They were hers, a part of her. And the scream was not.

The red-pitched sound ebbed, leaving behind a golden entrail. Irissa lay on some islanded floor, her senses wavering like water, yet hardening like rock into something stripped, painful, and skinless. She held her ears against the dimming scream and wondered why she could not open her eyes.

Chapter Fourteen

A bit of fur brushed by her hands. A voice came from the yawning blankness. "She is gone."

Talons gripped her elbows and tugged, pulling her down into a violent violet fissure in the ground. No, up. Drawing her up to stand on wobbly feet.

"Gone. She ushered us out into her primeval antechamber with little ceremony. Her towers darkened and drew back; the pavement became molten and flowed away like a golden river. We are some distance from Mauvedona. You can open your eyes."

It was Kendric's voice, of course, pealing over her consciousness more monotonously than a vaguely distant bell. Irissa thought her hands covered her eyes, but she discovered they cupped her ears instead. Then what had fanned past her vision in an erratic dimness? She willed the gestures that meant one opened eyes, looked at a specific point, and focused. It was a mental rather than a physical process, and the results were less than she had hoped for.

"Dim. It is night."

"Yes, darkening," Kendric agreed. "The sun was setting, after all, when we entered Mauvedona's walls. It's too dark already to seek a snugger place. We'll have to make the best of it here. At least the mounts were ushered out as unceremoniously as ourselves."

Irissa looked in the direction that his less loud voice indicated he had glanced. Yes, something glistened there, an eye perhaps. "What of Mauvedona?" she asked.

There was a lengthy pause; in it Irissa could hear the

bearing-beasts shift their weight and could hear their hooves crackle pine needles.

"She . . . stepped back . . . from us. From you, rather. And all her holdings retreated with her. Spell-walls, goblets, borgia—all. It was as if we stood in this forest place and the rest of the world rolled past us like a Tolechian rug, all of running colors. Mauvedona screamed—I have never heard such a cry, a terrible weaving of triumph and loss. I do not think Mauvedona acquired whatever she wished from daring your eyes."

"Or she gained more than she had anticipated," Irissa said dully.

She knew now that she stood among towering pines; the odor of their sap was amber-hard around her. Her memory painted them pulsating lavender, though her mind knew they were merely deep green, now muted by the night.

"You are weary," Kendric said, watching Irissa's head droop, an unsupported lily on the stem of her figure, a flower with all its weight borne by the blossom alone, and thus likely to snap its life early. "I'll make a fire here where you can rest. Sit. There's a convenient log."

Irissa sank until her knees seemed ready to greet her chin before the advertised log materialized under her. She moved her booted foot as Kendric's flint struck steel. In a vivid flare of blue, something white rocketed past with a howl as demonic in its way as Mauvedona's.

"Felabba! I'm sorry—" Irissa reached out and found only the pale warmth of an infant fire. She drew her fingers back.

"She's gone into the woods," Kendric explained. "Probably hungry, for she got nothing at Mauvedona's table." He moved again in the vortex of dark surrounding the fire's insipid glow, then came back again, dropping something ponderous upon her. "Your cloak. I'll settle by yonder king pine and keep watch for any sorcerous afterthoughts on our former hostess' part."

Irissa said nothing; she merely pulled the cloak edges together like dough and rolled her fingers into them.

"I've no brew to restore you," Kendric said apologetically. "And I wouldn't trust it if it had lain in saddlebags under that one's fiery roof, at any rate. Good rest to you."

Kendric moved away, each needle snap beneath his unseen boots breaking as loudly as a maiden's heart in a ballad. Irissa sat on her fireside log, somehow more alien than Finorian on her melting stones.

Kendric settled silently near a towering pine that was lance-bare almost to the top, where a barb of distant branches whistled softly in the evening air. In his own way, he was as drained by the encounter with Mauvedona as Irissa. And neither had learned anything that would aid their quest, save that even the wonder-makers of the old days felt the uncertainty that stirred the Realms like some clumsy ladle in a pot of simmering soup. The thought of food, other than road rations, stirred in him, also. He could almost smell the spices of a feast, of hot wine warming the hands through a cup, and sweet boughs on the floor . . . Then there was another scent, spiced but heavy on the air, a kind of incense.

She was curling into the air in front of him, like an apparition, yet he knew it was only another of her innovative entrances. Her hair wafted in a topaz fog around her, but the jewel that glimmered in the dim moonlight was violet—a great, square-cut amethyst that anchored her cloak across her collarbones. She was walking toward him in full stride, as if she had come all the way through the woods from her encampment to reach him—but pine needles were no carpet for those sandaled feet. He saw her toenails, painted dark, below the line of jeweled thongs.

Mauvedona stopped, having fully materialized by whatever method she had employed. She smiled. "You do not sleep, Kendric. It has been a trying night; in the old days, too, you were wont to sleep, after."

He did not rise to either her presence or her taunt. "In the old days, you were not wont to come to me again after your desires had been satisfied," he said, crossing his arms.

She laughed, a sound as brittle as a Rocklands dry-storm. She was Rocklands stock. One tended to forget that. Her skin had a vagrant golden glitter, that of crystals in common stone, and her eyes were uncut amethyst—semiprecious phenomena in an impassive face. He had forgotten that, too.

She laughed again and looked up. The dark boughs above swooped groundward. They instantly stood in a high-domed tent of striped forest green and black, Kendric's back against its ridgepole and his body reclining on soft-piled rugs and cushions rather than on mere pine needles.

He shrugged at her display of power. His indifference lighted its opposite in her gemstone eyes. She glittered. Braziers of beating flames sprang into life around the tent's circumference. And food appeared upon a low table, only the simple urban delights of Rule after a long journey, but what he had been thinking of.

"The Circle of Rule would spurn such witchery, Kendric, my old friend. But sorcery shakes you not; otherwise you would not travel with such an unreliable touchstone as that."

Her eyes flashed over her shoulder and his followed, knowing Irissa sat still by her fire. He saw only the engulfing sides of Mauvedona's conjured tent, the ensorcelled privacy she had draped around them. She had always had great concentration.

She came toward him, her fingers greedily wrapped around a goblet as golden as she. The scent of warm spiced wine rose almost palpably above its gilded rim. "It is a cold evening, Kendric. Chill."

He took it, his fingers unbending a bit as the metal warmed them. He quaffed the liquid, indifferent to its source. Wine was too simple for her now; it would be innocuous.

"Your faith touches me, Kendric. When Ronfrenc's emissaries came to escort me from Rule, they would not touch a drop of my brewing. They would not touch even me."

She was as close to him as a Slug Street harlot, one of those riverside professional women who used to ply their charms before the Circle rehabilitated them all to wormskin weavers. Their once-elegant hands would be toil-cracked now. Hers were supple and silk-shiny—and twined somehow around his on the cup. He extricated himself.

"I thought you had accomplished your purpose with yonder seeing, Mauvedona. You have no need of me."

"Kendric, you underestimate yourself. Another symptom of the Wrathmen's waning power. In the old days, you would have no doubts of my motives."

"In the old days, I was younger. And you were older. I think we have reached the same age now, Mauvedona. It strikes me your power has increased. You were once a bewitching practitioner of a few amusing sleights of the senses. But you are more now—and less. What did you do to gain your new potency? How many axe dances have you performed upon unwilling flesh? With whom do you meet when there is no need for dazzling a passing soldier?"

She laughed and snapped her short fingers; the goblet winked to bright air and was gone. "You have always seen through me, Kendric. That is somehow comforting. What bargains have I made since we last met? Not many, and most of them I would exchange for a simple soldier in my toils, my dear Wrathman. There are none like you left in the Realms, did you know that? I have long anticipated our reunion. Do you not remember our dalliance in the crimson castle I created for you?"

He pulled her supple hands from his shoulders. "I came to you in Rule wounded by the lance of loneliness, and your games made recovery sweet. I am not wounded now."

She walked away, the cloak burden dragging behind her, as if it were heavier than it looked. "Are you not? Are not the Wrathmen shattered, seeking, lost? The Circle has no need of heroes—only accountants. Reconcile yourself. Only I have need of you. And any passing hero would do. Even dull-witted Glent of my own people, even he is a man worth entoiling in these pedestrian times. I do not require you, specifically. Preen yourself not. Now Valodec— I have never encountered Valodec. The men of Clymarind are said to be quite inventive in more arts than war . . ."

Kendric shuffled impatiently and she whirled, throwing the cloak behind her shoulders and lifting up her arms, so that the full sleeves fell back from her dainty, pale limbs.

"But I do not mean it! None but you should satisfy me, Kendric. I am sentimental." Her mocking lips curled, and he noticed for the first time that she had taken to painting them a bright, bitter red. "There are few whom the likes of us can call friends in these days, Kendric," she entreated, coming close and pressing nearer, until she seemed to be a brimming cup and he must curl his hands around it for warmth.

The gown she wore was thinner than mist between his hands and the strong, silken lines of her body. She tilted her brimming red lips toward his face. She was not very tall; he would have to drop his eyelids and bend down. Her golden hair, thick and luxuriant, flowed down her back to her knees. He found his hand stroking it as if it were some exotic pelt. Kendric leaned toward her, aware only of the warmth she generated; he could almost hear a deep-throated purr . . .

His surrendered eyes flicked over something alien at the tent entrance—the small, quite commonplace figure of a cat. Felabba's eyes were all wide green iris in the glare of Mauvedona's ensorcelled lamplight—all iris and somehow all warning. Mauvedona's delicate hands caressed the sides of his face and pulled him down into her red mouth. His lashes fought upward for air and he glimpsed Felabba, not sitting, but stalking forward, and then out of sight beyond the figure entwined as close to him as armor. Mauvedona's scarlet lips split like an overripe cherry. Desire possessed him. He pulled away the enveloping cloak and caught her limpid warmth nearer. Something amethyst spun away—the unseated cloak pin. Mauvedona reached out a striking hand and caught it. Something white and vengeful streaked by. Mauvedona's hand blossomed tracks of red, and the pin arced from her fingers and quenched its glow among the floor cushions.

Mauvedona wailed. Kendric brought himself to her waiting mouth, but now the lure was fractured into a ring of black teeth. He was twined in the embrace of a moon-weasel wearing the remnants of Mauvedona's face. The eyes were amethyst instead of gold, and the pale skin and incongruous, painted red lips were on a noseless visage with those black teeth . . .

Kendric tightened his muscles for some attempt at escape. But the creature's shrunken, nail-tipped hands were even now pushing off him. The moonweasel slithered groundward and burrowed among the cushions with an obscene grace, its tiny, dark-clawed limbs, scratching across the dirt. It was busying itself in pine needles now, and only night tented them.

"Ahhhh." It was a hiss of triumph. Even in this form, Mauvedona's voice was golden. The moonweasel reared up, its pale front limbs clasping the amethyst pin clumsily. It was Mauvedona again, rising slowly from the supine position, her hair shrinking to its normal boundaries.

"Is that your price?" Kendric asked quietly.

She began to answer, and he saw that her teeth were white again. She raised a long, scarlet-nailed hand before her face. "Yes. To become a queen, one must become a slave to somebody. Or something. Leave my part of the

Realms, Kendric. I have seen more than I wished through
yonder Torloc window. And now, so have you."

She vanished. Kendric stood beneath his ordinary pine
tree. Shock had congealed the rising warmth of his veins
into something poisoned. He almost wished he were a
shape-slipper, that he could doff his current self like mail
and leave it pooled and abandoned in these woods. Yet
within his revulsion throbbed a pulse of pity for Mauvedona. She had been exiled from her simple arts in Rule
and had taken to darker ones in retaliation. Could not the
Circle see that its suspicion of the marvelous only made its
fears come true?

Kendric settled forlornly at the tree's foot again, unwilling to glance toward Irissa's night-watching profile. He
had urged her to accede to Mauvedona, perhaps at a cost
he could not ken. And had he used Irissa not only to spare
their lives, but perhaps to gratify Mauvedona, whom he
knew of old and was wont to gratify?

He would have dallied with the sorceress in her night-
forged tent, had not mere chance unveiled her alternate
form. Mere chance, his own headstrong desires—and
Felabba. He looked about and found the prescient creature
sitting not far away and regarding him gravely. Kendric,
too, was willing to make his bargains. He could not judge
Mauvedona. And he hoped the cat at his feet could not
judge him. There was something in those emerald eyes . . .

Kendric turned upon his side and drew the sillac cloak
firmly around him. The clean cloak was wholesomely lined
with saber-toothed beaver fur, but now the thick, dark
pelt gave little warmth. He felt a brush across his face and
opened his eyes. Felabba had thrust a coldly inquiring nose
and set of whiskers at his mouth. The cat sniffed deeply,
as if testing for contamination. Then she turned ritually
around and curled into the curve of his stomach. Kendric
dropped a fold of cloak lightly over the sleeping cat,
feeling oddly comforted.

Chapter Fifteen

✦◆✦

Kendric awoke in the morning, catless. Irissa still sat by the ashen fire, and he went over to her as unobtrusively as a man nearly seven feet tall could. He was nearly unobtrusive enough, for she didn't move until his boot squeaked. He tried for a robust normality after the night's excesses.

"Good morning."

"Is it morning?" Her voice was contained, like her posture.

Kendric found his eyes dropping to the top of her hair with a more superstitious fear than he had brought to bear on the shape-slipping Mauvedona. "Yes."

"Ah." Her pale hands clasped her knee. "I thought so. I heard birds. Though there seem to be few in Mauvedona's woods."

"Heard?" Kendric asked, though he had guessed—eons ago, it seemed—why she had sat up all night. He looked down.

She raised her face to his, or to where she thought his should be. Her eyes paused on only the height of his cloak clasp. They were a quiet attractive honey color. Kendric found them shuddersome and rustled in unease.

"I believe I need not avoid mirrors now."

"When?" he asked, knowing it would make no difference.

"It began as a kind of mist, just after Mauvedona and I exchanged—viewpoints. Rather pretty, really; gold like a fabled Clymarindian sunset . . . My mother had amber eyes, much lighter than yours, of course. Are mine—?"

"Yours? No, of course not. It's a mere phenomenon." Kendric's mind creaked as inefficiently as his boots. If it

103

had begun immediately after the two sorceresses' mutual looks, it could be no trick of Mauvedona's. "A passing sort of thing."

She let his optimism fall on silent ground.

"Temporary," he lied.

She finally compensated for her disorientation and brought her calm, sightless gaze up to the level of his face. "A glancing kind of blow, you mean—" She had no chance to complete her thought. A crash of unseen woodland shoots and the explosion of a dozen nearby sticks told her Torloc ears unquestionably that he had gone.

Irissa sank back into the bitter calm that coated her as Iridesium does its wearer. All she saw was unreflecting black, robbed even of its rainbows—Mauvedona's heraldic color. This was the cost of sharing vision with one blind to anything other than the everyday, visible, material world.

Irissa's clasped hands tautened until her knuckles whitened in the unassuming light. She did not see that. This, the inner voice droned, was recompense for accepting guidance from a marshlander, a mere mudwort from some bubbling morass called by so elevating a name as a Realm. There was no realm but the dark behind her eyes.

"You grow hard, Torloc, and that is the last thing that will aid you. Rue, I promised you, yes, but not ruin. Or if ruin, perhaps spelled another way."

Irissa's head remained unmoving, though the voice seemed to come from behind her. "Cast your runes, then, Felabba, and tell me what you see with your old cat's eyes."

"I see a man and four shadows of himself. I see a woman with no shadow. I see another woman with eyes that are slowly turning inside out because she drank deep from another's cup. Are you listening, troublesome one? I do not speak for my pretty, pointed ears' sake—"

"I'll box your ears if you don't come to the point."

"You have been overhard on Kendric."

"I? Hard? On Kendric? You turn senile, Felabba. Only days ago you carped on how unworthy he was of our company."

There was no sound for a moment, but when Felabba's voice came again, it was much nearer. "Ah, Finorian, give me patience! Truly, those who come into the world tailless come without the sense a mouse contains." Irissa felt the faintest furry flick as the cat's own appendage curled past her and doubtless around a pair of pillared forelegs. "You could not see this evening past, but I could—and did. She came, our lady of the flying blades, and bent her softer weapons upon yon Wrathman. Oh, she was skilled at it. I have not seen such subtlety since ill-fated Porphyria, who was Rocklands' queen before. But that is an old tale . . ." Another furry passing came, like the tap of an airy finger for emphasis upon Irissa's wrist.

"She had reason to come to our knight; they have met before, and she would have chained him to that former time and kept him from our future. But he resisted— enough for a mortal man. I assisted, of course, knowing his weakness and her power. But he fought her as fiercely as you, though on different ground, I admit."

"And what care I how many times Kendric of the Marshes kept the fog of Mauvedona from his throat?" Irissa stood in her fury and stamped her booted foot. Felabba yowled and arched away, sitting to lick her injured extremity.

"What he did mattered before, when he urged me to accede to Mauvedona's threats. What care I, who can mend mail with my eyes, for a few temporary slashes? I may now have no wounds to mend, but I have no eyes to rejoin so much as Dame Agneda's broken thread. Mauvedona has stolen my eyes; what care I upon whom she trains them? If the man from the marshes had any trust in Torloc powers, he would have known that I could have mended my own wounds, as I had succored his. There was no threat, therefore no need to concede. And look what it has brought me."

"If you knew humankind or yourself better, you would know why he could not let you challenge Mauvedona's axes. Sit, your log is at your heels. Trust at least me."

Irissa sank back onto her log and sensed the cat padding nearer again. Felabba's voice was slightly rough, the vocal counterpart to silverthistle. And now the bristly tones rumbled, soft and confidential, so that Irissa leaned forward into the black before her and squinted her sightless eyes at it.

"Torloc, have you ever seen a mirror?"

"No, it was—"

"Forbidden. Have you ever seen yourself in any mirror?"

"No, more than ever. My own reflection will drink my powers."

"So you have never seen yourself?"

"Seen myself? No."

"Oh, you know certain things of yourself: that you are taller than most in other Realms; that your hair is as sable as the dark behind your eyes and falls to your fingertips; that your hands are white and long and unringed. And your eyes?"

"My eyes are as clear as a mirror before anyone has looked into it. Finorian told me that once, long ago."

"Your eyes are silver—or gray, perhaps, as mortals would have it. I know that because I have looked upon you, as has Kendric—and, of course, Mauvedona. But you do not know that of your own inner knowledge."

"I know myself!"

"Oh, perhaps, but you do not know your outer self. And if Mauvedona's sharpened steel had creased your features, had made the *temporary* pain and blood twine to produce its own kind of fruit, what model would you use for restoration after? Yes, you would look inward and draw the shattered shreds together. You would sew in the dark and make a crooked seam, my girl. You would mend. And the mending would make your outer self a blending of raw edges so uncomely that they would rival Mauvedona's interior for ugliness."

The cat's words had buffed Irissa's wounded spirit as harshly as thistlepaper and had been hurled toward her like hovering axes seeking old wounds to wrench open. She was silent for a long time and spent it twisting the cord of her tunic around her pale fingers. She spoke more gently. "Felabba, be my mirror. Is my face comely?"

"Enough," came the gruff reply. "To some."

Irissa knit her brow and bent her face again to contemplate the bottomless black ground. "And what do mortals call this pride of face that is worth such risks?"

"Vanity," the cat replied.

"It is a pretty word," Irissa conceded. "And why would one mortal care for another's vanity?"

"Because they are weak," Felabba snapped, "and prone to ask the wrong questions."

Irissa felt the riddlesome creature bound away and soon

heard the reason for it. Something clumsy was coming through the underbrush. Her pulses guessed at moonweasels. Her instincts told her it was something more dangerous.

A pungent essence plummeted to her lap, where it crackled softly, as had the dying, unseen embers of the night before.

"Moonweaselbane," Kendric said. "I believe we'll have reason to wear it. The Rulians were right in festooning it to every door. I found some rinroses to take away the odor."

Irissa flinched as something scratchy circled her head and settled, necklacelike, over her shoulders.

"Careful, you'll scratch your face—" Kendric fell silent. "I've even woven one for Felabba, if the creature will wear a collar. Where is she?"

"Gone, I think. Hunting."

"You are troubled," Kendric said finally, reluctant to approach a wounding subject.

"I cannot see."

"Beyond that."

"I have lost both sides of my vision, that which looks without and that which sees within—and you ask if something more troubles me?"

Kendric sighed. "It is perhaps our kind's oldest fear—the night, within or without."

"Old fears are at least like old enemies—familiar. I have learned a new fear from you and Mauvedona—fear, not of what I may see, but of how others may see me."

"Feel this." Something cold and rounded blossomed in her hand at Kendric's thrust. It was metal, icy and impervious. Her hands caressed the unseen Iridesium and found furrows, ridges, dents, seams, and scars.

"That is why men wear armor," Kendric continued. "We do not use ourselves as shields. My helmet bears the scar of every blow aimed upon me. Your vision was your shield, and if you have lost it, at least you have not altered the self behind it."

"No? And what if your face bore the notches hammered onto this cold metal? Would you not be the same as what you are? Is not this helmet, however used, still a helmet? Do you not treasure it for the blows it has taken? Have you ordered another merely because its gleam has dimmed?"

"No—" he began. "But flesh will wither soon enough. It is too much to imperil. Mauvedona aimed at the critical chink in your defenses; she sensed it—"

"Not mine—yours! I, who care nothing for mirrors, have traveled half the Realms with a walking looking glass. You reflected a false image of me, Kendric, and I became false to my instincts and thus am punished."

Her hands smoothed the helmet in her lap as if it were a gazing crystal and she could see. A tear slid from each blank eye and fell to the ground, one briefly gemming her finger before slipping off. Irissa heard Kendric bend forward to capture the invisible coldstones. He was silent a long moment, probably weighing her grief and finding it wanting for such a catastrophe as loss of sight, she thought, blindly certain somehow that her Torloc tears even now rolled into his boarskin purse . . .

"Weep," he said, a strange tone in his voice. "Weep if you will and if you can."

"I never wept before you came to Rindell. And now Rindell is gone, Finorian, all the Torlocs, and my sight . . . All my tears are gone as well, Wrathman. Fill your purse with your own grief."

"Weep." His massive hands covered hers on the helmet, tightening for emphasis until her fingers tingled. Her head rose to face the darkness squarely.

"No. I would rather bleed than weep, but you have denied me that."

Kendric stood with a muttered expletive. "Then if you have no uses—if I cannot mine your eyes either way, I'll leave you to crawl back to whatever rin will hold you. I've done with nursing a treacherous Torloc and her mangy feline on a journey upon which Realm survival depends. Stay here for Mauvedona's furred legions, then. You will not see them, so your end should be merciful." He abruptly pulled the moonweaselbane circle over Irissa's head, a nettle scratching her temple as it passed.

She said something, a cry of surprise or dismay, but it was drowned by the crash Kendric made across the clearing. Then there was the lash of a tree shoot as reins were unfastened, the click of bearing-beast hooves against loose stones, and the falling away of all such sounds, until only the trees gossiped in the fall wind, softly.

Chapter Sixteen

Irissa sat, unmoving, as she had sat all the previous night. "Smokeshadow," she whispered once. She heard no answering whistle. Eight hooves—that was what her Torloc ears had told her. She did not need eyes to know that Kendric had taken both mounts.

She sat silently, hearing and waiting. She spoke again, another single word. "Felabba."

There was only a swish and rustle high above. Only the howls of silence answered. The cat was gone and would not come again; she suddenly knew that, too. She let her hands drop, fingertips brushing the ground. Nothing was there but dusty earth and pine needles to sliver behind her nails and no wreath of moonweaselbane anywhere. So he had taken even that with him.

Traitor! It was a word that had been tossed about before like a folg ball on some measured court. So Kendric had called Thrangar; so Glent had titled Kendric. Now she added her inner voice to the judgment: traitor. One could never trust these—marsh weasels. They were a backward, brooding lot—avaricious, vulnerable to the gleam of cold-stone or a Mauvedona's eye.

He had seen her uses from the first. If he had foreseen that Mauvedona's sight lock would drain her resources dry, he would have urged the axes at her as vigorously as he now urged himself away with both mounts. Somehow the vision of a craven Wrathman spurring his bronze mount in flight seemed to shake her more than the sight of her Torloc keep melting stone from eldritch stone. An unyielding emotion pounced upon her, tenacious as a moonweasel. She stood, shook it off, and moved a booted foot cautiously along the ground. She was walking, away from the dead fire, away from the direction in which Kendric had retreated, to the clearing's edge. Her branched hands abraded on tree bark, a lone, thick trunk like one worthless prison bar before her. Her feet sank into pine needles and she knew their color was yellow—sere, mummified saffron. Something other than pine scent lingered there, musky and lethal. She moved around the trunk and beyond, her ground-hugging feet shuffling a choking fog of dust and detritus into the air.

Irissa stopped to sense with her ears and fingertips. She felt a silent army of underbrush leaning in at her. Two steps forward confirmed it. Forked branches snagged her tunic and high grasses rustled on her cloak hem, clutched, and then let go, somehow a more contemptuous gesture than if they had tried to leech onto her. A sudden whip cut across her face. She stopped and fought to hoard her tears. Her fingers stilled a quivering branch.

She moved beyond, into unyielding black. Her foot turned upon some anonymous root. She stuttered forward, caught herself, and reached out to touch an ambushing tree trunk. She turned, moved sideways, stumbled, and slipped. She heard her unseen feet snap invisible twigs and heard birds break angrily from her lumbering progress. All was as black as the navel of a rin. And in the eternal ebony rin bottom lived the pale, scaled things that did not see. She would find a rin, fall in, and pine into a wail-wraith, to lure passersby with a keening as disembodied as her eyes. Irissa, she would wail her name, so shrilly it would whisper across the rin lips like wind through stone chinks. Irisssssssaaaaaaa. Hear if you cannot see. She would become a legend as remote as Finorian and the Torlocs who had long ago lived in the Shrinking Forest. She had begun to identify with the black, plummeting presence her imagination conjured. As Felabba had said, she did not know herself, else she could not weave such lethal visions. She did not wish to die, to cease . . .

Her clutching hands laddered along leafed branches, blindly loosing one only to seize another. It was forest here, a friendly place where one could even roam bare of foot— Then her boot plunged into inches of icy water, and her horrified retreat brought a sucking sound that froze her. Marsh! She was near the marshlands. Irissa wheeled, struck forward again, and felt sinuous weepwater strands entwine her face, hair, throat, and hands. She screamed, tore off the wisps, and edged around the hoary trunk that was velvet-garbed with moss. Green, it would be. Her boots slurped with every step now, protesting the mud that carpeted them and oozed between their seams into the downy lining. The waist-level foliage appeared to have drowned in the marshy stretch. Only air linked hands with her when she reached out—air, and sometimes the sudden bulk of a weepwater trunk, off which she caromed and then mindlessly bored into that open direction.

It occurred to her to despair, to cry, to sink to the base of a weepwater tree and join it in its lachrymose occupation. The ground rose sharply and she scrambled up it, half on hands and knees. It felt hard, not pulpy like the track she had been following. She expected the land to straighten after a bit, but it continued upward, even more steeply, so she had to grip her hands on small leafless sticks which projected thornily from the growthless ground. She finally reached a point where it seemed the incline was leveling off. There she paused, exhausted. Irissa crawled wearily over the hill's brow, oddly aware that her tunic must be ragged, her boots mud-soaked. She had never considered her outer seemliness before, and the very fact that she did now was but one more whip from an unseen branch.

She forced an inner stock-taking and found her self-esteem sodden, her pride lacerated, her faith as ragged as her tunic. She was betrayed, deserted like some crippled bearing-beast. Even the practical Felabba had dusted her whiskers free of the scent of her.

It was finally enough to make her weep, and she did, copiously, producing a brittle rain that made a molehill of sorrow at her feet. The coldstone tears clicked like coins on one another. The very worthlessness of her valuable tears only procreated more and still more, until she thought she had purged herself of all the water in her, yet still found that hot rising in her sightless eyes that welled into an outpouring as unwelcome as a Rocklands dry-storm. She was like the Rocklands for more than her gemstoned tears, she realized. They both were deserted, forsaken landscapes of the Realms . . .

Something made her raise her head. Through the faceted

glitter of her still-forming tears she saw green and brown; then a parti-colored world began to waver and form. She saw the hilltop forest, the tree branches shuddering through her uncertain vision, and one tall, thick, dark trunk, blacker than the rest, with strange spots of pale color upon it . . .

There was a faint yellow cast to her vision, and it painted the clearing features of Kendric the Wrathman waxy, like a corpse's. Kendric stood watching her through the trees, a spectator with the bowed, horned heads of both bearing-beasts behind him. All were waiting quietly, as if tethered there. And there, perched solemnly beside the Wrathman, was Felabba. The white cat's ears flicked forward in momentary recognition, then pricked erect, as hostile somehow as a cocked lance. Irissa looked down and saw her crescent of coldstone tears wink blurrily from the ground, as if they drowned in amber oil. She looked again to her silent former companions.

Then Kendric moved forward, until his shadow towered over her. He stopped and bent an inquiring glance, not on Irissa, but on the coldstones clustered at her feet. He ran his fingers through them, and she gasped at his unvarnished greed. His thumb and forefinger rose from that pile with a dainty glint of palest citron pincered between them. He looked at Irissa through his crystal as if he saw her magnified.

"You see now."

Kendric made it a statement, but she answered him as if it had been a question. "Yes, a bit. But—"

His fingers probed the shining pile and he plucked another coldstone from it, holding both stones paired before her, a set of gleaming golden eyes. She focused painfully, aware that it was important to do so for some obscure reason, then veered her cloudy gaze between the gems in his fingers and the foggy amber of his waiting eyes. There was no danger of perfect reflection there now; her sight was misted, only an immaterial veil of pale gold. Irissa of the Golden Veil now, not green . . .

"Look, Torloc," Kendric said softly, and she sensed a smile in his voice.

Felabba padded up to them and assumed a majestic seat near Kendric's crouching form. Her eyes gleamed diffused green. Irissa looked again to the twin gold stars Kendric had captured. Twin—no! One spoke with a deeper yellow sparkle than the other. One was ambered over, the other merely misted.

"This is the chronology of your tears," Kendric explained. "First this—" The deep gold coldstone dipped in his hand. "—then this. You see what is happening?"

Puzzled, she let her eyes twist from dark to pale stone, from left to right. Her first-shed tears were deep gall-colored emanations, her latter droplets delicate, like new honey . . . Of course!

"The first two you shed by the fire were the deep shade of a moonweasel's eye," Kendric confirmed. "If you can but weep a few shades lighter still—"

Irissa laughed, twisting to a sitting position and burying her woods-whipped face in her grimy hands. She laughed until the tears came trickling through her fingers, hardening as they formed and dewing the ground with a spray of white diadems clearer than rock salt.

"It was all so simple as that?" she finally managed to sputter. "A few tears to set right a spell gone awry? Mere mortal magic? What need have the Realms of Torlocs when the well is within?"

A small shower of tear chips still spiraled groundward as Irissa arose on Kendric's offered arm and surveyed the glittering pile of her grief—and her deliverance. She saw as clearly as she ever had seen, perhaps more so. She saw Felabba's cat mouth curl in satisfaction and Kendric's brow smooth a bit as if it had been braced for worry and found the cloud had passed.

They both looked down upon the coldstone pool gleaming from dark amber to untainted white. It was as if Mauvedona's soul had puddled there. Kendric probed his boarskin purse and extracted two dark topaz stones. He dropped them onto the ground and the gathered cold-stones, like a farewell. He and Irissa both stepped carefully away from the spot, as if it were a trap.

"But where do we go?" Irissa asked as they neared the patient mounts. "Me to my rin, you to your marshes? Our quest is at an end."

"Perhaps not." Kendric retrieved the trailing reins and began picking a way through the soggy forest. "Mauvedona dropped a stitch when she mentioned Geronfrey. He was considered mighty even in the days of my marsh-youth.

He dwells beyond Feynwood, beyond these two Realms, in the mountains of the City That Soars."

"Another senseless journey? We learn nothing but our own limits. Better to serve the Circle than to buffet from one mystery to another. I could sit upon a moonweasel-skin bench in Ronfrenc's vaulted chamber and far-see promptly at ten o'clock each morning. Felabba could wear a cap and do acrobatics."

The white cat leaped to Smokeshadow's back at this and cleaned her muddy feet.

"And I," Kendric rejoined, "if I served the Circle as it wished, I could take Moonbane here and polish its blade on you."

Irissa stopped, and so did the bearing-beasts. "Kill me? They really meant you to?" Her eyes for once were as open and harmless as a child's.

Kendric bowed ironically. "So I was commissioned by Ronfrenc. You forget."

"But why? I would not harm them. I wish only to find my own way in the world—or out of it. Why would they want me destroyed?"

"You are Torloc." Kendric had resumed walking, and his dark boots sucked emphatically in and out of the mud.

"But I barely know how to use my powers and could likely never learn well enough to threaten anyone with force. If I did invoke them, it would doubtless be to Realm advantage. I am, after all, as much a citizen of Rule as they."

"You are Torloc. And they are not."

Irissa walked silently along for a moment, listening to the liquid clutch of the mud at all their feet. The earth gave, but custom did not.

"How do you know this?" she finally asked.

"Because I, too, have hated Torlocs."

"Do you know why?"

"Because I hated myself. Hate always springs from within, I think, and therefore must be aimed at a target without oneself, before another discerns one's unworthiness and can direct his own hatred—outward."

"You speak as a tale weaver of the past."

"Yes. I was always uneasy in Wrathman's armor. It was as much a defense against that within as that without."

"Within, without . . . You turn philosophical, Kendric of the Marshes, and thus give me a headache."

Kendric smiled. "Your headache grows, I would think, from other matters. We need not make our journey a fell one. There are other ways to regard our lot. We are not cast adrift, merely set free."

"Free." Irissa contemplated her gray, woven trousers, sopping to the knees. "And so you no longer hate Torlocs."

"Not generically, no. As a breed, that is. I'm certain individual Torlocs are fully as detestable as, say, a starving moonweasel or a Gilothian fireworm or . . ."

But Irissa had snatched Smokeshadow's reins from his gesturing hand and now slurped steadily ahead, until Kendric's only view was of the mud-dappled hindquarters of her bearing-beast.

"Be wary of slimeholes," he warned. "They would engulf you rather more thoroughly than they would me—"

Kendric was answered with a resounding splash and Smokeshadow's sudden retreat backward. He smiled the smile of the prophetic and promptly stepped into brackish water up to his waist.

Felabba, high, dry, and handsome in the curve of Smokeshadow's saddle, looked pleased with herself and applied her tongue more diligently to her hind foot.

Chapter Seventeen

◆·◆·◆

They sat before that evening's fire, their booted legs stretched toward the licking flames. The warmth had hardened the day's mud until their trousers and tunic skirts were leather-stiff. Behind them, the bearing-beasts each stamped one delicately hocked leg, then another, trying to loosen leggings of dried muck. Felabba, the party's only pristine member, sat curled into her tail across the fire, green eyes windowslits of wariness. Irissa chewed a chunk of aged bread, which seemed soggy even though it had ridden saddlebag-high above the swampy strip that bordered Feynwood.

"Well . . ." She had to pause to chew more thoroughly. "Where now?"

Kendric dragged his boot heel across the dry ground before them. "Feynwood runs north and south, so. Ride along it far enough and we come to the verge of the Furzenland between these Realms and the City That Soars. It is there we will find Geronfrey. Somewhere." He leaned forward and rested his arms on his splayed knees, staring at the rutted ground.

"On so little does our quest depend now," Irissa said. "But if you are willing to go, how could I refuse? It is my quest."

Kendric's profile was cameo-still against the black, swallowing night. "I fear it is all our quests now." He sighed finally. "If Geronfrey is involved in it . . ."

"This man seems another you know of." She paused and kept her voice perfectly flat. "Like Mauvedona."

He looked at her, although the fluttering light did little to reveal the emotion, or lack of it, carved upon his face. "Not like Mauvedona, no. Unlike any Realm-born. I'd heard of him at my Nana's knee, that old woman who wove brambles into mats. I thought Geronfrey was another of her weavings. He would come and make a moonweasel of me, she would say, if I were not a good and proper son to her son, Halvag the smith. And then I grew beyond my father's forge, my grandmother's knee, and beyond believing in things that have nothing better to do than swoop down on small boys. I forgot about Geronfrey, until I took Wrathman oath on Clymarind with the five who were my bondbrothers. We heard of Geronfrey during those ceremonies, but he was even more secret than the rites. I cannot tell you more than this: If any in the Realms springs from a space beyond time, a place before and after what we know, it is not a Torloc, Irissa. It is Geronfrey."

Irissa shivered and drowned in the blackness of his unreadable eyes. "And you would ride to him?"

Kendric nodded. "I think I must. I quest for the Wrath-men now,—Torloc sorceress, and for myself. I will ride. If Geronfrey guards your gate, then your journey will not have been in vain."

"My journey, yes . . . I can see again now, at least—see to find I do not like the road." Irissa laughed, shaking out her tunic hem until clods of mud fell from it. "And I accused *you* of being a muddy mortal!" The fire crackled approval of her tacit apology. "What of—Mauvedona? Will she not—?"

"No. Her power has its reins, and they are furred ones. She has allied herself to the moonweasels and is as doomed as they."

"Doomed? Why?"

"Did you not listen to Ludborg? Hegira, he said—the moonweasels flowing in fanged waves toward the Abyssal Sea. My grandmother also told me of moonweasels and of the time when they mass together and overrun everything, ending only at the Abyssal, where they cast themselves into the water and crest the waves with fur, until they drown."

"I almost pity the wretched beasts," Irissa said, snuggling into the dry, unfurred collar at her neck. "But you still do not tell me of Mauvedona."

Kendric shifted as restlessly as the bearing-beasts; but because he now wore no Iridesium, he did not rattle. "Mauvedona made a pact with the forces of—what would you call it? Sorcery turned against itself. Who can guess what inner and outer demons she conjured? But she wished to remain powerful; and once driven out of Rule, she had lost her center. So she applied to another source for power and entered an unholy alliance with the doomed moonweasels. It is she who sends them on the City and causes the Rulians to dress their doors with moonweaselbane. Otherwise, the creatures would simply stream past without wreaking damage and plunge into the Sea."

"Could it not be the moonweasels themselves who made the pact with Mauvedona? They speak marvelously fair to mortal ears—"

"No, no, no," Kendric said impatiently. "They speak, yes, but only rudimentary phrases that give the semblance of intelligence. They are mimickers, like the Rocklands lizards who, from a distance, sound like a growling encampment of quarriers. No animal speaks, as such—or speaks thoughts."

On this pronouncement Kendric shifted again, missing the expression that crossed Irissa's fire-ruddy features and the look she threw the suddenly wide pair of green eyes across the flames.

"Hussshh," the cat Felabba said. Or perhaps it was merely the fire exhaling an unburnable rush of wood ash.

"You mean, Kendric, that the moonweasels may prattle human phrases without comprehending their meaning?"

"Exactly. I mean I would as soon believe yonder feline would of a sudden speak up and demand milk as that a moonweasel knows any more of the sounds it utters than a dog knows of its bark or a bearing-beast its whistle."

Irissa knew no other diplomacy than silence. Felabba rose then, stretched at her great and good leisure, and wandered away into the shadows.

"And are my powers as much a mirage as a moonweasel's voice?"

"Mauvedona does not covet mirages, believe me," Kendric said dryly.

"What happened with her? She had her will, and yet . . ."

"Having one's will is always more than one bargained for, especially if it's at the cost of someone else's will. I do not think your powers worked as Mauvedona anticipated."

"At least she seemed to have some idea of *how* my powers worked. That is more than I do. Verthane said I could initiate myself. I thought I had done so when I sight-forged this." Irissa's palm paused on the sword hilt at her side. "But I am annoyingly hot and cold of power, which seems to ebb and flow at its own will rather than mine. I would I had been able to grow green and vanish like Finorian," she added wistfully.

"What? And miss this meal?" Kendric masticated the last of his crusty bread and wiped the back of his hand across his mouth, almost as if to sweep up any spare crumbs. "I'll ride to a marsh village tomorrow morning and bargain for some durable rations for our northward journey. Food will be hard-found."

He stood and strode over to Willowisp. The bearing-beast sniffed hopefully at Kendric's empty palm, then rubbed his whisker-barbed muzzle across it. "No, nothing for now, my fine fellow. You sup like one marshlands-born now, bearing-beast of the plain. We all wear someone's bridle or another and must go where the unseen hand tugs us." Kendric swept his hand through the glossy strands spilling from Willowisp's arched neck.

"Whose bridle do you wear?" Irissa asked softly.

Kendric looked over to her and smiled tautly. "Mine own. That is a tighter rein than any other would put on me. And who is the maker of your harness? Whose tug do you resist?"

Irissa sighed as the flames rose and fell before her like breath made visible. "Finorian's. And Ronfrenc's. And Verthane's. And yours. And Mauvedona's. I wish I had a restraint to call my own, but I am merely what others wish to know of me. I am kept tethered for my own good. Perhaps that is the most treacherous binding of all. If anyone had trusted in me, he would have allowed me to explore the boundaries of my powers; instead, I am unleashed like a hound sent to fetch a pheasant or an earth-arrowed falcon. I do my duty and return only to find the snap of the chain upon me again my sole reward. If I only knew why my sight clouded at Mauvedona's intrusion and why my tears unveiled me and if it could be done again and if my powers have been strengthened or diminished—"

"You ask questions a sage like Verthane still ponders. You are like Ronfrenc, really. You think power springs up in a shape to be mastered." Kendric paced toward the fire contemplatively. "That it extends so many leagues this way or that and is so high." He stretched to gesture to the sky until he seemed to tower forbiddingly. "You think that it is so many Wrathmen allied or scattered, so many sorcerers exiled or conquered. You think power can be harvested like wheat and then doled out in well-milled allotments. Power is empty sustenance, else Mauvedona would not have needed to feast her eyes on yours. You rest better not knowing your power and would rest even better if you did not use it."

"Your entire life has been force, power in its rawest form," Irissa replied, standing. "You are a Wrathman of the Far Keep. Were, then. It is easy to renounce power when it has come so cheaply to one. I will find the borders of mine, and pace them off and call them my own. I will use it. I have not come this far not to."

"And I will come with you only until your power overpowers you," Kendric promised solemnly. "It will be an interesting journey."

Chapter Eighteen

Kendric left early the following morning, even while the coals still glowed through the gray of their ashes. He took both Willowisp and Smokeshadow. Irissa he would not take. She remained by the wind-stirring ashes with her uneasy sword at hand, her furless cloak for warmth, and Felabba for solemn company.

"Well, my old friend, my silent twitch-tail, you look as if you'd like to live up to Kendric's assumption of you. Silence! Speak, you ragged, loquacious, leering, sneering statue of a cat. I have not heard your grating voice since Mauvedona did me the service of temporarily removing you from my sight and you took my calamity as cause to deliver one of your more cryptic sermons."

Felabba sat before Irissa calmly, only her tail flicking soundlessly back and forth and stirring a whirlwind of ashes.

"Don't. You'll never clean your tail."

The green eyes regarded Irissa implacably, but it seemed that now she could see deeper into the bottomless emerald. Felabba the cat was being coy.

"It's you who are an irritating, irksome creature," Irissa answered the silent sylvan rebuke in the cat's eyes. "You were as helpless as a marshmouse in Mauvedona's palace.

And when my eyes were lost, you romped blithely after Kendric in his desertion, you—"

"It was for your own good," Felabba said. Or perhaps she did not say it. The firm pink mouth did not actually move, the fangs did not flash in the light, the whiskers did not waft up and down with each syllable. Yet the tones reverberated through Irissa's ears, an amplified purr made articulate.

"My own good," Irissa complained. "You and Kendric should share mottoes as well as forces: *For Honor and Irissa*, or some such formula that would appeal to a fraud like Ludborg the Fanciful . . ."

"Or Scyvilla the Rengarthian," the cat suggested, tilting her head obliquely to watch some insect scurry past her feet.

"Ah, more mysteries." Irissa stood and paced felinely. "Am I to believe that oozing pool of a personage, that chattering puddle of allusion and illusion? You told me I would meet rue, Felabba. And I have met it, and melted it with my tears. You told me the Circle of Rule would be closed to me, and it coiled as taut as a moonweasel around me. In both these things you were right. And I still know no more of my powers than a babe knows of the rattle with which it admonishes the world."

"You come to a cat for knowledge?" Felabba's ear-crowned head was bowed, her white whiskers brushing the ground and whatever moved upon it. She crouched suddenly, coiled to the earth like a spring, her sweeping tail the mechanism that wound all the muscle and fur to their tautest.

"Yes, please," Irissa said meekly, abruptly amused at her mentor's utter feline concentration.

A pale paw slapped out, and then the dainty jaws snapped at the ground. Something winged and wriggling vanished in the pearly interior of Felabba's mouth. A petal of tongue rapidly skimmed the whiskers and disappeared. Felabba sat up again and took a moment to launder her striking paw before speaking. "I trust our absent giant has the foresight to return with victuals appealing to a cat. At my age, he can't expect me to hunt all the time."

"What is your age?" Irissa asked narrowly.

"Enough," the cat sniffed, "to earn your respect."

Felabba rose and walked over, her sharp shoulder blades

roweling the air like a fish fin. Why was it that predators always carried their sharp anatomy about like a banner? Irissa looked at her nailed fingers and remembered Mauvedona. Clawed. We all come clawed, and, unlike cats, mortals cannot retract theirs.

"So you want to know," Felabba resumed. "Know, then, that your power is to see—not, to some, a very unique gift. Humankind is accustomed to assuming that everything sentient sees. If I go too fast or too deep for you, say so. These are matters I would discuss only with Verthane or his like . . . Now *there* was one who knew how to feed a feline. Do you remember those cunning little silver trays in Rule?"

"You are evidently old enough to let your mind wander, Felabba. Return to my gifts and say less of those extended to you."

"Ah, well. So, you see. All things see, really, in a certain sense, though mortals believe only scaled, feathered, furred, and skinned things see or have eyes. The eye of a tree, for instance, lies at its root; so, of course, no mortal would think of looking there for it. Do you know where a wailwraith really sleeps? In the deep, single eye of a weepwater root. That is why such trees give off their resinous tears; you would, too, if you periodically had a wailwraith curled up in the corners of your eyes. Some of them are not as wispy as they should be, by any means . . ."

"Felabba!"

"But I avoid the heart of the matter. You see, and see better than most, things as they really are—simply because you have not been subjected to a life of seeing things distorted. Part of this is the guardianship of the Torloc dames. Most of it is your heritage. Your eyes are—alien. They are a trait rooted weepwater-firm in an element different from that in which they perform their daily tasks. You see at right angles to the rest of those in Rule. You see through the mirror, edgeways."

The cat sank into her mounded bones again and rolled her forepaws together before her in the manner of a Soarian monk. "Now, then. To keep your true sight, which is bound to degrade in time as the link with its origin grows thinner and thinner—to keep your gift sound, you must not diversify it. That is why reflection would confuse you, drain your energies, and make you concerned with how you thought you ought to see a thing. You would have acquired the bane of mankind—expectations of how you ought to appear, how things ought to be . . ." The cat's fur rippled over her sharp shoulders, like a shudder. "A most troublesome malady, expectation. I can't tell you what damage it has done humankind. Shun it. Shun it as you would a mirror, for it is as illusory.

"But I wander again, as you so delicately put it."

Felabba's tail wrapped tighter around her curled forepaws; only the very tip wafted back and forth a bit as she continued. "Of course, your gift is simply to see things as they are; and because you see them more clearly than most, it is a simple step from that to seeing them as they were or will be. It is how you can knit flesh and mail; even, if your spirit is strong enough, forge new realities such as your weasel welter there. Your sword! Naturally, had not Verthane lent you the peephole of his webbed star, you would not have been able to tread on Was and Will Be, which are the only conditions under which you can actually create from a mind-image."

"Felabba, you knew all this and did not tell me earlier?"

"You did not ask." The cat's eyes winked shut a moment, then slowly winked open again on short white lashes.

"And Verthane's star was a window, then?" Irissa asked. "A window to the world without, where Finorian and Thrangar and the Torlocs have gone?"

The feline eyes flared wide suddenly, their vertical pupils yawning like a distant pit. Felabba did not answer.

"Felabba!" Irissa stood and confronted the statued figure by the softly stirring ashes. She felt the same slight breeze ruffle her hair; a strand brushed her wrist and she started. She whirled and looked behind her, to the fringe of fir trees that braceleted their clearing.

It rainbowed across her eyes then, a midnight curtain decked with gaudy stars—crimson, violet, azure, bronze, green, and black—a meshed metal wall of Iridesium she had not seen since—

"Kendric . . . ?"

He stepped toward her, the armored man-tree nearly seven feet high, the Wrathman in full array . . . Kendric. Why had Kendric resumed his Wrathman's garb?

The Wrathman advanced in a cacophony of metal, leather, and snapping twigs. Irissa backstepped, gasping.

The Wrathman wore a gleaming, scaled gauntlet with a great crest of violet and ruby feathers bristling from its cuff. Around that rainbowed wrist, choking all that luminous color as night strangles the sunset, were a pair of scrawny hands, as black and shriveled as a moonweasel's and as well nailed as Mauvedona's.

Not hands—feet! It was a dwarf falgon that perched upon the knight's extended arm. Even now the strong, bright feathers of its ruff and massive wings riffled as the creature gazed alertly from side to side, its hooded head seeming to sense the presence of prey.

Felabba growled menacingly from her lowly post on the ground. The falgon lashed its scaled tail. The sleek, iridescent hindquarters, as streamlined as an eel's, shivered as if shedding their skin. For even a dwarf falgon such as Ronfrenc and his Circle pressed into service for their games of folg or the common miniature falgons that could still be captured occasionally near the City That Soars were twice the size of a household cat and three times as rapacious as a moonweasel.

"I startle you, lady." The strange Wrathman came directly for the cold campfire, as if something other than material warmth drew him. His voice was unusually melodious and quelled Irissa's panic.

"Startled, yes," she agreed. "I have not seen a Wrathman of the Far Keep—for some time."

She sensed a call for caution even in the breeze that brushed past her lips. But the Wrathman simply put his wrist up to a nearby vacant branch. The blindfolded falgon edged obediently onto the offered perch, voicing a strangled gargle of protest muffled by the leather hood. The falgon's claws, Irissa decided, were about the size of her own hands. And the nails were as curved and strong as a Clymarindian scimitar.

"You are brave, lady, to venture alone. Let me rekindle your fire." The Wrathman bent to his task and Irissa looked down, avoiding the obsidian gleam of his smooth helmet, except to notice that, unlike Kendric's, it was unfurrowed. Perhaps no blade had ever dared approach him that closely.

"I am not alone," Irissa said.

The Wrathman's hooded eyes glanced quickly to Felabba and flickered with some emotion just as the remaining half-charred logs warmed to his flint and steel. "A cat," he noted approvingly. "I have not seen a cat—in some time." Such a melodic voice was a pleasure,. and Irissa basked in it. "Nor has my falgon. I must keep the creature hooded, for only then does it follow my bidding."

"Yes, I know the technique," Irissa answered dryly, thinking of hooded things other than falgons.

The Wrathman stood; Irissa sensed more than saw the rising flames dancing in the deep, rich colors of his armor. It was a pity Kendric had relinquished all his Wrathman's metal; it was a suit as glorious in its way as any falgon's growth of melded scale and feather.

"I have ridden down from the City," he volunteered; courtesy required that he give an accounting before demanding one. "And you?"

"I have just ridden up from the City. The City of Rule, I mean. You have been—?"

"Among the Soarians, yes. I spent some time in a monastery, being tended for moonweasel wounds. You had best turn back, Lady of the City. You are far from your turrets and byways, your palaces and stars."

"The stars are everywhere," Irissa said, gesturing toward the daylight sky.

"I mean stars in a purely architectural sense," the Wrathman said, bowing.

"I am afraid we have no room for stars other than celestial these days," Irissa answered, smiling.

The Wrathman's face, or what she could see of it—merely eyes, nose, and mouth, since the mailed hood hid the rest—that face stiffened. It was, she decided, quite different from Kendric's, although she was sore put to say why. She was beginning to see that, for all the Wrathman's similarity of stature, dress, and perhaps even orientation, they were, after all, points from different directions of the compass.

He frowned, and the brows that drew together were a silky brown that reminded her of softer sojourns and more civil places. "You are one of the sorcerer folk," he said then. "Only such as they talk of stars, especially in these days, when all that we see are falling."

"I am Torloc."

"Ahhhh. I should have seen, but I am distracted in these days. It seems the moonweasel wounds drank deeper from my will than even from my body. These are cold times. I

am Valodec of far, floating Clymarind, and of all my
brothers, I have the least reason to fear Torlocs. Then why
does the sight of you set my mail to grinding its rings? No,
don't move . . . I ask myself these questions only because
there is no one else to ask them. My bondbrothers are scattered, as sour as last week's milk, as pale as yesterday's
stars when the sun is out. I think I curdle at something in
myself. I have lost my faith in what I knew, and now it
seems that there are not fires enough in Rule to warm me
nor roads wide enough to lead me."

Valodec of Clymarind! Of course. There was something
of Verthane in his golden voice, something unanchored
in his melancholy.

"We have all lost direction, Valodec," she said to comfort him.

He shook his helmeted head ponderously and turned
without farewell to reclaim his falgon and leave her.

Among the farther firs—and this time there could be
no mistake—stood Kendric.

Chapter Nineteen

He was a pillar of homespun brown and blue, a thick, absorbing stalk of ordinariness. The two bearing-beasts stood
behind him, their horned heads drooping slightly, their
sleek backs heaped with stores, so that their silhouettes
resembled Ludborg's humped dray beast more than those
of war mounts.

Irissa almost willed the distracted Valodec to blunder
on past his fellow Wrathman. But before she could so
much as draw a bough of veiling evergreen across the
figure of Kendric, he himself stepped firmly into Valodec's
path.

The Clymarindian Wrathman paused, more confused than confronted.

"Valodec! I have not seen you since— Valodec, do you know me?"

"Kendric—you? Here? And without your Wrathman's colors? Why? Ah, I remember. You have broken your bond. We are like masts of a wrecked ship that crash against one another blindly in the waves until we sink, we Wrathmen. Let me pass, and I shall not look back."

"But, Valodec . . ." Kendric's arms came forward persuasively, his hands open, palms up, unthreatening. "I have been hoping to meet with you, of all Wrathmen, who would understand—"

"Least," the beautiful voice spat from between set teeth. "Our times are inside out. I, who had the most tolerance, find myself half-mad with loathing for anything that does not mesh precisely with my world as I see it. Yon Torloc witch has been setting my teeth on edge, and now you rise up like an effigy before me, the stench of your marshes boiling in my veins. Away! You do not know me, and I know only your treachery."

"It's true that I have renounced service to Ronfrenc and his Circle, but I never thought to forsake my fellow Wrathmen."

"But you did!" Valodec said, so straining to contain his anger that his mail rippled like water on his body. Something beyond Kendric caught his eye. His mailed right hand extended, palm open, cupped, but thumb demandingly splayed for something.

"You have not surrendered your sword. Give it to me to take back to Glent and Prince Ruven-Qal and the others, and I will spare you."

"My sword is mine." Kendric's voice honed itself on the edge in Valodec's.

"You have disgraced it. Give it to me and let me pass." Another note entered the Wrathman's voice and vibrated beneath the command in it. "I beg you."

"Then take it," Kendric said, whirling and striding to Willowisp. The bearing-beast whistled and shied as his master drew the great blade from its anchorage in one gesture and came crashing back into the clearing.

"Take it, Valodec." Kendric's voice rang with challenge. He held the long blade lightly, half-lowered, so that even now it could be construed as a gesture of hesitation. But his eyes were not at half-mast, and Irissa needed no far sight to read in them that Valodec had finally met a roadblock.

The Wrathman unchained his cloak and threw it off. It slid to the ground, violet silk lining up so that it resembled the exotic entrails of some creature. "Yes. Stand and face me. We will fight as we once fought in practice yards, Kendric, as we fought the barbarian seaskulls from the outer Abyssal. We have not fought enough in these last years, Kendric. It is why we weaken."

Valodec unsheathed the burden of the sword that lay across his back, drawing it over his shoulder in a long, sliding motion. He brought its point to rest but an inch above the hard-packed dirt between the two men.

Irissa never even thought to demur at what was taking place or to invent some device that would blunt the edge of battle. It was inevitable, as unstoppable as the tide of moonweasels pouring on Rule and then ebbing out to sea and certain destruction.

She drew back from the clearing to take a watcher's post with the bearing-beasts among the trees. Felabba sat at her feet, for once no advice pouring from her. It seemed to Irissa as she stood in the pine shadows that Valodec towered over Kendric. Perhaps only his armor made it look so. It was certain that Kendric was ill-armed to meet a mailed adversary. All he had was his sword, his helmet of hair, and the iron in his eyes.

Valodec clasped his gold-worked hilt with both hands and raised the massive blade. Kendric was still, and it was only when Valodec brought the elevated sword crashing down that the marshman seemed to believe battle was begun. He leaped aside, swinging his sword in an upward arc. Then both his hands were fisted upon it, and it swung back again and rang flatly on Valodec's tunic-covered breastplate.

"Ah, now you show your colors, my soggy friend. Now I can make my blade chatter across your bones . . ."

Valodec came slicing inward, the sword hacking back and forth, a vicious pendulum. Kendric, armorless, dodged him nimbly, partially distracted by the singsong threats that issued so mellifluously from his opponent's mouth.

"And wasn't Clymarind the Wonderful first-born from the Abyssal Sea? Is it not the navel of our round-bellied world? You would spit at Clymarind and oaths, marshman. We have heard the winds whisper against Madorian; our fleets have returned to harbor with their bows broken and their canvases torn. Storms! It is the storm of oath-breaking that beaches upon our Realms. Relent, false Wrathman, for once my blade drinks blood, it is relentless."

On Valodec's last words, his sword swept back again, its very tip drawing neatly across Kendric's retreating arm. The blood spread in a dark circle, turning the rent blue fabric purple. Kendric's sword quivered in his grasp. Valodec stepped nearer, his spurs chiming, his mail flashing, his sword a moving line of thirsty steel.

Irissa shut her eyes slowly. She heard the ring of blade on metal. Not Kendric's—he wore none. She opened her eyes and saw Valodec reeling from a blow to his shoulder. Now his own weapon sagged. But his voice continued uttering a melodious singsong taunt, both chilling and attractive.

"Yes, my lad. Some little nip out of the shoulder and your puny blade will sate its appetite. My blade hungers deep for bone and blood and all the madness left in Rule. Nothing oils a blade so well as blood, and marsh blood is as thick as mud!"

Leaping nearer, Valodec sliced about the clearing in a frenzy, his blade rebounding from bark as often as from Kendric's parrying sword. His very fury armored Kendric. Valodec's slashes fell wider and wider of the mark. And if Kendric's woven garb was little protection, neither did it glitter and draw the needled sword like a magnet. Kendric leaped and gamboled about the edge of Valodec's sawing blade, a puppet linked to it by a dark, unseen string, as if the bloody cloth upon his arm were only a place where the string had broken.

A clumsy push butted Irissa from behind. She turned to find Willowisp staring mutely at her from under lowered golden bristles. Her fingers twined the crimson forelock that ran in rivulets across the creature's long and noble forehead.

"I can't," she whispered to the mount, to Felabba at her feet, and to the sentinel pines around them all. No one heard. All they listened to was the clang of battle, the ring of the two Wrathmen trying to hew each other down like timbers.

Eluding Valodec's onslaught was clearly tiring Kendric.

His legs began to bow to the earth on each blow as if he stood on sinking sand instead of hard, high ground. Valodec's sword swung around his helmeted head, whistling like a bearing-beast. Kendric gathered himself in his retreat toward the encircling forest and riposted intently, mercilessly, his blade swinging left and right almost as haphazardly as Valodec's. The armored Wrathman retreated himself, stumbled, and lost the grip of one hand on his pommel. He retreated another step, and his unweaponed hand went up momentarily as if to signal stop.

Its motion ended as the pitiless arc of Kendric's blade, wielded as a blacksmith would wield his hammer hard and sweeping on the anvil, cut across the center of Valodec's body.

Valodec fell on his back, a tortoise still rocking slightly in the shell of his armor. His sword fell across him, the hilt impressing an ironic emblem on Valodec's tunicked chest. Around it, a sunset ocean of vibrant red flared outward.

Kendric's own sword dropped to the ground. He came and stooped over his fallen bondbrother. "Your eyes, quickly!" He looked to Irissa.

She did not move from her post at the forest's verge.

"Now!" Kendric urged, delicately removing the heavy sword hilt from the chest that still moved up and down a little. Red lacquered Valodec's hilt and Kendric's palm. It glittered in the daylight from far above on the now-motionless plain of Valodec's tunic.

"Why not?" Kendric demanded, even as he saw that Valodec was dead. "Why not?"

Irissa shook her head. "This is the working out of something older than any of us. It would be wrong for me to interfere, even though I did so between you and Glent. It seems that since I lost my sight for a while, I see that better. This is between you and your fellow Wrathmen, between your sword and their swords."

A sudden cry of rage abraded the clearing's wounded silence. It was the hooded falgon, beating upward on a raw burst of fanning wings, like Valodec's soul hurled skyward in some irrational fury. The creature's feathers arced a rainbow of momentary reflection as it burst above the tall pinetops into daylight. It streaked upward, a giant-flung stone spiraling blindly, until it was lost to sight.

The three beasts and the two people watched it until only the pale sky yawned above their heads.

Kendric sighed. "Take the mounts into the forest and wait for me."

Irissa led them away. Smokeshadow's already laden back carried the lithe white shadow that had leaped atop it. Felabba negotiated the tied-on bundles until she rode the bearing-beast's sinuous wither and could lean toward Irissa's ear.

"A bad beginning for a journey," the old cat's thoughts sounded in Irissa's consciousness.

"Valodec had the advantage! Kendric only defended himself, ill-armored as he was. It had to end in someone's death."

"We go from here to there," the cat retorted. "And when here is rooted in death, what will await us there, eh? A bad beginning."

"You always carp about our beginnings, Felabba," Irissa said sharply. "We should not even have left Rindell, had you been my advisor. We must go somewhere, do something . . ."

"More has been done by sitting in one place and letting the mind roam than by any peregrinations of restless feet. Ah, well, you are your own headstrong person, I assume, and I am but a cat. What do I know?" The green eyes glanced sideways, slit vertical pupils darker than a vein of malachite.

"Know? You know more than a decent housecat ought, Felabba. And I think you know more than I care to."

Irissa finally halted the beasts and waited. She waited a very long while until Kendric came crashing through the thick undergrowth. Regret was a potent poison for a warrior—regret that worked in the blood like borgia and festered the will.

He said little that day or the next. The provisions he had obtained at the marshland village were simple but fresh: thick, dimpled cheeses, moon-pale; hard-crusted, dark breads; and dried strips of meat. Irissa expressed her appreciation, but it seemed that Kendric had developed a certain deafness.

It struck her with irony—a seeress whose eyes were unreliable and a warrior whose ears heard not. He had buried Valodec behind them, in the hard ground bordering Feynwood. And once, when he was flipping back Willowisp's embroidered leather saddlebag, she caught a flash of shimmering falgonskin, tufted with stiff feathers—Valodec's Clymarindian glove, a gauntlet of guilt always before his eyes. Poor Kendric!

The nights grew colder, and then the days, as if a chill were contaminating the land. They caught their cloaks closer and kept silence. Their route led upward, and Felabba sneezed frequently from her perch atop the dwindling food bundles. So rough was the landscape now that they seldom rode. Both bearing-beasts kept their extravagantly maned necks bowed, picking out a path for their hard-hoofed feet.

It was sad to think of such noble animals as mere beasts of burden now. But every party member was diminished in some way, every eye looked down, like those of the people of Rule and the Circle of Rule. Was Ronfrenc warm in his pillared hall? Irissa wondered resentfully as she clasped her cloak closer and still felt the wind burrow beneath it like an unwelcome pet. She couldn't even name the moment when the snow claimed the ground. One morning they began their daily journey on frost-bitten furze, and that night they camped on hard-shelled snow, old from many weeks of crusting. It was all white around them—ahead in the rising, snow-capped crags, behind in the sweeping train of Furzeland that trailed the advancing party, above in the faceless sky that loomed moonless and sunless over them.

Irissa blessed her down-lined boots for their toughness and warmth. She hugged her cloak collar to her throat and dreamed of her long-lost moonweasel fur, all bloodthirstiness forgiven. Kendric hunched into the saber-toothed beaver fur that ringed his cloak until only his feverish, dark eyes showed between the sable of his own hair and that of the creature whose pelt warmed him.

Kendric reminded Irissa of some fierce, hunted falgon, dangerous and denying that his heritage made him so. She had not discussed the Wrathman with Felabba, almost afraid to unveil her speculations. She was convinced now that some potent, ancient force had set the Wrathmen's oath in motion and that its pattern had played out through the years and generations until its potency was all but forgotten, even by the men born to carry the eldritch swords and the bond that accompanied them. The meaning had been lost, but not the power. And now, when even the moonweasels circled back on their own mortality and when all Rule quaked with some malevolent disintegration, the Wrathmen were the fulcrum of the forgotten curse. And it all had begun when Thrangar the Torloc vanished somewhere between the City of Rule and Rindell, somewhere near Feynwood, where he had ridden, blind as a tainted seeress, past Mauvedona and her beckoning, flaming castle.

"Thrangar . . ." Irissa breathed to herself and the cold that companioned her. He was the cipher that translated mystery into a common understanding. "Thrangar . . ."

"Aye," Kendric said, coming abruptly alongside her for the first time in days. "He may lie dead as well. That leaves only four; and of the remaining three, Glent has already tried to slay me. I should keep my eyes over my shoulder and watch for the shooting star of Prince Ruven-Qal's burning powder projectiles."

He didn't believe his own words; they were merely an expression of a doubt grown rancid within. But Kendric looked up bitterly, then pulled back on the beasts' reins and Irissa's shoulder simultaneously.

"Look. Look up."

She did, unquestioningly. She saw no fireballs, no hail of enmity—only the wide, white expanse of sky and something black and tiny buzzing upon it.

"Another dwarf falgon," Kendric said, almost eagerly. "We near the City That Soars, though we are not bound there. Rule grant that we find Geronfrey; he cannot abide far from the City."

His face had lightened, as if merely seeing something soaring were a kind of new hope. He left his arm around Irissa's shoulders as he quickened his step again, and they moved forward in a body. Irissa thought it strange that a burden could be a comforting thing. She exchanged a glance with the nearest bearing-beast and met Willowisp's amber twinkle. It was not so bad to serve.

They broke through a notch in a pair of hunch-shouldered cliffs soon after and paused on the brink of a gleaming white abyss. A snowy saucer sloped evenly to a center far below, while ahead of them reared the polished ivory fangs of a distant mountain range.

"Falgontooth." Kendric pointed to the highest of the mountains. "And there is the City That Soars."

Irissa followed the arc of his gesture westward toward an unbroken giant's jawful of pointed white peaks. And there, caught between the crevasse formed by two of the tallest, perched a geometric construction of ice and rock, a gargantuan snowflake frozen between the mountains' teeth. Irissa's eye traced the confusing fretwork of icy, white bridges and balustrades to the windowed buildings carved into the mountain's very sides.

"We rode that path, six abreast, eh, Willowisp?" Kendric indicated a line as thin and black as a thread that snaked from the valley to the sparkling snowflake hung above it. "A tricky bit of business, even for Wrathmen. But it was important we impress the people of the City That Soars, else they would have impressed their will on those beyond their border. That was our function, more than might and main, to impress the Realm-dwellers and thus make peace-loving citizens of them."

It was as if Kendric had never explored these thoughts before and they led somewhere dark and tortuous. "The Six Wrathmen of the Far Keep! The Six of Swords. The Six of Sleight of Hand is more to the point. We were mere diversions, the hand the magician waves to one side while his other hand performs the trickery. We were never more than that. And now Ronfrenc has dispensed with even the need for illusion."

Kendric turned to his saddle and pulled his great sword from its mooring. Here in the chill mountain air, against an unremitting background of snow and ice, the weapon looked naked and crude, clumsy in its runic hilt, awkward in its length. Kendric lifted the sword over his head like a trophy, both hands fisted around the worn leather scabbard as if he would hurl it far and forever away.

"No," Irissa said.

"It is a toy," he said contemptuously. "An oversized toy, as we all were—are. I am grown old for toys." He made to throw the blade, but then his knuckles whitened. It was as if man hung from sword rather than the reverse. His hands tightened until it seemed the blade should bite through the leather and cut him.

"It is still a sword," Irissa said calmly. "And we need it."

Kendric lowered the length slowly, without turning to her. "A practical Torloc," he noted, wryness wringing his voice dry. "No embellishment in your words now, Lady Irissa of Rindell. Simple truth." He slung the sword back into place on his saddle and gathered up Willowisp's fallen reins. He resumed the trek forward without further comment.

Irissa followed, Smokeshadow's lead clenched in her cloak fold and her restless palm warming the emerald pommel of her mind-forged short sword. It, too, was a weapon, beyond whatever magic had made it and now resided in the metal. It, too, she felt, would be of use.

Chapter Twenty

In Irissa's dream, they had settled for the night in a cliffside cave; and that was not so strange, for they had edged into just such a niche that evening. In her dream, the bearing-beasts drowsed on their tired legs, their heads, horns, and eyelids lowered. Felabba curled near the curve of Kendric's elongated middle, and Kendric was only a somnolent shadow. His sword lay beside him, like a wife.

And Irissa was sitting by herself, staring into the unwinking green gaze of her one-eyed sword pommel, remembering Verthane of the golden beard. For a moment the sorcerer far away in Rule appeared in the unrippled emerald waters, his beard gilded, his eyes young under a forehead smoother than a cabochon. The eyes caught hers; they were as warm and honeyed as a moonweasel's, only much, much wiser. It was Verthane long ago, perhaps longer ago than even a Torloc could imagine, as he had been.

A frown rippled a forehead—not Verthane's, but her

own. The face staring back at her was not that of a distant mage, but her own. Irissa averted her eyes in an instant, her dream heart pounding against her dream ribs. Her hand tightened on the dream hilt until the metal pressed into her waking consciousness. She knew then the sudden power of being able to draw above this unreal reality and do what everyone did in the morning—wake.

Yes, a mere skewer of will, a certain intent, and she would be awake in a cave with three beasts and a man. Or—or she could linger in this lulling state. She glanced again at her self-created sword's emerald eye. Ah, clear, of course. Nothing in it. No Verthane. No Irissa. Nothing.

Oh, but something was flashing in the cave—something paired and glittering, like Verthane's night sky of eyes in the chamber with the royal purple curtain. Irissa the dreamer arose and walked into the cave's deep black throat, where the thing that sparkled waited. She knelt to it, her tunic hem touching ground and clinging there, as if loath to let her rise again. She reached for a pulsing, ruby-golden warmth. Something smooth and heated from within lay on her hand, as richly veined as an Abyssal island pear.

The dream Irissa turned her head this way and that to examine her prize, her dark hair dipping onto first one shoulder, then the other. She was rapt, her pale face underlit by the soft, fluttering light that fanned her features with its ebb and flow. Her hands seemed warm as wax, melting. Her will ran in malleable streams down between her fingers. No, it was the snowflake city she held, and it was melting, icy water coursing across her hands like coldstone tears . . .

She looked around, to the cold, starred sky and an open ring of mountain peaks. She stood alone in the snow, her feet bare. Unbooted, after all that Finorian and Kendric had done to see her shod. She sank into the cold; it squeezed through her toes, rode over her ankles, climbed to her tunic hem, hung on, spread upward, and clutched at her throat.

The mountain was a great snow-furred beast, rising up on sharp, icy haunches. The mountains were ravenous and the caverns were their eyes, gutted pits of gray—bottomless, pitiless, fatal. The mountains swooped down like a giant falgon and wound around her and throttled her in rope after rope of cold, coiling snow. And the warm oval in her hands—she could not unloose it; it immobilized her and throbbed with her own chill life . . .

"Back!" the rising shadow of Kendric shouted.

A length of arm caught Irissa's throat and hauled her flat against a wall of stone. "Back," Kendric said, his voice very feeble and far away. The bar of his sword rose horizontally before her, while wave after wave of the snowy mountainside heaved past her, the frozen rush of its passing fanning back the hair from her face.

The flood of white forms tumbled, undulated, swept, and squirmed past. The mountains were falling and taking the stars with them, for here and there something small glittered warmly and was whisked by. The tide came faster, white as hope and irrevocable as death. Irissa wasn't sure whether the barrier at her throat was arm or iron, only that it held while the ranks of unending white wavered past—the same thing, but many.

Only there, white and familiar, something lay near her feet, then was swept up in the streaming waves. Only there, the stars that fell were green and turned to her in appeal even as they drifted away.

"Felabba!" Her eyes swiveled to Kendric's, two dazed, hopeless pools in a face drained of blood or belief.

He answered her with one last, unspoken gesture, the impulse she had stopped but days before; he flung away the Wrathman's sword toward the small whirlpool of white with its haunted green center.

The sword balanced on its tip on the rocky ground for a fractured moment; then ponderously, slowly, it fell lengthwise amid the swirling foam that coursed past it. And the white split like a wound and flowed away from the steel as does water from oil. Standing there at the blade point, back arched, tail a bristling pennant in an unseen wind, was Felabba. The white cat stood by the sword while the endless pale waves rushed by. She stood and waited, until finally the foam swept past and there were only the dull gray walls and cave floor. Two bearing-beasts stood under the low ceiling, with an unemployed Wrathman and a marooned Torloc cowering against a rough rock wall. A cat was in the middle of the space, sitting at the end of an awesomely long sword, like a period at the base of an exclamation point.

Kendric gingerly retrieved his fallen sword. Irissa huddled by the wall for a moment, then darted forward to scoop up Felabba. The elderly feline writhed in Irissa's encompassing arms and finally plummeted to the floor, where she rearranged her ruffled coat with a frantic tongue.

Irissa still felt dazed, even when Kendric offered her a swig of marshwine from his goatskin flask.

Kendric smiled. "You look paler than yon herd of albino moonweasels that flooded past us."

"Is—is *that* what they were? I was dreaming—"

"You must have been, for I awoke to find you sitting and staring at the first foam of them gushing through the tunnel. It's odd. I looked over this cave last evening and never saw a chink a mouse could crawl through. But perhaps the hibernating moonweasels devoured all the small vermin, as they did in Rule, then grew so fat they forced a way through solid rock."

"It is not amusing," Irissa snapped, still shaken. Something oval warmed her hand; she glanced down to find her palm curled compulsively around the emerald sword hilt. No, something else—redder—had drawn the heat from her hands before. Something she had held in a dream. And Verthane's face had been there as well, his eyes holding hers . . .

She gathered her cloak closer and shook off Kendric's concern as haughtily as Felabba had spurned Irissa's a moment before. "Your wine tastes bitter. I need no more of it." She waved the flask away. "I hope we find Geronfrey soon." Her tone was as much accusing as wistful.

Kendric grimly recapped the bottle, his palm ramming home the stopper. "Perhaps Geronfrey will find us," he murmured. He glanced at Irissa's withdrawn profile, her closed lashes lying like a massed army of dark barbs across the peaceful valley of her eye sockets.

He thought of death's-heads then, of his grandmother's tales, and of moonweasels drinking human veins dry and regurgitating their grisly liquid trophies back into the Abyssal. He thought of Geronfrey, whom he had feared as a boy and dismissed as a man. His mind grew crimson, brimming with destruction, a red tide rising. And the face that floated upon the vermilion marsh that misted him was Valodec's. The grimness of his memories was so overwhelming that for a moment he thought the rock had wavered, like something dreaming and now waking . . .

Kendric glanced again at Irissa, totally lost in her Torloc sleep. He sought the cat Felabba and found her serious, wedged face settled near his elbow. In the morning, they would leave the bearing-beasts behind and explore the tunnel that had spawned the moonweasel tide. In the morning, he would have to decide what course to take to find Geronfrey. In the morning . . .

Both Smokeshadow and Willowisp whistled morosely after the party vanishing down the dim tunnel, a feeble lick of torchflame their only track now. Inside the narrow rock passageway, the creatures' keening sounded amplified and hysterical.

"I am glad," Irissa said, "that we unburdened them for a while. They can rest at the cave mouth until we return."

"*If* we return," Kendric noted calmly, taking the rude torch from her to examine the rock around them.

"If?"

"Look." He drew the torch along the wall in an intricate tracery.

"Iridesium! And so high in the mountains! I'd never heard of it found anywhere but in Torloc rins, deep in the forest . . ."

Kendric shook his head. "Not the substance. The pattern. This Iridesium is inlaid."

Irissa's long white fingers tentatively traced the shining colors gleaming through an obsidian black. She fingertipped a winding route, as meaningless as the paths that had led them hither.

"Is it a star-shape? And here, such a strange configuration—so large. These parallel lines each coming at an angle. And another set—does it depict something, something real?"

Kendric moved the flame along the lines Irissa's fingers had etched, but even his respectable length could not reach the inlaid pattern's limits.

"I feel we stand too close to see it," Irissa said. "If we could but—"

"Step back? Aye, and you step into solid rock. There is no perspective in the cave except the near one."

"But, Kendric, how could anyone have inlaid a meaning-

ful pattern with no way to gain an overview? Perhaps it is
only random, after all."

"Yes, as random as Ronfrenc's schemes, I warrant,"
Kendric said, laughing. "Well, I have my sword, and if it is
more trusty than rusty, we shall have it to rely upon. You
have your truncated stinger, though I've yet to see if it
will rend anything other than mind-weavings. And we have
our faithful feline to scent our way." His heavy sword
tip bowed at Felabba in benediction. "So we go forward
and worry about overviews later."

But the passing flash of Iridesium channels in the rock
walls around them grew more disconcerting, as if they
were being subjected to an invasion from the corners of
their eyes. They began to distrust their senses. Even Felabba hunkered down now and then at the torch's errant
flicker, her green eyes burning orange in the enveloping
darkness.

The cave passage widened suddenly, before anything
told them so but the sudden inrush of cool air. The dark
arched over them, throwing back no reflections now, for
there was nothing near enough to bounce back the flight-
less beating of their primitive flame. The dark was a pit in
all directions, a limitless belly of unwavering ebony. It
seemed that any footstep would sink into utter nonexis-
tence, that any hand reaching out to rend the nothingness
would be absorbed by—something.

"The Swallowing Cavern," Kendric said, swallowing
despite himself.

"That's why they call it such, if such it is," Irissa answered with false gaiety. "It can cause grown men to swallow. And cats to crouch," she added, taking in the white
lump at their feet that was Felabba. "And Torlocs—it
causes Torlocs to—step forward."

It was mere blind foolhardiness, but she stepped once
into the liquid obsidian beyond the tiny torchlit pool in
which they stood. Kendric's hand welded to her arm, each
finger a hook to restrain her. Felabba yowled, a primitive
feline warning her only message.

Irissa felt she teetered on some massive finger, like one
of Mauvedona's power-leashed stars spinning on its finest
edge. She was jerked back, if back indeed she was, to the
sputtering prison of firelight that circled them all.

"I know not what the Swallowing Cavern is, beyond

legend," Kendric growled in her ear, as urgently as if he
had been Felabba. "But we do not dip our toes in it. I
think we center under the Realms' oldest mountain, Falgontooth. I think we balance on the long, slow slide into
the mountain's belly. So do not challenge the darkness,
unless you care to be devoured. Torlocs!" he complained,
sensing that she no longer intended to test nothingness as
if it were only an unsafe bridge.

His fingers uncoiled, and Irissa was minded to tell him
that they left her arm throbbing. She was not of a mind to
mention that her foot was of a sudden icy cold. She was
uncertain, indeed, if she still had a foot, for when she
stepped forward upon the visible rock now, her foot
seemed to sink a trifle lower than her eyes said it ought
to. She would not mention this, for Kendric had been
testy of late, and would only grumble that he had fore-
warned her . . .

They edged to the right, always treading only on the
puddle of light at their feet. This dark had no Iridesium
glitter; it was hooded, falgonlike. Old Falgontooth would
not unhinge its bottomless black mouth unless to masticate
new prey.

Kendric handed Irissa the torch while he slung his
sword over his back, choosing light over the ability to in-
flict fatality. He was cautious in swinging the five-foot
length around so that the blade did not pierce the darkness, as if somehow the surrounding shadow were sentient
and might bleed, might attack in kind. He took the torch
again and Irissa's hand. She glanced back to see Felabba
mincing one foot after the other behind them, an old cat
walking a tightrope visible only to a cat's eyes.

They edged like tentative acrobats on plain gray rock.
Irissa looked at her foot once, the one she had dipped into
the endless depths, and saw it walking beneath her, white
and bare, bootless. But she never felt the rough rock she
trod upon.

Kendric paused so abruptly she walked into his back and
thought it a wall. "Here. Another tunnel. We'll take it,
for—never mind, but quickly!"

She was glad enough to spring after him into the confines of simple hollowed-out rock. The absence of vast,
unplumbed space around them was a relief, like knowing
the sky was blue and therefore, somehow, finite; the color

said so. They looked up to see the cheery flicker of reflected torchlight above them. Even the air smelled closer,
more comfortable, promising the warmth of burrowing
bodies and the skitter of rat claws along the hewn corri-
dors. Behind them, the dark stretched toward them hun-
grily, and there was a growling as of a gargantuan stomach or the grinding of stony teeth. It seemed the tunnel
shuddered, but they were running forward, plunging into
each new pool of torchlight on the blind faith that only
an ordinary tunnel would open before them . . .

They were wrong. When they came into the rock chamber with its central, massive wooden chair and the figure
slumped upon it like a reveler slouching into his tavern
nook, they were momentarily so surprised they forgot to
stop until they stood fully in the small room's center, where
there was no avoiding the man upon the chair or what lay
askew against his heavy thigh.

"Thrangar!" Kendric and Irissa said at the same time,
though Irissa had never seen the Torloc Wrathman in
other than a dream. And in that dream he had slept here,
precisely thus, even to the small skeleton upon his wrist!

The bones were there, frozen into a graceful, articulated
pattern, so one could guess at the living litheness of their
now-dead owner. Then Felabba was growling furiously and
leaping at the delicately balanced assemblage of skull and
diminishing tail. The bones scattered, dies in a colossal
game of chance.

"A dead falgon," Kendric said.

"What?"

"A dwarf falgon, I think, that settled here on Thrangar's
wrist and died."

"But Thrangar is not dead?"

Kendric strode over and regarded his fellow Wrathman.
"No. Not alive, not dead. Why did your cursed cat have
to spring at the bones? I do not like it. It's sorcery that
knits a dead thing's bones together and—"

"And sorcery that strikes them apart, my friend,"
agreed a voice that was none of theirs.

Chapter Twenty-one

◆–◆–◆

The speaker stood quietly behind them. It was Geronfrey, although neither knew him and he did not resemble what one might expect of so remote, so mighty, a sorcerer. He would have been tall—had the Realms not cultivated Wrathmen to dwarf him. His hair was light and shoulder-length, held back with an Iridesium circlet. He did not wear the magician's subtle, sweeping robes, but trousers and a tunic like their own, although his were woven of a fabric shot through with sparkling threads. The belt that waisted him was Clymarindian water-beast hide, gleaming as if wet even though out of its glistening element. He was not armed—visibly.

"A pity," Geronfrey commented, stepping forward. "You know him?"

Their eyes returned to Thrangar, frozen upon his mocking throne.

"Are you saying that you do not?" Kendric's voice was rough for use to perhaps the Realms' most powerful mage. But if Geronfrey's sensibilities were jostled, the effect did not extend to his demeanor. "And what magic of ours did you say disturbed the falgon bones that shattered?" Kendric demanded, sending rudeness after risk as if to buttress it.

Geronfrey's eyes lowered to the dismantled skeleton littering the rock floor in front of Thrangar's leaden boots. The motion left a trail of blue—sky blue—glimpsed as through a tear, so that it glittered.

"Your cat has a finer tuning to these things than you," Geronfrey said, regarding the crouching Felabba with a dispassionate azure eye. "I have taken the liberty of silenc-

143

ing her, my lady." He swiveled gracefully to Irissa and bowed. "This place is too much constructed of my own and more ancient spells to allow the old one full measure of her musings. She will only mew for now. No doubt you will find it a relief. I am afraid I am most old-fashioned in this regard, and believe all cats should be seen rather than heeded," he finished with a tight, polite smile.

"What is he saying?" Kendric demanded.

They both awaited Irissa's answer—Geronfrey with a patient, unblinking courtliness, confidence radiating from him like a frozen flame, Kendric bristling like a Wrathman in full armor.

It was to Geronfrey she looked as she replied. "Felabba speaks, it seems—something I did not know until we left Rindell. And now he has gagged her."

She tossed this revelation to Kendric almost offhandedly, over her figurative shoulder, without even actually glancing at him. Kendric looked bewilderedly from Irissa to Felabba, and found the cat as rapt in contemplation of Geronfrey as her mistress.

"I have not heard her speak," he protested.

"Nor have you ever seen an empress falgon in flight," Geronfrey said. "It does not mean such things do not exist."

"More mysteries!" Kendric snapped, even more careless of Geronfrey's power. He stepped closer. "Has she spoken? Answer me, Irissa."

"Yes, of course," she said a bit crossly. "You are perhaps merely too high from the ground to hear her, that is all." Her attention centered on Geronfrey once again. "Does what a cat can say so discomfit the great Geronfrey?"

"It is not my will, as many things are not, under Falgontooth. Other powers have ruled here long before, to their own solemn precepts. I am a mere tenant. Like him." He waved to Thrangar as if a motionless Wrathman were the most common thing to have lying about one's antechamber.

"He is a Torloc Wrathman," Irissa explained quickly, "who vanished from the Realms, much to the sorrow of his fellows, for everything seemed to come apart at that. And now we have found him here, ensorcelled. Are you not the sorcerer Geronfrey? Do you deny the evidence of your powers?"

"My powers." The man laughed, and it was an arresting sound, like fresh water trickling over a rock. "Oh, if only I possessed half—nay, a tenth—of the powers attributed to me! I am not the author of every ill in Rule and certainly not of any out of it. But come, leave this somber place. Perhaps we can devise some way to release our slumbering friend. I knew he had appeared there, but not how or why. Perhaps you both can enlighten me."

It was not clear whether Geronfrey referred to Irissa and Kendric—or to Irissa and Felabba. But Irissa and the cat immediately turned to follow their guide, leaving Kendric to glower pointlessly at Thrangar, then shrug and follow the party. They slipped through a cut-stone passage high enough for a Wrathman, but too narrow; Kendric was forced to doff his back-slung sword and carry it or risk being wedged between the walls forever like Thrangar in his chair. The way led up, and this tunnel was clearly man-made, for niches in the stone held floating candles of amber light.

"You come to me from the bottom of my burrow," Geronfrey said, pausing at a heavy gold curtain. "Now we reach the habitable part of my home." He drew back the curtain. They preceded him into a lofty hall, mellow with the arch of carved wood and thick-hung with tapestries, as if the owner had tried to create an indoor, woven woodland. Compared with Mauvedona's flame-built palace, Geronfrey's was an almost austere hall. It was huge, but human in its ornamentation. Even the massive trestle table was slightly rough-hewn, perhaps to prove that human hands had formed it.

Geronfrey pulled a tasseled cord, and a figure rustled from a shadowed doorway, a tray of common pewter goblets in its hands. The figure was draped in floor-length brown gauzelin and hooded, as Mauvedona's servitors had been. But a very human face came clear within the overdraping gauzelin oval from time to time.

"A mute," Geronfrey explained, after the personage had bowed, offered goblets all around the three, and scuffed away on clattering sandals. "A monastery of Soarian monks kept vigil by the Abyssal—until some sea-raider razed their holy place and scattered them. I—adopted—a few. Their life was apartness and service. I live apart; and, as you see, I require serving." His hands, as supple and golden as Mauvedona's in a masculine sort of way, swept around the empty hall. "And I am glad of guests."

Geronfrey saluted with his humble goblet and quaffed what lapped within. Irissa followed his example, although Kendric, newly reluctant to sip a sorcerer's cup, kept his bent elbow stiffly at his waist.

"There is no magic in my brewing," Geronfrey said, his pale blue eyes twinkling genially above the cold silver of his cup.

"Borgia," Irissa diagnosed after a savored sip. "Very old and likely of Clymarindian vintage. And quite nontoxic."

Kendric weighed the goblet in his hand, his suspicion forming on it almost visibly, like a mist. "But you *could* brew whatever magic you wished," he noted. "You could make the goblet one cut from—sapphire, let us say—and make the drink within it boil like an Abyssal monsoon and lick the rim in a burst of flames . . ."

"Could, yes. But I do not." Geronfrey set his empty vessel on the splintered wooden table and paced away. "You are right, I have access to powers some would call profound. And when one can draw deep from within the well, one does not skim the scum off the surface. Jeweled cups and ever-flowing wines within them! These are tawdry games taught in Mauvedona's school. Ah, you know her . . ." he said as both Kendric and Irissa started slightly.

"No," he went on, "the more complex a man can make his world, the more he longs for simple things." Geronfrey stopped moving and faced them again, his eyes resting on Irissa. "Guests. Friends. Kin of a kind, I think."

Irissa then did something she had never before done. She blushed. The pale red tide rose in her like marshwine in a rock-crystal goblet until the potion brimmed to her cheeks and pooled there. She looked to Felabba and kept her glance on the icy feline eyes and on the unspoken message there, until she felt a slow-moving glacier of outward composure frost over her flagrant color.

"You're telling us," Kendric said skeptically, "that you're a lonely, harmless recluse, as removed from Realm life—from Rule and its unruliness—as Thrangar on his wooden pedestal below."

"You put it a bit more belligerently than I would, my friend . . . And have you a name, both of you?" Geronfrey glanced expectantly back and forth until Irissa could stand it no longer.

"I am Irissa of Rindell, and yon quibbler is Kendric, once a Wrathman and still discourteous."

This time Kendric flushed, a dull glow of resentment suffusing his unsmiling face. Geronfrey ignored the phenomenon. "And the—cat?"

"Why, her name is—" Irissa glanced at Felabba and found an unfamiliar set of syllables clattering off her tongue. "Belfanna."

"And she does not speak," Kendric added stubbornly, regarding Irissa with amazement at her duplicity.

This exchange left Geronfrey unruffled. "You have a story and I would hear it. Sit and tell me. I obviously cannot rely upon the cat for elucidation now—if ever," he added with a conciliatory smile at Kendric.

They sank onto the indicated wooden chairs, suddenly exhausted. Felabba sprang onto Irissa's lap and coiled there in perfect feline content. They told Geronfrey what he asked. For one thing, he was utterly different from what they had anticipated, and thus seemed more harmless. He sat with them until the flames in his Wrathman-high hearth fell back to snap at one another rather than at the wood, his neatly bearded chin resting on a folded hand. His pale azure eyes sparkled equally on Irissa and Kendric as they talked. His brow was smooth in placid contemplation.

He was as sleek and uncontaminated by the grosser attributes of sorcery as his homemade goblets. And so they poured their subterranean anxiety into him, letting it bubble to the rim of his capacities. As he absorbed their tale, he stilled it and them. The flood of their confidences crested, and Geronfrey's calm visage let their outpourings pool into a kind of passivity.

"So." He smiled. "The Realms vie for the privilege of biting one another's throats. And this Ronfrenc plots for sovereignty. Perhaps the raiders that made my Soarian clerics homeless were not the seaskulls, but some fleet of Ronfrenc's sent against Madorian on Clymarind. Intriguing times, even for a recluse. And you—" he looked, sharp and straight as a pin, at Irissa. "You are even more intriguing to a recluse. The last Torloc in the Realms—an untutored

Torloc seeress. You are as rare as an empress falgon, my dear lady, and should be treated as one."

"What, a falgon?" Kendric jeered.

"No, an empress," Geronfrey returned with one unshaken look. "Scabbard your blade, my friend. There is no need to play the Wrathman here."

Kendric shrugged and returned to running his fingers along the cracks in Geronfrey's tabletop, a gesture that brought a sudden chirrup from Felabba. The white cat leaped atop the table and wafted over to Kendric to tap playfully at his restless fingers. Kendric's hand stilled, and his eyes remained cast down. But his ears seemed to prick almost as intently as Felabba's.

"Yes." Geronfrey sighed. "All things shift these days. Well, you are weary and travel-stained and also my guests. I have rooms for you with proper fires, and full of food as well. Withdraw and rest a bit while I give some thought to what you have told me."

Geronfrey nodded to a slightly stirring tapestry, and one of the noisy monks shuffled forth, beckoning them to sail the wake of his slapping sandals. He led them up simple stone stairways to the place's upper storeys. Kendric and Irissa were wordlessly ushered to adjoining chambers, each equipped with a heavily tapestried bed, a roaring lion of a fire, and a long table accoutered with fruit, cold meats, cheeses, and more borgia in stork-necked decanters.

"I like it not." Kendric lingered on Irissa's threshold after their guide had skated off.

She paused in devouring an outer Abyssal pear and watched Felabba make a frenzied march along the chamber's perimeter before curling into fatigue in front of the fire. "Why not? Even Felabba can sleep here."

"Who am I to rely upon a speaking cat?" Kendric asked, crossing the threshold to inspect Irissa's half-eaten pear. He handed it back discontentedly after finding no flaws and paced to the room's edges. "I like it not. Have you looked out your window, lady? Even an empress falgon could not fly through these apertures."

Irissa joined him in inspecting the arched stone niches set into the walls at regular intervals. Geronfrey's chamber windows were like bas-relief, mock openings carved into the mountain's adamant interior and hard upon a view of solid rock.

"He lives beneath the mountain. Did you expect vistas, Kendric?"

"No. But he is a sorcerer. I like the breed better when they flaunt their arts. If we looked through these arches and saw—say a green and pleasant valley where the winds shifted waves of dwarf falgons from one end to the other, or the glittering colors of another world, or even merely a deep, snowy chasm outside Falgontooth . . . He is over-anxious to lull us with ordinariness, with things as we think they should be in such a place."

"In your mind, then, Kendric, we sorcerers are doomed before we begin. Distrust us if we wave our powers before your noses like a battle banner; distrust us more if we do not." Her dark eyebrows were arched in bitter mockery as she bit defiantly into her pear with a moonweasel's vora-ciousness. Its pale juices ran like blood down her chin.

Kendric shrugged and left the room. Irissa wiped her chin on her mud-caked tunic sleeve, secret worry a cor-rosive acid nibbling at her confidence. She sighed and went to push the heavy wooden door shut—it had no latch—before advancing to the fire and the dozing cat.

"Ah, Felabba, I hardly thought I would ever miss your shrill sermons, but I think you would be favoring me with one now, could you speak. What do you think?"

She crouched to face the head so delicately set with its paired emerald eyes. Felabba stared back seriously, the flames leaping phantomlike in the rounded sheen of her irises.

Irissa had never dreamed of letting her gaze explore the complexities of a cat's eyes, but the nearby fire's rhythmic flicker and the puzzle of Geronfrey brought her drowsing glance to rest deeply on Felabba's own intent stare. She plunged, diving with a wailwraith's surety, into an ocean of evanescent green thicker than borgia. An alien con-sciousness clung to Irissa's exploring entity like lethal sea-weed; she seemed to be drowning in gelatinous strands while the red-rimmed world of the carnivore stretched around her. It was a mistake to plunge into such utter felinity. She was confused; she had thought Felabba much more than this predatory, unthinking puddle of primitive impulses. Or was it a trap, the facade behind which the old cat crouched, while deeper, farther in, lay the real entity?

Irissa forged her will into a screw and spiraled deeper into the watery green murk around her. She burst into ultimate blackness, then into a landscape as empty and mute as a desert. Here the light was peridot green—pale, diffused, even more alien than the other. Here was no wisdom or knowledge, only great antiquity, an age beyond blood lust or such mere considerations as survival. Irissa saw herself as a tiny figure calling into the soft green void. She called Felabba by her true name, and her only answer was the distant wink of a cold blue star. Otherwise, the place was muter than a Soarian monk. She retreated hastily, rushing backward past the enveloping portal murk like a falgon eluding the pull of the earth.

She was crouched before a blazing fire, staring into adamantly empty eyes of feline green. Irissa stroked the old cat's skull and stood, her knees creaking protest. She must have been absent longer than she thought while delving a possible mind-link with Felabba. Something had foiled it, whether the cat's nature or her own fatigue . . . or Geronfrey?

Irissa sighed again and slowly stripped off her tattered, mud-stiff clothes. It was as she bent to wrest off her sole remaining boot—odd, that no one had noted the other's absence—that her glance discovered that other, its mate, sitting sentinel by the bed. She went over, bowed to the boot's reality, and turned it in her hands.

Kendric had complained of Geronfrey's miserliness of power. True, he had handed them mere pewter goblets, ordinary viands, quite mortal fires, and unremittingly logical limits to his environs. Yet that one retrieved boot, presented wordlessly, a thoughtful host's offhand gesture, froze her nerve more than any mutterings of Kendric's.

She knew the pit, had dipped her foot into it, and so had lost this very boot. What she held now was not a simulacrum; she knew that irrevocably. It was the boot. And Irissa knew also that nothing in Rule or beyond it would or could compel her back to the pit lip to fish for her lost footwear. It was beyond mortal or Torloc recall.

Yet Geronfrey had recovered it for her as matter-of-factly, as mutely, as one of his monkish servitors. Mauvedona had said Geronfrey's towers were rooted deeper in hell than those of any other sorcerer and that they thrust higher at heaven also. On what did one rely—one's own instincts or the suspicion of others?

She dropped the conundrum with the boot to the pelt-carpeted floor and let the rest of her travel-tattered raiment fall there, too. She slid naked between the bed linens, closed her eyelids, and let the supple flame reflections dance over them until the rhythm lulled her to sleep.

Chapter Twenty-two

A creak awoke her when the room was dim and only embers warmed the hearth. It was the great, unlatched door swinging ajar. A goodly portion of the hall's shadow flowed inward.

It was Kendric, still wearing his traveling clothes. She had guessed that one who would not eat would not sleep either. A pale dagger of light led him to the great bed in which she rested, but he seemed uncertain that she would be there, for he whispered her name as he neared. "Irissa? Irissa."

"Yes?"

"Ah, then I was wrong about the pear—you haven't any left, I suppose?"

"Take your own risks, Wrathman," she answered from the tapestried shadows. "What is it?"

"Only this." He extended the faintly gleaming hilt of his sword. "It's started up again. I don't know—"

"Keep it from the hangings, then, or we shall all go up in smoke."

Kendric propped the blade against the table and pawed over the remnants of Irissa's food by its soft circle of light.

"Have you tired of your own?"

He glanced across to the place from which her voice came, although he could see nothing more than unarticulated shadow. "Perhaps the vintage laid out for me is different from yours." He plucked up a fistful of ruby grapes and ate them one by one.

"You are wrong, Kendric, to be so distrustful. Geronfrey has shown us nothing but hospitality."

"That is what worries me." Kendric came and sat at the bed's foot, still methodically downing grapes with an indifferent kind of appetite. "You seem to have no difficulty accepting our wizard at face value. Perhaps you know more than I."

He had finished the grapes and leaned across the bed to fling the denuded grape branch into the waning fire. A brief burst of flame from its passing lit up the bed's far corner, where Irissa half-sat, veiled in her sheets of glistening black hair.

"Nothing. Except—"

"Yes?" Kendric still leaned across the bed's foot, looking intently toward her face.

"What do you think of Thrangar?" she asked abruptly. She glanced out of habit at Felabba, but the old cat was utterly cast in the role of silent fireside tabby now; she dozed, a furred statue in the hearthglow. "Thrangar—we should think of how to release him."

Kendric frowned, as if considering the matter. He looked up again, from under slanted dark brows, his face fire-burnished along cheekbone and chin. "It has something to do with you, I think."

"What, Thrangar?" She was astounded.

"No. My sword. It became brighter as I carried it hither. And now look at it."

She finally glanced toward the table to see the hilt almost white-hot and casting a wide swath of brightness. It was more than fire that etched in Kendric's features, she realized; it was the growing circle of his sword-beacon.

"You looked upon it when it was water-mired, drew it out, and it became brighter than a lance of light."

"That was the blade, Kendric, not the hilt. No, the sword bears your magic, not mine. Besides, it is not important—"

"No?" He leaned more intently closer, his chin cradled in his fists and a melancholy certainty in his voice that was unanswerable. He was close enough to catch up one of her hands that fell within the faint circle of hilt-light. "You picked up my sword," he said, lifting her hand in like gesture, "and it is since then that things have gone—off-custom. I wonder . . . I wonder what I wondered above the stable at the tavern where they would not have us. I wonder if perhaps there was something I neglected to do that sets all these events awry. I wonder—"

He never finished the last supposition, for the latchless door swept wider and something bright and harrying swooshed through to hang like an angry disembodied terrier at the huge bed's side. The sending, or whatever it was, vibrated there, chattering with a chaperone's gusto. Another swooped in on its tail and took up an opposite post, while behind it scattered another dozen or so, circling the bed and hovering in midair.

"What—" Kendric began, stirring too late and casting a self-recriminatory glance at his sword, still glowing, but propped against the distant table as helplessly as a cane.

"Go away!" It was Irissa, risen to her knees behind him, her dark hair fluttering as she lashed her head around to confront the positions of their night guard. "Away! I won't have familiars outposted like the dames of Rindell around my bed. Away!"

Kendric swiped at one, and the wheeling, chattering thing danced away, only to float back into position as his gesture faded. "By Rule and all the under-gods!" he thundered, rising to the bait and his feet at the same instant.

He reached out to throttle a pair of hovering taunters and found the bed's tapestries swaying shut in front of him with a force that almost made them clang. He looked behind to see the opposite set of draperies doing likewise, and those at the bed's foot as well, so that he and Irissa were caged in a swaying, curtained alcove. He thrust a hand at the wavering material and found it unbendable and leathery, the fabric somehow stiffened against intrusion—or escape. He whirled to see Irissa lit by some light of her mind's own creation, her dark hair licking at her bare shoulders like a flame shadow. From beyond the taut tapestries, a faint chatter died into absolute silence.

"I will not have these interruptions," Irissa said, hardly masking her triumph. "Now, Kendric, if you would be so kind as to continue your supposition—"

She had never resembled a sorceress more, Kendric realized, never been more like Mauvedona, powerful yet feminine. Feline. Kendric lay back beside her and cradled his neck in his hands. He glanced over to find her still sitting, the bed linens drawn up inadequately to her breasts.

"No," he demurred. "It was a feeble idea, not worth pursuing, really. Since you are holding off our uninvited escorts so efficiently, and since I don't trust my accommodations at any rate, I will avail myself of a chance to sleep. I suggest you do the same." He closed his eyes and absorbed the long, immobile silence on her part.

There was a sudden thrash as she hurled herself down into the bedclothes and turned her back on him. Kendric let out his breath on a long, slow exhalation. Geronfrey was an imponderable, that he knew. But there was nothing so dangerous as taking up a sorceress' invitation on her own terms. That he knew as well, knew of old from Mauvedona.

Chapter Twenty-three

Even the light of his sword hilt failed Kendric when he crept out of Irissa's bed that night—or perhaps it was day as they reckoned it. Geronfrey's dead-end windows certainly made time a solid dimension, if an unenlightening one.

Kendric stumbled across something evasive . . . Felabba restrained a yowl of complaint and Kendric swallowed his emerging expletive. In the almost dark it seemed both cat and man concurred on the importance of not awakening Irissa. For with her sleep had come the relaxation of her spell. The tapestries had gone pliant again, mere limp folds for Kendric to brush back on his exit. He did not think Irissa would care to know how briefly her defiance had held.

He retrieved his now-innocuous sword, then paused to

raid the bounties of her table again. He still did not care to partake of what Geronfrey had left in his own room. The evening's events but strengthened this hesitancy. Kendric did not like the wheeling intruders that had spun between Irissa and himself at their moment for comparing notes, if nothing else. It confirmed his suspicion that the sorcerer kept better track of them than he let on. And there was one Wrathman already immobilized in the fellow's earthen dungeons. Caution, Kendric counseled himself, is ever the warrior's most faithful companion.

He slipped through the latchless door and into his own chamber without interference, except perhaps for the almost tangible brush of a shadow past his lofty shoulder as he crossed his threshold. Caution! The word walked side by side with Kendric as he boarded his own tapestried bed for a night's worth of tossing and turning, waiting always for the dawn that never came—would never come. He must wait, then, for some gesture on Geronfrey's part that what passed for day in these lightless environs was upon them all. But Kendric was allowed to sleep on undisturbed. And despite his tossing, slumber washed over him in strong, steady waves that kept his cautious mind submerged.

On the other side of the stone wall that separated Kendric and Irissa, Felabba paced the chamber's unyielding limits. She leaped onto the windowsill and gazed morosely at the vista of rough-hewn rock. Her supple white shadow bounded down again and sprang onto the tapestried bed, where she sat for a long while at Irissa's feet, staring expressionlessly into the curtained dark. In time, the old cat retreated to the embered hearthglow, where she rested her face disconsolately on her neat paws and finally slept.

It was only when all else that might be deemed mortal in the castle slept that Irissa awoke. Perhaps she was disturbed by the sound of a random shuffle from the passage. She slid out of bed into the chilly air, dressed, and wandered into the hall. Her sword she left lying angled across the long table, its emerald eye dim in the shadowed room and sleeping.

There was another scuffle. She trailed the sound into a nearby chamber, an empty room, centering on a great wooden tub steaming with hot water and some spreading mist of scent. The water still lapped softly at the tub edges, as if it had just been poured from some hot-bodied ewer.

But the chamber was deserted. There were no would-be windows carved into the surrounding walls—walls angled and five in all. The place was a pentagram.

She recalled Verthane's geometrically treacherous web and retreated. Her hands brushed some heavy folds of cloth behind her. She whirled, fearful of curtains she had not observed before, and found a long sable velvet robe hanging from a high hook, as had the clothiers' wares in Wormwinder Street, where she had acquired what she now wore. Her hands unwillingly explored the encrusted lengths of gray tunic and trousers that enveloped her. They returned to the sleek black fabric that hung above her as invitingly as any curtain; it begged for exploration.

Irissa turned again suddenly and went back to the arch-topped door that lay open against the wall. It was just her height, or a little higher, no door for a Wrathman, certainly, unless he stooped. This door had a latch, a thick iron bar set in scrolled brass fittings. She swung the door closed and then levered the bar into place. It clicked most satisfactorily shut. Irissa turned to face the room. It was empty as ever, save for the waiting clouds of steam from the bath and the lank, expectant folds of fabric near the wall. There was a small table against the other wall. On it lay the handled circle of a mirror. Irissa went over and elevated the ivory oval, turning it slightly. Its face was as empty as the room, vacant and unreflecting. Irissa laid the hand mirror slowly down next to the ivory-toothed comb that companioned it like a fanged guardian.

The room was hers, waiting for her to impress her marks upon it. She had but to accept it and it would begin to shape itself to her, to mold itself around her with the flexibility of a moonweasel. Irissa knew this, even as she advanced to the waiting water and shed her road-worn clothing. It mounded at her feet, gray and tawdry. She stepped into the mists and the water and sank below them like a wailwraith.

Time stood still in Geronfrey's under-mountain hall. No shadows crept across the room where Kendric the Wrathman turned fitfully in a sleep born of caution. No clock ticked in the deserted chamber where an elderly white cat who had been known to converse now dreamed in utter silence. But within five stone walls, the steam no longer wafted above the curve of an oaken tub, and the water that lapped at the swollen wood was lukewarm.

Irissa stood at the little table, her head bowed and her fingers pausing across the comb teeth as if they were an instrument she contemplated strumming. She wore the long dark gown with its pleated trailing train and heavy-hanging sleeves, with the wide, dark vee of it yawning across her pale shoulders, a great gaping mouth, and all that weighted cloth caught closed by a huge golden clasp between her breasts. Her fingers moved between toying with the texture of that massive brooch and rhythmically stroking the ivory-fanged comb. Finally she picked it up and drew the predatory rows through her long, still-damp hair, which lay docilely along her back and shoulders, another well-groomed dark train.

She turned again to the room and went over to the pointed-toed slippers curling expectantly against the wall below where the gown had hung. She paused before them, looked down, lifted the ponderous hem, advanced her bare white foot, and paused, like a cat on a foreign threshold. Irissa let the skirt drop to sway softly against the stone floor for a moment. It made a sound like a whispered "hushhhh." Then she lifted it again slightly, evenly, in both hands and moved to the door as if on glides.

The latch fell back at her touch, and the unprotesting wood swung open. She glided into the hall and down its empty lengths to where a stairway spiraled into darkness. She paused, smiled, and mounted the steps, quiet save for the scrape of her heavy velvet train over each tread. Around and around, up and up, the narrow stone stairs climbed. Irissa followed their every curl until her train was screwed into a thick, dark tail of fabric. And still she climbed, deliberately, confidently, inexorably.

She came at last to another door. Its wooden facade was carved, and a nearby wall torch etched an outré kind of movement in the figures graven thereon. Irissa dropped the hem over her feet and folded her hands in front of her. She waited. Slowly, the door swung open.

She entered a room whose sides were faceted, in the manner of her bathing chamber. It was small, this room, but the arched windows set into the exterior walls were not blind, as they had been below, but opened onto dazzling brightness. There was no dimension to the whiteness without, no near or far, no high or low. It was an undifferentiated expanse of mystery, as unrelenting in its way as the rock faces onto which the windows below opened.

It suddenly occurred to Irissa that such light was made for reflection; she turned her attention to the room itself. It was rimmed around by angled tables laid with an assortment of the typical wizard's paraphernalia—vials and tumblers, flasks and variously colored flames, token falgon feathers and several odd, shriveled trophy feet, great opaline dishes with dubious liquids floating within them, and a quantity of crystal orbs and brass implements of a peculiarly surgical nature.

Irissa's eyes only skimmed the surfaces of these many objects, for most of them were reflective, and the light seemed to vibrate like a mandolin string between the glittering accessories and the vistas of white beyond the windows. Geronfrey sat, quite pensively, on a high stool near one of the most elaborately decked tables, his elbows propped upon the wood and his bearded chin resting on his folded hands. He stared intently at a glass cone filled with some pulsing crimson fluid that crashed against the glossy sides containing it like a small sea pounding the beach.

"The color is completely wrong," Geronfrey complained to himself, as puzzled as a distraught chef considering his latest culinary failure. One hand unfolded and beckoned Irissa, although the sorcerer's eyes remained anchored on the swelling scarlet liquid before him.

"Come in, come in. I should have known a Torloc would find her own way. I did not expect you so soon." He glanced at Irissa then, his eyes sapphire-bright and pleased.

He reminded her of Verthane again, not merely for the human golden attraction of him, but for a certain calm expectancy, an annoying certitude of her own actions and reactions.

He sprang up, a remiss host, and extended her another of his pewter goblets. As if he read her thought, he then pushed the tray aside and brought forth a second pair of goblets, these carved of translucent alabaster. He poured their borgia from a ewer of jade.

"Perhaps we should wait for Kendric," Irissa suggested, watching the bubbling green brim to her goblet's ivory-colored edge.

Geronfrey stayed the ewer's tilt for an imperceptible

instant. "No, I fear not. Our overlong wanderer slumbers as soundly as a Clymarindian sleeping-water-beast. It would be a pity to rouse him."

"You were not afraid to disturb him last night—if, indeed, it was night. Your halls seem to be set for either full day or darkest night, so the creep of time is undetectable."

"Last night." Geronfrey poured his own goblet full and considered the pooling green liquid as thoughtfully as he had studied the red but moments before. "You have caught me out at my most indefensibly magical." Geronfrey lifted his goblet and sipped before replying further. "I could tell you that my veins ran as jealously green as this borgia and hence I unleashed my harmless pets to harass you when that great fellow below came lumbering too near you. But I confess, I have lived too long for mere jealousy to congeal my blood. I am sure that if you knew what I do, you would want your impulsive escort as harnessed as I do. You see, your powers, even to the small degree you have exercised them thus far, hinge upon a certain attribute of yours that would be quite easy to—alter."

"An attribute of mine? You intrigue me. I have never had my character read by a wizard. I have had it expounded to me by an elderly Torloc dame, yes. And by a cat. And, more often than once, by a certain hulking marshman you even now remind me to forget. But by a sorcerer, no."

Irissa trailed away, her twisted train unwinding convulsively as she walked. She was like a great, lean, black cat twitching its tail. That fact even Geronfrey seemed to appreciate as he admired the shimmering lengths of her dark hair and the sure, graceful way her fingers clasped the occasionally fatal borgia, even now gleaming slightly venomously.

"Surely you must have guessed," he said. "It was not for your eyes alone that you were kept veiled and remote from the world of mortal men . . ." Geronfrey paused, unwilling to continue.

Irissa turned to him, her face felinely unexpressive and her eyes burning past him, ever so slightly off-center. "I am not veiled now." Her fingers pressed the pale stone goblet until they were whiter than the alabaster. "Tell me."

His eyes dropped first, soft golden lashes falling across the honed sapphire edge of his glance. "Yes," Geronfrey murmured. He went to the window and looked out absently across the white unrolling in sheets before him.

"A Torloc seeress," he began, "if she is truly born to the breed, is a great gift to her race. She is rare even among Torlocs. And her vision must be protected, as yours was. Her powers are—immense. She has more to bestow than her eyes. If—*if* such a one brings the first flower of her womanhood to another of power, she can imbue him with resources greater than any he could acquire, no matter how he labored. But he must be a man of power, else the bestowal is wasted and only the fruits of the flesh grow from that union."

"I do not believe you," Irissa said, so flatly that Geronfrey had to turn to be certain she was still in the room with him and not some part of the stony walls themselves.

"Believe me," Geronfrey urged, setting down his goblet and stepping toward her. "That is why I must meddle with yon troublesome Wrathman. Do I care who finds whose bed in the dark? No. I went beyond the flesh long ago, when fatal Porphyria betrayed me, and my powers had to be agonizingly restored over eons."

"You are old," Irissa said, disbelieving it even as she spoke. "Older even than—"

"Verthane?" Geronfrey laughed then. "Yes, Verthane is old. He is my grandson by Porphyria, the only thing that came of that treachery. And he is doubly treacherous, for he counts me evil and would destroy even the powers I have husbanded since his Clymarindian birth."

"You do not look old—" Irissa began, studying the unlined planes of his face and the gilded hair unstreaked by any white.

Geronfrey waved a deprecating, impatient hand. "Looks, looks, looks! Appearances are the stuff of magic. So is a prolonged life. But that is not enough. I must shape my world, not withdraw from it. I would be beneficent to the Rocklanders, grant boons to the marsh dwellers. I would return fair Clymarind to its glory and call Torlocs back from their outer gate. I would depose Ronfrenc and, yes, even free Verthane from his narrow house. But I must have power, and things shift. They shift too far—"

"*You* shift too far for me, Geronfrey. No wonder the world seems to move overfast for you. But if my maidenhood is such a prize, such a goad to a sorcerer's ambition, why was I never told that, since I, and only I, can choose where to bestow it?"

"You were to be told. And soon. Why do you think shrewd Finorian had sent for Thrangar? Why do you think Thrangar dropped his bond to his fellow Wrathman and came away without word, bound for Rindell? You were to wed him."

"Thrangar? But I never knew him!"

"Knowing is the least in these matters. He was the only male Torloc of power suitable for you. Finorian had great hopes of such a match. Thrangar's powers, once enhanced, would have enabled him to stave off this disintegration that eats at the Realms. The Torlocs could have remained, and grown in power until they could openly inhabit the City of Rule once again. You and Thrangar would have reigned as king and queen over a vastly different land. But—"

"But Thrangar never came. You drew him here," Irissa accused.

"No more so than I drew you," Geronfrey protested, his hands fanned in denial. "Sit down, then. It is a great revelation I have draped upon you."

She sank without demur onto another stool, the dark train coiling around its legs and only the very tips of her unshod toes visible at the hem edge like a broken string of pearls.

Geronfrey's glance fell to her feet and he frowned. "You did not bring your sword," he noted, looking up again to the pale silver eyes she kept slightly askance.

"I did not think a sword was necessary to deal with an antique recluse."

Geronfrey's head inclined, acknowledging her irony. Irissa picked up a strangely engineered mechanism from the nearby table and toyed with it, her fingers setting the little gears whirling.

"Ambition never ages," Geronfrey said sharply. "Do not forget that, and we shall deal better together. I would not deceive you."

"No?" She risked a sliver of a direct glance at him.

"No." He stood then and dusted off his fingers, which she saw were powdered with a silver glaze. "I have told you forthrightly where your power lies."

"An interesting choice of words."

"Do not be foolish. This is no game. I have retreated here under my mountain, gathering my powers, ever since Porphyria fell. Now, more than ever, the Realms have need of what our kind has to offer—"

"I was refused," Irissa reminded him.

"By whom? Ronfrenc? Worse than a fool, an arrogant fool. Do you not know that our powers are always most rejected by those most sorely in need of them? This tendency is called human nature by the philosophers. Unite with me," Geronfrey urged, his voice ringing clarion, his hand reaching for hers. "Then we shall restore an order to Rule not seen since the days when the Outer Ones intervened in our affairs."

"Outer Ones? Are these they whose odd-numbered eyes peered past Verthane's curtain?" Irissa's fingertips balanced lightly in Geronfrey's palm as she stepped down from the stool and walked away. Geronfrey's hand closed convulsively at the gesture, but she moved beyond him, her fingers curled absently within her own palms, as if they required warmth.

"Verthane has managed to crack open a gate? Worse and worse." Geronfrey followed her to the wide, staring, white windows, a moth drawn to the power that radiated from her in the unfiltered light. His face showed a sudden strain, an infinitesimal compression of all its planes, a sinking around the bones that made him suddenly age an eon or two.

Irissa did not see; she faced the dazzle beyond his tower windows, and her eyes were shut against the glare and against the treacherous reflection he could hurl at her if he wished. He could destroy her in a moment, she realized, sensing his desperation and frustration growing almost tangible behind her.

She turned, more willing to face the all-absorbing ambition of the sorcerer behind her than the unshaped expanses ahead. "You could have seduced me."

Geronfrey's face lightened, a smile turning all his finely angled flesh youthful again. "I thought I was doing so."

She laughed, the sound reverberating from the empty stone walls as hollowly as the wind. "Clearly, you have been a recluse too long, sorcerer. Is there not some boon you can offer me, some magical suitor's gift with which to delight me, enchant me, captivate me forever?"

"I had hoped . . . myself alone would suffice."

There was raillery and truth in his tone. Irissa felt briefly ashamed for having taunted him. She was frightened of Geronfrey again, not because of the power he held, but because he admitted a lack of it and thus demanded her respect.

"I am not utterly immune," she confessed to the corner of his eye.

His fingers spread and rested, cobweb-light, on her arms, fanning starfish on the plush gown sleeves. She looked at his hands, aware of a disembodied strangulation rising to her throat. She leaned away, even as his voice came soft and persuasive.

"I am not as—indifferent—as I thought to the means to my end. I am not as old as I thought myself to be." His young hands inched up the soft dark folds, attained the summit of her shoulders, and paused, pulsing with the simple, unshakable power of mere maleness.

Irissa drew in a breath, suddenly sure of the dimensions of Geronfrey's trap. She risked a quick, lancing look at his hovering blue eyes, suspended like pitiless stars above the night landscape of her gown, the moonsilver of her flesh.

"You could force me," she suggested breathlessly, waiting.

His hands tightened on her shoulders, then loosened and ebbed away. "No," Geronfrey said urbanely. "For then I would have only flesh, not power. And that is not enough. You must agree to the exchange."

"Even magic is bound by the laws of ordinary transactions, then," Irissa observed, taking the opportunity to step away from the strangely intent sorcerer before her.

"You implied you wished to be wooed," Geronfrey said after a long silence. "But your eyes can rain more cold-stones than even I could shower upon you. You have a self-sufficiency that shrugs its shoulders at lust. There is only one thing I could give you—"

"And . . . ?"

"And I shall. I will give you yourself. Verthane, you said, allowed you a peep through the gate without. I shall draw back the veil within. I will show you yourself, the pretty painted thing the world calls a reflection."

"Your gift sounds more like a threat, sorcerer. You

know I must not see my reflection without losing my abilities to my own image . . ."

"Not any mortal mirror do I offer you. I have within my mountain's heart a pit so deep that even the night cannot find it." He neared her, his voice as enveloping as the velvet robe. She felt his hands again upon her shoulders, though she knew that they were not there. "And at that pit's blackest, deepest bottom lies a pool of water never warmed by the sun, never silvered by the stars. It is as thick and glossy as a drop of liquid coal, with the sheen of an empress falgon wing . . . I could bring a thin sheet of that pool before you, my sorceress, and you would see yourself and that sight would not be reflection, but absorption. There would not be the slightest danger to you or your powers, believe me."

"A pool? There is nothing to be seen in pools but ripples."

"So you *have* looked. Then look again."

Geronfrey's hand flashed in front of her, spreading some silver powder in a swath. The white outside the windows thickened like cream, grew ivory, then amber. Its surface curdled, clotted into a repellent orange, grew more flaming than Mauvedona's castle walls, soured into violet, then bilious green, and finally congealed into a viscous, wicked black.

Irissa put out a hand to the puddling show of color and saw a faint gray likeness of that hand reach out to her. She followed the pale gray up to where the ebony of sleeve merged with the window's now-midnight surface. She traced the inevitable path farther and found the triangle of unrobed flesh balancing on its tip atop the smoky, golden round of the great brooch. She traced the triangle tip to its shoulder-wide base, to the pale gray stalk of neck, and to another wedge of face beneath the dark river of hair that flowed on either side. Eyes—she saw eyes—her own eyes, light, opaque, and unblinking. Geronfrey's mirror neutralized everything and presented it through a distant gray gauze that was almost indifferent to reality, rather than another side of it.

Irissa tilted her head to view the apparition of herself better. The grayish ovoid tipped sideways also, floating on the sleek black surface like a wailwraith's face seen through the veiling water. That was it. What she saw of

herself was unembodied, mere spirit posing as self in its
daily physical form. Yet it enamored her. Truly had Geronfrey said his mirror absorbed rather than reflected. It drew
the light from her and winked back a phantom image.
Irissa stared in self-absorption. She moved her dove-pale
hands to her face and watched their liquid progress across
the deep black surface. She parted her hair and pulled
it away from her face. Still she saw only the innocent oval,
the dark of brows, lashes, nostrils, and slightly parted lips
floating on that almost phosphorescent face as dead leaves
might skim the ripples of a forest pond. She reached a
hand forward, intending to riffle the image and watch it
resolve back into itself, herself, again. The narrow fingers
grew whiter as they neared their foggy opposite image, the
straining fingertips inching closer . . .

"No!" The faintest of figures emerged from behind the
mirror-image Irissa; in the room, a soft ocher shadow
pulled back her wrist. "You must not disturb the surface.
It is not legitimately of this Realm."

Irissa directed her attention to Geronfrey, or rather, to
the elongated hazy portions of him visible in her looking
glass. His dark clothing, like hers, vanished in the limpid
expanse. His face was an unfocused circle of light far behind her; his extended hand seemed sharper, as much composed of bone as of flesh. She glanced again to her placid,
floating face. The features were clear enough now, if not the
expression. Ignoring the floating patches of Geronfrey, she
reached her pale hands into the ebony around her face. She
pulled out a swatch of hair, glimmering faintly along its
edges, and began plaiting it dreamily. She felt she bent over
the pools of Rindell again, only now their basalt depths
were silvered over and they had shrunk to one thin sheet
of revelation . . .

The blackness rippled, throwing off rainbow hues like
a falgon's back shuddering in the sunlight or Iridesium
mail quivering from battle blows. The colors swirled and
lightened. Irissa threw up an arm before her face and
felt the velvet quench her sight like night.

Moments later, Geronfrey's hand tugged inexorably on
the veiling fabric. She peered beyond her lowering arm
to the flat, white windows of his tower room and to his
elegant, youthful face. He was watching her as intently
as he had studied the restless crimson liquid in his flask.

Were her reactions more puzzling than the ceaseless motion of his ruby fluids? Was she a phenomenon worth encasing behind glass and infusing with first one reactive agent and then another? A fistful of powder thrown into the wind and—poof!—one Torloc sorceress drawn into the net of her own image and drowned. She smiled at herself, at her easy enchantment, her self-witchery.

Geronfrey thought she smiled at him. "It is the only bauble I can offer you," he said, resting his bearded chin on a self-congratulatory finger. "A betrothal gift." He waited expectantly, his power holding its breath.

"Yes," Irissa said. "I may accept it as such."

She walked to the room's center, her back to the semicircle of scalding white windows. "But you must allow me to absorb all that I have learned in your tower today— which, I think, is more than I ever learned in all my life. My will must be truly free. And so—"

"Yes?" He waited.

"Every suitor must be patient, even a powerful one."

"Most especially a powerful one." He smiled tautly, but his eyes glistened with triumph.

"It is a great change I contemplate. I ask only that you withdraw for the space of a few hours while I meditate upon it, so I may—"

"—prepare . . ."

"Yes, prepare. So I may prepare myself. I ask that you remain here, that you do not eavesdrop upon my meditation by any means, so that when I see you again, I shall be totally myself—as you have shown me here." She gestured to the windows.

Geronfrey captured her outstretched hand and used it to draw her to the tower door. "As you wish. I swear to leave you utterly to yourself. And you, in turn, will come to me again, utterly as yourself?"

"If you wish it."

She bowed her head, her eyelids dropping momentarily in the gesture. In that shuttered second Geronfrey's hands came to her shoulders, his lips to her mouth. He kissed her in an odd blend of fever and icy proprietorship.

Irissa withdrew from him as smoothly as her image in the dark mirror had glided from herself. She passed through the wooden door and down the tortuous steps, her velvet train wringing its length taut around each stone-hewn curve. In time she came to the long corridor and followed it, past the small, arched wooden door behind which lurked the now-chill tub of water and the stale scent of bath salts, past the threshold of her chamber, where the fire threw the shadow of a sleeping cat large against the floor. She came to the chamber of Kendric; and on that threshold she paused.

Chapter Twenty-four

The fire crackled like a mirthless crone muttering into the hearth. It threw a little light around the room, enough to show the great sword lying sheathed atop a chest and the neatly folded mound of Kendric's clothes. The tapestries stood bulky sentry at each corner of the pillared bed. Irissa moved to join them, standing wordlessly there until the soft rhythm of her breathing seemed to resonate in the quiet chamber.

"Who's there?" The shadows in the linens shifted, erupting as did the earth when something far below the surface shook it. The linens rippled, and Kendric's voice came clean and certain from the darkness. "Who is it?"

A hand edged into the firelight. Irissa watched the stealthy revelation of bare arm that seemed to stretch forever from the shadows toward the bedside chest and the sword hilt even now growing softly bright. The hand paused above the glowing handle, and the voice plunged into certainty. "Irissa!"

"Yes," she said, looking upward for interference and finding none. Sorcerers were prone to keep their word, even powerful ones—or, perhaps, most especially powerful ones. It was an arrogance that rivaled Ronfrenc's.

"Yes," Irissa repeated, unmoving as marble.

The covers quaked again as Kendric squirmed into the light, the spreading light of his sword hilt. "I thought it must be—"

He saw her fully now—the magnificent, heavy gown hanging from the white, rounded ledge of her shoulders like a burden, the huge golden medallion gleaming on her breast like armor, the dark hair flowing past a face as sure of itself as Mauvedona's, one lock of hair still loosely twined as if she had come fresh from some decadent experiment in front of a looking glass.

"Irissa?"

She knew what to do, but not how to do it. Somehow, after seeing herself, she saw him differently now. She realized that the Kendric she had traveled with these many days and weeks had been as dimly revealed to her as if he had been seen through Geronfrey's mirror. To her, Kendric had always been merely a vague parade of features, an unsatisfying pageantry of actions and reactions she had watched from somewhere far away. But now the magic circle of his sword threw light upon the obvious. She saw that he was not merely tall, but supple and strong in that height, not simply dark of mien, but endowed with raven hair as enamoringly soft and subtle as her own; his eyes were not a trap to be avoided, but warm, ale-dark pools deeper than any rin in the Realms.

She felt her fingers itch to reach out and touch the mirror image of another. This revelation surprised and pleased her. It would make what she must do easier, but how, how, how? All her life she had thought in terms of far sight; this vision was a nearer thing than any she had encountered.

"What has happened with you? Your clothes—"

Irissa picked indifferently at the soft, heavy-hanging skirt. "An offering, from him who waits. I—"

"He courts you? I see."

Kendric's face retreated into bed-curtain shadow, a motion that made the fine aquiline slant of his nose grow as pointed as a falgon's beak. Irissa slipped forward, her gown sweeping the floor, her mind certain she was losing her new view of him. How? How had Mauvedona done it?

The sword hilt glowed brighter, as if to burn its contours into the very air. It was a joint sorcery she craved, and in her at this moment was no magic but the overriding determination to foil Geronfrey's wishes, to break before his eyes the vessel he studied so assiduously.

He had lied; she knew it. He had drawn away her would-be bridegroom—whether to use Thrangar or simply to baffle his union with her, she didn't know. She resented the wizard's meddling with her future, as if her life were a river merely to be diverted into this channel or that. She would exercise her own will, make her own choice, however limited. She would become the passive and willing vessel Geronfrey craved—for Kendric. But how, how? She had discerned the faint stirrings of his desire in the past, but now they seemed as permanently quenched as the previous day's fires. And she had rained that discouragement on him as much as any outer element.

It was easy to say "No," she thought, picturing Geronfrey bowed in perfect complacency over his isolated formulas. It was not so easy to say "Yes," especially when the question had not yet been asked.

"Is there something the matter?"

Her attention focused on Kendric, a Kendric who looked puzzled and rumpled and totally innocent of guile. It was not the question she needed, but she searched herself for a reply. Her sensations centered finally, not on her need to defraud Geronfrey of his desires, but, oddly enough, on her bare feet growing icy beneath the rich, remote drapings that masked them.

"My feet are cold," she finally complained, like a child roused in the night by some inescapable physical need.

Kendric considered the statement dumbfoundedly. Then comprehension lit his features more brightly than the shining hilt, and he reached out and drew her into the bed, the gown dragging behind her until he pulled once on the bulky golden orb that anchored it and all that swathing black slipped into a puddle on the floor.

Irissa watched Kendric's arm and shoulder muscles ripple as he reached to draw closed the bed curtains in turn, flesh shaping fabric to its will. There were, she thought as dark enveloped them and even the intrusive sword-light vanished in a wink, occasionally more satisfactory ways of dealing with things than sorcery.

Chapter Twenty-five

Nothing so natural as morning would ever come to Geronfrey's under-mountain halls. So they did not sleep afterward in the way that lovers had sealed their bargain from time before the Realms.

Kendric finally sat up and jerked back a set of tapestries. Pale firelight flooded the bedclothes and Irissa lying dormant beneath them. Her feet, at last, were quite warm.

Kendric glanced at her, his face serene with fulfillment's aftermath. She regarded him soberly, uncertain of the customs governing their new relationship. Without his clothing, he was as unsheathed as a sword; she felt a dim relief when he vanished behind the undrawn tapestries to don his piled attire from the chest. He appeared again, clothed, drawing back the remaining tapestries like a magician exhibiting a particularly amazing manifestation to his invisible audience—herself.

Irissa tilted her face up on an elbow. "Would you mind venturing into my bathchamber and retrieving my clothes?"

"What of this?" He dredged a handful of torpid velvet from the floor.

She looked at it and shivered slightly. "No, my old clothes bought in Rule by my tears and your insistence. Fetch them, please."

She had sounded rather imperious on that last, but Kendric nodded and vanished. Irissa pulled a strand of hair through her fingers, winding the lock around them until it was taut and as shiny as satin. She was beginning to understand how Mauvedona functioned, with or without sorcery.

Kendric returned and deposited the uninspiring gray bundle on the bedclothes. "I trust you can dress yourself. Or perhaps I—"

"No. Certainly not. Go find some food."

He grinned at her dismissal as if he had expected it and left the room.

Irissa dressed hastily, afraid suddenly of watchful eyes from above. She paused before donning the boot that had temporarily deserted her for a sojourn in Geronfrey's pit, the place from whence he had called his night-bright looking glass. Her hands stroked the sides of her face. She had an image of that face now. It was as if her mind held up a mirror to her and as if she held that mental mirror before her real face and passed it off as hers.

She hurried to her own room, where Kendric sat on one end of the trestle table and picked at the cold food upon it. Irissa plucked her sword from the wood and donned it quickly.

"You seem impatient to be gone. Like a thief," Kendric noted, rolling up a strip of meat and presenting it casually to Felabba. The old cat attacked the morsel heartily, even as Kendric leisurely rolled another.

"The cat can feed herself," Irissa said. "Yes, we must leave. You heard Geronfrey; he knows no more of Realm matters than ourselves. Where is your sword? We must be off. We can take some food in a bundle—"

"You're as edgy as a cat," Kendric observed, swinging a rangy leg off the table and coming toward her. His large hand cupped her face and ran gently along the curve of her skull and down her back to where her hair thinned to tendrils. Irissa jerked her head away. "And as grateful."

"Grateful?" Her eyes flared, luminous with silver indignation. "It was *I* who gave you—"

He caught her shoulders and turned her to face him. Although his hands rested lighter on her than had Geronfrey's, they seemed too heavy to bear. "We gave to each other," Kendric said, his mouth a grim line. "I do not traffic with sorceresses who measure their tears by the carat or their love by who gave what to whom."

"What of Mauvedona?" she challenged, shocked to discover that the question had been trembling on her lips for what seemed like hours.

"Irissa." His hands tightened reassuringly. "Let Mauvedona burn away from rage in her flaming castle. And let

Geronfrey freeze into his lonely power here under Falgontooth. We have traveled together for some time; it seems
now our paths are only to be closer. I must admit I like the
road."

He smiled, a phenomenon that buffed the sharp edges
of his warrior's face into something more polished, more
precious. Irissa melted into his arms, perhaps because it
was as good a place as any in which to hide.

"Your sword," she finally murmured anxiously. Kendric
humored her, breaking away to pick up his weapon from
its sentry post by the door and sling it across his back.

"There. I'll gather some journey rations and we can be
gone, if you are so eager to avoid another session with our
host. Torlocs make most ungrateful guests."

It was too late. A procession of the previous night's sendings wheeled implacably through the open door, the whirling edges of their presence spurred with lethal stingers.
Now they were no gentle phalanx of supervisory phenomena, but intent and deadly emissaries that broke ranks
to surround and isolate Irissa from Kendric.

The marshman batted at the squadron as he would at
a cloud of drylands flies. He drew back his hand as if he
had interjected it into the sharp-edged path of a coldstone-
grinder's wheel.

"What—?" He looked, as always in matters of sorcery, to
Irissa. But she was still and pale within her own slicing
circle, her hands distant from her sword pommel, as if
she knew that no steel stinger was a match for the airborne
rage of the sorcerer Geronfrey.

A cry rent the place, one as agonized and searching as
that uttered by Valodec's falcon when it had hurled itself,
blind, at the devouring sky. Each stone in the walls and
floor seemed to grind itself against another. The entire
castle under the mountain trembled, grated, and shuddered,
creating a vibration so low and buzzing that it seemed
the growling of a giant stomach. The pitch and frequency
intensified and rose, until comprehensible syllables painfully emanated from those vibrating stones.

"Blind!" the voice complained thunderously. "Blind in
my shining tower! While I abided your wishes and awaited
the fulfillment of mine, you spent yourself on a common
betrayal of the flesh. Oh, devious sorceress! Oh, Torloc who
has learned to lie like mortal men—with mortal men! I

could finish Mauvedona's work—and now the threat would matter."

The axe-edged flock tightened on Irissa, its nearness drawing more color out of her draining face, until she was as ghostly pale as she had been in Geronfrey's black mirror. She stared in mute misery through the brassy blur of the enraged magician's emissaries to Kendric, standing stricken within his own vicious circle.

"Betrayed! And by one new to the game. You could have bequeathed the finest distillation of your powers to me, and both would have profited. Instead, you waste yourself upon an unmagicked mortal man. Waste, waste, waste! Beyond magic, beyond forgiveness. You have forestalled me, Torloc. That does not mean I shall abridge my next blow—"

The grinding voice growled in fury, and the hiss of the nearing blades sent Irissa's hair lifting around her naked face, flying away from the terror in her unguarded eyes. She cast those eyes once more at Kendric and saw only a distant, shocked expression retreating from her, amber eyes withdrawing in the same sense of betrayal that so stung Geronfrey.

"You lied to me!" she protested finally to the shivering walls, which still wailed in a low, grinding throb even when the words were not forming. "About Thrangar, about—"

"What if I did?" The stones groaned even more shrilly. "A lie can always be spun into truth. But you have cut the thread of my magic and yours; you have woven false, and everything that comes from you shall be warped henceforward . . . I shall cut you, Torloc, an outer mark to mirror your inward duplicity." His hiss-edged weapons drew maliciously closer.

Irissa looked to Kendric again, but the marshman stood stunned, silent, and remote within the limits of Geronfrey's cage.

The metallic creatures whined and tightened on Irissa, their motion slowing to display the variety of their bladed edges. She shut her eyes and saw the black, lucid length of Geronfrey's mirror, saw herself in it, and a thousand stinging stars falling from the pit's everlasting night sky to burn out on the pale pool of face she presented to it. Her fingers trembled at her sides, but remained there, even as the wind blew warmer on her face and the stones' throbbing hummed more deeply.

"Begone!" came a voice pitched somewhere between the shrill and the deep. It struck, lancelike, through the chamber's vibrating confusion and rang in Irissa's ears with the familiarity of a prayer.

It resonated in Kendric's hearing also, bestirring him from the spell that webbed him—a new voice, but somehow not unexpected.

"Begone, Noge who is knife and Rore who is sound and evil Yoner who is destruction pure and simple!" the voice continued lazily.

Irissa slit her eyes open to see the hovering sendings depart through the open door one by one, sinking lower and lower to the floor as they progressed. One, still before her, buzzed closer, glittering wrathfully; she felt the faintest sting along her cheek.

"And you, Ferog, vanish also. I have known and named you. I, Felabba who is Guardian, in the name of the Gate I expel you!"

They were gone, and the room's vibration had dimmed to a dying rumble. Irissa and Kendric stood anchored in their places, eyes riveted to the figure of the cat sitting between them.

"It spoke!" The hush of the believer trembled in Kendric's voice.

"It spoke despite Geronfrey," Irissa added, her own voice faint from her ordeal.

Kendric glanced at her on that, his eyes beaming betrayal, anger, and resentment as surely as had Geronfrey's lethal messengers.

"Most certainly," Felabba intoned by whatever means she communicated. "I am too old and canny to permit a mere youngster like Geronfrey to silence me."

"But you have been silent ever since we came here," Irissa protested.

"Only a subterfuge—as you allowed yourself to appear docile to Geronfrey's design, then foiled him so—effectively." The cat hoisted a fastidious paw and licked it while Irissa's eyes met Kendric's above the bent white head.

"Even the cat laughs at me—" Kendric began, his voice strangled.

"Not 'even the cat,'" Felabba interjected tartly. "Surely

you have seen enough of my endowments to tend me a little respect, Kendric of the Marshes and the easily injured sensibilities. Now stop this quarreling, you two great silly children. We must leave while Geronfrey still withdraws to lick his wounds. He will not stop at this."

Felabba trotted to the door and gazed sharply left, then right, then glanced back. Irissa and Kendric both rushed for the door after a mutual pause, arriving there together. Their gazes crossed like blades; Kendric bowed back and elaborately gestured Irissa through the portal. She hesitated, regarded him icily, and swept through, as if precedence were a kind of poison.

"Mortals." The sigh of the cat wafted up to them from the stone floor.

Felabba padded rapidly down the passage. They followed, dimly aware of the grinding walls about them and of the quaking from somewhere deep within the mountain, as if an ancient but still operative mechanism had been set in motion. They trailed the confident Felabba down a cascade of spiral stairs and reentered the deserted great hall, where the tapestries writhed to the walls' subtle motion until the figures therein leaped in a frenzied dance.

Irissa rushed across the stone floor, nearly sprawling when her foot turned without warning. Kendric's hand caught her arm and buoyed her up at the crucial moment, but when she glanced at him in gratitude, his brows and mouth were parallel, grim lines as unforgiving as stone.

They ducked past the gold hanging and down the slanting passage. The lamps were unlit in their niches. Felabba growled a meaningless syllable, and the flames flared up green. But even these hewn-rock walls were wavering. The flames flickered unevenly upon the opposite walls, until it looked as if tenuous gases were swirling through crevices and fluttering like festal ribbons in the passage.

"Felabba! We shall have to pass through the Swallowing Cavern again if we take this way," Irissa protested breathlessly.

"Do you know another?" the cat responded shortly.

Without warning, they broke into the high-ceilinged chamber that housed Thrangar on his immobile throne-chair. As their eyes adjusted to the dusk that ruled below, they saw the circle of falgon bones still white and splintered at his feet. And those feet were merely tattered rags of leather leading up to—more bones, bleached and bare upon the rotting wood. Bones particularly long and sturdy among the races of men . . .

The walls around them jigged for a moment while a moaning vibration mounted from the tunnel behind them.

"The sword. The great sword," Kendric said, his hand stretching, white and hopeful, toward the long weapon still undecayed. "We cannot abandon it."

"And who is to carry it?" Felabba snapped. "I? You have burden enough of your own to bear, Wrathman; do not pine for another's."

"Geronfrey's spell," Irissa said, thinking aloud. "He must have let it lapse when he . . . he . . ."

"On," Felabba said, practically snarling. "On!"

The walls around them ground inward and began crumbling. Dark chunks of rock came rebounding toward their feet. They turned and ran, straight for the way that they had come, headlong toward the Swallowing Cavern.

Chapter Twenty-six

◆◆◆

Behind them, a colossal dry-storm of clatter rained thunderously. They plunged on, wafted before the uproar like leaves before a flood. Suddenly the channel of passage yawned open, an immense toothless mouth. Darkness spread before them, palpable and inevitable. Depths yearned below them, and they felt the immeasurable distances of the Swallowing Cavern unrolling in all dimensions, perhaps even in some not invented yet.

"We have no torch this time," Kendric reminded Irissa as he paused at the passage edge.

"Then we have no hope of passing it," she answered. "For even now my foot throbs with the remembered horror

of the depths, the pit beyond pits, where Geronfrey found
his mirror and I my rue. Oh, Felabba, we are beyond
being guided even by such as you. Go back, as we all must,
and let Geronfrey grind us in his relentless teeth."

"A Torloc can alter as well as make," the cat said, her
voice piping from the blackness at their unseen feet. Silence
punctuated that remark, while Irissa wondered if her Torloc
powers still existed.

"It's a pity you wasted yourself on me," Kendric said
stiffly. "No doubt your powers are now as worthless as your
merely mortal consort. It's fit punishment for defying a
sorcerer as powerful as Geronfrey, and for the common
offense of turning a man into a fool—"

"Hush," Felabba hissed.

Irissa turned her vision inward, forgetting for a while
whatever she had seen lurking in Geronfrey's pit-drawn
looking glass. Her palm clung to the polished curve of the
emerald cabochon dewing her sword pommel. The jewel
was warming to her flesh; now her eyes saw it and painted
it a deeper green—the same limitless, lush green as Felabba's feline eyes.

A light leaked between her fingers, phosphorescent,
pulsing, as illuminating in its way as Finorian's great touchstone. Irissa's hand fanned open. The light touched all
within a six-foot circumference, painting the highlights of
every surface with streaks of liquid borgia.

Kendric looked out from the vivid green of his face.
"Let us edge along the rock ledge, then, and try for another passage."

Irissa nodded, her hair draped with green strands like a
wailwraith festooned with weepwater weed. The cat glowed
green at the tip of every pale hair, and her eyes were almost blinding in their amplified double green. Irissa lifted
her hilt-light before her and edged forward, her free hand
trellising the rock behind her, her feet stumbling along a
ledge the light revealed to be piteously narrow. One foot
was somehow yet numb and yearning to overstep the ledge
into the limitless abyss. Still they heard the mountain
grinding away at itself, but remotely, as if from a hollow
distance. And occasionally, when they paused for breath
and an interior reassembling of spirit, they heard the restless, oily hush of water sucked to and fro far, far below
in the impenetrable dark.

Irissa stepped forward again, her foot twisting bizarrely
and moving beyond rock into nothingness. Kendric caught
at her hair and held her, the light dancing eerily, her feet
dangling into the dark and one boot slipping inexorably off
her foot. The strands on her head slid through the Wrathman's fist above her . . .

A colossal jerk pulled her back until she stood shaking
on the rock ledge, the emerald's light smeared by the sweat
of her hand.

"Another passage ahead, thank Rule," Kendric said. "Just
ahead. That dark spot into which your sword-light doesn't
pierce. We'll try that."

Irissa inched forward, slowed by the drag of Kendric's
grip on her tunic skirt, but glad of it. She came abreast of
the velvet dark, then dived in, taking a great gasp of breath,
almost as if she expected to drown. Iridesium glittered
wickedly in the greenish glow from her sword. They were
in another of the man-hewed tunnels, one inlaid with cunning streaks of the rainbowed metal in untranslatable patterns. Irissa fanned her fingers along the metallic channels,
feeling the same regularity of line she had encountered
before.

"Now we have less light than ever by which to decipher
these inlays," she told Kendric.

"And less time, I think," he responded, nodding grimly
ahead, so that she was forced to continue into the long,
dark throat of rock they had happened upon.

Felabba had sprung to the lead and trotted nimbly down
the distances ahead, the reflection from Irissa's sword
handle painting the cat's scrawny white sides lambent
green.

"We all look as if the mosses were growing on us already, thanks to your wizard-light," Kendric grumbled.
"This tunnel narrows. But behind us—" He paused and
turned, as did Irissa.

Once they stopped, their ears registered the stony rumble behind them, the sound of a giant, rocky throat clearing.

"Geronfrey?" Kendric asked. The ravine of worry etched
between his raven brows took startled flight as an unmistak-
able burp of rock vibrated up the passage after them,
spitting pebbles against their hesitating feet. "Faster!" he
urged, prodding Irissa after Felabba's disappearing form.

But if distance delivered them from the earthy upsets of the Swallowing Cavern, it also narrowed their chances quite literally. Soon Kendric was running forward in a half-crouch, and even Irissa had to stoop—to avoid unintentionally combing her hair on the rough rock above them. "If it becomes much narrower—"

But Kendric never responded to her uncompleted supposition; when she looked forward again, she was almost on top of the cat, which had paused and now hung intently over an even narrower aperture that led off from the one they traversed at a sharp angle. Felabba cocked her head to regard the maw beneath her with both eye and ear. Irissa knelt next to her and stared as intently at the mysterious dark, the emerald of her sword casting no light into it.

"We can still go on if we crawl," Kendric suggested, resting his hands on his knees and peering into Felabba's discovery as cautiously as if it were the Swallowing Cavern itself. "I'm not certain this chink your cat has found will encompass us all. And it certainly won't let Moonbane pass unless I drop it down first, and that I'm loath to do—"

Kendric never finished his thought, for the center of Felabba's hole grew suddenly light and fluid. Something oyster-pale and slimy shot up from its depths on stringy tentacles which looped greasily around Felabba's lean middle and drew her rapidly down. The old cat's claws tautened on the rocky pit lip; Irissa clutched for the sadly short and deficient tail. A meager fan of white hair was all she salvaged. Kendric threw himself belly-down on the rocky floor and dangled a rangy arm toward Felabba's still-visible form. The old cat twisted so violently it looked as if her spine had been halved already, the lurid green light from above encapsulating her descending shape in a faint sort of ooze that grew paler moment by moment.

Kendric's straining fingertips brushed a portion of the writhing back, but could get no purchase. Then one of the tendrils wreathing Felabba lashed upward, a stringy gray snake that twined his arm. It resembled the stuff of Verthane's conjuring web, only now it was unmastered and hungry in its haste. Kendric ignored the wreathing tentacle and reached convulsively for Felabba, now that her descent had paused. The little of the green light still pouring down the passage wavered, withdrew, and brightened suddenly in a vengeful streak like a blow. Irissa's sword carved an arc that cleft the brief umbilical cord of gray still linking Kendric to the cat. The feline mouth opened wide, a kind of Swallowing Cavern itself, ribbed upper palette colored a sickly green and all those phosphorescent white teeth quite pearly against the drowning green. Felabba plunged, the remaining rubbery tentacles still wound around her.

There was no sound, save Kendric's meaningless epithet as the cat disappeared and his overextended muscles contracted into sudden relaxation. The thing twining his arm withered and dropped off, a harmless thread.

"Why?" Kendric demanded. "Another moment or two, and I would have had her, miserable guide that she is. But she's a graceful, furred thing, her conversation aside, and I would not have her swallowed by that slime from the pit."

He sat up and rubbed his strained arm. Irissa rested her short blade on its point, her hands folded over the pommel and the green light leaking through them to shade her face a sickly color.

"I have seen something like it before. And it was not anything to toy with. Your aid but prolonged her agony and risked—"

"And your aid is as unasked for as your bounty," Kendric interrupted, rising as high as he was able and starting off again down the passage.

Irissa gave a farewell glance to the opaque black side-passage, then rose herself and followed the marshman, her sigh reverberating off the rocks around them like a soft wind.

It was good they had not lingered to mourn the vanished cat. For hardly had they gone a few paces beyond the treacherous hole when the tunnel sides around them began heaving. At first they thought the upheaval affected merely the walls and learned to keep their hands from brushing them as they passed. But then they noticed that the floor flowed, too, in convulsive, gentle surges of oceanic swell. And yet no fissures opened in the rocks, no clutter of dislodged stones filled their path. It was all disturbing, irrational movement in the dark. Irissa was reminded of her first time aboard a bearing-beast, when her closed eyes couldn't distinguish the rocking motion from the sea's primeval pull. They were adrift in an undertow of rock, rushing tide-pulled toward some unthinkable point.

"Can we go back?" she queried of the almost unseen figure before her.

"No, for it ushers us forward. The passage itself is pushing, pulling us onward. Hand me your wizard-light." The vivid gleam dimmed when the weapon passed to his grip, then glowed on. "As I thought," Kendric announced, pleased to be right even when the outlook was grim. "This passage narrows to nothing. And we must be inevitably drawn toward those grinding rocky jaws ahead, as your cat was pulled to her bottomless doom. Tell me, do you think this is Geronfrey's work alone? Or something other?" he asked, hunching over to disengage the sword from behind him.

"I don't know."

"You knew enough to cuckold the most powerful sorcerer in Rule—"

"I didn't betray him! His own certainty of the effectiveness of his charms was the traitor. He says I betrayed him. You say it. But I never committed myself there."

"You used me to disarm him; if that isn't a betrayal . . ."

"Do you think he was simple to resist? All that power arrayed against me? And he was a most persuasive man, very fair in speech and face."

"Geronfrey?" Kendric snorted. "He was as pale and slope-spined as a marshworm. Bland as yestermorning's mush."

"He had presence. Surely you concede that," Irissa countered.

"He had the bluster that is to be found in Ronfrenc's ilk and comes cheaper from a moldy-bearded trickster."

"He is a great and powerful magician, perhaps the most skilled ever in Rule. His youth is illusion, yes, but not his power."

"In a moment you'll be running back to marry the fellow, or whatever rite you wizards perform to seal your bonds!"

Irissa's hilt-light had faded as her anger flared. It was only a watery blur of meadow green in the center of the enveloping darkness now. Kendric's and Irissa's voices rebounded from the dark like blows badly aimed.

"We are quarreling like great silly children," Irissa finally remarked. "And whatever Geronfrey is, no matter how foul or fair, it cannot do his cause but good to have us tarry and bicker here like the commonest marsh couple."

There was a lengthy pause.

"Aha!" came the voice from the dark. "Now you throw calumny upon the marsh-born." Another pause followed. "A point well made. You've taken blows enough against Torlocs on your shield without parrying. Peace," Kendric continued. "If we allow our own tempers to work against us, we deserve Felabba's fate. And, by the marsh king, these walls quiver whether we argue or not. I think I'll take sword to them. What think you, witch?"

There was enough raillery in his voice to disarm the epithet. Irissa shrugged in the growing green light of the emerald. "It is your weapon. Wield it as you please."

Kendric swung the sword upward until its haft and tip spanned the quivering tunnel sides. The blade wedged and caught. It bridged the unnaturally quaking rock and stilled it, though behind and before them they could still hear the nudge of shifting rock against rock. Kendric sighed the sigh of the relieved and, borrowing Irissa's lighted blade, surveyed the walls.

"There's still Iridesium here," Irissa noted as the light traced the same puzzling parallel lines as before.

"Iridesium, yes," Kendric agreed absently, kneeling to inspect the angle where rough-hewn floor and wall met. "And something else made by man. This portion slides, so."

Another ghastly grating sound came but it was only the rending of rock from rock. Irissa leaned over the struggling form of the marshman as he pulled away a huge block of stone to expose a low, cut-stone passage leading away at a right angle to their own tunnel.

"Hands-and-knees work," he muttered. "Our escape route grows narrower and narrower . . . Oh, well, Moonbane's long and needle-straight. And you're but a reed of a maiden. Marshmen have crawled ere this, according to Glent and Valodec and certain Torlocs."

"But your sword—can you dislodge it now without bringing a dry-storm of tunnel down upon us?"

"Into your warren, rabbit. I'll pull on the blade and slip after you. Perhaps."

Irissa felt the same abhorrence of backing into the discovered passage mouth as she did of dangling her foot into the Swallowing Cavern's unrevealed darkness. She crawled in, nevertheless, feeling that to argue with Kendric now would be redundant.

She kept her head and the thrust-out length of her sword hilt still within the larger tunnel. Kendric wrapped both hands around his rock-sheathed sword blade, planted his sillac-hide boots, and tugged. For an instant, the sword seemed immovable; then it cracked suddenly free with the resounding snap of a whip. And with it came the rock, showering down in ever-larger pebbles. Kendric scrambled headfirst into the new passage, driving Irissa back and drawing Moonbane alongside him. The thunder behind them built to a roar. Irissa twisted dexterously and crawled forward, hearing Kendric's scrapes and grunts behind her.

Their progress was tedious, and she could feel her trouser knees wearing thin. It was hard to keep a hold on her sword, short as it was. Its gleam was vivid now, as if the nearer walls reflected it back upon itself and magnified its light to uselessness. She was almost minded to cast it away, remembering then that it was a mind-made thing and that there might be danger in treating a projection of herself so cavalierly. There was little use in their talking now, much less quarreling. There was only their snail-slow progress and the drag of the rock on their skin and clothing, their weapons rasping alongside them like metal anchors.

Irissa abruptly somersaulted over herself—two, three times. She ended up sitting dazedly on the rocky ground, her sword still clutched in her fist, its light streaming into the unrolling black velvet of another cavernous place.

Chapter Twenty-seven

◆◆◆

"Another cave. We're through, Kendric! Safe!"

"Nowhere under Falgontooth is safe until the mountain's fangs are pulled—and Geronfrey's," Kendric objected, working his rangy frame through the last of the crawl space. He stood in stages, each joint unfurling reluctantly, a creaking token of the cramped spaces they had traversed. "The wizard's rocks still gnash their teeth behind us—" He paused as a sharp hiss sliced through the dimness.

Irissa's hand hooked itself onto Kendric's forearm in mid-flex. "Look, Kendric. Rows of them, veritable mountains, piled like folg balls stored for a million games. Kendric, look . . ."

The hush in her voice drew his attention to Irissa, who was looking pale and sick in her emerald light, then to the vague limits of the cave, where piles of shining white spheres lay pyramidically heaped against the walls.

"The moonweasels," Irissa said, suddenly inspired. "This is their breeding ground! These are eggs."

Kendric walked over to a waist-high stack, picked up one of the ovoids, and studied it thoughtfully. It lay in his large palm, fitting the curve as if made to size. "No, not moonweasels. They breed as most animals on Rule do—living young hatched within and delivered without through great travail. Not moonweasels, but—" His fingers curled slowly around the gleaming shell.

"Don't crush it! You never know what . . ."

"But I do know what," he interrupted triumphantly, whirling on her, his eye whites gleaming greenish in the unnatural light. "Not moonweasels—falgons! This is a dwarf falgon rookery, and one of a size beyond compre-

184

hension. I had no inkling that these creatures dwelt in the Realms in such numbers still. Those captured by Rulians must be the very unfortunate few. What a discovery!"

He snatched her sword and began striding along the egg-strewn walls with an abstracted jubilation. "Do you know what a sackful of these would bring in Rule? What Ronfrenc and his cohorts would pay for only a modest pile of them? Coldstones enough to make even a Torloc's tears redundant. By chance, I look on a fortune and am helpless even to cast the dice in my favor!" One fist slammed into the other in frustration.

"Fortunes. You Wrathmen are mercenaries, Kendric. Here, I will weep for your lost opportunity and give you coldstones anew. Oh, Kendric, I would give all these living pearls, and all my perished tears, to have Felabba back again."

"Would you, now?"

Irissa had buried her face in her hands as if to wash it of weariness; when that question came, it only danced at the rim of her consciousness. "Of course. Do you think I have no heart?" There was a silence, and Irissa answered it bitterly. "But that is precisely what you do think. I had forgotten our quarrel in these discoveries—"

"Great silly children!" the voice came again. Irissa realized then that it was not Kendric's, had never been his, and could only belong to—

Her head jerked intently about the cavern, just as Kendric's did, searching for the voice's origin. Something round and white unrolled from the base of an egg heap. It elongated into a luxurious stretch, waved a disreputable posterior plume like a battle flag gone tattered, and moved leisurely to greet them.

"Felabba!"

"Irissa! Kendric!" the white cat mocked sardonically. "I confess I am more surprised to see that you survived your own obstinacy than I am to have eluded the maw of this cursed underground digestive system. You're looking well." The cat sat and worked again on her ravaged tail.

"You also," Kendric said, just as sardonically and twice as formally.

"Felabba, how?" Irissa rushed over to scoop up the cat. The creature retreated hastily.

"Enough of your mollycoddling. Soon we shall have

more of your sharp-edged tears and waste but more time
retrieving them so as not to leave a trail for Geronfrey's
nomad devourers."

"How did you escape?" Irissa asked, baffled.

"By the emerald that embellishes your sword. Green is
the Torloc color of power. You as yet can distill it in but
feeble amounts, but enough of that light veiled me as I
was seized by the meandering maw-thing that I was a hard
and bitter morsel for it to swallow." Felabba applied her
lavatory motions to her forefeet. "Also—" The green eyes
arrowed up to Irissa's face. "I used the claws that nature
and Rule gave me," she added modestly.

"How did you arrive here before us?" Kendric asked.

"By another route, marshman, and my native grace on
all fours—something, I am forced to point out, in which
you surely do not share. I could hear you two lumbering
your way here minutes before you arrived."

"There are other passages?"

"Dozens," the cat replied. "Some small, and some even
smaller. I fear you two shall have to stoop to your work
again. There is one tunnel in particular that intrigues me—"

The cat padded past the falgon eggs, stepping delicately
over those that littered her path like unstrung pearls, and
paused near a darkened spot of rock.

"Another worm-way through the mountain." Kendric
groaned. "I don't know—but then, I'm listening to a cat,
so I might as well suspend all belief—and all hope of ever
walking upright again." He dropped grimly to his stomach
and inched forward into the dark opening Felabba had
found. At the last instant, the cat squeezed past him and
bounded into the lead.

Irissa dallied behind. The notion of corkscrewing herself through another entrail of stone oppressed her in a
way she could not name. And her feet hurt—foot, rather.
Her foot hurt—the one that had dipped into the dark of
the Swallowing Cavern. It ached as if a great iron chain
pulled on it. She felt a weight on her shoulders as well, as
if two heavy hands rested there and forced her down. It
would be too much to have all that rock pressing down
on her from above. It was too near a thing, that tunnel
that had so readily swallowed her companions. Narrow-
ness gave no perspective. And her sword was heavy. It

was burdensome always to hold it up for a torch. Perhaps she should cast it away . . .

She suddenly wished she could curl herself into an eggshell, that she could be a thing of potentiality rather than of realization—something calm and contained, smooth and uncracked, something passive. There was a distant rumble down the many passages piping their way into this placid rookery. The air was warm here, though, and embracing. The rumble increased and burst forth a smothered cough. A few of the falgon eggs shifted in their piles and rolled softly along the floor to a lazy stop. Others dislodged and rocked out of place, so that the pointed piles became blunter and melted into a wider possession of the space. One came bobbling roughly toward her foot, stopping only when it nudged her boot. She felt a spasm of protest in her leg, tried to backstep, and failed. The egg cracked in a ragged little hairline along its polished white surface. The emerald light buffed its curves eerily green. The fissure widened slightly, a crevasse in a silent and waiting self-contained world. The egg split dramatically, its halves rocking open and trembling at her feet, the viscous stuff within puddling in a jellified pool; then something red ran down its glossy sides.

Irissa turned blindly and made for the tunnel, throwing herself to her knees, then crawling doggedly forward into the blackness. The intermittent strike of her sword on rock was the only sound, ahead or behind. It occurred to her then that there might be a bending in the tunnel, a branching off that Kendirc and Felabba had taken that she might simply flounder past unknowingly. There was nothing for it but to clutch forward into the black that was as thick as oil. She had an impression that she was penetrating Geronfrey's ebony mirror from its reverse, coming upon herself from the other side of image. Looking glasses, reflections! They were her enemies. Yet seeing, looking, was her power. Why could she not apply her power to herself? It was always through another that she approached it—unwillingly, as with Mauvedona or Geronfrey or even Kendric. Her mirrors were her means, and they were always other people, other eyes. They took from her, if they dared read her at all, only what they put into her.

That was it. Mauvedona had withdrawn the utterly tainted waters of her frustrated ambition from her tem-

porary Torloc well. Geronfrey had sought to match Irissa's
own reflection with its magical opposite, but had seen
only his own high hopes within her depths. That was why
he had felt so betrayed. Kendric had yearned for something human and uncomplicated in a woman, mere artless
animal warmth. And he had found her deeper waters cold.
Irissa felt the nameless chains dragging at her heels loosen;
Geronfrey's hands lifted from her shoulders and melted
back into the overarching rock. And another weight, one
that hung somewhere at the back of her eyes, lifted slightly, swung around a bit in the fresh winds blowing through
her mind, and showed a friendlier face.

Irissa saw a circle of white light glittering ahead. She
made for it blindly, ignoring everything but its slowly
swelling dimensions. She crawled toward it, dived through
it, and emerged in another cavern, lit by a wash of shifting
albino daylight from somewhere far away.

Chapter Twenty-eight

Kendric and Felabba were nowhere to be seen. Panic
slithered out of the tunnel mouth with Irissa and entwined
her like a strand from Verthane's long-lost web. She held
her hilt toward the pulsing dark. This cavern was larger
than the others; its dimensions were a sable velvet mystery. Irissa plunged into almost palpable blackness until
her light ultimately reflected a fold of its fabric. More
rock! and—her heartbeat paused—a shadowy someone
stood, casting a shadow even darker than he . . .

It was Kendric, at last, his back and that of the white
creature at his feet obliviously turned toward her. Fear
retreated to give resentment center stage in her emotions.
They were not even fretted by her delay.

"Incredible," the cat Felabba was murmuring in a strangely feline way, so that the word ended in a purr.

Kendric's chestnut head dipped and he nodded sagely, as if conferring with a cat were the most ordinary of occasions. "It's as I thought. I suspected—"

"That you could readily be rid of me?" Irissa interrupted, stepping ahead until her light streamed upon their backs too directly to ignore.

"Irissa." Kendric turned as if drawn back to a present he had forgotten. He frowned. "Give me your light; we have need of it." His hand was thrust out, casually demanding.

Irissa passed the sword into it and pushed her empty hands up her narrow sleeves for warmth. "Perhaps I had better simply have sent my blade along with you and stayed behind, for all the use I seem to be to the both of you."

They confirmed their absorption by ignoring the comment and edging intently forward. Then the soft greenish light clung to the contours of what they had seen beyond them; Irissa dropped her hands from her sleeves and came cautiously after them. There was a faint hum in the heavy cavern air; they noticed that all at once. It was quite different from the stony grinding that had pursued them thus far, the friction like the mountain snapping its molars at their heels. No, this was a strange, hysterical hum, a lute string broken and trembling in protest. It was a portent sound, one that promised to end abruptly and signal some irreparable alteration. And it came from the high, polished sides of the great oval object before them—a single falgon egg, but as large as all the earlier eggs melded together. It was so huge that the shell surface was no longer perceived as utterly smooth, but dimpled by irregularities. It resembled a kind of pale rock—unyielding, any life it had held long ago hardened into something that defied change.

Kendric struck it lightly with the glowing hilt of Irissa's sword. There was the muffled click of a fingernail tapping at a tooth.

"Don't!" Irissa said, unsure why.

"I'll not hurt it." Kendric laughed at the thought. "It's as tough as Tolechian tortoise shell." He strolled around its narrowed end, vanishing below the waist behind the white ovoid curve, like a snow-skater who slips and disappears beneath a drift.

"Leave it. It must be some conjuring of Geronfrey's. We mustn't meddle."

"Yes," Kendric agreed. "Who else could hoard an empress falgon egg in some forgotten cave like a magpie stashing a coldstone?" His hand slid along the massive curve as it had once stroked the arched neck of his mount. "Now I know what configuration the inlaid Iridesium drew."

"It's a dead thing. Leave it!" Irissa was panicked again and knew it, but did not know why. Everything in her shied from Kendric and the cat bending their attention on the massive thing they had discovered. It was sorcerous, unclean—dangerous. She backed away, half-aware that her reactions were what was ensorcelled and tainted.

"Danger," came the warning voice of Felabba.

Irissa whirled to see a party of oozing maw-things sliding into the cavern from the tunnel she had just abandoned. They emerged as serpentine slugs thicker around than a Wrathman's waist; but once into the cavern's open air, they puddled into white, sickly blobs that spread toward their victims in slow, certain stages. They reminded Irissa of something skinned that had nothing outer to hold all the soft, warm, hungry, slimy innards together. They were not creatures as she knew them; they did not even have the flattened features of a moonweasel.

A green arc spiraled toward her, just as she heard the familiar rasp of Kendric's sword sliding from its scabbard. She caught the spinning emerald-topped hilt and felt her fingers clench nervously around metal still warm. The pale maw-things flowed forward, in an odd way somehow as appealing as warm curdled milk. In their tracks they left a searing mist of corroded rock.

"They must not reach us," Kendric shouted. Irissa glanced at him and saw that Felabba had astutely chosen to leap atop the empress falgon egg, from where she watched the battle with roughened fur.

There were only three attackers, but the first was tumbling over itself toward Irissa. She slammed her short blade into its knee-high back. The glossy skin quivered and flattened, oozing away unpierced. She struck again, dancing forward with less caution, as if, finding it impervious, she must risk more. She lashed out again, a blow that set the

shapeless ovoid pulsing in reaction. But piercing was like
trying to cut an egg white with a butter knife; the thing
simply slid from her blow and regrouped when the steel
was raised for another strike.

Kendric was hacking as fruitlessly at the first of the
other two. His heavier blade sliced a bit of something off,
but the tissue lay on the cave floor, a quivering albino
wart; then the trio of attackers flowed toward it and
merged with it and with each other, until a great, trembling,
amorphous mass loomed shoulder-high from the cavern
floor. Kendric crashed his great sword down two-handed
on the thing's apex, his blow nearly cleaving the matter in
two to the rock it reared itself from. Kendric drew back
his blade. The tissue oozed together seamlessly, slowly
rising again.

"It's time for Torloc weapons," Kendric said, retreating
from the slime that lapped at his boot toes.

"Magic?" Irissa asked distractedly. "I had little when I
met you and have less now. Perhaps none. Geronfrey
said—"

"Bother Geronfrey," Felabba snapped from her hard-
shelled safety. "Use your brain."

Irissa studied the thick, oncoming mass. Kendric was
striking doggedly at it from the opposite side, but his
sword no longer chewed off morsels of substance. The
entity was pooling irreparably toward the farther wall, toward the egg and Felabba and Irissa in its hissing path.
Behind her, she heard the low-key hum intensify; ahead of
and around her, the mountain's murmur grew loud again.
And sliding toward her was the blank white sheen of something beyond reason, beyond the Realms—beyond even
magic, if she still carried any.

Use her brain, Felabba had counseled. How? The word
finally triggered something in her mind. She was afraid to
call up any shape—afraid that it might be one that did
not answer to her, but to the person Geronfrey had
evoked in his mirror. To a previous shape, ready-made . . .
Her fist tightened on the sword hilt, and then she changed
grasp on the weapon in one rapid motion. She held the
blade high along the raw metal, where the edge was duller,
and brought the heavy hilt down hard on the nearest surface of the maw-thing.

The emerald flared feverish green, then hissed through

the creature, leaving a jagged, dead white track. The mass collapsed slightly, and paused. Irissa hit it again. The Torlockian green of the touchstone sizzled through the tissue. She bludgeoned it into tatters, until the blade edges were creasing painfully into her palms.

"Enough," someone counseled—Kendric, Felabba, or a face from the other side of the mirror. The mass was a pulseless pulp now, its sleek surface growing thick and opaque white. A strong, sour smell emanated from it almost as visibly as the steam of its passing. Irissa backstepped and distastefully changed grip on her sword. Her fingers curled reluctantly around the tainted hilt, as if death were something communicable.

The cavern was rocking again, loud with distant rumbles thundering closer and with a cataclysmic ripping sound around them through all the labyrinthine tunnels. Irissa thought fleetingly of the hoarded dwarf falgon eggs rattling against one another like lost teeth. Ronfrenc would find his supply of folg falgons diminished . . .

She heard an even sharper rending behind her and turned finally. Kendric was raising his blade and bringing it down on the pristine white slope of the great falgon egg. The cavern rang with the dull impact. The whine around them intensified. Felabba twitched her tail as she sat atop the trembling eggshell.

"Are you mad? This is only a falgon shell, no white, swallowing enemy."

"A falgon shell rightly." Kendric grunted between blows. "But not *only* anything. An empress falgon shell contains an empress falgon—and perhaps our way out of Geronfrey's crumbling chimney."

He glanced upward once, swiftly and grimly. Irissa followed his look up into the thick, sky-deep dark above them. A star glimmered there—just one, a coldstone solitaire, a facet of light, icy and remote. Around them the rock shook and quivered, ground together, made pebbles of itself, and gnashed together again to make sand.

"A bridle," Kendric ordered, his eyes clinging to the unruffled surface of snowy shell. "There must be one nearby, for if she is not controlled as she emerges, she'll eat whoever waits to master her like a gutterhawk snatching bread crumbs."

A bridle? Irissa ran wildly along the shifting walls,

searching for a thing her mind couldn't even picture. Each step she took seemed timed to Kendric's rhythmic blows on the egg that was his anvil. Something glimmered among a landslide of fallen rocks—something golden and serpentine. Inborn revulsion halted her. Then she darted out a hand, struck for it, and snared it—a supple, shining rope of braided something.

Irissa turned back with her trophy to see Kendric a looming shadow, pounding at the innocuous egg like a Shield-shaker raining a dry-storm on the Rocklands. His dark blade plunged, struck, and drew back, leaving behind the first fine trace of a mark. A dark, jagged line, finer than hair, fattened and grew thicker. Kendric paused in mid-stroke, and the blade hovered over the growing ravine, a stilled pendulum. It dropped finally to the ground; Kendric's arms trembled from his efforts and rested on the haft as much as they held it. The fissure in the egg yawned, split apart, and shattered suddenly, as if one breach were a thousand. The thing that remained was dark, coiled, and faintly, wetly, golden.

"The bridle—now!" Kendric extended a palsied hand into which Irissa looped all that she had found. Kendric dropped the long cord over the dark thing in a complex pattern. "We'll mount her now, while she's still dormant, else she might toss us off as Felabba does a flea."

"No fleas, Sir Wrathman," the cat retorted, mincing forward even as rockfall behind her eradicated the spot where she had been sitting.

"Then up, all of us, while we may," Kendric urged. Irissa hesitated, but he swung her atop the dark bulk, looping gilded stirrups around her muddy boots.

"We can ride upon this beast?" Irissa asked over the rising gnaw of rock on rock around them. "That's only legend, surely—"

"So are Torloc tears and talking cats," Kendric retorted, swinging the length of his sword over one hip and mounting the falgon ahead of her.

"But with what do you control it?"

"This. Geronfrey must have made it ready for the hatching." Kendric straightened from winding the shining lengths she had found around his own insteps. A snake of faintly glimmering gold trailed limply from his fist. "I've tied it around her neck, you see."

Irissa found it hard to isolate any part of anatomy as specific as a neck from the dark hump of still-damp feathers and scales upon which she sat. Something moved slightly ahead, a collar glittering in the dim light.

"What of Felabba?"

"She'll have to ride between us. Tie her to you, if you can." Kendric seemed engrossed in adjusting the endless loops of supple gold around the falcon. The rocks agitated madly, and a sudden hail shut forever the small tunnel through which they had entered the empress falcon chamber.

Irissa studied her position. She was tokenly astride the falcon back, although her legs were more splayed than gripping. She perched at the place where the sleek feather pattern changed into scales that grew ever-smaller, until they ran into the hindquarters and long, tapering tail in as tight an array as grains of sand. Kendric sat ahead of her, just behind the great, drooping curtains of dark wings lying folded like limp props on either side of the creature. Irissa unbraided the decorative belt around her waist to fashion a tie for Felabba. As if the thought had been spoken, the cat's form curved gracefully up from the cave floor, settling into the small space between Irissa and Kendric.

"But how will we escape the cave?" Irissa asked as her fingers shuddered on the knots and the entire chamber vibrated to the destructive tympany of writhing rock.

"There was always only one way out of this chamber for a falcon." Kendric pointed up to the hovering star of daylight. "A rock chimney. She'll have to spring straight up."

"But with a burden on her back?"

"An empress falcon soars for air just as a doubting Torloc prefaces every sentence with 'but.' I'll prod her now. Take care."

The cavern ground around them like a throat digesting an unchewed morsel it had to make quick work of. The dark mass beneath them stirred. Irissa twined her fingers under a harness length that circled the dormant body. Ahead of her, something loomed over Kendric's shoulder. There was a convulsive shudder through the falcon's body, a rippling wave. She could feel it quiver to the creature's very tail. A shriek circled the cavern. With a spring from powerful rear legs, the empress falcon sprang straight up,

giant wings beating once and then streaming back along
its sides like floor-dusting sleeves.

Irissa felt her legs slide a sickening number of inches
backward. Kendric was a hillock of fabric crouched close
along the falgon's back. She herself was almost lying back
along its perpendicular surface, the golden loops tugging at
her heels as if to slip free of her. The vertical motion had
rammed Felabba into her stomach, where every bone of
the cat seemed a spur arguing for immediate dismounting.
The air and the dark swam past them like combs meant
to curry man, woman, and cat from the rising falgon back.
Irissa's inner leg muscles clenched, stretched, and clung.
Her fingers wrung the cord until it grew warm and slippery.
She tried to shout something ahead, but the rushing air
gagged her with her own sounds. Her hair was a shifting
blindfold and the wind sucked at her greedily, a retreating
tide eager for some captive to its undertow.

The falgon's straight, strong glide upward slowed. They
all seemed to hang for a moment in an upright tunnel of
rock, far above the spray of crashing stones. The sound of
air rushing past them grew deeper and became a low
murmur rather than a shriek. They were still moving upward, but at a paralyzed speed dangerously alien to winged
things. In a moment their motion would wind down, pause
for a pulsebeat, then reverse and plunge falgon and riders
back to lie among the crumbling rocks and shards of ivory
eggshells below. Irissa turned her head around over her
shoulder to face their failure.

There was a blinding sweep of white, as dazzling as the
view through Geronfrey's tower windows. Irissa felt herself lean longingly to the side, until it seemed she would
tumble that way to her death—but not backward, at least.
Ahead, Kendric's dark blue back tilted. And beyond him
was more blue—the sky. Something white washed against
her face, as viciously glittering as Mauvedona's star-axes.
She shut her eyes and let it beat against her lids. Her
fingers buffed the harness dry of her own sweat.

Kendric shouted, but the wind detoured his voice and
returned it a shadow of itself. How had Kendric gotten
somewhere else while she still clung to a thread in a world
of tilting elements . . . ?

Irissa opened her eyes to vast, unimaginable depths. A
field of milk opals seemed to gleam below, crimson and

green in isolated spots, but mostly white, cold, and hardened into curdled creases. Above was the sky, blue, cloudless, and featureless. And to the side, if she glanced too far, the sun was a burning hole of gold, a coin cursed by an ignoble purpose, blistering always like a conscience.

Stretching away from her in the clean light was the bit of falgon back upon which she sat and two great, feathered wings lifted to the wind, the tip feathers tilted upward like splayed fingers. Kendric's back ahead was now more erect. Even as she watched, it shifted; he was accustoming himself to his seat. Seat? They had no seat upon this beast—only a shred of webbing to clutch at.

The falgon wheeled in its first-felt freedom and tilted inexorably sideways. Irissa saw the snow swallow her horizon in an Abyssal wave. She clung to the slender harness, aware of nothingness sloping away before her like a slide. Her sword hilt gouged her side until she thought she would die, pierced by the wrong end of her weapon.

The falgon completed its turn and slowly straightened. Relief knifed into Irissa's lungs on an icy, indrawn breath. Kendric turned a wedge of face to her.

"Still secure?" he shouted, though his mouth was below a hummock of shoulder and the words still seemed to come from far away.

Irissa nodded, dazed by the cold, silent air, her fingers and feet numb from clinging.

"And the cat? The cat?" he repeated as the wind delayed his words.

She glanced to Felabba crouched against her stomach, short fur rippling and ears flattened.

"I am as snug," the cat said, "as a flea in a wizard's beard." The voice came to their ears unruffled by the wind.

"Where now?" Irissa queried.

"Where her instincts take her."

"And that is—?"

"Solid land, I hope."

The falgon wheeled again. Irissa was growing used to such dizzying changes of direction and looked around confidently. Dark, emaciated elbows of rock thrust themselves from the snow-mantled landscape. Falgontooth itself shrugged a bony shoulder from the surrounding white. But no one aboard the falgon could spy the rocky chimney that had spit them out like a cinder. The falgon's wings

pulsed slowly in great, undulating sweeps; she rode the
upper air and glided as much as flew. She continued reeling leisurely, always dipping gently, until the regions below
began to take on character—this valley, that crag, this
snowdrift. Two dark rocks rolled remarkably slowly down
a long white slope.

"Look!"

"Yes, I see," Kendric replied. The falgon swept lower.
"Our mounts! They're retracing the way down the mountain. They've given us up."

"They're bright beasts," Irissa said, as much to herself
as to him.

She saw a spark of Willowisp's red coat, imagined seeing the mist of Smokeshadow's tail . . . A tear stroked her
face, icily, but coldstones always were frigid. A sea of
such gems seemed to sparkle in the white below. She wondered if her own fell to a soft bed among them.

The falgon beat its great wings in unison and climbed.
The two figures on the snow-road diminished to pebbles
again and rolled lethargically away. The falgon rose
higher, soaring effortlessly. Falgontooth slid by again,
belching rocks and a black smoke screen of dust. The icy
latticework that was the City That Soars wheeled by on
their left like a fan of coldstones. They flew swiftly now
over peaks and precipices and rumpled white foothills.
Nothing shared the upper spaces with them. Even the wind
was disembodied, an attribute of the falgon, not of the
heavens.

They swooped lower, Felabba murmuring protest. The
blue bowl of sky tilted to meet and blend with the liquid
that sloshed up its sides.

"The Abyssal," Kendric explained over his shoulder, as
if he were a guide for a party of Soarian acolytes on a holi-
day.

They soared straight over the endless dimpled ocean, a
feathered arrow launched into the sky. Nothing companioned them over the water, nothing but the shape of the
falgon's shadow as it skimmed the air.

"Where?" Irissa asked. Her only answer was the shake
of Kendric's head. She looked at her fingers, twined under
the golden rope. The cold stiffened the substance. Her
fingers grew red and the tips white beyond the strip of
harness across them.

Kendric was staring off to the south and the sun; she could see his forehead and nose angle in that direction. Irissa looked there. The sun lifted its blinding shield to them. Was there something dark on a level like their own? Perhaps it was only her own dark eyelashes seen in the instant before her eyes squinted shut to the light. They flew alone. Realmkind had not flown since the last legendary empress falgon had shed its feathers like gaudy snow and plunged naked into the Abyssal's icy water. Finorian had told her once, so long ago she had forgotten, of that last giant falgon, the last to be ridden, the last to ride the celestial currents. She wondered if Kendric's grandmother had told him the tale, too, and if that was how he knew the Iridesium designs had etched a giant falgon form into Falgontooth's forgotten tunnels. She wondered if Geronfrey still lived and if even now he tried to loop the creature with the strands of his sorcery.

"Another rider," Kendric shouted back.

Irissa blinked again into the wind that blurred her eyes and wiped coldstones from them like the hand of a nanny comforting a frightened charge. There was no comfort in the distant, dark thing she saw. Airborne, as they were, it was large and slow-moving, black and deadly—and, most likely, Geronfrey.

Chaper Twenty-nine

Kendric pulled on the rope, doubling the falgon's long neck upon itself; the creature reluctantly slowed, almost stalling before it swooped lower. This time Irissa found herself thrust forward, with the flattened length of Kendric's blue serge the only topography between her and the rumpled azure water below. Felabba tumbled forward also as the falgon continued her rebellious plunge. The pale feet clutched for leverage, but the downward angle sucked the cat forward. Irissa felt the tie at her waist tighten, then snap. The cat bounded against Kendric's back, the only purchase on the whole empty horizon. Felabba splayed four white paws and contracted them, tiny grappling hooks on whatever of Kendric was available to her.

"Aiiyeeeeee!" His cry of protest would have been comical if so much ruffled water were not awaiting them all.

The falgon screeched in fury and dived straight for the waves, which seemed to swell for them like great wet blue lips parting for the prey. There, between that ridge of water and another, they would plunge, flounder, and sink.

The falgon swooped upward, her great wings dipping into water and then flicking it off contemptuously. She soared higher than a Rulian tower, then leveled out and flew on with massive rhythmic thrusts. Felabba slid back into her niche at Irissa's stomach and waited without comment while Irissa laboriously twined the snapped line around her with one hand.

When Kendric turned back to regard them, his brows were two forbidding falgon wings, and what rode between them was a frown. "She tried to rid herself of us. Be ready

for another attempt. And curse that cat. I'd rather hear
her carping than feel her poisonous grip." He turned forward, wincing, while Irissa and Felabba exchanged glances.

But at least they flew evenly now, and at not too great
a height above the water. The wind was sharper, and the
falgon's passengers had to endure the steady beat of her
giant wings, fans ready to waft them into the abyss.

At first Irissa had feared the creature had responded
to some inner call of Geronfrey's. Now she wondered if
the falgon hadn't been simply unwilling to abandon the
upper currents. They skimmed the water with effort. Perhaps the falgon needed food. And what did empress falgons eat? She remembered Kendric's saying they needed
the harness for control or the creature would snap them up.
Geronfrey's devouring mountains seemed a less personal
means of oblivion than the unfettered beak of a hungry
falgon.

The falgon was gradually reasserting her right to the
upper air. They rose so imperceptibly that they were unaware of ascent until Kendric reached out a silent, pointing finger. It was difficult to see below between constantly
fanning falgon wings, but each time the feathered sky-
oars drew up, an expanse of ocean bobbed beneath them,
and now, upon it, lay a fleet of floating corks.

"Yes, I see." Irissa leaned into Kendric's back, shouting
over his shoulder. "We're higher than we meant to be.
Can't we—?"

His windblown head shook violently. "Not that—not at
our height. Look what's down below."

Irissa struggled to look again, the falgon wing teasing
her perception with its elegant, lofty strokes. "Clymarindian sleeping-water-beasts? Are we near the island?"

Kendric's head shook again, impatiently. "Those are
beasts of wood and iron, canvas-winged and fire-spitting.
It is a fleet from Rule."

"A fleet? Ships against Clymarind? Ronfrenc wouldn't
dare."

The wind whisked her words behind her, so that not
even an echo from the party above fell on the diminutive
vessels below.

But something dark from the party overhead did fall
on the valiant decks plowing the Abyssal—a shadow as

fleet as a cloud with a great crossbar that brushed over every head below. The sailors shivered and the rowers in the flagship paused in drawing back their painted oars. Tillack from the City That Soars stood near the shield-hung rail, his profile turned toward his home shore, the last bit of Realm-land the armada had clung to before striking out for the heaving, empty ocean.

Young Tillack shivered as if the sun played hide-and-seek with its warmth on a chilly day. When the shadow withdrew, the sun warmed him like yellow lava; he rubbed his cold, white hands together and felt the icy Iridesium mail lay upon his flesh and casket him, not arm him. He glanced to Ronfrenc, who sat under a scarlet-and-green-striped awning on the topmost deck. Ronfrenc wore no armor, for he expected little battle. A few Tolechian fire-jectiles at the airy Clymarindian settlements, and they would rend, weblike, and drift into the executive imple-mentor's fat and patient hands. Unless shadows . . .

Tillack tilted his face at the sky, a blue, blank space that mirrored the water below it. He had seen a shadow there. He once had seen Six Wrathmen ride abreast up the winding road to the City That Soars. He had seen and he had spoken. And no one had listened, just as no one had heeded Verthane's last warning: "Beware of that which sees without eyes. Most fear what you most despise . . ." Ronfrenc most despised the unpredictability of others, their common hesitations, and their rare brilliance. Either dull or gifted, in the end neither fitted smoothly into Ron-frenc's Realm-map. He would have no raw edges in his world.

Tillack screwed his eyes at the sky and the sun. He thought he saw a black and wheeling cinder—nay, two, spiraling across the vacant azure. Tillack sighed. He had learned to see and say naught. Otherwise, the ignominy of Verthane awaited. Tillack wrapped his stiff hands around the gunwale and shifted his shoulders under the spray-wet tunic. He looked finally to the vessel's wind-fat central sail, testing for slackness. All he saw was ivory billow and, upon the swollen canvas, two black, distant dots, burned into his retina by overlong looking. Tillack's right hand sought his sword pommel, as if for comfort.

*　　*　　*

High on the waves the wind made in the air, the empress falgon wheeled. She had put the tawdry bobbing fleet behind her and oared into the vasty spaces untrammeled by anything man-made. There were two burrs on her back and a loop of stubborn hair about her feathered throat. But after the long and unyielding dark, this was a petty price to pay to soar, wheel, turn, and ride the wind.

The falgon's brain was a simple one and still reverberated with the crash of steel upon her abandoned shell. That soft, damp darkness, so rudely splintered, and then the long, shadowed spring up her rocky birth canal. Now she tired. She sought a rest as static as that within her ovoid shelter. And some primitive longing stirred inside her immense body, then bobbed there on her empty inner waves like the armada of dark things that had wafted on the water below her. Those things . . . Her neck feathers roughened and she allowed herself a brief, birdlike bark. She did not like them. They spoke of fettering, and she was free. But still the gnawing inside and outside . . .

She glided nearer the water, even as the afternoon sun companioned her. The falgon slipped lower, her bright green eye fast upon another flock of dark things in the water. Some dormant sense told her that these were not man-made. She wheeled slowly away from the sinking sun and swooped over them again. She wished to make sure of them . . .

"Look! Clymarind the Wonderful!" Kendric's voice held the lilt of a harp string, the cry of the home-comer. And Clymarind loomed at them, a glittering falgon's back of earth breaking water. The island rode low in the waves, ringed with foothills that were as frosted purple as the grapes on Mauvedona's treacherous board. Its inner heart was softly green and golden. The waves washed around it and trailed it in a frothy wake, like paper lace nestling around a suitor's bouquet.

The falgon's circle stripped the island from their view. They rotated their faces, anxious to keep it in sight, reluctant to lose its iridescent wonders behind their eyes. The thirsty sun was burning hot and sinking toward the water. It grazed their faces with its terminal heat and painted Clymarind a hurtful, dazzling shape before them. They wanted to regard it; they fanned their fingers before their faces and tried to take the island unawares. But it was no use. The falgon slipped lower and they adjusted their bodies to the motion, ignoring all else but distant, golden Clymarind, so near . . .

A screech sounded, arrow-shrill. The falgon pinions lofted backward and beat frantically at air. Irissa and Kendric lurched again on her swiftly slanting back. The wings flapped downward and flung a necklace of spray against them, the droplets striking them more sharply than coldstones.

The water boiled as the falgon drummed her wings upon it, her cries strident and unabated. Kendric peered over her neck, then turned and thrust a demanding hand back to Irissa. "I cannot unsheathe my sword."

She saw the shape of his words rather than heard them. Kendric's face was riveleted with crusts of white. Her own eyes wept into the stinging veil of spray that lanced around them. The hilt at her waist seemed slick, recalcitrant. She bruised her knuckles upon it, and the splashing water stung them.

"Hurry!"

This time she heard him. She pried the sword loose and handed it to him. A moment later a sort of scaled root writhed out of the mist and lashed the falgon's side. Kendric hacked at its retreat. The root tip sprang through the air as if launched, oozing a comet's tail of red. Another, thicker tentacle swayed above them on the opposite side. It twined around Kendric's thigh and pulled him sideways toward the hissing foam. He sliced it desperately, heedless of his own flesh beneath the coils. The tentacle slid limply away in two pieces, and Kendric's trousers split red where his blow had fallen.

The falgon gave a raucous cry; her great wings slapped the water until they fanned an Abyssal gale. The creature lifted up momentarily, her riders seeing, above the tumult, Clymarind floating in a sunset pool on the horizon. And then the vision sank. The falgon was dragged back to the waves. Her voice became strangled and intent, and her head dipped to the seawater as if she drank it.

They looked up again for Clymarind, as drowning people might bobble above the swells, hoping to anchor their eyes on something solid, only to sink again. Clymarind bounced, baublelike, as the falgon's back bucked beneath their clinging bodies. Felabba, wet to her skin, lay half-crushed beneath Irissa, her prescient green eyes caked shut with salt. Irissa thought of how she herself had always been drawn to pools and knew now that she would perish in the world's greatest pool, the lonely Abyssal Sea. The body beneath them shuddered and arched out of the water momentarily. The falgon beat frantically for air beneath her wings. She lifted, sagged, and lifted again. She was above the foam, her wings dragging at the air, propelling her awkwardly forward. Her proud neck hung low under the burden of lifting herself off the Abyssal. Kendric pointed with Irissa's sword to the simmering water just yards below them. A benign herd of shiny corks bobbed in the waves, each slick brown back as shapeless as a slug, while snarls of tentacles wreathed the foam washing against the creatures' sides. The falgon emitted a triumphal screech and flew ponderously for Clymarind's dimming shores.

"Sleeping-water-beasts," Kendric said into the strange silence that hung over them now. "They graze upon the inshore weeds."

The water-beasts' featureless brown backs slid into the falgon's wake, to be replaced by dormant herds of shore-line rocks, each breaking from the surf with a surrounding furl of sea foam. The falgon ignored them and flew steadily on, until she lifted for the violet hills and crested them on laborious sweeps of her water-heavy wings. She made for the first deep crumple of valley and there, near a tinkling thread of stream, she pulled her wings sharply back and broke her flight. Powerful lizard legs touched earth, braking to a stop atop the limp, brown thing that hung from her arched claws.

Kendric and Irissa slid off the creature sideways. Kendric handed down the wet armful that was Felabba; for once Irissa was allowed to cradle the cat without protest. They hastily retreated from the untethered falgon and walked a distance away before turning back to regard her.

The sun's last rays were smoothing the creature's ruffled feathers. The falgon crouched upon her strong, scaled rear legs. The horn-barbed tail that trailed behind them swept gracefully sideways. Her feathers began halfway up the sharp-spined back and grew as rich as foliage along the now neatly folded wings. They were water-burnished, and shone borgia-soft and marshwine-red. The falgon arched her attenuated neck into a labyrinth of scale and feather and preened fitfully at her breast and wings. Her throat was scaled through its greater part, with the feathers resuming just below her long and lethal head. She wore a crown of stiff indigo quills between a pair of spiraled, barb-tipped horns. Her eyes were small and deep-set features on a long, feathered snout that ended in a horny, upward barb as long as a Wrathman's arm. The falcon leisurely unhinged her proboscis; a giant saw of angled ivory teeth lay along each jaw. She clicked her chewing apparatus shut and dipped her supple neck to the dark thing at her clawed feet. The noble neck rose and fell, the last daylight etching a subtle golden gleam around her throat, a rope of light that trailed impotently to the ground.

Irissa's hand found Kendric's forearm. "We rode that?"

"Yes. We rode it blind. Which was, it seems, a piece of foresight after all. Come, leave her to her meal. She earned it."

They retreated further to a bend in the stream far from the falcon's ritual dipping, raising, chewing, and dipping again.

Kendric sighed gustily. "Very well. Let us see what we salvaged from our stay under the mountain and over the Sea."

He dropped the great sword from his back and rummaged in the boarskin purse at his waist. "Solid hide," he noted, shaking it approvingly. "If my flint and steel are dry . . ." They came rolling into his palm, clicking like coldstone tears. "We can only try," he said, beginning to forage for wood.

Irissa laid Felabba by the sword and went in the opposite direction from Kendric, bending to the ground in the dark, her hands skeining for twigs, branches, nettles even, if they would burn. She gathered a scratchy armful and made her way back to Kendric.

"It's a pity we left our cloaks on the bearing-beasts," Irissa observed as she bent down to run a hand over Felabba. "She could use a blanket."

"We all could use a blanket," he grumbled, bringing a spark to the brittle sticks she had found. The fire snapped at them, weak but feisty.

Irissa moved an unprotesting Felabba nearer and sat

by the bristling sticks. Beyond them, the unseen stream trilled in the dark.

"Here." Kendric extended a square of cloth. "At least we've fresh water to wash off the salt sting."

Irissa passed the cold cloth over her stiff-feeling face, then wiped the edges of Felabba's eyes. The cat purred, a wordless, totally feline hum. Kendric sighed again and fed the snapping fire another stick. Felabba raised her sopped head and began listlessly licking the fur upon her bony breast. Kendric and Irissa drew their knees up before the fire to warm their legs and present chilled toes to the low flames.

Irissa leaned her hands and chin upon her peaked knees and thought. The crawl through Falgontooth's caverns had worn out the trouser fabric; she could feel the cold bones of her knees infecting her already icy fingers. She had come a long, long way from Geronfrey's steamy bathchamber or his bright, faceted sorcerer's nest—and longer even from the sable sheen of his dark mirror. Her hand moved to brush a strand of hair back, then paused. She pulled her hair across her cheeks, like a black velvet curtain, for warmth and for retreat.

Kendric noticed the gesture and misinterpreted it. "You have little reason to despair now. I think your gate is closer than it has ever been. And you are wise to take it; Rule has become as mindless as a moonweasel pack at the full. Nothing but destruction will come of it."

"Gate?" Irissa looked up numbly from across the fire. Of course—she was the seeker after gates who had embarked them on this journey. And for what had she longed? Something so simple she now viewed it as intricately distant—a mere matter of joining the Torloc exodus, fading away with her people, one of many vanishing like stars when day overruled night. Not so much winking out as simply no longer visible. But there still, as was Finorian, beyond the reach of this Realm, beyond Ronfrenc and Mauvedona and Verthane and Geronfrey, and beyond even Kendric, who sat across a fire and a broader gulf than that which stretched between herself and her vanished race.

And that was what stung her, thorned her more sharply than any of Mauvedona's darts. What lay between her and Kendric was of her making, hers alone, and it was an ill

thing. She wished she had never seen the dim side of herself—but, of course, that was what had made Geronfrey's
gift a two-edged offering. Her vain wish for an outer image
had planted the hook firmly. It resided there yet, cankering
her spirit. She suspected that Geronfrey had only to give
the proper tug and she would flap wordlessly to him on a
line as long and fine as any ever woven. Felabba would
have called it vanity. Irissa thought of it as pride.

She hunched away from the flames as she felt the
bucket of her emotions plummet into the bitter springs
within her. She spread her tunic skirt to muffle the impend-
ing coldstone hail.

"I'll fetch more wood," Kendric volunteered, taking
her huddling for mere physical cold.

She didn't answer, and he rustled away. His absence
gave her another inward wrench. There was no going
backward, no reclaiming what she had given him—and
taken away. Despite the darkness of her thoughts, the
coldstones would not come. She was an empty Torloc rin,
with nothing to be mined in her but reflection. Her gift
was her curse.

Kendric returned, the crunch of his step snapping her
head around.

"I've found a cache of dried bushes," he began, letting
his stark armload tumble to the ground. He glimpsed her
upturned, inquiring face. "You've been weeping," he said,
amazed.

"No," she denied, secure in the knowledge that no
betraying coldstones encircled her.

"Weeping, yes." He dropped to his knees in front of
her and traced a finger across her cheeks. He presented
the wet tip to her like a trophy.

"No," Irissa said, shaking her head until her hair flew.
"No."

Kendric brought his fingertip to his tongue and winced
slightly. "Salt. The sign of work. And of woe."

"No!" Irissa rose to her knees, as if she pleaded with
him. "It's only from the Sea, the salt spray. The price of
my grief is coldstones, not these worthless secretions, these
weak and stinging internal raindrops."

"Your face shines with them," Kendric said. "What is
worth so much water?"

Irissa drew her hands across her cheeks and examined

her trembling palms in the firelight. They glistened. She felt again the hot slide of a wall of something down her face. Not tears, no! Tears were chill, brittle things one could store up like coins. This was an alien outpouring, a spasm of the weaker things within her. And yet she knew irrevocably that, since their time in Geronfrey's halls, cold-stones had been lost to her. She remembered the icy rivulet she had shed to see the lone bearing-beasts make their path home below her. She had taken it for a brush-ing coldstone. Now she knew it had been only mortal water, frozen by the upper air. Mock misery! Irissa put her face in her hands and wept, no longer attempting to store her sorrow in whatever form.

"Irissa," Kendric coaxed, drawing her hands away. "You'll wear riverbeds in your face. You would make a wailwraith laugh . . . Enough."

"It's gone, my power. Worse than Mauvedona's blind-ness, which was something that she shared with me, this is that which stems from only me. I have seen my own re-flection and loved it. I have felt my own pain and hidden from it. Don't you understand? I have truly lost my powers. I am only ordinary now!"

The water trickled through her fingers and oozed slowly down her knuckles. Kendric's hand slipped from her wrists to rest warmly around the back of her neck. "Do you think we do not all duel with our own ordinariness? Yes, even wizards like Geronfrey, who was more than ordinari-ly stupid to let you slip away from him. That is the true mirror image, and there is nothing magical about it."

"Just as there is no longer anything magical about me," she wailed, her voice struggling against great gulps of air for exit.

"Yes, there is," Kendric responded, his smile apparent even through the waterfall that separated them. "And not the least of your magic is that you can be so wet and troublesome and still make a Wrathman glad he is by your side rather than any place else in Rule."

Irissa's hiccups stopped; her eyes slid evasively edge-ways. Kendric's arm still lay across her shoulder, and the other was lightly bridged to her arm. He hedged her, and there was no overleaping him—not with her conjuring vision, not with her razor-edged tears. His hand on her neck grew warmer under the heavy blanket of her hair.

The touch was an invasion, a reaching in, under, through, and surfaces were her specialty, her magic.

"I have forfeited my power," Irissa whispered to the ground between them. Even then, she wondered if it were Geronfrey's dark mirror or the polished brightness she had found in Kendric's arms that had defrauded her.

"Power is ours, whether we will it or not. There are other things more sweet. And those are the things that, turned bitter, make your tears flow. Not power. Power is a plaything for old men—and cats." He grinned over Irissa's shoulder at the slowly reassembling Felabba. He swept Irissa closer in his arms and spoke into the lengths of hair at her ear.

"It has been a sore goad to me, this lack of powers in Realms rooted on such things. Even when the great sword of the Six was conferred upon me, I knew then I had merely the width and breadth to carry it, not the heart. It is a terrible thing to bear what you are unworthy of, and not by your own choice. The great swords were weighted with the meaning and powers of an elder day. By the time Kendric Halvag's son claimed his, the link between man and weapon had withered. The sword has enough of its elder powers to know that and reflect it, as you yourself reflect a person's inadequacies back at him. Always, whenever my motives or hopes sink beneath those required of a Wrathman, the cursed sword gleams at me like a dazzling, all-knowing eye. It registers my most mundane weaknesses and winks them back at me—that is why I nearly hurled it off Falgontooth. And it's why you must not rue your power's loss. You cannot dance to human heartbeats and weigh your tears by clarity and number."

His words had staunched her newly liquid tears as effectively as a handkerchief. She laid her head on his shoulder and let the sure, ponderous beat of his heart soothe her more certainly than words. The alien dampness dried slowly on her face, pulling uncomfortably at her features, including the smile lurking on her lips. This, she thought, was something Mauvedona would never learn. Irissa lifted her arms around him and felt a momentary panic as he shrank away. Too late, was it too late?

"Your cat," Kendric explained, still wincing. "Your scrawny, lizard-eating, prattling, sorcerous cat. She nearly flayed me on our descent. That's what I get for trekking her across all Six Realms—I'm cast in the role of tree."

"Five Realms," Irissa corrected absently. "Kendric, perhaps . . . Let me try my healing spells—"

He pulled away. "It's naught but a pussyfooting kind of hurt. Why tempt your fading powers on so little?"

"Perhaps the little is all I have left. Let me see," she pleaded, unaware of her word's multiplicity of meanings.

Kendric reluctantly shifted his back to the firelight. Irissa unveiled a ragged set of crimson stitches under the worn blue tunic, the track of Felabba's salvation across his back. The wounds were not serious, but shallow pain sometimes stung the sharpest, a fact the whipmasters of the world knew well.

Irissa furrowed her brow and made her eyes tread the ragged edges of flesh. Healing was a kind of fancy work, a delicate mental featherstitch. She willed the skin to overcast itself into one seamless whole, desiring it with more than her mind and eyes this time. With her heart she willed it, demanding that some hidden spring of her compromised power bubble to her service. Perspiration shone like unfallen coldstones on her forehead. Kendric, seeing it, would have wrenched away, but her fingers clenched the rolled-up tunic edge as if it were a curtain to some drama she must not fail to see. Time was an afterthought. She saw the source she tapped within her suddenly overflow onto a purely immaterial plane and wash over Kendric's wounds, visible only as a kind of frosty breath. The scarlet roads across his flesh vanished in that mist and never reemerged.

"There." Irissa sat back on her heels, passing the back of her hand over her damp forehead. "You are healed, a little—and I as well, I think. My powers seem deeper now, but more my own. Verthane said that the rite of Far Focus was one I could take myself through. Perhaps I have gone further than I knew."

"It is near focus you need lessons in," Kendric said. He tossed a few more branches onto the pallid flames and sank down beside her, relieved to stretch full length without ripping loose the taut threads Felabba had basted onto his back. "You fret for your lost tears, my scratched back, and all the trifles in Rule, when the greatest question is where we should go next. But do not bestir yourself," he

added, waving a hand. "Clymarind is a small island, and
I believe I can find Valna again. That is where we should
aim ourselves."

"Excellent," Felabba commented, interrupting her ear-
to-tail tongue bath.

Kendric stared blankly at her. "Why, when a cat is wet,
does it wet itself more to dry?"

"Is that a riddle, Sir Wrathman?" Irissa asked, content
to sit at the fireside between two such preening creatures,
one contemplating its coat, the other its fate.

"No," Kendric said finally. "We will leave why and
where and how for our when, which is the morning. Now
the only riddle I wish to unravel is the intricacies of your
silken belt—" His fingers toyed with the frayed tie. "—the
satin windings of your hair . . ."

He pulled her down beside him, unfastening and setting
aside her short sword while she was sinking into his embrace as smoothly as a blade into a scabbard. The warm,
unseen winds of Clymarind washed over them. In the farther dark, the sated empress falgon tucked her bristling
head under a wing and slept. The fire snapped softly by
the stream, which gurgled and chuckled back. Felabba
lapped noisily at her still-flattened coat. Her hints went
unnoticed. She finally stretched and twitched her tail.

"Foolishness," she sniffed to all who would hear and
stalked stiff-leggedly into the shadows to continue her
grooming in a privacy that included, rather than excluded,
her.

In the flat grass, the hilt of Kendric's sword grew lambent and spent its light in a ground-hugging arc. It finally
dimmed, with the fire, and went out.

Chapter Thirty

The Oracle of Valna was the oldest and the only holy place left in the Realms. Here the Torlocs of elder Edanvant had come in solemn procession to administer the rite of Far Focus in those days when the birthing of a girl child was as likely to result in a candidate as not.

Here, under Clymarind's soft, purple-shouldered hills, all the Realm-born would hope to pilgrimage once in their lifetimes. They would queue up in lines that doubled back on one another so frequently that the latest arrival might brush tunics with the first. Yet the order of entrance never suffered; a petitioner would watch a competitor but a handsbreadth away enter the Oracle's mouth in polite, even awed, silence, while his own turn was still three snakes of the line away. Sometimes fully half would have to camp in the fragrant meadows until the silver chime rang forth at dawn and they could corkscrew into place again. Invariably, they assumed their positions in perfect order.

And what did Valna offer to earn such dedication? Surcease? Panacea? Even, perhaps, the hundred palliative trickeries of philosophical mumbo jumbo? No. Valna was empty and altarless. The Oracle had no priests, no vestal tenders, and no seeresses. No god was in residence. There was only a Voice. And no one could quite say whether that Voice was spoken, merely discerned, or simply imagined. Those who had been to Valna—and in time, they were only the rich, the ambitious, and the fearful—would come forth mouthing fragments of portentous-sounding phrases. But they were never certain of how they had acquired their prophetic passwords. Nor were they sure whether these words were directed at the future or were mere echoes from some still-reverberating past.

The magicians in Rule, and they were many, studiously avoided Valna and all mention of it. They might have sensed that they were of Valna, but apart from it. More likely, they hoped that those who would go to Valna would choose instead the nearer and easier mystery—the scarlet robe and the smoking powders or the web and the star.

Valna was only a gaping cave mouth, a purely earthen portal. True, Clymarind itself was a restless land, peopled by majestic, golden-haired men and women who lived in valley-nestled settlements rather than in overarching cities. Their simplicity, like that of the Torlocs, was another goad to suspicion. So, in the end, the throngs avoided the difficult Abyssal passage and left Valna to itself. Only the Wrathmen still came in those rare intervals when their number had been fully replaced and it was necessary to take sword-oath as had the original Six Wrathmen of the Far Keep.

Who these had been, and even where the Far Keep was or had been, were secrets reserved for the Oracle's stony mouth. Kendric had been the last new Wrathman among the Six and the youngest when they had voyaged to Valna. He had been as dazzled by the Iridesium glitter of his companions as by any wizardry within the Oracle. He had heard nothing, seen nothing. So Kendric did not seek Valna like a pilgrim, with any hope for its intercession. He went there simply because he could think of no place else to go. Perhaps that was always an Oracle's greatest power.

Dawn came to Clymarind over lushly rippling hills. The early rays picked out a pair of figures trudging inland.

"Rue," Irissa complained good-naturedly. "If Felabba could speak but one word, that would be it. And, in most cases, it would be true."

Kendric glanced over his shoulder to the rangy white cat stalking behind them. "I imagine Ronfrenc is ruing his foray against Clymarind. Feel the wind? This island ship is ruffling away from his war fleet," he guessed. "They do not all sleep on Clymarind."

"How can you tell?" Irissa stopped and cast up her eyes to the pale sky. Clouds skimmed the rosy surface, as fleet as Smokeshadow's tail riffling the wind. "I grow dizzy looking up," she complained, dropping her glance from the swirling heavens.

"Then look down, as most do on Rule, Torloc," Kendric advised, nevertheless seizing her elbow. They paused to catch their breath and study the unpeopled landscape.

"It's a beautiful land, Kendric. Gauzy, iridescent. The very leaf veins seem to pulse with some slow-oozing ichor. The ground almost hums beneath my feet. I feel that the entire island is a giant sleeping-water-beast, and one more attractive than those that sentinel her coast."

"Yes, Clymarind is full of wonder, but wonder is best viewed at a distance. Remember the empress falgon."

His words brought Irissa's eyes skyward again. A fleet shadow spiraled into the heights. "Look!"

"Yes." Kendric shaded his eyes and stared up while Irissa consulted the stark lines of his profile, worry written large upon it. "The falgon is free," he said, smiling finally.

"I did not like her," Irissa confessed, shuddering in the chill dawn. "She was dangerous."

"As are we." Kendric shifted his shoulders under the burden of his great sword and walked on.

Irissa caught up in a few quick steps; behind them the old cat broke into a trot. "Only to ourselves, Kendric," she said when she strode alongside him again.

"And to each other."

They smiled at what had not been said. The cat Felabba overtook them with an audible sniff.

"And Valna, Kendric—can you find it?"

"Valna draws its seekers to itself. In a sense, it is as mobile as is Clymarind, almost springing into one's path unannounced."

"Like a bearing-beast?"

"Bearing-beasts are not noted for—" Kendric's glance had finally caught up with her nod into the oblique distance. A bearing-beast stood there, horned head dropped to the fragrant grasses.

"Ah, my lost Willowisp," Kendric mourned in tribute to his left-behind mount.

"There are no four-footed beasts on Clymarind," Irissa observed in mock rote as their pace quickened toward the tethered animal.

"This is no mere four-footed beast, my unobservant seeress." Kendric was trotting himself now; Irissa had to run to keep up with him. "See the great folded burdens at its sides? The creature is winged."

Felabba had already reached the bearing-beast and had dropped her inquisitive muzzle to the ground before its fanged mouth, so the two appeared to be whispering to each other while companionably sipping through straws of grass. The beast was tied to a blossom-brimming rubyheart bush, heavy with pulsing crimson flowers. It continued its placid munching, a creature of steel-shiny hooves and horns. A glossy blue-black coat inked its bones in one unfaltering shade. Its curling mane was sea-foam white, as were its faceted eyes. Felabba leaped suddenly to its back and stretched luxuriously on the unsaddled black surface.

Irissa reluctantly averted her eyes from the creature. "Its coat is so sleek I feel I could find reflection in it . . ."

In avoiding the polished curve of sable belly, her eyes chanced upon something even odder but a few yards distant. "Kendric, look!" She trolled for his sleeve and towed him away without glancing back at beast, cat, or man.

A wagon waited in the shade of several towering rubyheart bushes. Wagon? It was more a chariot, with beaten Iridesium wheel rims and one low, almost cradlelike seat lined in pumpkin-colored sillac hide. Harness lay puddled in front of it, so many limp leather snakes. A particularly heavy bough of pendant rubyhearts hissed softly against the wagon's side, until it seemed the vehicle was clearing its throat for their attention.

Kendric's finger traced a nonexistent pattern on the wagon's shiny painted side. "I warrant I could put a name to the owner of this equipage. But no face."

"Geronfrey?" Irissa whispered.

Kendric's finger moved to her face and traced the mythical course of a tear down her cheek, but he smiled as he did it.

"Mauvedona?" Her chin lifted as his finger dropped.

He shook his head. "No, they all adhere to the tight arc of their own desires too much to meddle in matters that don't affect them. Whom else have you met in your journeys, Torloc? Besides me?"

"Why . . . Ronfrenc. Verthane . . . And Ludborg, Ludborg the Fanciful, who dropped hints at our feet like rain and then left us in a skyborne wagon. But this is not his—"

"Nor shall he himself remain unchanged, I think, when we see him next."

"What are you saying?"

"Only that Valna opens its mouth to us, as I predicted." He pointed past the wagon. Irissa turned to see a yawning dark cave mouth flanked by stands of deep purple rubyhearts.

They walked toward it without further words, their boots crushing the ripe, fallen petals to a shiny pulp. Outside the low portal they paused while the scent of rotting blossoms perfumed their nostrils. They bowed to the entrance and stepped forward into the flat dark. Instant blackness surrounded them. And more startling than the quenching of all light was the absence of all smell, as if the broken flowers outside were an attribute of some time and space hideously distant from that in which they now stood. In the emptiness, their hands met as if guided by a sense other than sight or smell, and they walked forward together, their handclasp tightening before each step was planted firmly on the invisible ground ahead.

"Another Swallowing Cavern," Kendric said. His voice echoed in a hundred unnatural pitches from the unseen walls around them, some reverberations as high-pitched as bat cries, others deep and ominous, like the rumblings of Geronfrey's tormented mountain.

"Hush," Irissa said, unwilling to hear his voice bounce back at her like an attack. And her own soft syllable whistled shrilly into ultimate space and returned a knifing, hissing wind.

They stopped, aware of the pointlessness of moving or talking into the face of such a mystery. Kendric caught Irissa's other hand, and they faced each other in the sightless dark.

"I think we have stumbled into the Outer Abyss," he whispered into the night of Irissa's hair so that the sound would not splinter and spray them with its echo. And yet it did, the softness degenerating into a kind of mocking cacophony.

Irissa didn't attempt to answer, save by a pressure on the warm palms that enfolded hers. She felt a calm, fearless love well up from the deepest emotional rins of her body. She felt that she made a bridge with her hands, her heart, her mind, and that no ground could ever melt from her

feet again. It had taken utter darkness for her to sense the
bridge between her and Kendric. The mere temporary
blindness of her eyes had not done it, nor even the flirta-
tion with her vaguer self within Geronfrey's night-struck
mirror. No images existed in this absorbing dark, no reflections or illusions. Only feeling swathed her, and that
was as real as a cloak or a touch.

A pale oriflamme of light, moth-shy, blurred somewhere above her. It was moonsilver-white and unresolved,
but the glow strengthened until it lighted a highlight along
Kendric's shoulder, hair, and ear, so that his features were
mottled by light and shadow, and her own face warmed to
the glow upon it. The light elongated into a bar and loomed
above Kendric's right shoulder like a dagger. But it was
only a hilt—his hilt.

"Have you conjured the moon?" he asked softly, and
this time the echoes threaded themselves into a pleasant,
contrapuntal chorus.

"Only for the eye of your needle," she answered, pointing behind him.

He turned his head, startled, as if he had seen a snake
rearing to strike behind him. "My cursed sword! It never
leaves me in peace, never leaves me anything that may
be totally my own. It is like carrying a stranger lashed
to one's back." His hands snuffed the rising light as he
drew the blade, perhaps meaning to hurl it away.

"No! No-no-no-no-o-o-o-o-o-o-o-no-no-no-no-no-noooooo-
ooo."

An unfurling ribbon of blue light leaked along the edges
of darkness. It slid through a forest of stalactites and
stalagmites among which Kendric and Irissa stood, lost
children in a world of boughless, windless trunks.

"No." This time there was no echo. A figure grew, shaping itself around a ball of blue light. It wore silver samite,
great lengths of cloth that draped it as a cobweb would
swathe a pumpkin.

"Ludborg." Perhaps it was only the certainty in his
voice, but no echo rebounded from Kendric's greeting.

"Ah, my fine, attenuated friends. Still high, I see, as I
am your lowly servant." The figure extended its samite-
draped arms wide; the blue light uncurled and snaked up
its arm to twine around its shoulders.

"Ludborg? Really?" Irissa stepped forward into the dark

that now vibrated with electric points of blue light. She was aware of tall, narrow mountains of icy rock thrusting up at the cavern's sky and of mirror-projections of stone daggers piercing down toward them.

"Of course." He rolled forward, the blue light now trailing from a sleeve. "None the worse for your travels, I see. Excellent. We shall need keen minds and sharp swords. Or vice versa. The chords have reached the appropriate length, as was decreed eons ago when the Outer Ones first named the Realms and those who inhabit them."

A sweep of samite encompassed Irissa, and she felt an undefinable squeeze. "And I can use a Torloc, oh my, yes. So, ye evil-doers, tremble whether ye be within or without. Scyvilla the Rengarthian has his means now. And his methods." This challenge was directed upward to the ever-brightening stalactites that shone, like steel-blue teeth, from the cavern's upper palate. Then he turned to Kendric.

"And you are Halvag the smith's son, but it is not he whom I depend upon at this moment. You are the Wrathman from the marshes—yes, do not debate me—and it is a Wrathman I require as key."

Ludborg swept Irissa forward with him, as if he knew that would draw Kendric after, and the party advanced further into the jaws of the deep blue dark. Ludborg wheeled suddenly and regarded their rear sternly.

"Felabba." Irissa's voice rang with appeal, but the firm pressure of samite restrained her. Felabba looked on the vanishing party with eyes of intent green distance.

"That is quite right. You are only Guardian, Felabba," Ludborg said to the cat. "You must remain to watch over whatever it is that will—remain. Ah, me, these ceremonials are so tedious; I quite tire of saying ponderous things. But one can hardly summon the Outer Ones without resorting to a few formalities. Come, my friends, it will all come plain to you."

The blue, trailing light slithered to the cave floor and rippled along. An entire flock of such things reared from around each stalagmite, curling into their places like well-trained torches.

"We must move to the vocal heart of Valna, who is normally tongue-tied to routine supplicators."

"*Who?*"

"Ah, you sound like a Feynwood owl, my looming friend. Well, then, escort her yourself," Ludborg acceded, unentwining Irissa as Kendric insinuated himself between her and her encompassing escort. "Yes, Valna is a who, though not in the, well, individual sense you Realm-dwellers are accustomed to thinking of. There is Valna." He pointed to one of the luminescent blue-worms. "And there." The samite, with presumably an arm within it, rose and indicated a stalactite fang above. "And there as well." This time the silver sleeve lay along a line leading to the sword on Kendric's back. "But do not twaddle. We have work to do." Ludborg skated ahead, a pulsing silver ball emitting sparks of azure light.

"There is Realm-battle on," Kendric protested to the well-rounded back. "Ronfrenc leads a fleet against Clymarind. You must marshal your powers against that."

"Against that? When there is *this* to contend with?" Ludborg spread his arms upward, making a horned circle of his body. An oval of blue-worms sprang to vibrant life around them, illuminating the cavern's inmost ring of stalagmites and stalactites, a series of ice-blue teeth that glittered coldstone-pure.

"Here," Ludborg announced, and it was not so much the echo returning as a note being struck on the same tone as he had spoken. The sound pulsed around the various projections, as if each one had to register it separately. Irissa had the odd feeling that she stood among a council made up of many individual members.

"Six each," Kendric said tersely, tugging at her sleeve. "Six point up, six down. It is a Circle of Rule with twelve members."

"Members? These are rocky formations, a sort of earth-weeping, a kind of crying stone. They have no sentience," Irissa argued.

There was a crystal ripple, as furtive as distant cup rims nodding acquaintance. Ludborg's robes quivered.

"Hush! The wind comes, and once it arrives, we must hold our ground by any means. You with your sword, Wrathman. Unsling it now and let the hilt do its work. And you, my Torloc, you must use your powers. It will be fearsome, fearsome. We will raise the living and some who are not. At some time, Torloc, your gate will open. Take it when you see it, for sufficient wind to blow it ajar comes but under special, yea, ceremonial, circumstances. Drat these sleeves, so effective but most inconvenient."

Ludborg tossed back his dripping garments—Irissa and Kendric glimpsed waxy limbs—and uttered a high, sustained note. Kendric had unsheathed his sword again as requested and held it before him. The hilt reflected a bit of the prevalent blue luminescence but little else. It appeared reluctant to glow.

"Now, Wrathman, now," Ludborg instructed. "The cavern is a tumbler and your hilt is the key—"

Kendric's knuckles whitened around the metal. "It slices against my will, whether I unsheathe it or not. I would be happy to relinquish the burden of it, but not to Ronfrenc and his kind."

The samite quivered in impatience. "Oh, you marshlanders were ever the soul of indecision. I cannot understand why the Outer Ones seem to set such store by you. Think of your companion, then, Kendric the Equivocator. If you use your sword but one more time, you will unlock her gate of escape. There are none powerful enough left within the Realms to release her—none but a true Wrathman willing to make the gesture."

Kendric glanced to Irissa. She was watching him as intently, as mutely, as the cat Felabba had looked after them both when they had disappeared down the tunnel to Ludborg's assignation with powers beyond the ordinary.

"You have ridden far to find this gate, Kendric. Open it," Ludborg urged.

"And what will I let in?"

"That I cannot tell. But you will let her out."

Kendric's eyes anchored again on Irissa's. She was minded to read what lay behind them, but found she couldn't dip so much as eyelash-deep beneath their amber surface. Too greatly were her powers diminished; even the simplest reading now was gone. The thought crossed her face, leaving a ripple of anguish behind. Kendric saw it, clenched his teeth, and squeezed his eyes shut to all reservations. He gave himself over to the sword clutched in his fists by its awkward, runic crossbar.

Chapter Thirty-one

—◆◆◆—

Kendric had never made such a leap into magic before, had never plummeted off the summits of his imagination. His senses wavered. He felt a sharp descent and would have pulled back his outstretched arms to break his mental fall. But his own will stood behind him, a wall more solid than fear. He saw a shifting haze of bronze. He felt the center of his body pull toward it, draw taut, and twist him fine and strong, a thread prepared for the weaving on some colossal loom.

That was what he felt most—distance, size, and immensity beyond comprehension. He knew now why those who had set the Fellowship of the Far Keep in motion so prized the Wrathmen's size. He suddenly apprehended that the very sword he held was a mere toy within the vaster worlds of that without.

Into this Irissa wished to go. Kendric's brow took on the ripple that had crossed hers but moments before. He was not certain he ought to allow—

That one negative thought ripped him from whatever mental moorings he had found in the misty copper world around him. He felt wrenched about as if by a giant hand and set spinning over some seething abyss. He hung from only a sword—his sword. His palms grew slick upon the crossbar. All his great weight was suspended from that suddenly alien metal; now he knew it for what it was. Behind his eyes the copper boiled. He knew that if he opened them, he would awake in Valna. That would be epochs, eons, away from where he dangled now; there would be one instant in which his ranging consciousness straddled both worlds, and then he would snap like a rotten strand and shred into lint for all the Outer Ones who waited.

No. He would only think of hope, trust, and belief. His hands would hold the sword, and his mind would hold to its anchorage in his sanity. Irissa would see her gate yawning before her and melt from his mind as efficiently as Finorian's long-ago-lost green mist.

His thoughts painted the clouds around him a calmer color, faint green. Even that simmered away, and some brighter illumination rose, sunlike, on his sensibilities. Kendric tried to shut the eyes within his eyes against it and could not. He knew the blindness of one who is drained by another. It was too long, too late.

"Your eyes are the gate. Open them."

Kendric responded instantly to Ludborg's voice; his eyes snapped open. For a fine-sliced second, what they saw was streaming away from him in a fast-moving meld. Then he focused on the open throat of Valna, with its circle of stalactites and stalagmites.

The place was dazzling now; each stony fang glistened blue-white, studded with a thousand coldstone refractions. Ludborg, or whoever he was, scintillated in the center of the ringing, pointed pillars. Kendric saw that the light that silvered them all came from the hilt projecting above his fists. He looked to where Irissa had been standing last and found her there still, her eyes brighter than silver blades and somehow as sharp when they looked at him.

Kendric shook his head wearily and lowered his aching arms. A wind was hissing through the cavern, growing more strident. It was a clean wind, icy and purging. He felt that somewhere a copper chaos spread into fog at its approach. Ludborg's robes whipped into a flurry of flashing motes. The stalactites and stalagmites lightened from within, grew translucent, and melted into snow-season ice-daggers. The upper fangs began to drip clear, crystal liquid onto their lower opposites. The thin milky cords grew together, string-straight, until each set of formations was linked by an umbilical cord of water. The wind shrieked louder, slashing through the viscous strands until it axed them into a thousand suspended drops. Each gust splintered them infinitesimally; each slackening allowed them to flow together.

As the wind's pitch and howl through the cavern grew

louder, Ludborg spread his robe-winged arms. The howling
hushed a moment until only a strand of wind plucked one
rock-linked cord. In the foot of the glistening stalagmite, a
slender needle of image formed, grew, and was magnified,
until its pointed apex touched the thread of water suspended to its tip.

"Valodec!" Kendric's cry was as much joy as disbelief.

Valodec stepped from the stalagmite's glossy, wavering
surface into the cavern—Valodec, looming Wrathman-high,
wearing full armor, as in life, with the falgonskin glove
looped through his belt. It was the very falgonskin
glove Kendric had so solemnly tucked into the bag on Willowisp's back . . . Willowisp, now only a fading ember rolling down a distant white mountainside. And Valodec—

Kendric stepped toward the apparition, whose Iridesium
glimmered silver now, more than black or any rainbow
hue, and who looked as if he had been somewhere very
cold.

"No, Kendric. Touch him and you make a bridge that
will not hold you."

Kendric nodded and drew back. Valodec slowly unsheathed his icy blade and stood frozen by the stalagmite
that had birthed him, sword point arrowing to the ground
in a mirror image of the pale tooth of stalactite above.

A hand closed on Kendric's arm and he started, his palm
automatically curling around his sword hilt, though the
light it still gave off repelled him. It was only Irissa, and
while she pinched at his attention, her own was directed
to another of the mighty stalagmites, where a thin green
line was broadening into substance. A skeleton was being
born in this formation, a phosphorescent linkage of swelling bones that gradually clothed themselves in silvery webs
until they, too, wore Wrathman's garb.

"Thrangar!" Irissa whispered, totally unaware that this
was the first word she had uttered when she had found
Kendric wounded near a weepwater root. "Thrangar . . ."

The Torloc Wrathman, his bony face more frozen than
any rock around him, stepped through the stalagmite's shim-
mery veil into the cave as if piercing a fog. His once-vivid
Iridesium was as frosted as Valodec's. He had no five-
foot-long blade to unsheathe; perhaps it was still trophy
to Geronfrey. But Thrangar's long bow and quiver lay
across his back. He doffed the bow wordlessly and took

position, ready to thread one of his pale arrows to its taut, lean string, which quivered with as eerie a life as the liquid linking his womb-fang to the one above it.

And so, in silence, with no word of recognition between them, the Six of Swords slowly reassembled in the Oracle of Valna. There was Prince Ruven-Qal, who grew from a tiny red pulse to his full seven feet and stepped, courtier-calm, into the circle. There was a stingy charcoal lump in another stalagmite, and subsequently, a figure swelled there and stepped forward—Glent of the Stones, now as silent as the rocks for which he was named. Glent named no one traitor now. And Fiforn the Lesser came, growing in a lavender haze and slipping through a slit in the stalagmite in his unquenched Iridesium.

"Fiforn lives. Good!" Kendric commented under his breath. "And Glent—him I cannot credit to my sword, thank the Ones within or without that govern such things. And the Prince. But Thrangar and Valodec have been called to life despite themselves, despite their—condition."

"You call this life?" Irissa objected. "They are like statues."

"They are called," Ludborg said. "They did not come as you and Kendric did, hence they have less will left to them, Lady Irissa." He rustled over, then turned and gazed fondly on his work. "Either of you two may still muddle my plans. It is an honor to hold even that much power. It is because you have tested yourselves in your journey. That is why, after our confluence with the Outer Ones is past, you—Irissa—will be able to pass through your gate."

Ludborg's robe wafted as he emitted a sigh. The shadowed visage swiveled to Kendric, the seemingly empty hood askew as Ludborg tilted what passed for his face up at the looming marshman. "And you, Kendric. I think you made a most contrary Wrathman, otherwise you could be consigned to the life-in-death and death-in-life awaiting these, the last of their kind. You are a flaw in the fabric of the immortals, but woven in well, and so we must wear you as best we may. Your marshlands will be the only Realm to grow beyond this time. It will be a spawning ground for the survivors and their descendants to come. I will have you conveyed there, when your duty here is done. And you will grow old and shrivel by your father's smithy and remember when Clymarind was nomad upon the waves, when the City That Soars clung to the mountaintops like a great white web, and when Torlocs walked, bare of foot, the further forests—when the people of the Realms abided by their Circle of Rule, and Ronfrenc was not.

"There will be many Ronfrencs in your marshes now, Kendric. They will spring up as friends and neighbors and breed unchecked. It took more time than you can comprehend to spawn but one such creature in Rule. And he has brought it all down. He will not know it, of course, even as he plunges with his fleet to the Abyssal depth, where the exiled wailwraiths will wreathe his bones with the chains of office he so loved. The Realms were built upon the rainbow and mirrored a spectrum of what may be, each Realm pure and undiluted. So the Outer Ones intended. But Ronfrenc introduced a new color into their palette, and the shade was rust, the hue of shed blood. So all shall shatter, Kendric, all but your mud-brown marshes, which have little within them to threaten the equilibrium between here and there."

Ludborg pointed to the empty ground surrounded by six miniature mountains of rock rearing up from the floor and thrusting down from the ceiling. "Take your place, Kendric, and serve the Circle, the true Circle, one last time. Now that your Realms are shattering, the evil without can enter and swallow them whole. Repel that, you and your fellows, and the marshes shall have a few millennia to grow to their own accounting day."

Kendric moved slowly to his place between Valodec and Thrangar, between the true living and the true dead, seeming almost as drugged as the stalagmite-summoned Wrathmen. As he entered the circle and the arc of blue-white light within, it bathed him with a simulacrum of Iridesium mail, a glittering web of illusion that attired him once again identically to his fellow Wrathmen, so that they were once more the Six, rather than any one.

He took position with the sword tip resting on the ground and glanced down to see if it didn't pinion a spot of Torloc green, as it once had done in Ronfrenc's chambers. In fact, an island of olive moss grew there, and the point dimpled the velvet surface. Kendric's glance passed over Irissa, then focused ahead on the empty air.

Chapter Thirty-two

"There is one tooth in Valna left unborn," Ludborg said, moving in Irissa's direction. "Because your Wrathman came on his own two legs, he cannot claim it."

"He is not my Wrathman," Irissa said dully. "But you want something of me. Say it."

"I will need your mind-loomings to face off what sword and arrow cannot pierce," Ludborg continued unctuously, his voice dropping. "You have great potential; I cannot deny that. But you are not in the Realm that feeds your powers directly any longer. Your magic is patchwork, tattered. And you have been sorely tried."

It was odd, but Irissa felt that Ludborg stared directly into her eyes then. For an instant, the vacant black within his hood grew silver like his robe, silver and flat as a mirror. She looked away.

"You see, until you learn to overthrow false caution, you will always glance sideways at your powers. Even Verthane could not teach you more than that."

"You know about Verthane—?"

"My dear, I was there!" Ludborg laughed, his draperies sparkling with the quiver of it. Irissa thought she glimpsed three bright points of light twinkling in the cavern of his hood.

"Ludborg, my powers—you want to use them, but they have drained into some other place. I have nothing left."

"Perhaps." The samite squeezed her again, as much as anything that felt so inwardly gelatinous could exert pressure. "But be still a moment. It begins."

Irissa watched a small, black fissure open in the navel of space encircled by the impassive Wrathmen. It was diffi-

cult, but she identified Kendric among the stolid figures
that still wore unfrosted Iridesium. His sword hilt was the
color of cold iron between his entwined fingers. And his
face was as quenched.

The small, black hummock in the ground grew larger
and taller. It was so unrelievedly black that it held no dimension. Yet she knew it spun with a wild compassless
vertigo. It expanded, a thick, black, rising column, until it
spanned the cavern from floor to ceiling. And then its unseen motion stopped. Irissa could not say how she knew
this, but she did.

"Another gate," Ludborg explained in a hushed voice.
"My gate, in fact, if yon warriors are festy enough to hack
a way free for me."

"For you?"

"Not for my sake alone, dear no. I am not that self-taken.
Nor do gates of such magnitude open merely for misplaced
Rengarthians. But I may slither through at the apt moment,
as you may worm a chink into your new Torlockian world.
Alas, brave Thrangar shall never be your consort. Even
Finorian could not reconstitute his corporeal form, I fear.
But you will find many other Torloc warriors on the other
side of that gate. And one of them no doubt will suffice to
complete Finorian's plans."

Irissa was conscious of a slithered side glance from the
hood.

"Ludborg, you ramble on about hypothetical betrothals
and do not explain this sable pillar before us. Mauvedona
was right, you are senile—"

"Senile! In my own time and place I am younger than
you, Lady Impudence. Nothing I say is quite as purpose-
less as it seems. Remember that, should you ever encounter another Rengarthian, though that is doubtful. We
are famed for our enigmatic ways. But heed me now. Yon
basalt stalagmite is a gate, and one not cracked for vast
times and distances. That it has opened this far means
the Realms must shatter beyond reknitting. And if the
Six Wrathmen do not repel what may enter with the gate,
not so much as a scintilla of anything sentient shall remain
to tell the tale. Watch."

But there was nothing to see except for the somber
Wrathmen and the great black bar rising in their midst, a
narrow, foldless curtain. Then the formless dark rumpled

in opaque waves. It swelled and rent, emitting a noxious barrage of fumes into the damp cave air. The odor was ripe with dried blood and congealed entrails; it reeked of rotting vegetation and the fetid, heavy damp of putrefaction.

So overpowering were the smell and its associations that Irissa clutched her midsection and buried her face unhesitatingly in Ludborg's broad samite shoulder. Nothing solid stopped her, but an endless diving into slack folds of samite seemed worse than inhaling the stench. She reemerged in time to see Prince Ruven-Qal pull a hammered Iridesium flask from his belt. With a loose-limbed, easy grace, he dropped to one knee, balancing against his upright sword. He drew flint and coursed it once down the lethal metal ribbon of blade. Sparks scattered like burning moths and clustered at the open mouth of his powder flask. They expired in a conflagration that spat out stiff tongues of flame from the narrow neck. Prince Ruven-Qal rose fluidly and blessed the great black column of stench with an arc of shooting sulfur. The fiery spray cut the column in half, spreading straight through the heart of the visible cloud of odor. It penetrated the still-belching mist, and vanished, instantly damp, leaving behind only a growing stench as of a thousand dwarf falgon eggs rotting. The dark pillar split from top to base while a flood of rank fumes poured out in a swelling sea that was slowly overpowered by the burning acridity of Prince Ruven-Qal's noxious powder.

The gathered Wrathmen stood impervious to this stultifying exhalation, Valodec and Thrangar at attention once more; even the Iridesium-arrayed living warriors among them were as indifferent to its passing as if dead themselves, save one who clutched his sword hilt close to his Iridesium-webbed chest and bowed his head over the crossbar, coughing and retching.

Irissa glanced accusingly to the samite orb at her side. The hood tilted to meet shoulders raised in a shrug.

"Yes, I fear our friend feels the battle a bit more than the others. As I told you, he was not called, but came willingly. No spell shields him from that without, except the conjured Iridesium I gave him; and that contains only its normal properties."

"You are as deceptive as Felabba, Ludborg."

"I do not deceive you when I say you must call upon reinforcements. Look to the last pillar. Its heart is blank, but potent as a witch-womb. You can reach another sorcerer through it."

Irissa stood unmoving, refusing to edge along with Ludborg to the untenanted stalagmite. The dark of the alien's hood swiveled point-blank toward her. "Whom should I call?" she asked, finally stepping after him. "Verthane?"

Simply uttering the word sent the frozen silver surface of stone whirling with inner chaos. It became a milky mirror, with one dark, star-shaped window winking high in its narrowing point. A soft, shadowed mist moved deep within the curves. Irissa looked harder. She saw a five-pointed coldstone web starring the ashy floor and a ghostly figure brushing to and fro upon that pallid surface.

"It is Verthane's conjuring-chamber, and that is—" Irissa watched the smoky mist pace methodically across the white stones, not one wreath of it disarranging even the tiniest coldstone of pattern.

"The City of Rule sits south of the Rocklands," Ludborg reminded her, sounding like a geography tutor. "And the Rocklands now cough fire and blood as they did once immemoriably long ago. They aim nature's firejectiles at Ronfrenc's City, where even the moonweasels have ebbed away with the last Abyssal tides."

"Verthane is white, therefore . . ."

"Verthane is dead, as are most in the City of Rule. You could summon this remnant, of course; some power clings to it still . . ."

"No!"

"Then find me another, a living, sorcerer."

"Will a sorceress do?" Challenge rang in Irissa's voice; she was wearying of Ludborg and his riddles: "I call upon Mauvedona."

Her heart beat as she invoked her enemy, unsure whether the wish to disconcert Ludborg or save Kendric was stronger.

Flame spurted upward in a triangular fang through the icy dagger of stone, so vibrant that Irissa backstepped and brought her arm to her face. But it was cold flame that warmed the stalagmite with its color only. And in its heart gleamed a violet wraith that was Mauvedona, a great amethyst inset into a circlet at her brow.

"But she is half-mist, like Verthane."

"Hmmmmm. Mauvedona has surely enough power to

manifest herself in our fanged mirror more concretely than this—" Ludborg's hood tilted even more violently, as if he leaned a faceless chin upon a boneless finger.

"It is her face, her figure," Irissa continued. "She even wears the same gemstone she wore when she tried to usurp my sight."

"Ah, the stone. I see it, token that it is of her treaty with the moonweasels and whatever ancient evil spawned them. She is worthless to defend our gate, Torloc, for her bargain with a magic lower than her own has left only this aura untainted. Would you defend your life with a gauzelin sword? Then take Mauvedona as your ally and watch her violet mist soak up Wrathmen's blood."

"They are not fully present, you said. How can they bleed?"

The samite shrugged appeasingly. "Those who are fully of the here and now can become fully—dead."

"Those?"

"Well, one."

Ludborg was silent, and Irissa glanced back to the inner circle of contention. The central black pillar had sprouted a hundred writhing tentacles, each one mottled with pale simulacrums of the Wrathmen's colors—anemic pinks, grays, greens, and mauves, in all shades of the flesh and its decay. The tentacles branched, split, and curled, until they twined around the stalagmites and stalactites and around the feet of the circled Wrathmen, who raised their swords and hacked at the entwining members.

One figure, pale even against the pale colors, stood in the center and grappled with the most aggressive of the headless, eyeless, noseless snakes. His right hand rose and fell with the swings of his heavy-edged sword. His left hand was gloved in falgonskin, the cuff's feathered crest rising and dipping to its prey as rhythmically as the living empress falgon devouring the sleeping-water-beast.

It was Valodec, dead Valodec, wearing the shadow of the gauntlet Kendric had taken as a memento. The shadow man and shadow glove moved together as lithely as the spiraling tentacles. Valodec's gauntleted fist choked the gangrenous colors, and they ran molten and oozed down a withering trunk. Where the Clymarindian gauntlet had tautened and relaxed, a living tendril died and fell, brown and broken, to the cave floor.

Irissa recognized Thrangar, standing wreathed in a host of the prehensile things, one thick, salmon-colored coil around his throat. Thrangar fell, his frosted Iridesium picking up none of the cave's clinging humus. Another Wrathman, one wearing unfaded Iridesium, came hacking toward the fallen Torloc, whose bones even now seemed to glow through his armor. A hungry root of tentacle wove restraint around the rescuer's every limb. The great sword he carried lowered; a rubbery vine coiled down the knight's arm, snaked across his fingers, and pried open his grasp. The thickest tendril had wrapped itself moonweasel-fast around his neck; his face flamed protest, then paled helplessly as air became a memory.

"It is Kendric!" Irissa advanced, then paused and projected the impulse of her mind instead. A fiery serpent writhed to the floor in front of her and slithered hissingly into the circle. There, a rope of mottled flesh fell upon it. There was a searing sound, but the tentacle weaved triumphantly up from the floor, a thin ashy scar its only damage.

An angry squadron of fire-snakes hissed into life at Irissa's boot tips, but Ludborg reared a samite wall ahead of them. They scaled the shining surface, transmuted into blueworms, and dropped harmlessly to the ground again.

"Reinforcements!" Ludborg insisted, stamping whatever passed for his foot. The samite robes quivered, but no sound came from the gesture. "Your powers are only stopgaps. Fret not about this uproar. Look to your summoning-glass."

Irissa's glance was torn between the fallen Wrathmen—one dark, one pale—and the icy dagger of stalagmite before her. In the circle, she saw the Wrathman who was once Valodec hack his way to the two fallen warriors. His falgonskin gauntlet closed convulsively on one thick tentacle after another. The fiber around Kendric's throat slackened and fell away. The marshman's face remained as pale and mottled as that which had attempted to strangle him.

"Now."

Something prodded her, although it was not sharp. Irissa let her mind focus on the spire of rock before her, on its viscous, gleaming surface, within which rippled—

"Call another."

Another? Who was left to call? Who but . . . ? No one, save . . . In the end, it was not even left for her to call the name into her consciousness. Geronfrey wavered into image on the rock's crystalline undulations of surface. This was a calm Geronfrey, a certain Geronfrey. Geronfrey was no longer raging in his white-windowed tower. Geronfrey seemed to have been waiting for this moment from the first instant of his disillusionment.

"Do I know you?" Geronfrey lifted a vial brimming with a scarlet liquid to his eyes; he appeared to be regarding Irissa through it.

"You know me. But not well enough. I fear that is your fault, not mine."

"This is no time to talk of faults," Ludborg interrupted querulously. "Get on with it."

Geronfrey seemed unaware of Ludborg's promptings. He still sat in his tower chamber, the arches behind him looking out as blindly as ever on depthless nothing. He finally set aside his vial and also his feigned indifference. He ran a long-fingered hand through his golden beard, but the fingers shook almost imperceptibly. Perhaps it was only the water sheeting the stalagmite surface.

"I know you," Geronfrey conceded. "You are the thief of my present and my future. I am old, as I told you. But for a moment I became young enough to lay plans, envision results, dream, and hope. I had all the empty emotions my aged brain had rejected eons ago. I miscalculated. But do not sorrow; you have cured me of my ambitions, my interest in anything but my endless, pointless amusement. I have finally come to terms with myself and my place in Rule. I am neutral."

"You have answered my question before it was asked, Geronfrey," Irissa said. "Surely that is the mark of a great sorcerer. One who should not stand aside impotently when the Realms quiver and dissolve—"

"Ah, my vanity. You would appeal to my vanity. I grant you I have spent some centuries refining it. And what of yours? Your fresh sprig of vanity so vulnerable to an early frost, a sudden snapping of its life-sap—?"

Geronfrey's pleasant visage rippled smoothly away on soft silver undulations. Irissa stared into his empty, blank windows, mystified.

She did not even know when a steady, faint infusion of dark began to appear beneath the light, the waters thinning to a mere pearly skin over some inward heaving of black. It was only when the ghostly image surfaced through the ripples of stone, water—whatever the pillar was—that Irissa recognized the enemy Geronfrey had chosen to send against her.

Herself!

Chapter Thirty-three

On the stalagmite's dark, reflective surface, the figure had a pale translucence that was almost spell-binding. It moved toward Irissa, paper-thin, seeming to peel from one layer of nearness to another. It was as if, by her having stared once into Geronfrey's dark mirror, a skin of Irissa had formed like scum over its surface and plummeted down again with it to the nadir of the Swallowing Cavern.

There it had lain, put away, forgotten, gently wafting on the soundless ripples, drawing near oblivion each time some faceless beast of the pit came to lap greedily at the brackish water. What slimy, scaled back had brushed briefly against the underside of that floating image? What unthinkable cavern spawnings had come perilously close to swallowing it—her—whole?

And that shaving of herself still lived, ready to be called up at Geronfrey's whim to dance, mock-life upon the vanquished white of his windows. He presented it to her now—herself, wearing a gown of ebony velvet still, walking toward her other self, dark strands of hair tentacling her throat, choking, tightening . . .

Irissa was minded to face off this false remnant of herself, minded to make it serve her and turn on Geronfrey. Its eyes were pale in its pale face, silvered, like holes in the mirror, through which she saw more deeply and power-fully than anyone had ever . . .

No! That was the trap of Mauvedona; even Irissa would not, could not, feed upon her own power. She threw up a hand before her face, expecting the heavy velvet sweep of a black sleeve, but it was only modest gray silken stuff. She dropped her arm experimentally. Only a stalagmite was before her, with water veiling its rugged surface, until it seemed to be a shifting, elusive, clear-running mirror.

"You've lost him! Our last amplifier. And it was an army he offered you. I saw it massed in his chamber, the fiercest army in Rule ready to come to our aid," Ludborg bewailed.

Irissa regarded him strangely. "Yes, he had an army. Its general was Illusion, and he has rarely lost a battle. Let us try to win one without him."

She felt finally free, knowing that whatever Ludborg had wanted for her had failed, and therefore her chances of succeeding were correspondingly greater. She turned from the now-empty stalagmite and moved closer to the swirling events in the center of the circled Wrathmen.

The tentacles had vanished. In their place was an out-pouring of the foulest misbirthing of elements in Rule that could be conjured in the most fevered imagination. She saw empress falgons with a dozen heads, many of them half-severed and spouting fountains of indigo blood. Everything that lived appeared to be represented and con-torted into a visible, gory parody of itself. Giant moss-green sea-slugs bore the heads of rabid housecats. Citizens of Rule wore every deformity and disease plainly on their visages and limbs. With them were bearing-beasts, whose flowing manes were braided with ropes of muck and whose sleek configurations seemed to have been bent into a hun-dred unnatural positions.

All these creatures came out of the black pillar, gibber-ing and slavering at the Six Wrathmen. Their rolling eyes glittered as fiercely as stars with a remote, vindictive gleam. And no sooner had a Wrathman's blade severed one bloated limb from a disproportionate trunk than the limb would sprout limbs and a miniature leering face and come nip-ping, ratlike, at the knights' beleaguered heels.

The entities poured from the pillar, heaped pyramidically on the cavern floor by the very rush of their entrance. As an outer ring of Wrathmen struggled to contain the invasion's spreading edges, so one remained at the portal's dark center, driving his great blade into every bit of bone and muscle it could penetrate. Even as he hacked one-handedly at the onslaught, it closed shut behind him and rose at his rear.

The surrounded Wrathman wore unquenched Iridesium; Irissa feared it was Kendric, had he survived the tentacles. But then she saw the blackwood lance the Wrathman dug into the cave floor like a standard he rallied to. Its tip was steel so shiny it sang with a violet highlight. She remembered then a Wrathman she had never met—Fiforn the Lesser of the City That Soars, who carried the lance of his forefathers and had brought it home in Kendric before she had stumbled across the marshman in the Shrinking Forest.

A latest abomination reared over the mound of anomalies clogging the portal. It was a maddened bearing-beast, with hissing snakes for a mane and great carbuncles of wild, sightless eyes. The creature's bloody hooves beat the air and came crashing down like drumsticks. Fiforn stood his ground and raised his barbed lance. Its point drove deep into the bearing-beast's descending chest, all the way to Fiforn's fist midway up the lance shaft. A great gout of blood fountained to the floor and painted the bearing-beast's predecessors crimson. The tide evaporated, taking with it everything that had been there a moment before. It was all gone in the wink of a carbuncled eye. And Fiforn knelt, braced on one knee, his stalwart lance piercing empty air.

"Ahhhhhh." Ludborg's tension sighed away, but the assembled Wrathmen were permitted no such natural release. They merely resumed their stations mechanically, each waiting the next challenge of the pillar alone, though not alone.

But the pillar remained still and black. Nothing seeped from its base or poured through its center. It was motionless, reined, and waiting. Above each of the pointed stalagmite tips, the narrow threads of liquid vibrated and hummed a high, fluted sound, pleasant and distant and demonic. It picked up tempo, until the cavern rattled with the thunder of a Rocklands dry-storm. Sound pounded from wall to wall, rose, fell, shrieked, and howled. It divided itself and rushed off into two precisely opposite ranges that set the teeth grinding in time to its cacophony. Screams came rolling down the noise's mighty concourse, wails and keenings so sharp they cut like invisible whips, sound fashioned into lethal corkscrews to skewer into ears and then run whistling around the empty, echoing brain.

Irissa's hands were at her ears even as she recorded the withdrawing litany of Ludborg's "Oh dear, oh dear, oh dears." His hood sucked inward, as if to stop whatever he carried under it for ears. The circled Wrathmen dropped their weapons and ground their mailed palms against their head mail, eyes squeezed shut against hearing so painful that seeing would only amplify the torment.

It was odd, but seeing all the Six together made Irissa aware that, despite the uncommon size that united them, there were distinguishable differences in each Wrathman. And one who filled out his Iridesium a bit more broadly than the others, whom she instantly identified as Glent of the Stones, stepped into their center. Slowly, as if contesting an insuperable force, Glent pulled first one hand, then the other, from his ears. He drew the longsword that had ridden unsheathed over his back and retrieved his fine-bladed axe from the floor where he had dropped it. The sword he impaled on the ground, an inflexible anchor, while he sent the axe winging and sighing in an intricate arc around his head.

The axe blade was a wonder of design—its outline an angular embroidery of steel. Its spurs of finely honed metal goaded the air and wove through it like harpist's fingers through invisible strings.

The general howling increased, an abiding, immobilizing uproar that stopped all senses but hearing. Irissa drew her sword, her one exposed ear twisted into her shoulder, and still the onslaught of sound attacked. Her blade vibrated slightly, as if wind shook it. She glanced to the unoccupied pillar and thought she saw Geronfrey's empty tower chamber reflected in it yet, with one dark window among the pale, blazing wilderness of light. She let herself slip toward that remembered, silent safety for the merest instant. She still saw the chamber, but all sound had hushed, save for a liquid gurgle as the crimson fluid suddenly swayed in its abandoned vial. She leaned toward the reality of the room, her sword unconsciously thrusting ahead of her like a blind man's cane. She glanced at it finally. The blade tip was a shadow swallowing brighter metal up to the hilt, the hilt with an onyx jewel impressed into it—

She withdrew her will, and Geronfrey's dark mirror slipped off her shoulders, as a heavy velvet gown once had. She came bobbing to the surface, dizzy and gasping, the noise of the cave breaking back into her reality as she felt the last lick of Geronfrey's control at her heels.

In Glent's pale face, his teeth were set, grinding as stubbornly as Geronfrey's masticating tunnel walls. The spinning steel of his axe edge was tearing the enemy sound to tatters; the cacophony rent in narrow shreds of screaming, attenuated sounds, growing shrilly fainter, that played crescendos of chills along every living spine present —and along some present but not living. Even Ludborg twitched in his shapeless robes. But Glent's axe played a destructive tune upon the ragged-edged sound, until it wailed into high-pitched retreat and was sucked, faintly vibrating, up the liquid ladders between the stalagmites and stalactites, finally fading into bat-high cries on the cavern roof.

"Ahhhhh." Ludborg's hood shook, its folds floppier than a hound's ears. "Most fortunate. I confess it gave me a bit of an ache. And most unfortunate. I see you have lost your link to any magical alliance," he added, his unseen face a blank but somehow recriminating force in the silver hood's center.

Irissa merely shook her head, perhaps to scatter the last shreds of sound, thinking that some unexiled remnant still rustled vaguely between her ears. She knew the sixth stalagmite rose solid and stone-frozen from the cave floor behind her—calcified, a window or door to nothing.

"I think you assembled defense enough in your Wrathmen," she told Ludborg. "Perhaps you only required a witness in me."

"There is more to come," Ludborg intoned portentously. "And more to go. You see but a tenth of the battle's dimensions, for the forces without threaten on levels below and beyond the mere five senses. Or even the sixth, Torloc. Had any of these Wrathmen's weapons not stifled the attack, we would have all been overwhelmed and swept into an existence as scattered as the stars. Oh, but my wits tell me, here comes yet another wave!"

As usual when Ludborg predicted great upheaval, there was nothing immediate to be seen, except the sentinel Wrathmen against their partnering stalagmites and the battle-strewn floor with its shapeless scum of the minions of sight, sound, smell, and touch littering it.

"Ludborg, these are monsters of the senses—mere perceptions—that they duel."

"Quite so. That is why mere perceptions of Wrathmen, such as Thrangar and Valodec are now, serve as well as the real thing to make up the necessary number."

"And each is armed with an ancestral weapon that is potent against the sense his particular race embodies—but what sense must Kendric fight? We've seen, heard, scented, and touched more monsters than the mortal mind can birth from the most perverse of imaginary couplings. What is left for Kendric?"

"And Thrangar." Ludborg's robes were sinisterly still. "You overlook that the Torloc champion has yet to step into the circle's center. The black gate does not forget it."

Irissa glanced at the dark navel around which the Wrathmen still gathered, at attention. Her own mind swirled as certainly as that within the featureless column of blackness. There were five senses and Six Realms, though only Five now, as Finorian had insisted from the first . . . And the sixth. But forget the sixth; only four had manifested themselves here. First the smell, then the hideous vision, the tearing sound, the suffocating tentacles of touch gone lethal—

Ludborg seemed to be reading her conjectures as he would a pair of transparent Tolechian dice. "The least. The other Wrathmen were right. Marshlanders always were the least among them, the least among the senses . . ."

"Taste! Ludborg, Kendric's enemy will be taste."

"Yes, taste has always been considered the most dispensable of human senses," Ludborg said dryly. "Especially to a well-fed lot."

"But Kendric is without an inherited weapon, other than his sword. He does not have the Prince's stench-smothering power, nor a singing axe that outkeens the wind, nor anything differentiated to slay a particular foe . . ."

"Other than his wit . . ."

"As he once said."

"You mistake the signs, Lady Irissa," Ludborg said,

rolling comfortingly closer. "He is better armed than any of the others, though his weapon bears no cutting edge. You have seen it—"

"I?"

"You most of all. Do any of the other great swords bear a torch within their hilts, a light of unreason that shines in the most labyrinthine of depths?"

"But Kendric said his sword hilt but throws light upon his shortcomings, his failure to match the races of old."

"All light throws shadow, Torloc; a forest dweller should know that better than most. And nothing can cast a longer, stronger shadow than the proper light well held."

"Riddles, Rengarthian? Riddles will not lead us from this Swallowing Cavern of the senses. You said the pillar never rested. It rises again. Look."

Irissa pointed to the circled stalagmites' vacant center, just as the revolving darkness whirled into blatant motion. She suddenly recognized its composition. It was not an absence of everything, as she had thought, but a total concentration of it. Geronfrey's ebony mirror had been the merest, finest layer of what comprised the pillar, only dark gossamer to web her untried mind. This was the bolt from which his bewitching fabric had been cut, and now it spun, unspiraling yard after yard of the blackest forces within Rule or out of it.

"And have you solved the riddle of the Torlockian challenge? Thrangar may be grateful to his bones for your kind of aid. Because sorcery and not flesh knits his skeleton together does not mean that he cannot suffer dearly." Ludborg's tone had become taunting, almost goading.

It penetrated only the edges of Irissa's consciousness. What, she was thinking, could the minions of taste do against a flesh-and-blood Wrathman with a five-foot-long blade? And even as her mind told her such an adversary would be a mere tang on the tongue to a Wrathman, all of her senses—eyes, ears, skin, nostrils, yes, even taste—exploded around her with a lethal dazzle, whipped into tidal waves of motion.

Floor! She stood on the cave floor and felt it undulate under her in mushy, sinuous waves. Sounds sawed across her mind in an unharmonious parade of squeal, piercing shriek, and throbbing, maddening growl. The pillar parted like a curtain—no, like dark sheets of hair, her hair, drawn aside with a grinning, phosphorescent, green skull there, wearing an Iridesium circlet across its bony white temples.

She reached up to her own, almost forgotten circlet and grasped a ring of fire. Her hand fell away, dripping blood that fell, coldstone-brittle, to the floor and collected, rising to her knees in a sparkling ruby tide. The crimson cold-stones webbed her, climbed her, and dewed her hands, arms, and face. They marched in military rows of four down the far furred, golden back of some undrowned moonweasel. She followed the wreathing form downward and saw it extend far, far into the distance, a furred stalk upon which she was some fragile, snapping blossom . . . She fell, screaming into darkness, straight for the oily waters of the Swallowing Cavern. Down, down, down into the deepest pit. The waters slid over her, greasy and thick. She rose to the surface and looked. It was not water, but earth she lay upon, slick from head to toe from the passage of a huge, rippling slug which even now turned and began coiling toward her.

Ah! Her senses were under bombardment. And she, a Torloc, was sharing in the Torloc Wrathman's ordeal. Far sight was always the core of Torloc powers, projection beyond the physical, beyond the senses. And so they were attacked.

Irissa drew away from the sensation shaking her as a cat belabored its prey. She drew back far enough to find the ringed Wrathmen once more visible before her. They wrestled the physical overflow of the visions being heaped upon Thrangar, those visions so disturbing and strong that any other Torloc near the beleaguered Wrathman would focus upon them as one with him. But if she shared in his confusion, she only amplified it. No, she must resist so he could weld himself to whatever force still lay within her and draw it from her as a sword from a sheath .

She felt the steady, frightening tug of Thrangar's meld-ing even now. "And he is not even alive, Torloc," some enemy in her mind whispered to her. "He is but an ani-mated, ghostly puppet of bone and mail." She shuddered and the pull almost broke. Then some inner portcullis dropped on either side of her mind, and she was a mere tunnel to Thrangar's needs, her mind honed into a staff for him to lean upon. It was a thin, dark line between them; at the end of it, Irissa saw a tiny Thrangar flare to ghostly life, an agile, distant figure going through motions too obscure to be meaningful. He grew in her sight, as if drawn toward her on some steadily pulled rug. Child-high, he was, and his movements held more purpose. She saw him clutch behind his back—but his sword was missing, held still within the power of Geronfrey's spell. Yet he was reaching back as if all the weight in Rule hung from that single arm and tried to keep it immobile. Then Thrangar wrested a long stick from the air behind him. Not a stick—a bow! He fought his arm backward again, and this time it returned bearing an arrow—no peacock-feathered arrow, but one whose shaft bore a crest of white now. He nocked it and drew back the string, which was as taut and glistening as any that linked stalagmite to stalactite.

Thwannnnnggg! The arrow whistled straight for the heart of the invisible emanations. It passed through and pierced the pillar of black. And it did not exit. Another pale lance arched the air and buried itself in the deadly black. And another, until Thrangar's quiver was as empty as the sword sheath that flapped across his back like a vacant wineskin. Then the dark pillar split from top to base to reveal a blinding sheet of light.

"Done! Beautifully done, my Torlocs. Our day is almost finished. Take your gate, lady, as I take mine. These others will remain here . . ."

Irissa watched a samite globe catapult to the chasm of light. She saw Ludborg quiver on the threshold of the split pillar, his silver gown almost lost against it.

She wheeled, knowing the stalagmite behind her now etched an image on its surface. Not tower walls, not sorcerers, but a verdant veil of vegetation shimmered there. And in the foreground stood Finorian. Irissa felt a surge of power and warmth from the sword pommel at her side and turned instantly toward the peak of stone glowing so refreshingly green now. It was her gate, as Finorian had promised even while she faded from the sight of Irissa and Kendric on a Rindell day unthinkably different. Finorian was silent because no words were needed to meld with one's kind, to flow stream-strong together as destined.

Kendric!

Irissa risked a brief glance over the shoulder at Ludborg, who seemed to be revolving slowly in the central shaft of light.

"It is over?"

"Almost. The forces necessary to challenge Torloc powers have cracked both our gates. Take yours while you may. Such gates are hinged on impulses, not on long thought. Mine own wavers shut. Ah, blessed Rengarth again—"

"But what of the last sense?"

"Taste? What weapon has taste to hurl, my dear Torloc? Go in good conscience. You have done well."

Irissa licked her lips and tasted the slight salt sweat of her uncertainty. It was so green and sylvan ahead, so dark behind. And weren't the days of the Wrathmen done, with all to remain immured in Valna? Kendric would find a way out when he was finished. None would accompany him, of course, for all others would stay. Her hand reached for the stone, into the stone. She felt a warm zephyr pat her hand in passing, heard bells nodding acquaintance and leaves gossiping at the treetops. She saw safe, four-square towers hulking over distant pinetops and waves of gray and orange birds beating across the pale mint-green skies. She scented an eternal season of spring. She saw Finorian's calm parchment face with nothing written upon it but peace.

Irissa darted her eyes backward again to the edge of Ludborg, still vibrating there, now clearly off the ground, or what passed for it. "What of Kendric?"

"Take your gate—quickly! It closes."

"Not until you prophesy of Kendric." She had wrenched her head over her shoulder to face him, to force him to give clear reassurance that all would be well, and then she could step into the stone and—

She felt the withdrawing pressure on her fingers, as if a warm hand grasped them, closed tighter, and slid away, leaving a narrow, empty channel behind.

"Gone!" Ludborg shouted. "You have lost your gate! But I told you your Wrathman would be well armed!"

Irissa didn't turn back to stare into the stalagmite; stone made a very limited mirror. She watched instead as Ludborg whirled into a chubby orb of spinning silver samite, blazed suddenly, and disappeared behind the falling curtains of the midnight pillar.

The cave was dark. Somehow, Ludborg's blue-worms had extinguished with him. The black pillar was intact again, one unseamed bar of menace whole and wholly threatening again. The place was oddly bereft now of Ludborg's pseudo-comic presence and the living drapery of his extinguished blue-worms.

One faint light did glow from the Iridesium that garbed the silent Wrathmen; Irissa traced it finally to one of their number, to a hilt between folded fingers.

Kendric would be the next, the last, to do battle; Ludborg had confirmed that much. There was no need to speculate upon whose weapon the attack would fall heaviest now, no necessity to guess the identity of the next figure to step into the circle's center in contention with the black pillar's spewings.

Irissa's mind remained a seesaw balanced across a bulwark of speculation. Taste was perhaps the least, yet the most human, of the senses, a luxury among senses, more geared to satisfaction than to raw survival, one would think. What could taste send forth as an advance guard? Wormwood? Gall? The cloying grimace of the oversweet? The rancid? The sour? Of course, the pillar attacked through physical evocations of the senses, exaggerations! Distortions . . .

She had forgotten that taste was the one sense that could turn back upon itself as lithely as a moonweasel, the only sense through which a fatal administration could cloy the entire body. Poison! Poison made physical—that was what the pillar would draw from its darkest recesses for Kendric. She shivered then, almost feeling some icy meandering down her veins, almost sure that she knew what the crimson fluid was that painted the sides of Geronfrey's vial.

Chapter Thirty-four

———◆◆———

Irissa bent all of her purely human senses on the quiescent black pillar. It was again a column of inactivity, but that did not reassure her. Dark clouds and quiet always came before the storm, even a dry-storm. Despite the cavern's new dimness and the shadows natural to a cave, Irissa suddenly became aware of a heart-stopping difference in the scene. It wasn't only the absence of Ludborg's conjured lights and illumination of garb, it was . . .

It was the Wrathmen. The Five who had been called by Kendric's leap of faith were—altered. Somehow, they had all ebbed into the stones behind them. Each had hardened in some senseless way, becoming engraved upon the stalagmite looming at his rear. Each, his sword held formally before him, had become a bas-relief of a knight upon his tomb. They were—gone. Only Kendric remained of the Six of Swords—the merely human *One* who had been least and now was the last. If that one human could not halt whatever might crawl, ooze, or undulate through what was left of the gate, then there was little point to the survival of anything human in Rule.

The pillar vibrated faintly, a self-satisfied, hissing hum that dropped to a lower, growling pitch. It spun again, its motion more difficult to discern in the dim atmosphere. It rotated clumsily now, as if its hinges were screeching almost shut and had no need of oiled caution.

The gate let loose its last monster of the senses. It was as thin as a serpent's tongue and vividly green. It *was* a tongue, a long, forked tendril, slithering through the last crack, a somehow tentative thing, made of subtlety and sly deference. It was a courtier among monsters, ready to make a fine knee, even as it entwined for the kill.

The last Wrathman raised his heavy sword and brought it roughly down upon the encroaching, sinuous member. It hacked across the green tendril that was now as thick as the Wrathman's blue-clad arm—Ludborg's phantom Iridesium had vanished with the Rengarthian; it hacked the thing fairly in two, exposing an emerald-dark core which bled black ichor on the cave floor.

Well done, Kendric, Irissa thought, as frozen in her watching as the stony, encircling Wrathmen buried in their stone sepulchers. Well done.

And then the beast of the pillar, the ignoble bearer of the most humble of the senses, stuck its whole, long, scaled snout out the pillar door to see who had stung its tongue. Its face, if one could call the Wrathman-high visage of mottled green mold and scabrous scales that loomed there a face, was drawn upward into a grimace of rage. It was a true monster, a flesh-and-ooze kind of thing of pure malice. It sparkled, it hissed, and it bit at the dull cavern air with scintillating teeth. It caught the incorporeal and worried it like a moonweasel, then cast away air and lunged for the man. It shone, bright and glossy, its coat dewed in cabochons of green. It was somehow as translucent as a bottle, with something shifting and lethal within it.

Kendric's sword crashed down upon the quivering neck and chipped the hard, gemmed surface. Sparks flew off, dazzling emerald. One spun across his foot and he leaped back, stung, the fine dark leather of his boot eaten away to the glimmer of undefended flesh.

Kendric moved again, farther away, as far as the circling stone teeth permitted him. At least Kendric moved. Irissa did not. She watched the thing that was more physical, perhaps, than any of the pillar's previous sendings—and more fascinating. It was a monster of myth, this glittering, encrusted creature. Would some fragment survive, some tale passed on to marshfolk by marshwives regaling children at their knees as the women wove bramble mats? They would not prattle of moonweasels—moonweasels were drowned now, with most of Rule—but of Kendric. Or would it be Cedric, the name even distorted with time and distance? Of Cedric and his battle with the Scale-demon that hissed green fire? Of how the Scale-demon won and left

only a few broken fragments of blade upon the cavern
floor; and of how the hero escaped into the high, snowy
halls of Falgontooth, where he walks to this day, leaving
hot, hissing footsteps in the ice as his only trace? And whenever the wind sighed through a highlands crevasse, would
it be the hero Cedric pining for his lost sword, his lost
battle? Would they tell of how Clymarind had once sped
nomad on the waves—or would they call it something other
than Clymarind? It was a long word to remember rightly.
They would talk of wizards, of sorceresses in crimson
castles, and of a simple, strangely gifted folk—Torlocs,
Worlocs, or some such like—who could build stone on
stone from their imaginings, and some, belike, cry coldstone tears. No, perhaps there would be no coldstones
then.

Irissa watched the creature's glimmering bulk emerge
from the pillar and coil its sinuous limbs around the inner
circle of stalagmites, driving Kendric and his puny sword
out into the cave's vaster darkness. This beast acted as if
it owned the center; it acted as if the entombed Wrathmen,
still visible in their slowly hardening stalagmite capsules,
were its honor guard.

She was not meant to see this, she who had seen so
far on occasion—into eyes and even into the very "I" of
herself. She was supposed to be safe in Finorian's green
land by now. This was Kendric's battleground and no
other's. Had anything gone aright, he would have been
here alone with no witness to record that final, fearful
thing that had gone agley. No, she had been wrong; there
would be no surviving marshlands to memorialize his duty
or his death. All would be gone, swallowed whole by the
borgia-monster.

Yet she *was* here, the last Torloc, with the remnants
of her powers and with her wits, at least. And Kendric
still had his, for he had circled around the creature and
darted between the stalagmites to strike it deep upon the
coiling flank. Now a cloud of hissing, acid steam cast an
eerie green light upon the cavern, upon a grim-faced
Kendric, and upon a motionless Torloc standing in the
shadows, her hand on a polished stone hilt of her own
manufacture.

Then Irissa whirled and stared into the opaque limestone

of the pillar that had promised her exit and which she had rebuffed once already that day—or was it night?

"Geronfrey!" She spoke his name, a call that had not been necessary before, and nothing happened, save the hiss behind her of Kendric's futile forays against the armored poison that confronted him.

"Geronfrey, I call you. By your name I command you, if merely to hear me out."

The stone cracked a bit, as if held solid by some terrible force from within.

"Geronfrey." She shut her eyes and imagined the ghost-pale reflection she had glimpsed once in his dark mirror. It was hard to conjure that shining, sightless surface. Her mind continually wanted to glance off to her own image in it, but she held to the misty, gray outlines of the sorcerer until she opened her eyes and saw him, clear and aloof, before her in the towering stone. Both of his long, fine hands were trellised around his blood-red vial, which he cosseted like an oversized goblet containing some rare vintage. He looked finally to her eyes over the brim of his concoction.

"You would not be seeing me now," he told her, "save that you were astute enough to conjure some vague sliver with your vision-made-concrete. Careless of me to have mooned in my own dark mirror like some overcome swain. But I have been careless of late. And now it seems, dear Torloc, that you have joined me in that lapse. Why linger you here? Has not Finorian's gate long since swept wide for you—"

"And shut again," Irissa interrupted quite coldly.

"Shut? Yes, we all have a propensity to gaze upon gates closed to us."

Geronfrey's blue eyes dipped momentarily to the scarlet brew shifting between his hands. "Do not tell me, my marooned sorceress, that any loyalty to yon blade-man even now dulling his steel upon some conjured atrocity behind you is the reason for your tardiness in slipping through gates? Surely such a dull fellow was merely a means to one of your astuteness. Leave me at least some of my illusions."

"Even a means to an end must be well treated if it is to serve, Geronfrey. That is only astuteness. I would not leave Rule and one to whom I owe—gratitude—so sorely beleaguered. If you would help him—"

"You cannot leave Rule, Torloc. That is the only truth that swings upon your gate. You are bottled here, like my rosy potion. And here you will stay until I decide how you can serve me." He capped his pliant fingers over the vial's narrow neck like a stopper, and shook the ruby fluid until it foamed.

"It is a borgia-monster he fights. It is all the poison that lingers within the folk of Rule, all that waits lapping at our boundaries without, made incarnate. Verthane is a wraith and Mauvedona a mere veil of violet. Yet you remain stone-solid, Geronfrey. You will survive this, but only if something of Rule survives—and only he can—"

"He can do nothing! As I would do nothing to save a dust mote of this weary world. Yes, I survive and shall sleep below Falgontooth as long as anything remains of that mountain on or below the water, over or under the snows, in or of the air. And with the certainty of that behind me, I tell you there is nothing that I can—or will—do to strike so much as a sliver off what you have so rightly named a borgia-monster. I will not aid you. And the pleasure of telling you so, of seeing your face cave inward into darkness, as it did in my night-colored mirror, is the only thing that brought me back this one last time."

"Luckily, Geronfrey, that was sufficient." Her tone had changed. Though the clangor had risen behind her, though even Geronfrey's eyes winced from time to time with the view of the battle continuing behind Irissa's back, she stood indifferent to it. All her attention, the focus of her bland silver eyes, was pooled on the sorcerer with the bloody vial in his hands and his ice-blue eyes warming themselves over that liquid fire.

"You have eluded me—again?" He did not believe his own charge yet; he could not.

"Yes. And once again, you have confirmed that which I only guessed. Once again, Geronfrey, I have conversed with a master sorcerer, and now I have my means—"

He stood, the curves of his robes caught halfway through the motion, so that he seemed a carving of a man, half-crouched in stone. His long hands tightened convulsively on the neck of his vial. "You have guessed—" His arms raised as he dashed the glass container to the stones of his tower floor, the fluid arching into a crimson rainbow that scattered into splintered red drops. "No!"

He glanced triumphantly back to Irissa, with her dark hair breaking away from a face gone gray with concentration, her hands folded prayerfully at her gray breast—folded, surely, not grasped around an empty glass vial of precisely the shape and size as the one shattered at his feet? The outline of the container wavered against her body and grew firm. Horrified, Geronfrey looked to the floor and saw his as yet unfallen liquid siphoned up into the air, drawing itself into a thin and flowing vein of red that breached the stalagmite between them and poured accurately into the vessel she had created, as if being dispersed from some friendly wineskin.

"My antidote!" Geronfrey wailed, thrusting out his hands, heedless of whatever barrier reared between them. They broke through solid stone, those hands of his—reaching, clutching, clawing—almost to the wrists. Irissa, still willing the red fluid into her vial, marked them only with the outmost vision of her eyes. Skeleton hands, they were, the price even a wizard of Geronfrey's powers had to pay for crossing gulfs of mere inches and of great magic. Irissa watched the last of the potion levitate from the stones at Geronfrey's feet and curve into her vial, leaving only shattered glass to sparkle coldstone-bright. The liquid rose almost to the vessel's very brim between her hands.

She finally looked again to Geronfrey. He was drawing his hands back from her, through the stone; they were worn to bone encased in skin like cracked parchment. They were two thousand years old. It was only then Irissa realized that while she had used the stalagmite to see into Geronfrey's chamber, he must have conjured the dark mirror from the Swallowing Cavern to give himself reciprocal sight. He had seen her darker mirror-self always, and thus read her motives as if through a murk. Forgetting himself, he had thrust his hands wrist-deep into that oily surface, exactly as he had once prevented her from doing. Magic's greatest risks were always its greatest wonders.

He stared only at his unensorcelled hands, twisted and weakened as if natural time had finally wrung its due from them. Geronfrey thrust them finally into the wide sleeves of his robe. His face was still dignified above his yet golden beard. His eyes were older than Mauvedona's.

"I thank you for your antidote, Geronfrey, though it was unwillingly given. Now perhaps you know how it stings to be forced." Irissa turned carefully toward the cavern, so as not to spill the vial's contents. She paused. "Your hands. Perhaps . . . My Torloc powers are arbitrary, but I believe they are the only ones that could restore you. What I have seen, I can make or remake—"

"No," Geronfrey said with infinite coldness, deliberately moving his hands deeper within his cloaking sleeves. "You probably speak the truth. But—no."

He blinked away, leaving nothing but the adamant limestone surface behind him. He vanished utterly. Irissa was suddenly aware that her flesh had warmed the red liquid to the heat of blood, and that she held the glass neck so tightly it seemed to throb in her hands. She turned, ready to face the borgia-monster, and found that its piled coils had risen wall-like behind her. It was this fact which had flickered in Geronfrey's eyes even as he forbore to warn her of it.

Irissa stepped forward, planning to circle around the creature's back to Kendric and the front line of battle. Her precious liquid sloshed within her hands and overflowed, running through the cracks of her clenched fingers and onto her knuckles. It was warm and thick, like honey heated over Dame Agneda's wheat-cakes at Rindell. Rindell. The word somehow made her look up, perhaps in search of an evaporating fortress tower. She saw instead the beast's twitching tail rearing above her, its stinger as sharp and as triangular as one of Mauvedona's fanged castle fenestrations. The stinger was borne up and over the monster's back and weaved above like a lethal standard. It descended toward her, heavy as a mace, growing larger as it neared. Her arm spasmed; a splash of red lashed toward it. Antidote or false hope? The liquid dewed the descending hard, green glitter—dewed and ate it into a dozen scattering shards. The central plate fell, dull and black, beside Irissa and leaked a trail of bilious green. Irissa leaped over the widening pool, her eyes measuring the level of antidote in her vial even as she landed. Splash! More precious liquid gone, scattered worthlessly on rock. Somehow, with Geronfrey withdrawn, Irissa doubted her recalcitrant powers could be goaded to brew a new batch. It was Geronfrey's magic she bore, and an unwilling servant to her, constrained to new service in the vial of her mind's making only because it was a gift, meant to serve a need other than her own. That was perhaps the most powerful magic of all and something Geronfrey would never learn, if he and his withered hands lived yet another millennium or two.

But where was Kendric? Impatient, Irissa threaded the vacant stalagmites and the monster's writhing coils, which promised greater contention ahead. The head—that was where she should deliver her vintage potion. All the rest of the red vial must go straight to the center of the poison that seemed to be swelling, larger and larger, enveloping the cavern, until it was almost caught among the place's serpentine tunnels. She heard metal ring off rock and rounded a last dagger of stone to find Kendric wielding his blade two-handed. Bits and pieces of the thing lay scattered around him like summer leaves, early fallen. There lay a toe, perhaps two feet long, ending in a long, curved nail like a Clymarindian scimitar. So the creature had feet? Irissa studied its long, coiling belly and spied many such appendages, each foot ending in a strong curve of claw, dyed emerald through the center by a poisonous vein of what passed for its blood. Some of those feet were upon the monster's forward portion, even now rearing above Kendric. Those myriad claws wriggled yearningly toward their single-barbed enemy.

She couldn't wait until the prudent moment when she faced the monster's fanged snout and could fling her potion directly at its throat. She sent it in a vindictive arc straight at the face from where she stood, the sweep of her arm as forceful as Mauvedona's throw with her spelling skirt. The vial broke on the monster's cliff-high spine and neck, cascading into paltry drops to burn a thousand red-hot sparks into its glittering green length. The creature's writhing paused, then burst forth renewed, its hide shrinking away from the dancing red droplets until the entire thing seemed to dwindle. Kendric's sword remained raised, his brows frowning and his mouth half-open, as if surprised in a yawn. The creature curled into itself, withdrew, even pulsed with a more venomous green brilliance. It was then Irissa felt the chill at her side.

A line of cold, ice-dagger-sharp, pressed along her hip. For an instant she feared she had leaned too near the window to Geronfrey. She had almost let her sword pierce through, before drawing it back. The sword! She glanced down. The emerald touchstone on its pommel was glowing green, but not as it had glowed when it served as a torch in the Swallowing Cavern. This was a drained, unhealthy green that infected even the blade, a green built on bile, with clear yellow as lethal as venom underlying it. She moved to touch the weapon and found her palm hovering over the pommel but an inch away, chilled as if by all the snow on Falgontooth. Even as she watched, a thin snake of crimson wavered across the cavern floor and stuck out a tremulous red tongue to touch tips with her sword. She shuddered. Her sword, forged from the danger of Verthane's web in his star chamber, paused a moment, then slowly, steadily, drank the thread of crimson into itself. A darker, brown shade appeared in the blade's green center and was absorbed upward to the hilt. Beyond her, just as she had drawn the antidote away from Geronfrey's grasp, the crimson gathered itself together into a mass again and drew in a halfhearted trickle toward her feet. Irissa was stunned to see what she had done so arduously being undone. She stood shocked, her hand still hesitating above her sword's haft, not daring to touch it, not daring to let that poison seep into her fingers and up her arm to her shoulder, a treacherous infusion. Why? The sword was hers. The antidote was hers. Why should they turn on her? Unless her sword had been tainted by its momentary immersion in Geronfrey's dark mirror. His hands had crossed the barrier for only an instant, and had undone centuries of instants. Green had always been the badge of Torloc powers, yet it was also the color of the deadly borgia. Was poison perhaps as much a power as any of Finorian's? Or was power a kind of poison?

She shook her head and let the vial in her hand drop. It did not break, but melted from the air as her thoughts abandoned it. Magic came from the same well, always. She drank from a different side, but she shared the same cup with Mauvedona. They all drew from the same source—Verthane, Geronfrey, herself, even Finorian. It was only how they used their powers that made them different. And here in Valna—which was a great Oracle indeed, and being great, took no sides—here, power called to power, beyond the mere uses of it. Her talisman was linked more with the destructive nature of the borgia-monster than it was with her. She had made it, and it would not serve her. No magic would serve her here, in the presence of its own kind of raw, devouring force—

Her fingers twitched. Already her hand was turning white. If she dared grasp the sword despite her instincts, perhaps . . .

"No."

Her mind had been so busy inwardly that she was surprised to hear a spoken word. She almost looked to the borgia-monster for its source.

"Irissa." Kendric had come closer, drawn by the phenomenon that engrossed her. Near them, the borgia-monster shut its bilious eyes and waited for the antidote to its power to be drawn from it. It almost purred. "Irissa. Don't look at the creature. Don't touch the pommel."

"It hangs on me!" she couldn't help rasping. "When it has drunk its fill, it will overflow into me! It is mine. I made it, and it will come back to me." Even now the sword blade was filling with fresh green at its tip, the color rising inexorably through the metal. "I must try the pommel while something of mine still clings to it. If I wait—"

"But wait," Kendric ordered, approaching cautiously. He glanced over his shoulder to the borgia-monster, which was steadily diminishing into a vivid green pool, lying on its heaving side in semicontent.

"You grasped hold of your sword hilt once, against my advice, and no harm came of it," she argued, desperate for agreement.

Kendric's stern face relaxed momentarily. "I did not forge my own sword, so it has less reason to turn on me," he said almost humorously. "Besides, I see now that my own glowing hilt is a healthy phenomenon, whereas yours is sorcerous, slippery, double-edged, and elusive." He let his hand drop below the crossbar of his weapon, and she saw that its hilt was alight once again, with a pure, white radiance.

"It does not feel hot?" She had to wonder even at this moment of extremity.

"Oh, sometimes it waxes exceedingly hot, as it did the night we almost burned down the innkeeper's stables beyond Rindell."

"We?"

"Aye, we," he said, grinning, his eyes never leaving the sword at her side.

"You seem of a sudden merry," she said suspiciously, but her voice broke on the last word.

He risked a quick glance at her. "Observe yonder beast. I will watch your sword, never fear."

She looked over as he instructed and saw only a flat pool of fetid scum, twinkling moss-colored in the glow of Kendric's hilt. She begrudged him that clean, searing glow momentarily, while she was anchored to the venomous green twinkle of a sword that had turned on her. She glanced to the thorn of steel at her side. It had drunk deep of the borgia-monster. A dark rust, the result of the conjured red and green, suffused its upper third almost to the still-lambent emerald pommel. Although she knew more than most that magic had no volume, she couldn't believe that her sword was not about to burst and spill its deadly pus across every inch of her. Her throat tightened.

"Irissa." Kendric's voice was very low, very cautious. "Look at me."

She did, through a veil of the quite human tears she had shed since coming to his bed. The veil thickened to a sheet, and she had enough pride left in the center of her peril to color a bit at the odd fact that she regretted certain events that would never take place again for her in Rule more than any missed gate to somewhere else.

Kendric was slowly raising his sword. What—to scabbard it, since she was beyond the help of any sword, unless it grant a swift death? Or was that it—the Wrathman of the Marshes performing his last duty before returning to his mud-soaked lot, as Ludborg had predicted? She straightened her shoulders.

Kendric smiled. He smiled down at her, with the great sword that he hated slowly levitating above his shoulders. "You missed your gate," he said.

"You saw?"

"I was still half-spelled. But I knew. My sword knew."

"Your sword, your accursed sword!"

"Never mind your gate," Kendric said. "I shall split open another for you."

She stared into his face and at his upraised arms looming over it at as sharp an angle as Falgontooth's slopes. She glanced to the poison bloating the sword at her side. She looked at him again, aghast, only beginning to guess what he intended.

"Through the hinges, Torloc. Straight through the hinges. Few gates can hold shut after that."

"Kendric, you can't."

"But I can. I have discovered my specific weapon, and nothing can gainsay it."

"Your weapon?"

"I never had Valodec's magical gauntlet, save in my saddlebags, where it does me no good. I had no lance, no ancestral powder, and no singing axe. I had only what I had all along, and they shall suffice—my sword and my wit."

His arms drew back slightly.

"Kendric, I see what you mean to do—sever me from my bewitched sword with a single blow. But it hangs by a thin green satin cord you can hardly see in this light; it hangs by my side like a Siamese twin. You will cut me in twain if you strike."

"Once, in a line as straight as Thrangar's arrow. And then we are free of it."

"Kendric, your sword is a monster of iron; its edge alone is too thick. You will have off my arm and half my side . . ."

"I let you sew my skin together with your eyes before I had known you for half a day. I am a swordsman by trade. Do you not trust me to cleave as true to my calling as you to yours?"

"No one could do it. Why should you try it? Oh, I may live from such a blow, but would I want to?"

His hands tightened on the hilt for answer; she could see that in the glow that leaked through his fingers. "Put your arm aside," he said through his teeth.

In her agony of doubt, she did, and met his eyes full on with no thought of diving beyond the surface by any Torlockian skill. She didn't need any deep reading now. His eyes were pure, burning certainty, like the hilt that gave no heat between his fingers, like the morning that always rose over the shoulder of some hill or other, and like love, whose face was as bright and cool as the moon's or as hot as the heart of its bearer.

"Is that what your magic is, Kendric? So simple? The

only magic that will survive?" She shut her eyes. "Then strike now."

She was wafting away on her insight, standing on some fragile web in some dim place with no up, down, floor, or ceiling. She was faced with whole constellations of adversary eyes. They all shone silver and glimmered back at her. Her lips curved in a smile, and the sword cleft the vague air around her with a sharp, certain hiss. She felt it pass her face, and her face serenely peeled away from its passing, her hair riffling past her cheek like furred smoke. It stroked the fabric of her upper arm, a glancing kiss of a passage; she felt it suck by her waist, missing by a great distance, and then down past the dangerous, out-thrust ledge of her hip, there no matter how she willed it away. She felt a ricocheting graze and then a tug. The great, thick blade netted in the satin sling of her belt; it pulled down on its honed edge, rebounded for the mere distance of a hairsbreadth, then drove down again. The dark green satin frayed, twisted, and snapped. The blade rippled past the gray silk around her leg, past the tougher barrier of her boot, and down to the earth; there, precisely parallel to the very edge of her foot, it struck ground, rebounding up, calf-high. She felt its passage; then it plunged earthward again to exactly where it had fallen the first time, held firm finally, harmlessly, in damp, dull earth.

Someone had her by the arm and was pulling her away. She opened her eyes, through which somehow those hot, human tears had managed to squeeze out. Her sword lay like a bloated green stinger on the cave floor, trailing severed tails of green satin cord. Kendric had pulled her back from it with him. His sword point was lowered now, and she measured the length of it and its width and was glad she had not seen it skimming her body edgewise, with any wobble liable to drive it sideways into her. Kendric's brow was dewed with sweat. She caught one drop on her fingertip and tasted it. It was salt, like tears. He shook his head at her and nudged her back down the passage as officiously as Ludborg. Behind them, the harp strings of water that bridged the stalactites and stalagmites whined the keening of the lost.

Chapter Thirty-five

At the very lips of the cave mouth they found Felabba, facing outward, her insufficient tail wrapped as efficiently as possible around her forelegs.

"Back at last, marshman?" the cat inquired calmly without turning.

"Aye. I was lonely for the sound of a human voice," he rejoined, thrusting his sword back into its scabbard. The hilt shed just enough remaining light for Irissa to catch his wink at her.

"I see you shall be as amusing as my former companion. Ah, well, I assure you our alliance is very temporary."

"Temporary, perhaps. But not as former as you might wish, Felabba," Irissa couldn't resist interjecting, coming around to show herself to the cat.

For once the unruffable feline displayed discomposure. Her bony back arched suddenly like a footbridge; her green eyes narrowed and her ears flattened. Felabba growled softly. "Finorian take me, but this is pretty. Not gone? When we all have taken this great trouble to see you gone? And why not, perchance? I cannot believe you lacked for opportunity."

"Oh, some door opened to my knock—or to opportunity's. But it was a hard, unforgiving portal. And I could not abandon you, Felabba, for I know how dependent you have grown upon the likes of Verthane's buffets, or even Kendric's crusts."

"I? Dependent? Hmmmm. Very likely, very likely. I'm not as young as I used to be. And now I suppose it's up to my old nose to sniff out yet another gate, and no easy

257

chore that will be. For you cannot stay. No Torlocs will prosper here."

"Another gate? Is there no end to escape? Perhaps I will forget gates."

"No," the cat said, almost hissing. "You cannot stay."

"Cannot?" Irissa's hand went to her side and clenched at empty air.

"Cannot," the cat replied, her tail lashing the rough stones. "You see, even now you reached for the proof. You grasp at your tainted blade that has dipped in Geronfrey's dark mirror in one moment of forgetfulness, else it would never have required being cut from you like a gangrenous limb."

"How did—?"

"The question is not how did I know what transpired within, but rather, how could you have not known? It would have been best to have taken yourself through the gate to Finorian. By remaining behind, you remained a conduit to forces more ill-intentioned than a moonweasel. Oh, why did you not go? You cannot claim lack of opportunity."

"No," Irissa began. "Only—"

"We'll have time enough to parse our actions later," Kendric interrupted, prodding Felabba impolitely on the flank with his scabbard tip. He caught up Irissa's elbow equally inelegantly. "Valna's teeth are grinding as angrily as Geronfrey's. We'd best escape the cave before it crushes us."

Neither Torlocs nor cats tolerated unsettled arguments. Felabba and Irissa exchanged one significant glare, then joined Kendric in scampering the short way out of the cave, inarguably in retreat from the new silence of a darkness once populated only with echoes.

It was as if they had been caught in the great, gauzy, black wings of a gigantic moth. They felt faint ripples of movement even as they ran, all unaccompanied by any sound. Between the instant one foot struck solid ground and the second foot did, it seemed as if everything might have surreptitiously shifted an enormous distance, so that their own sense of time and space was kept deceptively consistent while all around them chasms of discrepancy were opening up and closing in rhythmic, voiceless waves.

A sudden reek of rubyheart blossoms struck their faces.

Their heads reared back, even that of the white cat, and their eyes batted automatically shut for an instant. They opened them to bright daylight and to a hot sun distilling endless scent from the crushed petals at their feet and painting the emerald leaves pale out of sheer brightness. Yet those leaves rustled, as if shaken by some vestige of the cavern's screaming wind, forced to shiver in a fluttering natural hiss worse in its way than any long-drawn-out sibilancy from a borgia-monster or a moonweasel or even an angry sorceress . . .

"The island moves?" Irissa demanded.

Kendric's eyes were cast up to the cloudless and relentlessly aquamarine sky. He looked puzzled, an expression he kept even as he carefully settled his sword across his back.

"And that rustle, Kendric, that hiss of a hundred thousand leaves. I thought I loved forests, but there's something so steady, so . . . so huge about it—" Irissa put her hands to her ears, as she had done with greater effect inside the cave. Now she seemed only to trap the sound inside her head, where it washed back and forth like an angry red tide in a bottle.

Kendric spun on his heel, slickly pivoting on the fallen purple blossoms; he hardly noticed. He made a tight, reined circle, finally pausing as delicately as Willowisp and tossing his dark hair abruptly.

"Moving, yes! But not forward. Curse the Rengarthian! He meant you to leave by your vacant pillar, and me to become immured in it after all. Our only hope is the falgon!" Kendric had caught Irissa's wrist and was dragging her after him as he ranged in wide and wider circles, always looking up to the vacant and blazing sky. "No clouds. If there'd been clouds, we should have seen it instantly."

"Seen what, Kendric? It's not the sky that mystifies us. What's puzzling is the sound, that irritating hiss, like some gigantic nurse trying to hush us to sleep."

For answer, Kendric pulled her up the incline arching over the cave mouth, so that they finally stood Wrathman-high above the nodding and hissing rubyheart bushes. "There is your hushing, and perhaps the most natural phenomenon we have felt today—pure nature at the boil. And we are in the pot's center, waiting for the bubbles to reach us."

Irissa looked to where he pointed, then made a quarter turn and stared ahead again, repeating the movement until she had arrived at the first vista once more. It did not matter how she turned herself. What she saw was the same —always, ever, the same. A rippling ring of blue water was drawing slacker and then tighter on Clymarind's golden sands and green hills, water pursing its strong, foaming lips slowly at the land, consuming it with the certain, leisurely savoring of a Rocklander sucking the finest juices from a rare Abyssal island pear. Now it was the Abyssal itself in search of rare and tasty fruit—one golden, fallen island to preserve forever in its whispering, salty brine.

"We're moving, all right," Kendric said grimly. "Down!"

Around them was nothing but water, calm for an ocean but always heaving gently, always edging nearer. The stream where the empress falgon had rested was gone; there, a patch of something dark was drifting by, perhaps the floating remnants of their previous night's campfire. Did bones float? Irissa wondered, and turned to ask Kendric.

"If you do not mind forsaking the view," a haughty tone came from somewhere behind them, "I have made myself ready for our departure."

Felabba's certainty brought them both around, their breath taken in with mutual annoyance and let out with relief. They rushed down the slope through the heavy-scented outgrowths to the cat, who sat on the sillac-hide upholstery of Ludborg the Fanciful's splendid but abandoned chariot.

"Felabba, will the creature fly for you?"

The cat gave Irissa the look it reserved for the most elementarily stupid question and minced delicately along the chariot lip to pause above the drooping reins. Her lean form arched suddenly forward, landing atop the bearing-beast's inky flanks. The creature's intelligent, dark head loomed over its withers, and its crystal eyes glittered, momentarily reminding Irissa of her lost facility in crying valuable tears.

"Bearing-beasts are native to Clymarind," the cat began magisterially. "At least native to Clymarind before this land became nomad, or indeed, even an island. The land bridge broke—eons ago—while the stones of your fading Rindell bridge were merely dust motes. Even I was but half

a whisker wide at the time, being a mere kitten. The land
bridge broke, I say, and bearing-beasts, being a good deal
brighter than they look, were wise enough to stay on the
stable side of the issue. That, of course, was Rule, until
recently. That silly Rengarthian rover was right; all bearing-beasts hail from Clymarind, and hence are adept at
finding gates. So the Rengarthian counted on his beast to
bring him hither. As long as any kind of gate remains in
Rule—no matter how miserly—a bearing-beast can lead
us to it.

"And as long as an unauthorized Torloc lingers in Rule,"
the cat added, casting an unforgiving look over her sharp
shoulder, "some means to see that Torloc well gone must
remain. Oh, Finorian take it!" The creature snorted, sav-
agely tonguing its paw and making impatient swipes at its
coarse white whiskers. "Take it into whatever world the
rest of the Torlocs have found and leave this one to
such dull folk as the marshlanders, and me."

Kendric laughed. "Another gate! For once I trust this
disreputable-looking feline. And if a cat can ride the
spiny ridge of a bearing-beast, I imagine I can trust to
even an alien's rather showy equipage. Lady Irissa, you'll
find this vehicle a bit more secure than our last."

He ushered Irissa into the seat, bounding up beside her.
Kendric gathered the snakeskin reins into his hands; immediately they tautened. The dark bearing-beast walked forward, hooves grinding rubyhearts beneath it and the clumsy,
folded contrivances at its sides rustling open.

Felabba bounded prudently into the chariot with them,
managing to pucker Irissa's gray silk with her claws at the
instant of arrival. Irissa smoothed the fabric while her
forehead snagged to match it; then she laughed and
shrugged. Kendric reached out to deposit Felabba on the
floor, but the agile cat climbed instead to his shoulder,
from where she continued grooming her always ruffled
coat, occasionally catching Kendric's ear in the pass of her
thistly tongue.

He shrugged and grinned at Irissa. She smiled back and
thought her heart lifted—or at the very least the earth
seemed to. They glanced forward and saw the black bearing-beast taking long, loose strides right out over the hissing
water. Its wings were unfurling to unbelievable lengths,
then fanning in strong muscular swoops that made rain-

bows of iridescence from the azure, green, and gold highlights of its glossy, ebony feathers.

"We'll drown," Irissa concluded grimly, leaning over the chariot side nevertheless to watch the dancing waves seethe but a few feet below.

"Only if you fall in," Kendric retorted, hauling her back by winding a hank of her hair around a fist and tugging insistently. Irissa sat securely in the seat beside him, but he did not untangle his leash upon her. She tossed back her side braids and shook the rest of her hair until it whipped as gracefully into the wind as the streaming mane and tail of the flying bearing-beast ahead of them. One thick lock remained anchored around Kendric's hand. He finally unwound it; the lock sprang back to its owner, its end lying snake-coiled, his gesture still bent into it. Irissa brushed this last lock over her shoulder, so that her face was free to the wind, and stared ahead toward the endless horizon of blue.

"You are not afraid?" she asked.

"No." Kendric crossed his arms and stretched his legs as best he could in the cramped vehicle. "I am growing accustomed to magic—or at least to the kind that produces no more than what we marshmen might call monsters. Why should not a bearing-beast sprout wings and take us off to dance among the clouds, were there any? If it suits a wandering Rengarthian with most likely a pumpkin for a head, why should it not accommodate a knight with a sword for a crutch?"

But Irissa was uneasy, and found it hard to lounge against the smooth orange sillac hide. She wanted to fidget, but didn't want to test the length of Kendric's pull on her.

"This is worse than the falgon," she said abruptly.

"Worse? I still remember Felabba's almost-slip. Don't you recall how that unbridled creature soared and wheeled, how little control we had of her? This is a nice, pretty pacer that knows its business."

"That's just it. The beast climbs the sky in neat increments, as if it rode the road of logic. The phenomenon is too mannered. It smacks of . . . science."

"You must leave Rule—or whatever we shall call it hence. For once I concur with Felabba," Kendric said, laughing and tossing the cat on his shoulder a wink. "You have learned to mislike magic."

She did not deny it, but simply did not answer, watching in the meantime the bearing-beast ahead climb some methodical incline of air with purposeful strides and matching wing thrusts. Irissa tightened her lips and seemed about to speak finally when, directly and literally out of the blue —the great cloudless blue arching and blazing above them like some tauntingly distant bridge—came a shadow.

It was suddenly dark in the chariot, the kind of dark that permitted one to see and yet wonder how that was possible. Kendric and Irissa exchanged glances; then they crashed together utterly, shoulder to shoulder in the shadow, while Felabba catapulted to the chariot floor.

The vehicle listed like a ship, suddenly heavy in its weightless element. It dropped roughly for what seemed several feet, just as a tremendous impact caught it sharply on the side. They could hear one of its wheels whining uselessly through the air. Ahead, they saw only the great, rhythmic sweeps of black wings, looking opaque in the shadow, all their luster snuffed.

Sunlight sheared off all their senses with a lightning-sharp illumination. The chariot's rocking slowly subsided. Off to the side came a wild, veering screech as the great empress falgon wheeled away and into the sun, her scales and feathers sizzling in the unveiled daylight.

"Attack?" Irissa gasped.

"Accident," Kendric said, his arm around her shoulder tightening reassuringly. "Different prey, I think." He nodded below and this time did not intervene when Irissa carefully leaned over the chariot rim and looked down.

The falgon was clearly diving now, sleek and attenuated, a glittering arrow of muscle and hollow bone and brightly feathered, single-aimed need. Perhaps that was why she had not seen them, but had whistled past and into them like some mindless projectile loosed too long before to be diverted. Straight for the little waves far below she dived, where a few bits and pieces bobbed amid the dainty ruffle of spray—the humped backs of sleeping-water-beasts that used to sentry Clymarind. And where was the island? It was gone—as vanished as Ronfrenc had once wished it, absent from the Realm-map with a silent, telling finality. There was not so much as a grain of sand afloat beneath them. Irissa had not even glanced behind to see it go. It was simply—gone. And so the pilgrim sleeping-water-beasts, pale, sluglike, massive things that they were, milled around the empty ocean, easy prey for a landless empress falgon forced aloft by a nest that sank under her.

"Poor creatures. They still convene around what used to be. The falgon is making many catches," Irissa told Kendric over her shoulder.

He leaned forward for a closer look. His fingers suddenly curled into her arm. "Not sleeping-water-beasts. Even they, dumb as they are, are not as helpless in the open water as . . ."

"As what?" Irissa asked, though she knew, and the question was merely a way to lock knowing into its early stages of unwelcome speculation. "What?"

"Man. Men. Many men. Enough to outfit a fleet. The island must have created a whirlpool when it sank—tide enough to overturn a few pretty, painted ships. Ronfrenc's Realm-map will require amending."

The falgon wheeled away from the things bobbing in the water. She was distant enough to resemble a dwarf falgon now, one engaged in a particularly grisly game of folg. She dived again, her scissored beak splitting to pluck a small gray ball from the remote, level, azure surface. She circled away, too far off to show the working of her beak. But she always circled back for a deliberate and accurate dive at the dwindling supply of small gray spheres wafting gently on the waves.

"Ronfrenc—" Irissa began.

"—is but a name upon a map. And yonder creature is etching a new geography with only the impulses of its simple animal hunger. It is not unlike him, I think, and it is also the last of its kind. As we are."

"What will happen to it?"

"It will eat. And rest. And fly. Someday it will drop to the water and never be seen again. And then we will remember it."

Irissa sat back in her seat, content at last to watch only the huge plumes of black before her sink and fall. The more she saw of worlds within or without Rule, the less she cared to see.

"When you fought within the stalagmite circle, did you

sense anything of what you battled?" she finally asked Kendric.

He thought a long while before answering. "I did not even sense myself," he confessed ultimately. "We were tangled in some old pattern, some not-quite-seen web—myself and the others." Irissa doubted he would ever call them—or himself—Wrathmen again. "And, like ensnarled things since the beginning of time, we fought to our greater enmeshment. But—somehow I did feel that it was our energy, not our winning, that was required. Yet it was not fully sorcerous energy. Simply ordinary—human—struggle. As if that were the point . . ."

"But it was! Don't you see, Kendric?" Irissa leaned forward, her gestures backdropped by the vacant, crease-less curtain of sky around them. "Quest without end! Struggle without victory! Where have we gone in our wandering but full circle upon ourselves? And, ultimately, what has driven us but vast and pointless energy? One by one, my powers have dropped from me; what was originally effortless is kept only by great struggle. That is why the sorcerers are driven to the edges of things. Rule will no longer tolerate the easy, empty gesture; mere magic will not suffice any longer. Our world has cracked to let that element out—and in doing so, has almost allowed much worse in. That is why you and the—others—were literally set guard to stuff the crack shut, like so much Iridesium-clothed cement; why only you had a hope of escaping that eternal vigil. Ludborg was right. You had no Clymarindian glove, Kendric, no burning powders or rainbow-feathered arrows. Your greatest flaw was always your salvation. You were what you always suspected. You were ordinary."

To Irissa, her words were the unraveling of a blinding revelation, and she uttered them with joyous intensity. To Kendric, they were a kind of condemnation. He watched her noncommittally from burned-almond-bitter eyes.

"And you. Doubtless you were permitted to roam the length and breadth of Rule, leaving a coldstone trail across half of it, because you, as well, were weaponed with—what did you call this virtue, this salvation?—ordinariness."

"But yes! Oh, I was heir to extraordinary powers, but I could set about using them only in the most ordinary of ways. You all expected such magic of me—you, Mauvedona, Geronfrey—but you never expected me to be quite . . . ordinary. It was by a most ordinary means that I eluded Geronfrey's trap, after all. And it was a horrible trap, for he would have kept me as a favorite fly in a bottle . . ."

She paused, contemplating this, and Kendric allowed the silence to stretch until it bowled them, like the unwinking sky. Irissa finally sighed. "The last Torloc in Rule has been the weakest. Felabba is right. I must move into my proper element; there is no longer room for even my blundering sorcery in what remains of Rule."

"And little of that remains," Kendric said, nodding to the horizon ahead, bitterness bleached from his face by a stronger emotion—dread.

Chapter Thirty-six

Irissa glanced over her shoulder, then stiffened.

The heavens had bleached themselves white ahead and were rinsed pale in the glare of the sun. Yet, beyond the bearing-beast's ebbing and flowing dark wings, a charcoal-gray pair of even more gigantic wings stretched from one horizon rim to the other, forming a lofty topography of feathered white and gray, like distant foothills.

"Some gargantuan sorcerer has outdone himself," Kendric commented. "A display of smoke and powder to overwhelm a world, were it not a bit off-balance already. I think Geronfrey's under-mountain keep waxes warm now."

"Geronfrey? *He* made these wings of wind and smoke?"

"And ash and dust and a fine trail of molten red, rolling like entire herds of Willowisps down whatever snowy trails remain. All Falgontooth has become a choking, cinder-spewing chimney. I do not think many dwarf falgons will

fly up some neck of rock to freedom. We have seen the
last of the large—and the small. It is an even-handed ruin,
at least."

"All those thousands of eggs! I held one once, in a
dream. It throbbed with a red life as mysterious as Geronfrey's fluid. One could not expect the last empress falgon
to outlive her immortality—she was half-legend already,
anyway—but the ordinary things, the taken-for-granted of
life in Rule . . . must they perish, too?"

"If you would be rid of Mauvedonas, you must sacrifice
moonweasels, too," Kendric said tersely.

"And Torlocs," Irissa said, and he was silent.

There was little to say, at any rate. Their flight had
quickened, as if the bearing-beast misliked the scent of
sulfur so high in the atmosphere. The creature veered
southward uncommanded, where they could see the sham-
bled snowy sides of what had once been the most soaring
of mountains.

Falgontooth had exploded in a fit of geological apoplexy.
The summit had shown first an ashen pallor to the world,
then the underlying choler that ruled its volcanic temper
tantrum. Perhaps, deep within the now-blunt profile, labyrinthine passages were crumbling upon one another. Perhaps the fragile white pyramids of the dwarf falgon's destiny
were even now shattering between descending jaws of rock.

Kendric liked to think one chamber remained unfallen,
and that within it lay a random pile of bones and one
great, unrusted length of sword. Irissa did not think of
that rock chamber at all. She thought of the yawning dark
that lapped at a ledge, and a black, slimy ooze somewhere
at its depthless bottom. She saw Geronfrey in a silver
boat trolling that murk for his lost hands. For he would
not perish, he had said. Geronfrey would wait.

"The shore! Is that possibly the shore?" This time Kendric forgot himself and stood; the chariot reeled in the
heavens, and the bearing-beast turned a rebuking muzzle
over its barely visible shoulder. Kendric sat, as if the air
had been slowly siphoned out of him. "But it's new land.
The waters must have drawn back. The Abyssal is shrinking. And for a moment, near the mountains that border
Tolech-Nal, I saw a great, shattered coldstone splintered on
the highlands. It must be ice, set adrift by Falgontooth's

fiery spitting. Ice seems to shape itself quite architecturally at times."

But he did not believe himself, and neither did Irissa. She leaned below and saw the fine, distant geometry of a snowflake scattered about the desolate ash-and-snow-salted landscape.

"If soaring things like falgons are too rare for Rule now," she said, "why not soaring cities, too?"

"We rode," Kendric said in a voice so heavy it seemed to drag their chariot a trifle lower in the air, "we rode six abreast, up the undulating road to the City That Soars, the sun sparkling on our Iridesium and our extraordinary pride."

"You will ride again, Kendric," Irissa said, looking down and seeing that it was not his despair, but a natural descent, that made them seem lower.

To their right, Feynwood was a charred picket fence of needle-stripped pines. From the heights, it looked like the boar pits Rocklands men dug and then armed with lethal spikes. Falgontooth's fires had licked southward, and had likely devoured Mauvedona's more fanciful constructions made of the same hot-throated element. Beyond Feynwood should stretch the barren Rocklands, but the routine blue-gray hummocks that broke the surface below were waves. Water had claimed the desert place and drowned it. Nothing was the same below, except the familiar bogs and low places of the marshlands, now a vast, watery plain. It was an empress among marshes, spreading with the revelation of rising lands to its west and newly sunk farmlands to its east. Where the City of Rule had stood—proud as a sinking sun on land's farthest point, impaled into the Abyssal like a spear—there was only a stark headland, flat as a tray above the sharp cliffs, as fine a place as ever was for the headlong rush of suicidal moon-weasels, had such legendary creatures still—or ever—existed.

"He was right, that cosmic charlatan," Kendric muttered. "Only the marshes remain. Only marshes, and marshmen, and marshwives and marshchildren . . ."

They were low enough now to see the only people visible during their whole, rapid overview of Rule. Emigrating folk, leaving waterlogged land or plodding toward the newly beached acres given up by the retreating Abyssal. There were carts on what passed for a road, two-wheeled contrivances pulled by knots of weary villagers. And there, in the center of the sorry little tide of refugees, was a larger, four-wheeled wagon; leading it were two four-hoofed beasts, one ashen gray from Falgontooth's eruptions, the other as powdered, but with a dull flash of red beneath. Kendric's knuckles whitened on the chariot lip.

Irissa leaned near and spoke into his ear, like a temptress. "You will be a great man in the marshes now, Kendric. The last of the Six, though the folk below will not remember who or what or why the Six were, even as we in our time had already lost grasp of that. But you will still have your sword and, if your faith or hope or charity is strong enough, it will take on the glow of these most ordinary virtues and bedazzle the simple souls below. You will be king, for which Ronfrenc gladly gave his fleet and his life and a thousand other lives. You can command respect, as Mauvedona fought for it in her crimson towers and in my eyes and sank under the weight of its absence. Ludborg did predict your lot, idle gossip and irresponsible traveler that he was. Even a windbag can work a bellows: It will not be so bad."

"No," Kendric agreed.

The chariot was descending, skimming past the folk left in Rule, who, like all Rulians, did not look up to see that last great wonder of the Realms—a winged bearing-beast drawing a glistening chariot wherein sat a knight, a seeress, and a ragged cat, perched on its forward lip, her tail streaming like a particularly disreputable pennant. The equipage sank lower and lower over the water, almost grazing bogs fenced by reeds that were home to nothing but stick-legged birds.

"We fly east, to where Rindell was," Irissa decided with a quaver in her voice. "We were ever near the Sea, and now the Abyssal has claimed the last Torloc place. Perhaps my remnant of gate is a watery one."

Irissa stared at the still water passing but a few feet below them now. She felt the reminding tug of Kendric on her hair and waited. The water puddled into sullen ponds and shallow pockets. Some last high ground extended soggily around them, firm enough to create the illusion of a lake at its center.

It was a calm, wide lake, large enough to support the solid presence of an island in its center—a rock-gray island, curiously shaped, tumbled really, like stones. The chariot was bouncing roughly along the water's margin, slowly sucking to a halt as its wheels mired, the decorative spokes choked with snake-slender green weeds. The bearing-beast stood still and docile, head drooping and sides heaving. Felabba leaped down and waded through the mud to join brief muzzles with it. She was back beside Irissa and Kendric in an instant, her whiskers tipped mud-brown.

"Release it," the cat ordered. "It cannot pause long on an element now foreign to it."

"How will I return across this wilderness to the marshes, where I will be king?" a reluctant Kendric demanded.

"Hurry!" the cat insisted. "It has served you. Would you see it suffer?"

Kendric turned to unfasten the chariot poles without answer. He moved swiftly, and barely had the traces fallen free when the iridescent ends slipped from his hands like melting rainbows. The bearing-beast was moving, already distant and glossy as a crow, striding upward in the air toward the still-unclouded horizon.

"Where does it go?"

"To the air that is its own, just as you will no doubt run headlong back to your marshes, knight," Felabba said sourly. But she showed the great sensitivity of her kind by not calling Kendric a Wrathman any longer.

"King," Kendric corrected, his eyes wrinkling into humor but his mouth a very straight line. "I have the word of a seeress on that."

Irissa felt the sting of his last sentence and turned to face the wide, soft, blue water. It was untroubled stuff, unclouded. However it had arrived here—in a series of awesome swells or in one crashing wall—it was still water now —ordinary. A lake.

"Those stones—I know them," she finally announced. "I can yet see them melting one from another in my mind's eye. That means I could erect them again into their former semblance, live on here alone . . ."

"That is what you offered Ronfrenc. Retreat from Rule, but clinging to Rule. I do not think it will suffice any more now than it did then," Kendric said.

"Ah, you will go far, marshman," Felabba interrupted

ironically. "A veritable emperor, with such wisdom. Yes, this is Rindell, Torloc, and your eyes will play no tricks with the shape of it. For one thing, it would be an exhausting chore. For another, I will not permit it."

"You—?"

"Yes, I. Now, we must get you to that rock, for it is the last thread to Finorian, and the only thing you could have sliced it with was the mind-sword you left in Valna. So even if you would defy me, you have no weapon now with which to defend your defiance."

Irissa turned incredulously to Kendric. "You severed me from Rule. With that sword I could have chosen whether to stay or not . . . ?"

"All things cut against themselves best," the cat said. "There is no finer whetstone for magic than magic. But yours has dwindled. You must take the gate."

"And how do we get there?" Kendric demanded. "Swim?"

Felabba honored him with a look of pure feline venom. "There is still a particle of magic left in the world, and it is behind you, oaf."

Kendric turned with slow skepticism. He saw only the abandoned chariot, then noticed that it had shrunk and widened somehow to become a boat—a most plain, ordinary rowboat. Irissa stepped docilely into it, automatically reaching out to hold her sword aside, then dropping her empty hand. She studied the far-off abutment of rock as the cat hurtled into the bow and began a frenzied bathing of her muddy forepaws. The boat creaked protest as Kendric's boot swung over the side and planted itself on the planking.

"There is no need for a gatekeeper now," Irissa said without regarding him.

"I will row." Kendric grasped the two homely wooden oars, vaguely aware that they corresponded mysteriously to the chariot poles that he had loosened but minutes before. He flexed his hands more firmly around the oars, as if he could help hold a spelled thing to its current shape by sheer pressure.

They struck smoothly from shore across the quiet water, into the silence. The rocks looked more like steps the nearer they came, great gray risers leading up from uncounted depths below and breaking off quite accidentally into the air. The little boat grunted as it scraped to a stop against them. Irissa could not believe she stood on the edge between one world and another. There was no gate but her own desires, and those she had kept securely shut.

"Now," Felabba instructed, having whitewashed her feet as if for a sacrifice and taking a commanding position at the vessel's prow.

The lake was so still that the boat rested docilely against the rocks, almost as steady as they. Kendric kept his hand along a rock edge nevertheless, surprised to find the surface warm, as if it had stood in the sun for a long, long time.

"Now!" Felabba said, so imperiously her whiskers seemed to vibrate with the force of her speech. "The rock is the gate, and you are the key. Go to it."

Irissa stood slowly, while Kendric steadied the boat. Her gray, loose tunic and trousers blended with the rock. She leaped atop it and took an experimental turn, watching the wide, empty water.

"This water—I know it. It is my Rindell pool, where I sometimes used to troll for glimpses of wailwraiths when I dared not see myself. It has swelled and flattened to cover everything I knew of Rindell. And of all the things that I knew and saw vanish, including myself—moonweasels, empress falgons, and the great flocks of dwarf falgons that even you will grow old enough to call legends, Kendric—of all these things, I think that which was the most unreal was the wailwraith. I have never seen one and never expect to. There was more illusion in my simple forest pond than in any dark mirror Geronfrey could levitate from the Swallowing Cavern. And yet, when I am gone, the marshfolk will prefer to believe in wailwraiths rather than in anything so magical as a Torloc. Remember me, Kendric," she urged, "and do not go fishing for wailwraiths, or hear them in the midnight winds. It is Irissssssa the gossiping leaves whisper, who was once of Rule but is now—gone."

He had risen to hear her, but kept one foot on the rock to hold the boat from drifting away, for some deep current had sprung up and was eddying the water that washed the rock. An archway of spray shot out of the lake, a sort of misty rainbow that hissed, lancelike, through the air and went to ground at the rock's other side.

Irissa stared up at the pulsing curve of spray bridging

her. She stretched her hands wide and they vanished into it up to the wrists, so that they seemed gloved in Clymarindian snakeskin. Irissa appeared pinioned between the sparkling shafts of light and color, holding them apart. Behind her, the air was burnished a soft green, as if a thousand tiny leaves were shivering beyond some distant archway. She looked one final time at the pale cat in the prow.

"It seems, Felabba, I am fated to leave you behind—"

"On the contrary," the cat said calmly. "It is I who leave you behind. But you will not fret about that for long."

Irissa's elbows dropped. The shimmering walls of mist drew closer together, rustling taffeta wings slowly falling closed.

"And, Kendric. I would see you crowned. It will be a rigorous world, without magic, but I have grown used to that." She stopped speaking. Her eyes, still silver-gray, were misting over, and some of the wild colors around her were reflected in them. "It is elsewhere, behind me. I can feel it, Kendric, but I know not if it is a haven for a thousand borgia-monsters, or worse—three Finorians and a cat that speaks. I feel it enveloping me, like Geronfrey's velvet robe . . . No, wait—" she said, looking up again to the shimmer tightening upon her form like a gown cut to fit her.

The hiss of Kendric's sword sliced the air as he drew it, though metal would be a poor weapon against mere mist.

"Wait!" Irissa implored the greedy sparkle that webbed her, her fingers fanning to thrust it back a moment. "Kendric, I have solved it. I know it now. I must tell you—"

"Tell me what?" He angled the sword across his body, as if to strike the iridescence bluntly, crosswise.

"The Far Keep. I know where it is. Not beyond Valna's black pillar or under Falgontooth. It is that which is most distant, because it is most near. It is that which, when it fails, is the stoutest prison in Rule or out of it. The heart, Kendric, that which waits at the end of the longest quest . . . Wait, I must tell him!"

The veil around her fell in ever more tangible lengths of violet and crimson and borgia green; the colors seemed to pile up along her shoulders like so many cloaks being tossed upon them until the weight grew too great and she sank under them forever. Her eyes welled with ordinary salt water and overflowed. They appeared to be the only part

of her still free to flow where it wished. Her tears stabbed
through the scintillating air, sparkling, hardening into
coldstones at her feet, and shattering on the adamant gray
rock. Kendric stared aghast at the rock, aware of Irissa's
restoring powers, though she was not. The coldstones
rained faster, bright hail to thrum an aggravating drum-
ming in his head.

"I have no magic!" he finally brought himself to shout
to the sky bare of any winged thing, to the silent water
empty of anything but a few floating coldstone fragments
glittering under the glassy surface, to Irissa flickering before him as implacably as one stone from another, as a
fading Eldress or a great emerald touchstone, winking out.

"Wrathman!" Irissa cried. "You bear more magic than
you know. This world will have no real need of you."

She stood on the stone, wavering like a memory already. Kendric watched the greenish circle of a growing
flame that ringed the rock. He had a vision of such as she
ringed by more lethal flames than that, circled by a devouring fear of old ways, old legends . . .

"If the marshlanders are the sole surviving Realm, I must
stay with them, serve them as my oath—"

"Your oath was made on more than mortal metal. Your
sword!"

She had attained something of the authority of Finorian
in her going; Kendric automatically thrust the plain pommel
of his great sword toward her, mirroring the gesture she
had made to him when they first met in Rindell's forest.
Irissa caught hold of the hilt. The weapon bridged them,
even pulling Kendric's boat nearer to the rock that glistened,
as if Iridesium-coated, in the sunlight . . . The sword, which
glittered in the sun also . . .

Kendric watched his unadorned pommel and blade glow
with more than reflections. Rubies blossomed along the
length of it, ripe drops of blood. Coldstones cried into tears
along the metal. The sword was scabbarding itself in gem-
stones, in celestial sapphires, amethysts as vivid as Valodec's
island mountains, and emeralds as green as the Shrinking
Forest of Rindell, where Irissa had once drawn this very
sword from the mire and brought it, light as a whisper, to
him.

"Kendric!"

Her eyes gleamed unallayed silver; at least she escaped

this ruinous world with her gifts intact. She had never regarded him so fully before, reflection no longer her enemy. But her image weakened now. Kendric saw it through a rising rainbowed miasma.

Two more jewels materialized in the dimming light, more coldstone tears that flashed down her cheeks to the rock at her feet and then minced into radiant shards. So much was shattering now—this world, the Realms themselves, old faiths, new faithlessness . . .

His hand was sliding off the suddenly unfamiliar sword, and the boat was wafting away from the rock. Her hand still wavered through the iridescent fog.

"It is gone from this world, Kendric—magic. Come into another. You will find it hard to live without magic now, Wrathman."

Kendric's eyes glittered with an alien resolve. "Torloc trickery, sorceress," he challenged. "But I have developed a taste for things Torloc."

He clasped her hand and leaped. His boots struck rock, and green flames hissed at his cloak hem as he vanished into mist, into something waiting within it.

The sword fell to the stone and balanced there on its gem-encrusted side. It seesawed gently on the dimpled surface, like something vibrating into eternal stillness. The mist cleared, the liquid flames subsided. Air dissipated to reveal nothing but the deserted rock and the empty boat butting patiently against it. The sword angled toward the water, pommel weight drawing it inevitably into the teasing blue.

With a last, long rasp, as if it were being invisibly sheathed in its natural element, the great sword slid across the rock and into the water. For a flashing moment, it seemed as if a pale and tapered hand caught it and drew it under. There was a remote, piercing kind of wail, like the screech of a high-wheeling empress falgon. But the cloudless blue sky was empty of witnesses. It was a quite ordinary world. Water, sky, rock, and earth reflected back nothing more than their ordinary solidity. The rainbows were gone, except for a fugitive glimmer arching the distant blue.

Something white sprang out of the drifting boat and onto the rock—the cat Felabba. She arrayed herself in the sunlight and began cleaning her narrow paws, pale red tongue rasping across her fur like an echo.

There was nothing magical about the old cat. Old—she had always been old and always would be. Her thinly furred pink ears angled back a moment, but there was nothing to hear. Her tongue darted out and wrung her meager whiskers of some last, undigested morsel. She settled onto her haunches in the sunshine, tucking in her feet and composing her sour face into an imitation of serenity. She did not look as if she could talk.

The slitting emerald eyes opened once, suddenly, a jeweled flash. Then they dreamed shut again. Her insufficient tail plumed itself, then deliberately curved around her hunched body and covered her feet.

The cat Felabba was waiting.

ABOUT THE AUTHOR

Born the daughter of a Pacific Northwest salmon fisherman, Carole Nelson Douglas grew up in landlocked Minnesota with an affinity for water, cats, and writing, not necessarily in that order.

Her majors at The College of St. Catherine, St. Paul, were theater and English. A finalist in the *Vogue* magazine Prix de Paris writing competition, she gravitated to journalism upon graduation in 1966 and is an award-winning feature writer for the *St. Paul Pioneer Press*.

As an ex-actress, she treasures an extensive collection of vintage clothing almost as much as her Arkham House editions and hardcover Lord Peter Wimsey set. She and her husband, an artist and furniture designer, make their home on sufferance with a trio of white cats, a lone—and somewhat confused—Lhasa Apso, and too many books.

Douglas has written all of her remembered life, but began writing novels in 1976. Garson Kanin, a newspaper interview subject, took the manuscript of her first novel to a New York publisher; it debuted in 1980, followed by her second. This is her third novel and first fantasy.

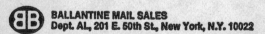